REALMS

Also from Phase Publishing

by
Colleen Kelly-Eiding

Favoured by Fortune
Face of Fortune

by
Christopher Bailey

Without Chance
Whisper

by
Dr. Robert Melillo & Domenic Melillo

Einstein's Desk

by
Emily Daniels

A Song for a Soldier

REALMS

by

PATRICK MORGAN

Phase Publishing, LLC
Seattle

This is a work of fiction. Names, places, events, and incidents are either the products of the author's imagination or are used in a fictitious manner. Any resemblance to actual persons, living or dead, or actual events is purely coincidental.

Phase Publishing, LLC first paperback edition
March 2021

ISBN 978-1-952103-23-0
Library of Congress Control Number 2021901026
Cataloging-in-Publication Data on file.

For my parents.

Chapter One

The last things I remembered were the flowers; rich, gold, and glowing, the sunlight streaming down through each and every one. Tiny red bugs, no larger than pinheads, moved along the fragile petals, weightless and silent. They were all around me, countless, tickled by a soft breeze that made their hairy stems bob and weave rhythmically against one another. I could feel that wind on my face, but I couldn't feel my body anymore.

The flowers were large, larger than they should have been, swallowing up my vision, but I didn't mind. I had never seen such color before, nor could I remember a time I had ever gazed upward at them from this angle. They had always been beneath me, around my ankles and my feet, and I had been careful not to tread on them, threading my boots delicately between the stems, feeling my way through this endless field of life. My steps were always slow but precise, eyes on the ground around and in front of me, shuffling through irregular patterns of flora at my own steady pace.

Now I stared in silent awe at my friends, the wildflowers, and my heart felt like bursting for joy.

PATRICK MORGAN

Why had I never seen them this way until now? The architecture of each and every one took my breath away, from the thin veins running up the stalks to the glorious ring of yellow at the top, fanned out and reaching up toward the sun. I tried to lift my head to see what they were seeing, to gaze up at the sky, but my neck was stiff, dull, and unresponsive.

No matter. I was right where I needed to be.

Something had brought me down here, first to my knees and then to the ground. But already, that memory was fading.

There had been something, though, some pain... 'ache' perhaps was the better word. I had felt my fingers tingle and then go cold. My careful feet had stopped moving forward as my balance left me in a rush.

But how I had gone from up to down was a mystery to me beyond that.

I wrestled with my brain, but it wrestled back and won. The memory was there somewhere, but I couldn't find it, and for some reason unknown to me, I wasn't sure that I wanted to anymore. This was too peaceful, too idyllic, lying prone on the solid earth.

The sun grew brighter, and the rays seemed to crackle now, hissing and sputtering like popcorn in a kettle.

That was odd. I had never *heard* sunshine before. Maybe somewhere nearby, someone was in fact making popcorn.

No, that was ludicrous. I was alone out here in the middle of a large field of sunflowers. Where would anyone find popcorn out here? Or a kettle to pop the kernels?

My ears strained toward the sound, which was all around me now. The golden rays vibrated, shaking with the growing noise, and the two became connected somehow.

One by one, quaking sunrays came lancing through the flowers, and like hot spears through butter, they made their incisions fast and smooth. First one petal fell, then another, and then another. Before long, the whole field was alive with yellow petals falling toward the ground, severed mercilessly by the sun.

I opened my mouth to protest, but nothing came out. My lips were sealed, literally, by a hot wax that oozed out from within my cheeks.

With a growing sense of alarm, I worked at them with my tongue, trying to pry them apart. But now my tongue, too, was immobilized, a victim of the same sticky substance that found its way to my lips.

It wasn't the heat that bothered me so much as the taste, some strange combination of vinegar and mint. The thick consistency coated my teeth now, working its way between my gums and the little cracks between molars. I wanted to vomit it out, but it was strongest at the front by my lips and nothing could pass through, I just knew it. Swallowing down a gag, I accidentally brought the wax even further down my throat.

Thinking about what was happening only made it worse, so I decided to shift my attention back to the flowers.

The crackling had stopped, as had the quivering rays. But their damage was done, and with what would have been a soft gasp if I could open my mouth, I took in the destruction.

A carpet of yellow petals stretched out before my

eyes as far as I could see. They buried half the stems, like snow around tree trunks, and above the beautiful wreckage sprouted new creations: tall spindly green stalks with fuzzy black caterpillar heads. Not a single petal was left attached; the popcorn sunlight had laid waste to my field of friends and left strange replacements in its wake.

I wanted to like the verdant columns and their naked black nests, but they were wrong.

The sun was coming back, and stronger still. This time, it was one steady press rather than a series of random attacks. It baked the alien landscape before me until tendrils of steam came from the exposed pistils, and the fallen petals below started to melt into one another.

Before long, they were all one big paste, and I was tasting it now inside my mouth. The flower paste and the hot wax were the same, and I tried to better enjoy the sensation of ingesting it, now knowing where it came from.

With a little concentration, the taste became bearable, and what once was nauseating now was simply bland and thick. The consistency was the worst part, and I shut my eyes to try and swallow it all down again in one fell swoop.

When I opened my eyes again, the field was gone. Everything around me was absolute darkness. My pupils dilated to try and let in more light, but there was nothing for them to see.

I tried to reach forward with my hands, and then to kick back with my feet, but I was weightless, suspended in the void. My limbs flailed every way they could, and I was happy to feel them once again; but truthfully, I was also quite frightened at the sudden disappearance of gravity.

Vainly, I tried to swim forward, but my fingers found only hollow darkness, and soon I had wriggled my way upside down and onto my back. Panic sunk in, as thoughts of the field and the flowers within became lost, forgotten in the threat of this new danger.

Maybe the wax was gone, at the very least. I opened my mouth to cry out for help, and though my lips actually parted this time, no sound came out from behind them. The muscles tightened in my throat as my vocal cords vibrated against one another. I knew that I was yelling, but the sound just wasn't there.

The black gulf around me compressed, and the air grew cooler, to the point where goosebumps broke out across my skin.

For the first time, I began to question my reality. Maybe I was dreaming.

No, of course I was dreaming. How else could I explain the vanishing field, the weightlessness, the absolute loss of control over my muscles and my memories?

Sunlight didn't have a physical danger to it; rays were something you could see and feel as a pleasant warmth on your skin. The idea that they could move like they had, produce sound, and ultimately carve up a sea of flowers, was all impossible. I had to be dreaming... it was the only plausible explanation.

My eyes shut and opened once again.

Still nothing. Just more all-encompassing, cold, black nothingness.

I had woken myself up from dreams all my life, and I knew this wasn't supposed to be so hard. So, where was that power now?

Over and over and over again, I shut my eyes and opened them, but nothing changed. I no longer knew if I was upside down or right-side up. All I knew was that I was still weightless in the empty space.

And then there was a new sound; short and soft and different, and completely unrecognizable.

What was that?

Quietly, I held my breath and strained my ears against the sound of silence. I had heard something… something just on the edge of my mind, barely more than a whisper. I was sure I'd heard it.

Hours ticked by—days, maybe—until finally…

Yes. There it was again.

It was a woman's voice, soft and simple; a voice that was familiar to my ears, but that I couldn't quite place. I racked my brain for answers, trying to shake the connection loose. It was right there, just beyond my reach…

I had to stop for a second. The effort of the search was beginning to hurt, and I felt a migraine coming on. Why couldn't I remember that voice?

It's me.

But who?

Someone was speaking to me in the blackness, but there was nothing there. The voice seemed to linger in the cool, stale air, bouncing around my head like an echo until it grew too soft to hear. Someone, somewhere, was speaking, and I could only assume that they were speaking to me.

Where were my memories? Where was my mind?

"Hello?"

It was the first time I'd heard my own voice in

decades, if not longer. I decided to try it again.

"Hello?"

Relief washed over me, as finally I was able to create sound again. My throat felt sore, rusty somehow, and I struggled to bring my fingers to my neck. When they finally made contact, it felt like someone was pressing icy metal forceps against my windpipe, and I couldn't help but cough.

Something wasn't right. My breathing became labored, and I felt myself choking on liquid cold.

It's okay. You're okay.

I caught myself mid-cough, holding my breath even though it burned my lungs to do so.

That was a reaction. The voice had reacted to my coughing.

Perhaps I was interacting better than I thought I was, and true contact *was* possible.

There was only one way to find out. I started coughing again, artificially at first, forcing the air out from my tired lungs in quick staccato bursts until the real thing kicked back in.

Before long, I was wheezing up a storm, and chunks of the yellow paste wax flew from my lips like escaping bumblebees.

It's okay. I'm here with you.

"Hello? Who's here?"

I spat the words out through hot tears and rasping heaves. Speaking was still difficult, but I didn't dare stop now that I realized I could do it.

"Who is that?"

Utter silence.

Why? Why wasn't she responding to me?

"I can hear you! Can you hear me?"

Maybe I just wasn't being quiet enough. With prodigious concentration, I managed to regain control over my breathing until the spasms subsided.

Bits of sunflower goo dripped from my lips and fell into the void below and above me. I waited to see if I could hear them land somewhere, like drops of black water falling from stalactites in an empty cavern.

But if there were in fact pools below me—or if there was anything at all below me—I still couldn't tell.

I twisted my body until it began to rotate, spinning slowly in midair. My blind eyes looked for something, anything, to identify, but there was nothing there. Just complete and unequivocal darkness.

Perhaps it was time for me to begin contemplating what total surrender might look like. Here I was, a useless body and mind, revolving around an invisible axis suspended in the infinite void. Dumb flesh and an even dumber brain.

Why couldn't I remember anything?

The voice. I had to remember the voice at least. That felt familiar; that felt right. Nothing else made any sense.

Time wasted by again, and perhaps, I fell asleep.

Or, wait—I was already asleep. Maybe it was sleep within sleep, like a dream within a dream.

It didn't matter, because when I came to again, I was still there, floating in the black hole of my missing identity.

I resigned myself to my fate. Maybe this was it.

Maybe I was dead, and this was hell. Or purgatory. Or, worst of all, maybe this was actually heaven. Just a great abyss. The negative of life.

Embracing the cold, dark truth of the mystery, I

shut my eyes and gave my full being over to it entirely.
That was when I woke up.

Chapter Two

White light, bright and blinding, everywhere all at once. It was just too much.

Was this the white light people talked about in those near-death experiences? The light at the end of the tunnel? If so, had my time finally come?

A vague smile crept across my face. At long last, someone or something had come for me, and I wouldn't have to be stuck here forever in the dark.

The first thing I did was feel gravity again... and boy, oh boy, did it feel *good*.

As the saying goes, you never truly appreciate something until it's gone. I felt the weight of my own body against a surface, and the sensation was exquisite. It was like I was a baby again, being held in my mother's arms. I was safe at last.

And my body... I could feel my body again.

I wiggled my toes, and they responded. I felt the digits squirm beneath what felt like silk. There was pain there, just that dull ache again, but it was worth it to feel movement where before there had been only nothing.

I decided to try my hands. One by one, I tapped the pads of my fingertips. I counted one through ten, starting with my left pinkie and working all the way across to my right pinkie before going back again.

The index finger of my right hand seemed to have some kind of thick plastic clamped around it, but other than that inexplicable anomaly, everything seemed normal enough.

I must have counted my fingers at least four times over before repeating the process again, this time with my toes. Everything was thankfully accounted for.

Hastily, I tried to open my eyes again, but only the right one responded, and the brutal white light came charging in stronger than expected. It made my eye water and my temples throb.

Patience. I had to be patient and take things slower than that.

Wherever I was, and whatever I was doing, it was clear that things weren't the same as they had been, and I was going to have to adjust to this new realm of existence gradually.

I shut my eye and felt the sudden relief of darkness once again.

Maybe I could focus my attention on my breathing.

But almost immediately, that turned out to be a mistake. Something was forcing air in and out of my lungs against my control; stale, sterile air that tasted like mildew and wet plastic burned as it went through my nostrils and up and down my throat.

What was I breathing in? Oxygen, poison gas, or stardust?

Whatever it was, there was no use fighting it anymore. The struggle only made the pain worse, and I couldn't bear another coughing or choking fit.

Slowly, laboriously, I allowed this foreign substance in, and out, in, and then out again... until, after a while, it became something almost involuntary.

What else could I do that didn't involve breathing on my own or opening my eyes? I had checked my fingers and toes; they were all there. What else was there?

My heart. I should check my heart.

I went to move my right hand to my chest and instantly met resistance. Something was tugging at the flesh on the inside of my elbow, some kind of sticky wire or plastic.

I tried to pry myself free of it through force, but the thing was in my forearm good and deep, and my strength wasn't what I remembered it to be. A weary sigh escaped my lips from all the effort.

Maybe my left hand, then.

Yes, that was free. Rather than head for my chest, I let my hand slide straight across my abdomen and head for the intruder on my right arm.

It was harder work than it should have been, because my muscles weren't responding like they were supposed to. My left arm felt like a soggy noodle getting sucked through a straw. Several times, my fingers got stuck on something, some bit of fabric maybe, and I had to shift their path to keep the movement progressing.

Finally, after a minor eternity, I felt the skin meet between my left middle finger and my right arm. Slowly, curiously, my feeble fingers made their way to the alien presence. A thin plastic tube ran along my arm until it dead-ended in a tight circle of bandaging.

I couldn't help it; my right eyelid flickered open on

its own, and through a haze of moisture, gooey lashes, and crust, my vision centered.

The bandaging was white medical gauze, though it looked discolored in places; more beige or cream than pure white. My eye traced the tube out of the gauze and up along a sloping path through the air until it connected with a plastic reservoir, hung from a hook on a metal pole. I tried to read the words inscribed in faint black letters on the bag, but it was too far away. Either that, or my eye was still too weak.

Nevertheless, I recognized the instrument for what it was and what it symbolized: an IV drip, which had to mean that I was in the hospital.

A soft groan escaped my throat, and it was strange to hear my voice again.

I had heard myself speak in the darkness, in that weird, black vacuum. But it had been dreamlike then, and extremely painful.

Now, it felt like I was shaking the dust off some old, familiar tool in a woodshed, and I cleared my throat intentionally. The sound vibrated around my lips and cheeks like a buzzer.

What was that?

My right eye rolled downward until it found a transparent wall where my nose was supposed to be.

Well, my nose was still there, but it was fainter, paler than I thought it should be, obscured by some kind of mask.

Was that what it was, a mask?

Curiosity one-upped the pain and the fear, and with effort, my left eyelids finally slid away from each other and allowed in the harsh white light. I focused both eyeballs downward on the clear plastic substance and made a grim, uncomfortable revelation. Not only was it a mask; it was also responsible for regulating my breathing with the controlled pumping and sucking of air that I'd fought against earlier.

With panic creeping in on multiple fronts, the muscles in my body tightened and tensed up again, and from somewhere deep inside the knot in my stomach, there came a sort of frantic whimper that trickled out from my lips.

Was that my voice? It sounded different than how I remembered it, different even from the distortion I had heard in that nothingness. The tone, the pitch… they were both higher. Freer somehow.

Giving in to curiosity, I ramped up my courage a step further.

"Hello?"

It was the first word I'd spoken since the light, but it came out all funny. Sure, the mask wasn't helping at all, but even from within it, my voice sounded strange and unnatural.

"Hello."

I spoke the word as normally as I could, and yet it still sounded foreign to me, so I decided to try and whisper it.

"*Hello?*"

Still weird.

It was time again to switch my focus to something else; that, or face the possibility of a complete and utter mental breakdown. Which would be warranted, of course, given the remarkable situation I was in.

Still, it wasn't something I wanted to give in to just yet. I had already made a good amount of progress since the initial shock of the blinding white light.

There we go, that's what I could do. I could figure out that light. What it was... or at least where it came from, perhaps.

My eyes started to shift upward.

And there it was, in all its merciless glory, right above me. Why was I looking at a row of fluorescent light tubes behind a glass rectangle in the ceiling? Who in their right mind thinks white fluorescent lighting is a good idea for hospital rooms? As if there aren't enough reasons to be uncomfortable in these places...

But I was making assumptions now. Just because I was lying in some kind of bed under a sterile light with an IV drip attached to my arm didn't necessarily mean I was in a hospital. I could be dead still. This could be purgatory, or heaven, or hell, and I had no real way of knowing it.

Maybe I was even still dreaming. Perhaps the second I convinced myself I knew where I was or who I was, this whole room would shudder and slip away, and then I would be back in that terrible abyss, back in the field of petal-less flowers, or somewhere new entirely.

I squeezed my eyes shut and opened them, over and over again. My left hand still rested against my right arm. I used two fingers to pinch it, harder and harder until the pain became unbearable and the skin turned reddish-purple, but nothing happened.

At least for now, it looked like I wasn't going anywhere. If this was still a dream, I wasn't going to be able to wake myself up, at least not yet. Might as well accept this room as reality and just see what happened next.

Slowly but surely, I brought my body back to life. I

rolled my head from side to side on a pillow, feeling the vertebrae in my neck and upper back creak and crack as I went.

Everywhere I went and everything I tried was met with resistance, but I didn't care. As long as I could move it all, as long as all the parts were working, I could grit my teeth against the pain and live with it.

But it was everywhere, the pain. It was as if I was learning to move everything again for the first time. Except instead of doing this with the fresh, eager, exploratory limbs and muscles of an infant child, I was doing it all with the tired, old, dusty bones of a mummy.

More than once, I imagined actual rust on my joints, and wondered if I might be better off trying to find a canister of oil to use as lubricant. The idea of squirting some magic black mechanical fluid into my knees, my ankles, my spine, my wrists… it sounded so easy. I wished it was possible, and not just some weird fantasy cooked up by a brain I no longer trusted.

The IV attached to my right arm wasn't the only piece of plastic growing from my body. My heart stopped when I found the thin black tubes running between my thighs, all the way up to an unimaginable destination. The thought alone made my stomach twist, and for a second, I wondered if I might pass out entirely.

I had to remind myself that every tube attached to me had been done so with a purpose… probably. Either that, or terrible experiments were being conducted on my body by extraterrestrials, in which case I was *really* in trouble.

After a bit of internal debate, I decided to remain

optimistic and continue believing that I was in a hospital, and that the tubes all had perfectly reasonable medical explanations behind them. I tried my best to put them out of mind, particularly the ones down below—which was much, much easier said than done.

What was that sound? Had it been there the whole time? It was so soft and soothing I hadn't even noticed it till now. It sounded like…

Rain. It had to be rain.

My head rolled across the pillow until my eyes took in the source of the noise.

Outside the small window, little droplets of water routinely collided with the black glass and then rolled down and out of sight. The sky was dark beyond them.

Dim branches of what could only be trees were silhouetted faintly against the night, bouncing up and down with the impact of the storm beating down upon their leaves. I waited for the familiar sound of thunder or a flash of lightning, but nothing came; just steady rain against the window and a constant rustling in the trees.

My neck was starting to stiffen up again, so I rotated my head back the opposite direction until my left cheek kissed the thin fabric of the pillow.

Everything took so much effort and concentration; it was infuriating. Why was my body so slow to respond? What had happened to me?

For the first time, I noticed a small bedside table to my left. On top of it were two rectangular plastic devices, a book of some kind, and a bouquet of dried and dying flowers. I decided to investigate each new finding one at a time.

One device was larger than the other, wireless and

black, and looked like it might be a remote meant for a television. A slow turn of my head revealed a wall-mounted TV unit facing my bed, so my suspicions appeared to be at least partially confirmed.

The other remote was more ambiguous. It was a little white thing with two plastic buttons, one yellow and one bright red. Both of the buttons were marked with a plus sign, which I thought I recognized as a symbol for medical care. This device was connected to a thick, cream-colored cord that disappeared beneath the side of my bed. Most likely it was some kind of tool for paging nurses or doctors, and it reinforced my belief that I was probably in a hospital.

The paperback novel looked worn, but the title was still visible from the side of the book's cover as well as the crinkled top: *Rip Van Winkle and Other Stories*. The words meant nothing to me. Below them were two more words: *Washington Irving*. Again, nothing. No comprehension there.

What was this book doing on the nightstand, though? I reached for it slowly with my free hand and arm until it was within my grasp, then brought it across my body so it was closer to my face.

The plastic contraption on my right index finger made opening the cover awkward. I contemplated removing it, but the fear of what might happen to me if I did ultimately overruled that notion.

Inside the book's cover were more printed black words on white paper. But it was the inscription on the left-hand side, the reverse of the book's cover, that immediately drew my attention.

There, in small, squiggly, hand-written blue letters, were two words: *David Abbott.*

What was that supposed to mean? As far as I could remember, I'd never met anyone named David Abbott in my life.

Then again, I couldn't really remember much of anything at the moment.

I skimmed through the first few pages to see if I could discover any more clues, but there was nothing there. It just looked like an ordinary book.

Discouraged, I set it back on the nightstand and turned my attention to the final item: a cheap-looking bouquet of flowers propped up in a plastic vase.

For a second, my brain flashed back to the yellow flowers and the field, and I felt a strange searing pain in the back of my skull, like someone was prodding the soft flesh of my brain with a fire poker.

But the flowers in front of me now looked nothing like those sunflowers had. These were of an assorted variety, with multiple colors, shapes, and textures to them.

The only real constant was that they all looked like they had seen better days. Dried petals littered the area around the bottom of the vase on all sides.

Again, there was a momentary glimpse of a vision somewhere buried in my brain: a quilt of fallen yellow petals that stretched out and covered the ground in every direction, melting slowly into a congealed substance I almost felt like I could taste somehow in my mouth.

Quick as it arrived, it was gone though, and in its place, back came that scalding brand on my brain that seemed to forbid further thinking on the matter.

Tucked in amongst these flower stems on the bedside table was a bright blue plastic wand with a clip on the end, and in that clip was a small piece of folded stationery with a green dragonfly design on the front.

Another clue!

I extended the shaking fingers of my left hand toward the paper, removed it from the clasp, and opened it.

There were words inside, but the handwriting was different from what I had seen on the inner cover of the book. This was neater, more professional, and done in elegant cursive rather than the uneven printing from the book.

David,

Words cannot begin to describe how much we miss you. Dad and I keep praying that you'll come back to us soon, and that you're just enjoying a little preview or a special tour of heaven. We know you'll have some incredible stories to share when you decide that it's your time to return. These past five weeks have been the hardest of our lives, but you need to know that no one here is giving up on you. It's time to come home, though. You are needed here again. We need you here again. We love you more than you'll ever know. Come back to us already, okay?

-Mom & Dad

I read the note over and over again until my eyes hurt and my brain throbbed against my skull.

There was no use ignoring the multitude of evidence surrounding me at this point; it was time to begin drawing conclusions. If I was to assume that the David in the note and the David Abbott inscribed on the inside of the book were the same person, then it only made sense that that person was me.

But my name wasn't David, was it? I had another

name; at least, I thought I did.

What that name was, I couldn't remember. But I didn't think it was David... was it?

Could my mind be trusted right now, though?

The line between reality and fiction, between conscious and unconscious, was precariously thin at the moment. Assuming I was no longer dreaming, the physical, tangible objects surrounding me had to be taken more seriously than the vague recollections and impressions I'd experienced prior to the white light.

Puzzling over these mysteries was only making my brain hurt, so I shut my eyes again and squeezed the lids together against the headache.

I also needed water badly. My tongue scraped and scratched against the dry walls of my mouth like an archaeologist digging up bones in a desert.

What a miserable feeling, this overall concoction of helplessness, fatigue, pain, and confusion. I wondered if it actually might be better to try to fall asleep and surrender back into meaninglessness.

That world had been strange and sometimes terrifying, but at least now, I knew it wasn't real. This present universe was all too real with its unpleasant physical sensations, unforgiving environment, and rapidly expanding catalogue of basic human needs I found myself in the throes of.

I tried to sit up, but somewhere along the neural journey, the message my brain sent to my body got waylaid or just fizzled out entirely. Stubbornly, my spine refused to do more than shift a few millimeters from side to side to accommodate the movement of my slightly-more responsive extremities.

If I didn't get water soon, I was going to die,

though, so I needed to figure something out.

A fleeting image of the milk-colored remote on my bedside table came to the rescue, and with mild exertion, I tilted my head back in that direction. Cautiously, I reached my left hand out and touched both of the buttons on the device simultaneously with my fingers.

Nothing happened.

I was expecting a buzzing sound, or the symbols to light up or do something to confirm I had indeed pressed them, but there was none of that.

Again, I tapped the buttons, then held both down together at the same time for a few seconds.

Was it even plugged in? I tried to follow the thick cord from the remote's base down the side of my bed, but I couldn't move myself far enough to see where it ended below.

Beads of perspiration dotted my forehead, and one of the larger drops suddenly felt inclined to go for a slick ride down the front of my breathing mask. I slowly wiped it away with the back of my right hand, and realized that my entire body was sweating through the sheets and blankets cocooning me in their embrace.

It was time to get all these covers off of me; they weren't helping at all. I wiggled one foot and then the other, trying to use my toes as claws to pull the linens away from my torso and down toward the foot of the bed.

It was difficult work, but so far, I was having more success with my hands and feet than any other parts of my body, and there was no denying my sense of satisfaction in seeing the soft, pale blue cotton coverings slide little by little down the framework of my body.

Less satisfying was the slow reveal of what that body actually looked like beneath the bedding.

My chest caved inward like a sinkhole underneath a thin, white hospital gown I'd never seen before. The fabric jerked up and down occasionally with my ragged, shallow breathing, but it alarmed me how small and frail I looked and felt now that the majority of my body was exposed.

My stomach and waist were similarly nonexistent, and with substantial fright, I discovered the two protrusions flanking my pelvis were my hipbones. I allowed my fingers to make contact with both of them, then ran the tips of my hands along other strange areas like my belly button, my sternum, my nipples, and finally, my privates. The self-examination came to a quick halt at the reintroduction of the black tube connected there beneath the hospital gown, and my hands abruptly returned to my sides.

I managed to drag the top of the covers all the way down to the middle of my thighs before finally stopping to rest.

Unfortunately, the work had left me even sweatier than I'd been before. Panting and glistening, I let my eyes drift back to the obnoxious fluorescent lights above me, and my ears to the sound of the steady rain against the window.

One thing at a time. I couldn't hope to do too much all at once.

Clearly, my body wasn't capable of anything more anyway.

I recounted all the progress I'd made so far: moving all my toes and fingers, moving my arms and legs, getting both eyes open, exploring my surroundings, liberating my body of those sheets and blankets.

All things considered, I had a lot to be proud of.

And at the same time, what a ludicrous idea that any of these common, everyday tasks should be so difficult to accomplish in the first place. I wasn't paralyzed, so why should any of this be so agonizingly awful to do? It was just opening eyes and wiggling toes, simple stuff a baby can do the moment it comes into being, after all, and presumably without much thought or effort.

My ears pricked at a new sound distinctly different from the pitter-patter of raindrops against glass.

This sounded like footsteps, and it came from outside a door I had previously been unaware of, across the room from me and directly below the wall-mounted television set. Though the door itself was closed, there was a small window in the upper midst of it that looked out into a nondescript white hallway.

The footsteps grew louder and closer until a face slid into view in the window, and then there was the sound of the handle turning and the door swinging open into my room.

Chapter Three

A small woman in lilac scrubs emerged in the vacant space of the doorframe. One hand clutched a clipboard, the other was still on the door handle.

Her eyes met mine from behind thin wire glasses, and immediately, the color drained from her face and her lips split apart. She seemed to murmur something to herself, but her words were inaudible, so I figured I'd give it a try myself.

"Hi."

I croaked out the easiest thing I could think of behind the mask. My voice still sounded strange and high-pitched to me, but it did the trick nonetheless.

The woman brought both hands to her cheeks, clipboard and all, and for a moment, I thought she might actually explode.

"Oh, my God! You're awake!"

I nodded feebly, not quite sure how to react.

Ostensibly, this woman knew me in some capacity, though nothing about her seemed the least bit familiar.

She took a halting step in my direction, shook her head vigorously, and let out an audible gasp.

"David... you're awake!"

There it was; there was no mistaking it this time.

This woman, who had some existing relationship with me, had called me by name and confirmed all the evidence I'd compounded to this point.

Some part of me had still been holding out hope that there would be a different explanation for the book and the dragonfly card, but it now seemed pretty obvious that whoever I was and whatever I was doing in this place, at the very least my name was in fact David, whether I liked it or not.

The woman waited for me to say or do something. Unsure of what she wanted or how to properly react, I decided to try and smile as best I could.

The action was a little painful to complete, as my cheek muscles felt just as rusty and tired as the rest of me, but I managed to curl my lips into what I hoped could pass as affirmation behind the walls of slick plastic.

She laughed then and found her legs beneath her, gliding quickly to my side and dispatching the clipboard next to the flowers on the table. Her hands came for mine, and I was surprised at how cold to the touch her skin was on my fingers.

I also became aware for the first time of an unpleasant odor coming from her…

Cigarettes. That's what that was. She smelled like cigarettes.

I remembered what those were and what they smelt like, and then recalled that I was bothered by the distinctive smell. I wanted to pull my hands away from her and tell this strange woman that she stunk of tobacco, but her grip was firm even in its excited quaking.

"Do you know where you are?"

Definitely not. I had a hunch, but didn't want to take anything for granted.

The woman was waiting for a response though, so I had to say something.

"Hospital?"

In my mind, I'd asked her: "Am I in the hospital?" In reality, all that came out was the final word.

It seemed to work, though, because she looked delighted with my response, and her head bobbed up and down with fervor.

The strange woman decided to pry me further.

"Do you know which hospital you're in?"

That was a harder question. I shifted my eyes to try and search the room for clues, for words that might ring some mental bell and cue me in on the right answer.

It was absurd, this little game-show routine I was performing with a total stranger, but my earnest curiosity and desire to re-acclimate myself to reality could not be contained.

All the same, it was of no use. Other than the wall-mounted television, bedside table, outside window, and various medical tools and supplies arrayed around the room on clean white countertops, there were no signs or pieces of artwork on the walls.

Even the interior paint seemed freshly glazed, so the best I could do was assume the hospital was newer or at least recently renovated, and that still meant nothing to me. I also knew there was no chance I'd be able to convey a thought that complex with my infantile brain and unreliable voice, so instead I just shook my head no.

Her face was a picture of empathy and patience,

but it bothered me for some reason. Perhaps it was the accompanying smell of cigarettes that continued to plague my nostrils and make my stomach turn.

A wave of nausea rolled through my body, and again, I was stricken by my thirst and physical discomfort. I turned my head away, partly because of the smell, and partly out of fear that I might vomit all over her.

She didn't try to stop me, though she did squeeze my hands all the harder.

"It's okay, David. You're going to be okay. You're at Carolinas Medical Center in Charlotte, North Carolina. My name is Loretta Jean, and I'm your nurse."

The words just didn't make sense. None of them.

"Do you know why you're here, sweetie?"

Now, *that* was speaking my language. Those words reverberated through me like a tremor in my bones.

My head rolled back around on the pillow to face her, and with my best effort, I attempted to squeeze her hands back, signaling my interest in this particular subject. Until I could lubricate my mouth with the curative power of water, speaking was just too difficult.

Maybe she understood, because her face wrinkled into a smile, and her eyes gleamed with an even deeper patience that felt genuine and timeless.

"You had an accident. You haven't been with us for nearly two months now."

Did that explain the vacuum—the void I'd spent what felt like an eternity in, suspended with no sense of time, place, or purpose?

Maybe. But what was the accident, then?

There was the hot paste, the sunflower petals, the

soft breeze… what came before all that, though? Something must have happened; some kind of mishap must have occurred.

Again, I racked my brain for answers. And again, I came up empty-handed. If once I had possessed memories before that moment—that melting, dreamlike haze of color, smell, and sensation—those memories were long gone now, and trying to summon them back up only caused me further physical discomfort.

"What… happened?"

My voice still sounded foreign, but at least my words were coming out smoother now and with less strain.

Loretta Jean kept my hands firmly within hers, and every now and then, she would send a little pulse of a squeeze through both of them at the same time.

"You've been in a coma, David. You had a bad accident."

"What… was it? Did I… did I… fall?"

That was still my best guess. After all, there had been an ache, a dizziness, and then that shifting perspective: seeing everything from the ground up, which had been beautiful but unnatural at the same time. I had lost movement then, too, I thought, and control over my arms, legs, neck, and ultimately, my very thoughts and senses.

Loretta Jean paused and stole a quick glance toward the doorway. It was as if she'd heard or seen something, though as far as I could tell, there was nothing there.

When she looked back at me, her expression was different. While her face was still a picture of compassion, there was a tinge of uncertainty now in her chocolate-brown eyes, and the wrinkles of her face seemed more pronounced than they had been before.

"I should get the doctor—and, oh Lordy, *call your parents!* I should have done it already."

She squeezed my hands once more, released them, and then used the backs of her fingers to gently brush some of the hair off my forehead where it had become plastered with sweat.

"Now, sweetie, I'll be right back; I'm just going to fetch the doctor and to tell your mom and dad what's happened. If you need anything, though, anything at all, just press one of the cross buttons on that white remote right next to you: yellow for non-emergency, red for emergency, okay?"

She hadn't answered all of my questions, and certainly not the most important ones, but it appeared her mind was made up. After being alone for so long, I had to admit that the last thing I wanted now was to find myself again devoid of human company and interaction. But at least she'd given me more to think about.

I nodded feebly, she smiled warmly in return, and with another "I'll be right back, now, you hear?" she was out of the room, closing the door softly behind her.

My mind turned to the most important revelation Loretta Jean had shared with me: I had parents.

Well, of course I had parents; everyone has parents of some sort, even if they never know them.

I tried to reflect back on who my parents were and was unsurprised to find my memories resisting me once again. For some unknown reason, a faint image of a woman with springy red hair and freckles kept flickering up and then out again, like light and shadows from a candle flame set at the base of a great wall.

Was this my mother? Or were the wires in my brain so crossed and deep-fried that the woman was entirely fictional, something conjured up by a reeling mind desperate to find meaning and familiarity in something, anything, at this point?

Still, the little red wispy curls, freckled dots across her nose, and rosy cheeks were awfully specific. I hoped that when these parents did arrive, the woman who introduced herself as Mom would look exactly like the picture of this woman in my head. It wouldn't solve everything, but at the very least, it'd be a small victory for my poor beleaguered temporal lobe.

The doctor came quicker than I thought he would. After Loretta Jean's departure, I'd tried flexing the muscles of my body again, working out the kinks and testing my physical limitations. It was slow-going work and obviously quite painful, so I was pleasantly surprised and relieved when I heard a quick knock at the door, glanced up, and beheld an older man poking his head into my room.

"Well, hello there, David. Good morning, and very, *very* good to see you."

This man was bald, save for a few patches of short white hair on the sides of his head. His ears were large and pink, and there were light violet circles beneath his tired grey eyes. The lilac scrubs, white lab coat, stethoscope, and plain white sneakers conveyed that this friendly soul was probably a doctor, and most likely my doctor.

He walked over and patted my arm good-naturedly, speaking while at the same time checking the readings of the various instruments around me.

"My name is Dr. Walter Frye, and I've been taking care of you the best way I know how for the past seven weeks. Loretta Jean told me you must have paged her yourself, is that right?"

I nodded slightly.

"Wonderful. Just wonderful. Miraculous, actually. You know, David, it's exceedingly rare for coma patients to wake up after being under for more than four weeks? And even if they do, they're almost always still in some sort of persistent non-responsive state. Or, best-case scenario, they need months to regain basic motor functions, and sometimes even years of full-fledged rehabilitation."

He leaned in closer and squinted his eyes at me.

"So, you're something of a wunderkind. Am I to understand you're even speaking out loud already?"

I cleared my throat, feeling a bit like a specimen under a microscope. But the doctor's gaze was not unkind, and if everything he said was true, I supposed I couldn't blame him for being incredulous and inquisitive.

"Trying... to."

That was the easiest way to say it. I burped the words out, and a broad smile spread across his face.

"My goodness."

His spine straightened, and there was a noticeable touch of amazement to his tone. I wondered for a moment how long Dr. Frye had been practicing medicine, and if I was the most astounding case he'd ever encountered. He certainly looked like he could easily be in his sixties or seventies, and if he'd been a doctor most of his life, it gave me a strange sense of pride to know that I was responsible, even unintentionally, for shocking a man of his presumed experience.

"Did Loretta Jean tell you where you are?"

I nodded.

"And does that make sense to you?"

This time, I hesitated and licked my lips. What were the words she'd used? Obviously, I knew the word 'medical', but there had been a string of other words in there that had gone right over my head.

I wanted to respond by saying the words: "Not exactly," but the idea of pronouncing that '*zacht*' sound made my palms sweat and my mouth start to dry up again. A simple shake of the head would have to suffice.

Dr. Frye nodded serenely with infinite wisdom.

"Don't worry, David. That's completely normal. In fact, there may be many things in the days and weeks to come that won't make sense to you. But again, it's all completely normal. All that I ask of you is to try and remain optimistic; and above all, remain patient. You've already displayed incredible progress just in the short time you've been awake this morning, so there's every reason to believe you will make a complete and total recovery.

"However, these things do often take time, effort, and dedication, so don't get discouraged if you find yourself confused or mixed up at times. You've got a lot of people who love you, and they've been by your side and rooting for you from day one."

He smiled and patted my arm again.

"As a matter of fact, two of those people are on

their way to come see you right now—your mother and father. They should be here within the hour. I can't begin to imagine what they must be thinking and feeling right now, but I'm sure they can't get here fast enough. You're so incredibly loved."

The doctor inhaled deeply through his nostrils, and his face grew ponderous again as he studied me.

"You're also very lucky, David. Very, very lucky; and very, very loved. That's a winning combination you've got going for you there, young man."

His shoulders sank as he exhaled audibly, shaking his head from side to side as if he were marveling at something wondrous.

I didn't know how to react, so I just gave him the same smile I'd used on the nurse earlier. He smiled back, his fingers fidgeting with the stethoscope around his neck absentmindedly.

"Do you want me to stay here with you until they arrive?"

It was a tempting offer, as I remembered the sudden pang of loneliness I'd experienced when Loretta Jean left my room to fetch him and call my parents. Save for the faint background noise of steady rain hitting the window, my room and the hallway outside were both eerily still and quiet.

That said, I was far from being an adept conversationalist in my present state. Dr. Frye had also made it abundantly clear that he had no intention of rushing me back to reality and divulging everything I'd missed.

I had half a mind to ask him to turn the television on, but fear of what I might find on the screen made me second-guess that urge. Besides, if the medical practitioner thought it best to ease me back into the world slowly, flipping on the TV probably wasn't the smartest idea.

"I'm... fine."

It was only half a lie. I screwed my face into my best impression of a winning smile, and the doctor returned it before walking back to the door.

"Just page us if you need anything; anything at all. Your vital signs all look terrific, and there will certainly be a time very soon to run some more comprehensive tests. But for now, I think it's best that you just rest up and think about the fact that the next two faces you'll be seeing at this door will belong to your parents. Now, isn't that something to get excited about?"

Actually, it only made me anxious.

Left alone with my thoughts, tenuous images of the red-headed woman with the springy hair and freckles danced in and out of my brain. Who else could she be but my mother? There was no other logical choice.

I tried to think then of my father, hoping to pry loose some similarly-familiar recollection that might hint at his appearance, personality, or history with me.

Try as I might, though, nothing came; only empty darkness, and then mounting frustration at the fruitlessness of my endeavor.

Discouraged, I rolled my head back until my gaze fixated on the fluorescent light above me.

Maybe it was easier to just surrender to mindlessness again. Coming back into this so-called reality had been such a tedious and pointless process so far. It made me wonder whether existence hadn't been easier after all in that endless state of suspended animation I'd left behind.

This was the white light that had brought me out of that place. Maybe it could bring me back in. I just wanted something, anything, to feel right again. Or at least feel easy.

But the light didn't want me back. I stared at it without blinking until my eyes started to water, and still nothing happened. Then, I squeezed my eyes shut against it and tensed them until black and gold patterns flitted in front of me, but nothing changed. My brain and body still ached, and now my armpits and the creases behind my knees and elbows were beginning to sweat. Worst of all, my mouth was turning dry again.

Time stretched on and on, indifferent to my suffering and my solitude. At times, I found my condition so unbearable that I wanted to scream out for the doctor or the nurse to come running back. On other occasions, I hated them both so completely and so irrationally that I never wanted to see either one of them again.

How could this have happened to me? Who did this to me? Who could I blame?

I was so lost in my miserable infinity that I didn't even hear the door open. Instead, it was a voice that snapped me out of my paralysis—a woman's voice.

My heart thumped rapidly as my brain tried to place it, desperately hoping it was the same soft, gentle voice I thought I'd heard calling out to me while I'd been hanging in that void. I thought I knew that voice, just like I thought I knew the freckles and the red hair. This had to be the moment things would finally start to make sense again.

Sharply, expectantly, I twisted my head toward the

doorway to find my answers. There, leaning against each other, stood two figures.

One was a man, tall and thin, with deep brown eyes and a neatly-trimmed beard that flowed upward into slightly shaggy hair. He looked as if he'd just woken up from a long sleep and hadn't bothered to wash his hair or comb it down. His clothing seemed to confirm as much; baggy grey sweatpants, black tennis shoes, and a white V-neck t-shirt that made his chest look slightly sunken in beneath it. He had one hand on the door handle, and his other arm was wrapped tightly around the upper shoulders of the woman leaning against him.

She wasn't significantly shorter than the man, but the first thing I noticed about her was her hair: smooth, straight, long, and black, it framed a face full of worry-lines that was sadly devoid of any freckles. Her eyes were dark like the man's, and they glistened behind thick tortoise-shell glasses. She wore a royal blue long-sleeved shirt that had the words 'WCHS Marching Band' emblazoned across the chest in white block letters, and below that, she had on denim jeans and dirty white tennis shoes.

The voice I heard must have belonged to her. With tears welling up behind slightly foggy eyeglasses, she took a halting step away from the man's side and spoke again.

"Davey?"

The voice sounded nothing like the one from before; the one that had called out and assured me I wasn't alone in the darkness. All I could do was stare blankly back at these two individuals and try to conceal the crippling waves upon waves of disappointment that crashed down on me.

It seemed the woman could contain herself no longer. With a lunging heave, she rushed to my side and threw her arms around my neck, burying her face in the nook of my shoulder as unbridled tears dampened the thin cloth of my hospital gown.

The man wasn't far behind her, shuffling over with a quivering lip and ragged features that had long since surrendered to emotion. He wrapped strong arms around the both of us, pulling himself down and merging our three separate bodies into one big, trembling mass on the bed.

As the sound of the rain outside coalesced with the sounds of stifled sobs inside, three things became abundantly clear to me in that moment. First, this woman was my mother. Second, this man was my father. And, third and worst of all, I had absolutely no memory of either of them.

Chapter Four

Contrary to what my parents thought, I didn't mind seeing Dr. Eiding at all. She was an exceptional listener, which made sense, given her chosen profession.

The middle-aged psychiatrist had been practicing her craft all her adult life, and she had a simple ease with which she did all things. Soft-spoken, bespectacled, and usually clad in brightly-colored, hand-woven knits, there was something undeniably grandmotherly about the doctor.

More than anything, she also always seemed to know just how far to press me on any given topic of conversation.

Dr. Eiding would start by asking me something relatively simple, like an open-ended question about my physical therapy progress, my reaction to the current weather, or what I'd had for lunch that day, and then our discussion would gradually delve deeper of its own accord.

It was not lost on me that the therapist was a master of subtle manipulation, and on occasion, I'd recognize her gentle attempts to steer me a particular direction.

But for the most part, this never bothered me. And if there was ever a time that a subject grew too frustrating or too difficult to concentrate on, she would expertly chime in with a segue that both made logical sense and also served as a welcome relief.

If anything, I had actually grown to relish and look forward to these twice-weekly visits. Our sessions offered me opportunities to grapple with subject matter that was still either too painful or too confusing for my parents, as much as they truly wanted me to help them understand.

For obvious reasons, though, I realized it was easier for me to admit to Dr. Eiding that I couldn't recognize my own parents' faces than it was to tell either one of them that myself.

On the day I'd been released from the hospital, my parents—or, more specifically, my father—had insisted on picking me up from the hospital in a bright blue car identified as a Mitsubishi Eclipse. The vehicle apparently had been my dream car since I was fourteen, and my parents had given it to me as a gift the day I got my driver's license. Thus, it was no accident that this had been the transport of choice waiting for me in the hospital parking lot, looking as shiny and new as I'm sure it ever had.

I had given my father the best smile I could muster up in that moment, but truth be told, I found the color of the car kind of obnoxious, and the ride home from the hospital was made all the more unpleasant by the lack of interior space inside. Even with my mother gallantly volunteering to sit in the far back so that I could ride up front and stretch out, the vehicle was claustrophobic for three people.

My dad had excitedly listed all the fancy features and gimmicks he swore I treasured about Mitsu—the name I'd evidently given the car once upon a time.

I did my part in nodding my dumb acquiescence whenever he paused for breath or checked to see if his words were landing. But to me, it was just another simple machine.

While Mitsu hadn't done much to impress me, the greenery outside had been a different story. Whizzing by my window in a lush verdant blur, I had kept my forehead pressed tight against the cold glass in order to better take it in.

The view was dizzyingly beautiful, and the trees alone were taller than any trees I'd ever seen, at least that I could remember, and so thick! Everywhere around me was endless forest, and I'd been positively enthralled by it. I couldn't imagine trying to make my way through some of the thickets and woods on foot, and silently, I'd wondered to myself if anyone ever did.

That ride home was one of the first instances I remembered my parents looking at me funny. As hard as I had tried to feign interest in the car, my father surely must have realized that something just wasn't clicking entirely on my end, and I could see in his face that it worried him.

It wasn't like he was disappointed in me or anything. There had just been a pity there in the dark brown wells of his eyes, and an increasing sense of alarm in his voice as he pleaded with my memories to come back to me.

I couldn't blame him for being frightened, as I was downright terrified and ashamed that these two people who had literally brought me into the world were still nothing more than complete strangers.

Preternaturally, my mother had seemed to sense this burden in a way that only mothers can. She kept insisting that everything would come back to me in time, pleading with me not to worry. But every time she said it, she sounded more and more like she was saying it to herself and her husband than to me.

Their concerns had mounted as we entered the city limits of my hometown, a place they called Lenoir.

We'd passed a reddish-brown brick building where I'd attended preliminary school, West Lenoir Elementary. I'd learned basic reading and arithmetic within those walls, and had enjoyed countless hours of running, jumping, and climbing outside them.

Did I remember my first-grade teacher, Ms. Price, and how she used to always reprimand me for talking too much in class?

Or how about my best friend Jacob? "The two of you were inseparable until he moved to Wisconsin your freshman year of high school."

Or what about his parents, who often graciously hosted our sleepovers and made us French toast the next morning because they knew it was my favorite?

Further up Main Street had been the Dairy Queen where I'd gotten my first job, a small little shop I worked in all summer while saving up spending money for a trip to Ireland that our marching band took the following spring break.

Did I remember how I hated the trumpet at first, but after watching YouTube videos of Louis Armstrong, I decided maybe it was "an all right instrument after all?"

Oh, and look quick out the other window—that's

the park I fled to the day I decided to run away from home for good, only to sheepishly end up back at the front door of our house thirty minutes later.

Tirelessly, my parents had poked and prodded at me, hoping against hope that sooner or later, something I saw or heard would be the magic key that would unlock my memory vault and make me *me* again. They'd tried all manner of visual aids: old photographs, school essays I'd penned on subjects I was passionate about, various childhood mementos, worn-out stuffed animals…

One morning, I had woken up to find a folded map of Lenoir slid underneath my bedroom door with a sticky-note attached to it that read:

It's not a treasure map, but hopefully, you'll still find it useful. XOXO - Dad.

Unfortunately for my father, I had not found it useful, nor had I even begun to know what to do with it.

Eventually, I'd started contemplating lying and faking mental connections just for my parents' sake and overall peace of mind.

But I was also worried that they'd be able to see right through my façade, because the awful truth was that even though I didn't know them, they unequivocally knew me, and very, very well.

The worst part had occurred when we'd finally turned onto the street I'd grown up on, parked my car in the driveway, and walked into the house I had called home all seventeen years of my life.

From the outside, it had done nothing for me, and

from the inside, it was more of the same. My poor mother led me through every room, every closet, every nook and every cranny, pointing out this detail or that, always turning to me expectantly afterward, waiting, wishing, praying. But it was just no use.

They saved my room for last, of course. My mother opened the bedroom door as if she were a gameshow host presenting the winning contestant with a marvelous prize.

Everything inside had been made immaculately clean and organized. The bed was made, the window blinds were drawn, the carpet was vacuumed, the bookshelves were dusted. It would have been hard for an outsider to believe that this had ever been a teenager's bedroom, considering just how pristine it was. Even my father joked that it was the nicest the room had looked since they'd originally bought the house.

It wasn't that anything in the room disagreed outright with my tastes or sensibilities—whatever those might be, anyway.

It just hadn't felt right. There were all sorts of pictures, toys, electronics, collectibles, and other belongings that stamped my existence as valid and indisputable. But for whatever reason, all those objects felt more like artifacts than keepsakes, more like props than souvenirs.

My bedroom—and, in particular, the sleep I got there—was always one of Dr. Eiding's favorite topics of discussion. She would start our sessions by warmly greeting me and my parents at the front door of the cozy ranch home where she performed her practice, heeling her two Labrador retrievers behind her as she held the door ajar for us to enter.

Ever the gracious host, she'd offer cups of coffee or sweet tea to my parents and invite them to stay and watch television in her living room if they so desired. Sometimes, they'd agree, but more often than not, they'd kiss me on the cheek and promise to return in an hour's time.

Then, she'd put the dogs outside, and the two of us would climb up the creaky wooden stairs that led to her home office. I'd take a seat in a plush leather chair that always felt just a bit too big for my body, she'd sit down in an oversized armchair behind a small wooden desk, and then we'd begin with the same question.

"So, David, how'd you sleep last night?"

The gentle rotation of the ceiling fan above us had a calming, hypnotic effect on me, and I wondered if that, too, was an intentional method employed by the psychiatrist to put her patients at ease.

Closing my eyes, I tried to recall my previous night's sleep.

"Good. I slept pretty good."

We both knew that answer wouldn't be enough, but at least it gave me time to collect my thoughts.

I had been suffering all manner of physical aches and pains as I'd worked my body back into action, but none of it came close to the severe headaches I often encountered when scratching at the walls of my memory, both short- and long-term. Even the simplest mental exercise sometimes felt like my brain was being pulled apart on a rack over a raging fire.

At the end of our very first session together, Dr. Eiding had suggested I begin a journal to log all my dreams, thoughts, and memories for future reference and analysis. It was a great idea, and one my parents loved so much that they surprised me at breakfast the very next day with an elegant leather book I could use.

The only problem was that I kept forgetting to fill it out, and I worried that sooner or later, my psychiatrist would find that out.

"Can you remember any dreams you had?"

I was expecting the question; it's why I had given myself a head-start earlier with the generic response. Nevertheless, it was hard to summon this information up on command.

Out of the darkness behind my closed eyes there came a kind of flash—more sensation than image, if it was anything at all. My mind raced after it, fearful that if I didn't pursue, I might lose it altogether.

And yes, there it was again. It was a *texture*, and I could feel it on my fingers and in the recesses of my palms. Instinctively, my hands curled into loose fists, and I was holding it again as I had in my dream.

"I dreamt that I was asleep. But it wasn't me in the dream. Well, it *was* me, but I just felt different somehow. And it wasn't my bed. It was bigger than my bed at home. And I had a blanket…"

My fingers flexed as I imagined the material between them.

"Like a wool blanket, or a quilt. Different from what I have in my room at home, or what I had at the hospital."

I could feel the weight of the covering draped over me again, and I stirred restlessly beneath it.

"It was thick and old and heavy, but still soft and warm. Kind of like a protective cocoon, I guess."

The feeling was fleeting. And as dreams and

memories tend to do, it suddenly wisped away from me as quickly as it had come.

My eyes fluttered back open, and I noticed my hands were still balled up tight from clutching the imaginary blanket, so I relaxed them and spread my fingers out over my thighs.

"Do you remember anything else from the dream? Were you alone in it, or were there people there with you?"

That was a tough question. I tried to revisit the blanket and the bed in my mind. The clearest takeaways from the memory came through the sensorial form of touch: the blanket most of all, but also the gentle springs of the mattress against my spine, the soft cotton of the pillow beneath my skull, the heat of my body radiating under the layers…

Was someone there in the room with me? I couldn't be sure. It was certainly a possibility, but more than anything, I was just aware of my sleeping self, swaddled in the dense fabric.

"I don't know. Maybe… it's still so foggy."

If I were Dr. Eiding, I'd be sick and tired of hearing that response by now. I must have said it at least a hundred different times over the course of our sessions this past month.

But it was true. Everything was foggy these days. My mind, my memories, my dreams, my past…

This was the game we played every Monday and Thursday, just me and the psychiatrist that Dr. Frye had recommended I see before I'd been formally discharged from his care. The name of the game was to unearth David Abbott's memories, and the rules were simple: Dr. Eiding asks an easy question, David Abbott gives a simple answer; Dr. Eiding asks a harder question, and then David Abbott tries to answer it as best he can. With any luck, something new is discovered by both parties, and another piece fits into place in the puzzle of my past.

"That's all right for now. Maybe something else will come back later."

It was one of her best traits—she never pushed me too hard, and she always knew when to redirect our conversations. As a result, I felt like I was safe with her.

"How about your parents; would you like to talk about them? How's everything going at home?"

I was grateful for a line of questioning that could focus my answers on the present rather than the past. It was always easier for me to talk about events, thoughts, and feelings that occurred *after* I woke up from my coma, as opposed to before or during.

"It's okay. Things are all right. My… father started working again this week, which I think was a little hard for him. Not that he doesn't like his job or anything—at least I think he likes it, he seems to—but he keeps saying how much he wishes he could stay home with me and my mother. I suppose he just doesn't want to miss out on anything… like if anything happens, you know? With me."

"Has anything happened? Have there been any moments since we last spoke where things fell into place for you?"

I swallowed hard and thought about her question.

"What do you mean?"

"Anything at all that's made more sense to you, or connections you may have made with your parents, your belongings, your life in general. Have you discovered an affinity for a specific kind of food, or found an interest in a specific television program, or sensed some kind of meaningfulness in an old toy, or in an article of clothing? Anything at all, really."

Her suggestions were all good ones, but none of them offered much promise in the way of insight.

On the first night I'd returned home from the hospital, my father had cooked my favorite meal: steak, asparagus, and macaroni and cheese. My parents claimed I loved these three dishes most, so the dinner was planned as a special treat for me.

By the time we were finally ready to eat, I'd been famished, and I had to admit that the spread before me both looked and smelled extremely appetizing.

The meat was tender and moist, the vegetables were salty and flavorful, and the pasta was creamy and rich. Everything was exactly as it was promised to be, and from a rational standpoint, I could easily understand why a person might have craved all these individual foods as well as enjoyed their confluence together.

It just hadn't done anything for me, though. I put on the brave, appreciative mask I'd started wearing so often, nodding and smiling, licking my lips and working diligently as best I could for about an hour. But I couldn't have done any of it without lots of water to wash it all down.

The juices and fatty liquids leaking from the slab of beef privately nauseated me, and I began averting my eyes from the sight of my own serrated steel knife edge slicing and tearing apart the bloodied flesh and gristle from the bone.

That crunching sound that came from biting into

the asparagus stalks bothered me, and I ended up avoiding the leafy heads of the plant stems altogether after the first one nearly made me gag.

The macaroni was by far the most tolerable of the three items, but even that left me with a stomachache and a bloated, gassy feeling by the time I was done.

My father could only watch helplessly as I labored through my favorite meal, a combination he swore I'd voraciously devoured hundreds of times before. If my lukewarm reception offended him, he did his best to hide it. But none of us had been particularly adept at concealing our obvious disappointment that evening.

What was Dr. Eiding's second suggestion? Something about television programs?

The TV in general had played a fairly nondescript role in my rehabilitation process thus far. Dr. Frye cautioned against too much immediate exposure to television, for fear that what I found there might overwhelm me.

Nevertheless, my curiosity had gotten the better of me, and since I had a television of my own in my bedroom, there was nothing stopping me from flipping it on at night and meandering through the channels with the volume turned down low.

Dr. Frye was right: it *was* overwhelming at first. Hundreds and hundreds of different stations, shows, news reports, movies; they all jumped out at me from the screen like screaming ambassadors from some faraway country I'd never known existed.

While most of it was nonsense, there was a comfort in the common language I shared with the talking heads. At least I had that. I couldn't imagine how alienating it would have been if I'd awakened from my coma in a world whose inhabitants I couldn't literally understand.

The vast majority of the words I saw and heard were comprehensible. It really was just the proper nouns—the names, places, brands, and cultural concepts—that defied easy understanding and still felt strange and foreign to me.

All in all, I was less than impressed with any of the offerings I ever came across while 'surfing the tube', as my father called it. The comedy shows my parents watched after supper, the ones they called 'sitcoms', failed to tickle my sense of humor. The more dramatic offerings felt contrived and uninspired, and the evening news broadcasts created a puzzling mix of confusion and boredom in me, punctuated with occasional flares of outrage and astonishment.

By far, the most fascinating thing I had found on television was the channel I discovered one night alone in my room, a station that focused on capturing exotic animals, plants, people, and locations in breathtaking footage.

"I do like this one show on TV. I'm not sure what it's called, but there are all these crazy movies of animals in different places around the world. Like last night, it was all about these birds called penguins that live on the ice caps and lay eggs and swim to eat fish underwater. It's always a different place they go to on the show, like a forest or an ocean or a desert, and they each have different types of animals living there: birds, monkeys, frogs, snakes... Some of them I can recognize right away, and that's always exciting. I'll be like, 'I know that one!', and it makes me feel good, like I'm coming back to the world.

"And other times, it's just completely... blank. It's still amazing, and I'm still fascinated by what I'm seeing on the screen, but I have no idea what it is, what it's doing, or if I've ever seen it before. And I don't know if that's just my memory not being right, or if I've actually, really never seen it before. So, I keep watching, waiting, hoping that if I keep taking more of it in, maybe eventually something will snap, and I'll remember all of it again perfectly."

Dr. Eiding waited politely to see if I had anything more to say before speaking herself.

"Do you watch these programs with your parents, or do you watch them on your own?"

"Mostly on my own at night after they've gone to bed. Not all the time, either, just every now and then. I would watch it with them, but I don't know what it's called."

I thought back to the last part of her initial question.

"You wanted me to talk about my clothes, too, right? Or about the stuff in my room?"

"If you'd like. You certainly don't have to."

I brought one leg off the ground and draped it across my knee. It was getting to that point in the session where my muscles would grow restless and achy. Even with all the ongoing physical therapy, my body continued to find new ways to resist my command.

"I don't really know what to say. The clothes in my closet all fit me fine enough, despite being a bit baggy in places. I've gone through all the old toys and pictures and things in my room, with my parents and by myself. I know that it's all mine; I can understand that. And I get that I did the stuff they say I did. It just hasn't really done anything for my memories, I guess. Like… it feels like I'm trying to be someone I'm not."

"You know, David, that's a fairly common theme in a lot of the talks I have in this room. You're not the first person to feel that way, and you certainly won't be the last. So, hopefully, that knowledge offers some form of solace. The feeling you're experiencing may seem like a direct result of your coma, but it's actually pretty universal to the human condition."

Her words were well-intentioned, but I had a hard time believing these other patients suffered the same kind of perpetual identity crisis I found myself mired in. How could they? When I looked in a mirror, the person that stared back at me wasn't just some altered variation of myself that I was trying on for size or that I'd come to disagree with over time as a failed social experiment.

No, the person staring back at me was a total stranger, a mystery I could only briefly escape from at night through the distorted hallucinations of dreams; dreams that somehow meant more to me than anything real in my waking life.

The rest of the session went quickly. Dr. Eiding, perhaps sensing my increasing physical and mental restlessness, asked if I wanted to end our hour together five minutes early.

Happily, I obliged; less because I wanted to stop talking with her, and more because my legs were starting to kill me.

I swung my suspended foot back onto the ground, flexed the arches of my feet, and wiggled my toes until the pins and needles subsided along the long muscles.

After a minute or two, I felt confident enough to stand, and with one hand using the back of the chair for support, I eased myself back up to a vertical position.

Dr. Eiding waited patiently for me at the door to her study. She smiled as I shuffled past her and down the creaking steps, and she made sure to stay close behind so she'd at least be within arm's reach should I lose my footing and suddenly stumble.

Going down the stairs was always harder than going up them for me, and the slow descent made me dizzy and lightheaded. I always felt like I was falling forward, like all I had to do was let go and close my eyes, and I'd topple headfirst back into that spiraling black oblivion I'd left behind before waking up at the hospital.

When we reached the base of the staircase, Dr. Eiding moved off quickly into the kitchen, beckoning me to follow her with a look of impish exuberance on her face. It wasn't until I caught up with her at the kitchen counter that I realized why she was so excited.

"Here, I want you to take these home with you. I just baked them a couple hours ago. They're chocolate chip, which I know your dad said he's particularly fond of. Personally, I can't eat more than four of them or my stomach will get mad at me. More than one cookie, even, and my waistline gets mad at me, too; but that's a war I'm not going to win anymore. Who's picking you up today, by the way?"

I took the bag of cookies from her and shuffled forward a few halting steps up to the window above her kitchen sink, where I had a clear view of the street outside. Parked right at the end of the sidewalk leading from Dr. Eiding's little white house was Mitsu, and I could make out my mother's figure behind the car windows.

"Just my mother, since my father had to go back to work today. It looks like she's here already."

Dr. Eiding joined me at the window and waved at the car outside. My mother saw us and waved back.

"That's right, you said that earlier. Well, say hello to both of them for me and enjoy the cookies. As always, keep using the dream journal, and remember that you can always call me if you think something significant has clicked back into place for you or if you really need me. Otherwise, I'll see you next week."

Chapter Five

My mother immediately raised an eyebrow at the goodie bag of cookies when they hit the passenger floormat of the car.

"Good lord, did she send you home with more cookies? We still haven't finished the ones from last week!"

"I know. I didn't have the heart to tell her that, though."

"I think I've gained ten pounds since you started seeing Dr. Eiding. At this rate, I'm going to need to see a psychiatrist myself just to talk about my compulsive overeating problem."

She let out a soft chuckle at her own joke, then slapped one hand over her mouth and went silent, her cheeks blushing a deep rose.

"I'm sorry, Davey. That was inappropriate."

To be honest, her physical reaction surprised me more than anything she'd said. I wasn't even really sure what she was apologizing for, so I awkwardly reached over to pat her knee.

"It's okay... Mom."

The word still didn't sound completely natural coming out of my mouth, and we both noticed it.

"I've probably gained ten pounds, too. Her cookies *are* awesome."

This time, my mother let out a quick scoff.

"Yeah, but the difference is that you're *trying* to gain weight, while I'm trying to lose it. You should probably just keep that whole bag to yourself. And whatever you do, don't let Dad see it."

I smiled. In the short time I'd been back with my parents, I felt like I'd already picked up on a number of the nuances and traits that defined their relationship.

My mother, for example, took great pleasure in teasing my father about his weight; which was ridiculous, of course, since my father was tall and slender like a streetlight.

While neither one of my parents needed to worry about their weight, the major difference between them was their respective appetites. My mother ate sparingly and in rationed portions, and began every day with a morning jog around our neighborhood. On the other hand, my father ate like a man possessed, always went back for second-helpings, and regularly claimed that the only exercise that interested him was the mental kind he performed every morning while working on a crossword puzzle.

"Superior genetic makeup." That's how my mother chalked up her husband's thinness despite his nonexistent diet and exercise habits. She had no alternative but to rankle him by predicting the inevitable demise of a metabolism that so far had shown no signs of slowing down, while she herself continued to count calories and lace up her sneakers every sunrise.

The ribbing was all in fun, though, and my parents'

relationship seemed to be nothing short of a model marriage.

Every morning, my father would ask his wife what she wanted for dinner that evening, and every night, he would make it for her without fail. If she couldn't tell him what she wanted, he would surprise her, and his choices always seemed to hit the spot.

I liked the fact that my father cooked our family meals rather than my mother. It wasn't that my mother couldn't cook; she claimed she was no good, but it was a statement my father vehemently denied as false modesty.

Rather, my father did the cooking because he knew his wife didn't enjoy it, whether she was good at it or not. And so, it was therefore one of the many ways that he could practice his chivalry and showcase his romantic side, I supposed.

They had their own little ritual during the evenings, and it was fascinating for me to observe it, though I'm sure I'd seen it many, many times before.

He would begin dinner preparations in earnest around seven o'clock, right around the same time their favorite sitcom began. She would turn on the television set, crank up the volume so it was audible from the other room in the kitchen, and then offer to help out in whatever capacity she could as his 'sous-chef'.

My father would invariably hear none of it, shooing her out of the kitchen with soft whacks at her rear end and obscenities uttered in some indecipherable language and accent. Laughing, she'd retreat back into the living room, where she'd snuggle up next to me on the sofa under a blanket instead.

We wouldn't see my father again until five minutes

before the food was ready, at which time he'd sweep into the living room and announce it was time to set the table and wash up. If we were going to eat inside, my mother would set up a small, circular wooden table off to the side of the kitchen area. If it was a nice night, she'd do the same thing, only outside on the patio table.

On weeknights, my father drank cranberry juice— "for the sake of my kidneys"—and on weekend nights, he treated himself with a light beer or two. My mother drank the cranberry juice, too, out of solidarity with my father, but she would also indulge herself with half a glass of chilled port after dinner most nights.

They tried to get me to drink skim milk with my meals, as it was supposedly my own personal drink of choice. But after I gagged and nearly threw up trying to drink a glass three days after returning from the hospital, my mother reluctantly removed it from her weekly shopping list. Pure, simple water was good enough for me.

After dinner, my mother would clear our plates and begin the dishes. My father always tried to help, only to have his offer rebuked with a curt reprimand, something along the lines of "You know the drill, Steven. You cooked, I clean. We've been doing this dance for twenty years now, so get out of here."

If his appetite was satiated, my father would lumber into the living room and flip on the nightly news or weather forecasts. If it wasn't completely satisfied, he'd do the same thing, only with a spoon and a carton of chocolate chip ice cream smuggled under one arm.

Originally, neither one of my parents allowed me

to help them with any parts of this routine, insisting that I just relax and enjoy myself. Over time, however, I convinced my mother I was at least healthy and strong enough to assist her with the dishes.

We had a little black radio box tucked between the microwave and a kitchen counter TV. She would turn it on and slowly spin the dial until she found the smooth jazz station she always listened to while scraping plates and loading the dishwasher.

"It just calms me and helps with my digestion, I'm sure of it," she'd whisper confidentially to me as we worked our way through the simple chore.

And when we were finished, she'd turn the radio off, start the dishwasher, and together we'd join my father in the living room for another hour or so before it was time for bed.

The chocolate chip cookie bag slid across the floormat as my mother turned the car at an intersection. I recognized that we were maybe about halfway to our house, and I wondered if my father was already home from work and preparing dinner.

He hadn't said much this morning about going back to his office for the first time since I woke up, beyond the fact that he wasn't looking forward to spending the day away from me and my mother.

To be honest, I barely understood what he did exactly. I knew it was some sort of government or civic job and that he worked in a wide brick building on Main Street, but that was about the extent of my knowledge.

"Davey… can I ask you something?"

The tone of my mother's voice sounded softer and more cautious than before. Her fingers fidgeted on the steering wheel, and she alternated quick looks between me and the street in front of her.

"Of course."

She hesitated a moment before speaking again, and it was clear that something on her mind was making her uncomfortable.

"I know you don't remember a lot from before the accident, and that it's going to take time for everything to come back to you fully. I just… I can't help but wonder if we're doing the right thing, driving around in this car."

It wasn't what I was expecting at all. As a matter of fact, I didn't even know what she meant by it. And maybe she could see the disconnect on my face, because she felt the need to elaborate and soldier on.

"You've always loved this car so much, since the day we bought it for you, and that's why Dad thought it would make you happy for us to pick you up from the hospital in it, rather than taking his or my car. I told him I wasn't sure it was such a good idea, to see it first thing like that, but he was persistent; all this about 'getting up on the horse again,' which is silly, really, and I told him so.

"Anyway, I just want to make sure that it's okay with you, and that it's not too… painful… or anything. I'm obviously more than happy to use my own car. I just don't know what's best for you, or how you feel about it all. Or if you even have an opinion for that matter, which you might not…"

I was still confused by what she was asking.

From a variety of conversations with my parents, my physical therapist, my psychiatrist Dr. Eiding, and even from Dr. Frye back at the hospital, I'd gathered bits and pieces of information regarding 'the accident', as everyone always labeled it.

My mother and father spoke the least about it, and whenever it did pop up in conversation, they always lowered their voices to an apologetic whisper when murmuring the two words together, as if their mere utterance aloud was enough to send me spiraling back into the coma.

Apparently, I'd suffered some kind of severe head trauma. In the hospital, I'd wondered about the cause of it, even going so far as to ask the nurse if I'd fallen. That sense of lying immobile on the ground in a field of flowers was one of the few memories I could latch onto from time to time. She hadn't provided me with an answer, and since then, no one had made any complete attempts to illuminate me.

For my part, I had no reservations discussing 'the accident' whatsoever. I did understand the reluctance from my parents, though, given Dr. Frye's suggestion of easing me back slowly into the life I'd left behind for nearly two months.

But now I found myself impatient, and since my mother had brought it up herself—albeit in the vaguest of ways—this seemed like the perfect time to finally try and get some more concrete answers.

"What happened exactly... Mom? With the accident?"

Her jaw clenched reflexively, and worry lines deepened in her cheeks and along her forehead above her tortoise-shell glasses.

"Maybe I shouldn't have even said anything. We don't have to talk about it—"

"I want to." The conviction in my voice surprised

even me. "If that's okay with you…"

I tacked that last bit on as softly as I could. My relationship with my mother, like my relationship with everyone else at this point, was still a work in progress, and I didn't want to risk damaging it just to slake my own curiosity.

We were very close to home now, and she drove slower, taking her time accelerating at green lights and cruising just below the speed limit.

"Of course it's okay. If it's okay with you, it's okay with me."

I realized I was staring at her from the passenger seat, so I turned back to the road in front of us as casually as I could. The interior cabin of the car suddenly felt charged, the still air crackling with energy and suspense. Time seemed to freeze as the world outside our little metal shell drifted by in slow-motion.

"Well, Davey… you were in this car, of course. It was just a normal day; you were driving home from band practice after school. It was raining—quite a bit of rain, but nothing too out of the ordinary. And, well… I'm not exactly sure what happened, to be honest. The police said you probably lost control; maybe you hydroplaned and overcorrected?"

She glanced at me, perhaps looking for confirmation, then continued when she saw it wasn't coming.

"The car crashed into a beech tree, on the other side of a bridge over Lower Creek. When the rescuers got there, you were unconscious. They brought you in an ambulance to the hospital and did everything they could to revive you, but at that point, you were already in a coma. And then, after a few days, they transferred you to CMC to run more tests."

She paused again, taking a deep breath and smiling sadly at me before returning her gaze to the road.

"Those were the worst forty-eight days of my life." My mother cleared her throat quickly. "But it's okay, because what's important is that you woke up… right? You're here now, back with me, and with Dad. That's all that matters."

She jerked her right hand away from the steering wheel and offered it to me, palm up, and her fingers and wrist were shaking.

It took me a second to recognize what she wanted. Tentatively, I moved my left hand into hers, and she grasped it fiercely and slipped her fingers in between mine, squeezing our hands together into a tight ball of flesh and bone.

"Don't ever leave me again, okay? Promise me that, Davey. I wouldn't be able to take it."

The naked desperation in her face and voice cut through me. Suddenly, it became clear to me that our roles had reversed, if only for an instant. She was the suppliant child, oblivious to everything but the comfort and security of a parent's unquestioned and unfailing love, and I somehow held a power I couldn't even begin to describe—the mysterious and terrifying power of a person whose unfortunate life experiences had already aged them well beyond their teenage years.

"I promise."

Those were the feeble words that trickled out of my mouth with our hands still enmeshed. My voice sounded funny to me again, in the same way it had at the hospital when I'd first woken up, but the sentiment was sincere.

My mother smiled and gripped my hand tighter. Taking my cue from her, I did the same, and realized we were home already. The last few blocks had been a daze.

Chapter Six

My Froot Loops were getting soggy.

The colorful cereal had quickly become a staple of my mornings, much to the delight of my father and the surprise of my mother. Both agreed that I had never been much of a cereal person before my coma, preferring instead more home-cooked breakfast items like bacon, eggs, sausage, and toast.

Similar to the dinnertime experiments with my favorite foods, though, they'd tried to re-introduce me to these old standby favorites only to quickly see through my false politeness and remember once again that my tastes had truly changed since the accident.

But even my father hadn't expected me to take to Froot Loops the way I did. "You've never liked Froot Loops; not even as a baby," he'd remarked not that long ago. "But this is what I eat every day. Give it a shot, and if you like it, I'll go to the grocery store right now and load us up."

With both him and my mother watching carefully, I had shaken a handful of the bright, multicolored sugary rings into my hand and cautiously put a few into my mouth to chew. It was instantly amazing, just the right amount of crunchiness, sweetness, and flavor, without being overwhelming or too filling.

Before long, I was shaking whole heaps into my open palm and gobbling them up. My father had laughed, grabbed his car keys, and departed for the store, crowing "That's my boy!" as he danced out the front door.

This particular morning, I'd poured a bit too much milk over my cereal. The rainbow 'O's paid the price for my overzealousness, growing waterlogged until the sea of milk started to leech them of their color, form, and texture.

Absentmindedly, I sailed my half-submerged spoon around the bowl between the tiny little life rings, using the rounded end of the silverware to dunk and drown an orange ring here, a purple ring there.

"Quit playing with your food."

I looked up from the bowl and saw my mother watching me from the other side of the table. Her amused expression and the playful tone in her voice indicated she was just teasing me.

My father had left for work maybe twenty minutes prior. As he often did, he had forgotten to turn the small kitchen television off on his way out. It wasn't a big deal to me, but it seemed to be a pet peeve of my mother's, who preferred jazz on the radio over morning news on the TV.

I didn't blame her. The news rarely made much sense to me, and even when it did, the stories always seemed depressing. Just now, the man on the screen was grimly asking viewers to share any information they might have on a missing person: a local girl who looked about my age, and who hadn't been seen in over twenty-four hours.

"That's enough of that."

My mother switched the monitor off with a remote.

"So, Davey… what do you want to do today?"

I figured there was a good chance that she might ask me that particular question this morning. In fact, ever since our brief conversation in the car yesterday on the ride home from Dr. Eiding's house, I'd been counting on it—and I'd long since begun planning an answer for it.

The question in and of itself wasn't anything out of the ordinary; in fact, it was something my mother usually asked me after breakfast most mornings, since she didn't work like my father did, and I certainly didn't feel ready to go back to school just yet.

Every other morning, I never had a definitive answer for her. I'd just mumble something about being open to whatever she wanted to do with the day, and then we'd eventually go about it after a whole lot of meaningless back-and-forth.

Trips to local Lenoir landmarks, deep dives into family scrapbooks, board games in the living room… these were some of the many activities we usually did together, either to foster our growing relationship or to shock my old memories back into place, or both.

This morning, however, I woke up with a crystal-clear conviction that I didn't want to spend my day traipsing around the town or digging up old family heirlooms hunting for memory clues. The idea had spread like wildfire through my brain ever since yesterday's car ride. It was the only thing I could think about now, but I would need my mother's help to make it happen.

"Actually, I have a favor to ask."

I kept swirling the milk and cereal bits around in my bowl with the spoon, and it struck me that I was feeling kind of nervous.

"Do you think you could tell me how to get to where my accident happened?"

My mother stared blankly back at me. I wasn't sure what she was thinking, so I soldiered on, still fiddling with the cereal bowl, the spoon clinking softly off the circular porcelain walls every so often.

"If that's okay with you?"

Another *clink*, and I reminded myself to keep breathing, and that this wasn't going to be a big deal.

"It doesn't have to be a big deal. I can go alone."

And now, for the hard part…

"I kind of want to go alone, actually, even if it's weird. I can handle it."

She studied me carefully from across the kitchen table for a moment before folding her arms in front of her chest and leaning back in her chair.

"I don't know if that's such a good idea."

Maybe I needed a gentler tact.

"I really think I can handle it. And I think it'd be helpful, too. It might bring something back… and it kind of makes sense if you think about it, since it's the last place where everything was normal, and where my body and brain were still intact. Maybe going back there will connect the dots somehow."

The woman looked far from convinced. I let go of the spoon and slid my hands out slowly across the table in a gesture of supplication, palms up and fingers trembling slightly.

"Please… Mom."

That word had weight to it. Very rarely did it spring organically from my lips, and we both knew it. I hoped that saying it out loud right now would make an impact on her and aid my powers of persuasion.

My mother's shoulders lifted and then fell again as she let out a deep sigh. She ran her hand through her dark hair and tilted her head back slightly, looking up at the ceiling as if she might find some guidance there. When she brought her chin back down, there was a soft gleam in her eyes.

"If that's what you want to do, Davey, then that's what we'll do."

Her decision was a victory on a couple of levels.

It meant, first and foremost, that I would get a chance to test my brand-new theory: that ground-zero of 'the accident' held the key to unlocking my memories and my past.

But it also meant that my mother loved and trusted me enough to give in to my wishes, even if they went against what she thought was best. That, in and of itself, was an important step forward in a relationship that grew stronger by the day.

"Well… are you ready to go now, or do you want some more Froot Loops?"

For some reason, the question made me laugh. Her face seemed to indicate it was a legitimate question, so I shook my head.

"No, I'm full, finally."

She started to reach out for the bowl of soggy cereal.

"It's okay. I've got it."

I enlisted one hand to push my body up slowly from the chair and the other to pick the bowl up off the table, then brought it over to the sink, washed the remaining contents down the drain, and placed the bowl and spoon both in the dishwasher. When I turned around, my mother was still seated at the table, watching me in silence.

"I know this is going to sound silly... but I can't begin to tell you how happy it makes me, just seeing you up on your feet again, even doing something as simple as washing a bowl out. It's surreal."

I didn't know what to say, so I just smiled back at her. There was a brief stillness while we held each other's gaze before she stood up and walked over toward the staircase.

"I'm going to put on a sweater real quick. You should do the same, and maybe grab a jacket, too, while you're at it. I think it's really coming down out there."

She was right. I'd been too focused on my breakfast and on my plans for the day to look outside. Now that I did, I could see the tree branches outside our house bouncing up and down under a steady barrage of raindrops. The sky was one big swirling mass of grey, white, and blackish green; a peculiar mixture of colors I thought I'd never seen before.

Just looking at it all made me feel chilled to the bone, so I decided to heed my mother's advice and bundle up with a wool pullover I found at the back of my closet. And just to be safe, I tucked a denim jean jacket under one arm as well before heading back down the stairs and meeting my mother at the front door.

We shared a deep breath to steel our nerves, then bolted out into the elements toward the safe haven of Mitsu. I reached the passenger side and grabbed at the door handle, but it was still locked. Incredulous, I looked over the top of the car's roof and saw my mother fumbling with the keys, one hand shielding her eyes from the downpour while the other struggled to find the right one. In the midst of all the chaos, she laughed, and I didn't know how I felt about it exactly.

The collar of the wool sweater was already itching and irritating my skin, but now it was getting damp, too, as it absorbed the rain. It didn't take long to identify this as a terrible sensation—scratchy, wet, cold, clingy, and relentless, the collar just wouldn't let my neck forget it was there. I pried at it with two fingers and tried the car door handle again. Mercifully, it was unlocked this time, so I clambered inside and sealed the whirling elements off behind me.

We found refuge from the rain, but not the cold. My mother either noticed me shaking or felt the same way, because she deftly cranked up the heat dials as soon as the engine revved into motion. Beneath a thousand pitter-pattering impacts, the windshield slowly fogged over from bottom to top.

Absentmindedly, I reached out the tip of my finger to touch the glass. It was cool and wet, as expected, and as I dragged the tip downward, a small clear path emerged showing the world outside. Satisfied with what I'd created, I lifted my finger and pressed it to another place, not too far from the first, and brought the two lines together for a moment, before sending a third line down and away from both of them.

When I was done, I saw I'd made the letter K.

"What does that stand for?"

Her voice startled me. For a minute there, I'd completely forgotten there was another human being sitting beside me. I looked at my mother quizzically, and she nodded her forehead back toward the scribbled shape I'd drawn.

The fog along the inside of the window was quickly receding back from all the edges. Before I could formulate an answer, the K was gone.

Honestly, I didn't know what it was supposed to stand for, if anything at all; it came without any real thought or intention. All I knew was that it made me strangely happy to see it there, but I certainly couldn't say that to my mother. She'd probably nix this whole idea and take me straight over to Dr. Eiding's house for an extra round of therapy.

"I don't know."

The truth was the easiest thing to say.

She didn't press me further on it, turning her attention instead on backing the car out of the driveway and getting the wiper blades moving at the proper cadence. Once everything was set to her liking, she added the finishing touch by pressing the button that turned on the radio, and soon we were gliding through the deluge in style, accompanied by a comforting combination of soft jazz and circulated hot air.

As was becoming my habit on these car rides, I spent most of my time with the crown of my head resting gently against the side window, staring out into the world streaking by. This occasion was a little different than the others; my vision took turns alternating focus between the passing scenery and a hypnotizing screen of shifting water beads and rivulets of rain shimmying along the glass.

Occasionally, my breath would fog up a small

patch of the window in a manner similar to what had happened on the windshield earlier, and with it came the impulse to draw another K again, and see if maybe this time, other letters would follow. If nothing else, maybe some semblance of logical meaning might be unearthed, or at least a shred of a memory, like the texture of that blanket I'd dreamt of and recounted to Dr. Eiding.

Tempted as I was to doodle again and test the boundaries of my subconscious, the idea of my mother catching me out of her periphery and then asking me more questions was enough to stymie the compulsion, at least for now. So, I kept my hands warm and incubated between my thighs and the car seat.

It didn't take long for the landmarks and checkpoints I'd worked so hard to familiarize myself with to start vanishing. Somewhere along the way, we must have passed through the intersection we always turned at to get to Dr. Eiding's house, and now I was definitely exploring uncharted territory.

First, it was just the buildings and the street names that were different. Then, the spaces between those buildings gradually grew longer and larger, as whole swaths of undeveloped nature began occupying the bulk of what I saw whizzing by. It occurred to me that we were leaving the town limits of Lenoir behind us and venturing out further into the country.

My pulse accelerated with the swelling thrill of adventure, just as the window steam from my exhalations began to appear more and more frequently, both physical byproducts of a heart and a pair of lungs working overtime to keep pace with a frantic brain that raced far out ahead of them on the open road.

"I'm sure it's a little hard to tell in this weather, but does any of this look familiar to you?"

She turned the radio down to speak, but it didn't really make a difference. Her voice was muffled, smothered by the incessant percussive rainfall hammering against the metal car. Somehow, I still managed to piece together what she'd said in all the din.

"Not really. Should it?"

She smiled ruefully at me.

"This is the way you drive to school every day. Remember? Highway 64 to Beecher Anderson Road, and then the first right after the gas station? Then a left on Caldwell?"

The hope was fading fast from her eyes.

"You follow the curve up past the football field until you see the high school on your right?"

These were the moments when I most wanted to lie, if for no other reason than to bring solace to the people who loved me. Watching a mother lob meaningless words at her son in vain, desperately struggling to reconnect with the person she'd raised since childbirth, would be enough to break anyone's heart. It certainly made a mess of mine.

But while it pained me to see her like this, it also strengthened my resolve to follow through with this experiment. If I could just find something—find *anything*—at the site of my accident, then maybe a path to reconciliation wouldn't be so hard after all.

"How much further is it?"

Changing the subject was better than lying to my own mother.

She squinted through the rapid back-and-forth of

the black wiper blades.

"We're almost there. Just a couple more minutes, I think."

My heart pounded inside my chest. A shrill anxiety crackled like lightning through my muscles, and I shifted in the car seat to try and find a more comfortable resting position, but it was futile. Every fiber of my being was wound tight with anticipation for the event to come, and soon my calves and shoulders cramped up painfully too. I tried rubbing the nervousness out, but it was useless; I'd have to dwell in this tense state of bound energy at least until we reached our destination.

Agonizingly, the closer we appeared to get to that destination, the slower my mother seemed to drive. Already unable to sit still, I couldn't help but turn in my seat every thirty seconds or so to visually check in with her, wondering each time if the deceleration was a response to the driving conditions or if it was a signal that we were finally approaching the site of 'the accident'.

It was always the driving conditions, though. The rain would intensify to the point where you could barely see out the windshield, or the path would suddenly veer into a sharp and unexpected turn. Certain lower areas of the road were already flooded, and I watched with fascination as plumes of water sprayed up from the car's wheels on both sides.

With the radio turned off, we continued to drive in relative silence—relative only because there was nothing silent about the cacophony of the storm beating down upon us. I wasn't paying particularly close attention to the digital time display on the car's middle control panel, but it had to have been longer than a couple minutes already.

Maybe we missed a turn somewhere? I tried to remember what my mother had said about the location of my accident. She had mentioned a bridge over a creek, with a large tree on the other side. That's where they'd found me, in this very same car, smashed into the side of that tree and already lost to this world and the life I'd always known.

A thought occurred to me. How did my mother know the exact location where it happened? She wasn't with me during the accident, and she certainly wasn't the person who found me or who whisked me away in an ambulance. Presumably, she also wasn't with the people who had to tow the car away; she would have been at my bedside in the hospital when all of that was happening.

Realistically, the only way she would know exactly where the accident happened was if she had come and visited the location herself. Had she done that? Had she come here before? And if so, how many times?

These questions would have to wait. We were slowing down again, but this time, we were also pulling off the road completely.

My mother angled the steering wheel to the right and brought the car to a gradual stop along a loose gravel shoulder on the side of the pavement before cutting the engine. The overhead interior lights brightened as she unlocked all the car doors with a soft click.

"This is it."

What an apt choice of words. I knew she was only saying we had finally arrived at the spot, but it also perfectly encapsulated the gravity of what I was experiencing right now.

My insides felt like how I imagined a person might feel standing at the top of an extremely high cliff, knowing full well that they're going to have to jump from the edge eventually... because there's no turning back now.

My mother reached out a hand and rested it on my shoulder.

"Listen to me, Davey. This is a very brave thing you're trying to do. But there's nothing that says you have to do it right now, today, tomorrow, or whenever. I'm already so proud of all you've done, and of all the hard work you've put in to get to this point. You certainly don't need to prove anything to me, to your father, or, I'd even venture to say, to yourself."

She lifted her hand, rubbed her thumb across my cheek, and smiled.

"Plus, it looks awfully cold and wet out there."

I smiled back at her and reflected on the advice.

She was right; there was nothing forcing me to follow through with this idea. It wasn't as if the creek, the bridge, the tree, all of it would just disappear if I waited too long to revisit it. I could come back another day, any other day, along this very same road to this very same spot.

My mother was also right about the weather; it looked absolutely miserable out there. Maybe it *would* be in my best interest to come back on a warmer, sunnier day after all.

But no, that was just the fear talking. Fear of the unknown, fear of what I might find out there... or worse, fear that I wouldn't find anything at all.

I could come up with a million different reasons not to get out of the car and to postpone this exploration for another day, but I knew in my head and in my heart that all those reasons were really just excuses.

And if I allowed myself to give in to those excuses, did I really even deserve to learn the truth? After all, I'd come through much worse than rain to get this far.

"Thanks, Mom." It was the easiest and the truest the word had sounded yet. "I'll be fine."

I took a deep breath and opened the car door. The wind wasted no time in greeting me, and goosebumps broke out all along my skin as brisk air rushed into the warm cabin. Raindrops came sliding in sideways to speckle my jeans, sweater, and the leather interior of the car.

I had one foot swung out onto the wet pavement before I remembered I'd brought a jacket with me as well, which I must have tucked behind me at some point on the ride over. It was often difficult enough getting my arms and legs to do what I wanted them to do in good conditions; now, the task of putting the jacket on was even harder, since I was shivering from head to toe.

After much wiggling and writhing, I managed to fit it on atop my wool pullover and button it shut in front. Another deep breath, and then I grabbed the doorframe to pull myself up and out of the car and fully into the storm.

For my mother's sake, I quickly closed the door behind me to seal it off from the rain, but the window slid down as she leaned across to look at me from the driver seat. Her voice was raised, so I could hear it over everything outside.

"That's the bridge up ahead. The tree's on the other side, right next to the road. Are you sure you don't want me to come with you?"

I shook my head solemnly, squinting my eyes and hunching my shoulders up close to my neck as my body continued to react to the cold. The bridge wasn't that far away at all; I could see the guard rails on either side of it, along with a small yellow sign where it started. Something was written there, but I couldn't make out the words from this distance.

"Davey!"

The sudden exclamation startled me, and I bent over to bring my attention back to her.

"Don't stay out too long, okay? We can always come back again."

I patted the roof of the car twice to let her know that I understood, tucked my hands into the pockets of the denim jacket for warmth, and started walking toward the bridge.

Chapter Seven

Even bundled up as I was, the rain and wind opportunistically found chinks in my armor, licking at little cracks of exposed skin around my waist, wrists, and collarbone. All I could do was keep moving to stay warm, rubbing my knees closely against one other as I walked in a desperate effort to create heat from the friction.

A garbled sound came from behind me. I stopped in my tracks and turned back to look at the car. My mother lowered her own window this time and cautiously stuck her head out of it to look at me.

"*What?*" I yelled the question back at her as loud as I could.

"I said: let me know if you need me! Okay?"

The words were still muffled, but I comprehended them this time, and nodded my head before turning back to the road in front of me.

It had been over fifteen minutes since we last saw another car, but I still took care to make sure I walked on the right side of the white line that marked the outer boundary of the driving lane. The gravel was loose and slippery beneath my feet, and there was a steady film of water running off the main road and down the slope toward the grass on my right.

Every now and then, I'd look down and see a crumpled aluminum can, bottle cap, cigarette butt, or some other colorful bit of trash littered on the ground. It upset me to see any of that out here, considering how beautiful and pristine the natural landscape was in all directions, and I had to suppress the urge to pick up some of the larger and more out-of-place debris pieces. Maybe I'd grab them on my way back to the car.

The closer I got to it, the more the bridge came into view. I could make out the inscription on the sign now; the biggest word was CAUTION at the very top, followed by an image of a car streaking from side to side below it, and then the smaller words BRIDGE SLIPPERY WHEN WET placed along the bottom.

Had I seen that sign or its identical twin on the opposite side of the bridge the day of my accident? Evidently, I should have paid it more mind, because even in the blinding downpour, the bright reflective yellow was hard to ignore.

The road narrowed as I threaded my feet carefully across the bridge, hugging the protective guardrail that rose up just below my right hip. Occasionally, I'd steal a quick glance behind me, just to make sure there were no approaching cars coming. I'd already survived one vehicular catastrophe along this bridge; making it through two would be pushing my luck.

Fortunately for me, the only car within sight was the blue one parked along the side of the road, the flashing lights of which grew dimmer and dimmer as I continued my trek away from it.

Everywhere around me was water. Irregular patterns of it crisscrossed through me from above, dowsing and dissecting me from the head down. Some of the rain came at me sideways with the wind, beating me back and slowing my progress. It even seemed to splash upward at my legs and ankles like it was actually coming up from the ground, ricocheting off the glossy pavement until the hems of my pants felt glued to my shin bones.

There was water further below me as well. Maybe ten feet under the bridge, a gurgling stream swelled and shook under the assault of the storm. It didn't look particularly wide or deep, but the current moved swiftly.

My eyes followed a dead leaf floating along the surface as it zipped around a rock obstruction and then disappeared out of sight beneath the shadow of the bridge. I looked further up the creek to see where the water originated but lost sight of it amongst the heavy forest and thickening fog

As I approached the end of the bridge, it struck me that I wasn't entirely sure which tree I was supposed to be looking for. Several large specimens clustered together on both sides of the road, and none of them stood out at first glance as the obvious culprit I had come for.

In my fantasy of how this confrontation of sorts would play out, I imagined the guilty tree as larger than life: tall, thick, and twisted, its identity instantly revealed to me on a deeper level because of the pain we'd shared in that fateful moment of our collision. From the scene I'd played out in my head, the tree was still gashed and broken from the accident, weeping sap like blood from an open wound in its bark that just wouldn't heal.

And then, in the vision, I'd touch my hand to that spot, and like magic, all the memories would come whizzing back in a flash, working backward from the instant we'd first smashed into each other and the damage had been done.

It was all so cinematic and profound that I'd convinced myself it had to be true; not just a fantasy, but an actual premonition of what was surely to come in this climax of revelation.

And here I was now, the moment finally upon me, and I wasn't even sure which tree was mine.

All my mother had told me was that *the* tree was on the other side of the bridge, and that it was right next to the road. For some reason, I assumed it would be on the right-hand side of the road, the side I would have been driving on, but that was another unsubstantiated idea. What if my car had skidded across the road and crashed into a tree on the left-hand side? There was nothing implausible about that scenario, either.

I tried to reflect back on anything my parents might have said in the past that could be helpful now, but per usual, it was a difficult and ultimately fruitless exercise trying to force my brain to go backward.

Maybe it was time to ask my mother for help? She'd offered it several times, and if she knew this was the bridge I'd been driving toward the day of my accident, she surely could identify the tree I'd hit as well.

I turned around and looked back in her direction, searching for any sign of blue or flashing lights, but the rain and fog had completely swallowed up everything on the other side.

Somehow, the idea of slogging back across the

bridge through the storm seemed more arduous and daunting than the journey here had been. I decided that the best course of action was just to move ever forward and to try and discover the correct tree organically.

Starting with the group directly in front of me, I plodded through the muddy grass until I came face-to-face with one of the largest of the bunch. Slowly, I circled round the trunk, occasionally allowing my fingers to trace abnormalities along the surface.

Unsurprisingly, there was no mystical connection, no opening of the mental floodgates, no surge of recognition or remembrance. Just hard, wet bark beneath my fingertips.

So, I moved on to the next one. And then the next.

Trunk after trunk, tree after tree, my tiny body revolved like an orbiting moon around these great wooden giants, patient but purposeful in my quest to explore all possibilities.

A welcome side effect of this process was the temporary shelter from the storm each examination provided, because the rain had a much harder time making its way down to me through the interlocking patchwork roof of leaves and branches. Some of it still came in the cruel, wet gusts that blew parallel to the ground, but at least I was no longer getting hammered from all angles.

After inspecting maybe a dozen trees, I realized I'd moved a good distance away from the bridge, to the point where it now seemed highly unlikely my car had made it this far. It was still possible, perhaps, but I kept hearing my mother's voice in my head telling me the tree was right next to the road on the other side of the bridge.

Maybe it had been on the left-hand side of the road after all. If the weather that day was anything like it was now, it was absolutely within reason to assume I'd lost control and veered across to the opposite side.

The ground beneath me squished and burped rainwater as I meandered back toward the bridge, timing my walk to minimize the intervals I was unprotected and exposed between tree canopies. When I was back to where I started, I looked both ways up the street, checking again to make sure there was no oncoming traffic. Safety assured, I splashed across the black pavement to the soft grass on the other side and took refuge under the closest tree.

Quivering with cold, I tried to warm my body up by rubbing the palms of my hands over my arms, thighs, and torso.

It didn't work. If anything, the friction just served as an uncomfortable reminder of how thoroughly soaked I was. The rain had worked its way past the outer defenses of my jacket, pants, and shoes, and now it seeped through my wool pullover, socks, and even my underpants. Layers of soaked clothing hung over my bones like wet rags, dripping and dragging me down.

My spirits were sinking, too. The resolve and determination I'd initially armored myself with were both fading fast, washed away in the maelstrom like helpless sand castles on a beach.

Why wasn't this easier? The tree I stood under right now looked like it fit the part: it was tall, its trunk was thick, and its branches were definitely twisted.

But there were no signs of damage or impact, no scratches or dents, and no broken foliage. Even the ground around me looked pristine and undisturbed. The car surely would have left muddy tire tracks where it went off-road and skidded through the grass, but there was nothing of the sort on this side or the other.

It was better to keep moving. Standing still was good for avoiding falling rain, but all it really did was remind me of how cold, wet, and miserable I was. At least if I was moving, I could distract myself into focusing on the task at hand... however unsatisfying that task was proving to be.

So, I continued to shuffle my soggy feet around the bases of the trees, taking care not to trip over exposed roots and fallen branches, gazing wildly around my surroundings with no true sense of comprehension.

Wandering. That's what I was doing now. I was wandering through the woods without direction or purpose. More than once, I completely forgot what I was doing in the first place and had to stop, take a shuddering breath, look around, and start moving again just to try and stay warm.

Gradually, a new thought surfaced in the back of my mind, a thin whisper of a suggestion that I tried to stave off. But as I stumbled deeper and deeper into the thick forest underbrush, it became impossible to ignore the nagging sensation that I was lost.

My ears pricked as a faint hissing sound came from behind me, and I whirled around to confront the danger, hot blood rushing up into my cheeks.

But there was nothing there except green and black, the blurred colors of the dense plant life swarming in from all sides.

Vaguely, I wondered where the bridge had gone...

or, for that matter, the road. It was all gone now, suffocated and snuffed out by the overgrown wild that had come to life around me.

There was that hissing sound again, and this time, it was a crackling, too. The sound grew louder until it was a mountainous thunderclap that rumbled through the air and shook the foundation of the very world itself.

Dumbly, I looked upward at the sky and at the dim grey light piercing in through the darkened treetops, half-expecting to see some sort of monstrous and magnificent beast up there, as if only a mythical creature could be responsible for making such a titanic boom.

Of course, there was nothing to see there but more rain, and a pair of drops scored simultaneous perfect hits by splashing into my eyeballs at the exact same time.

Blinking, I brought my chin back down toward my chest and rubbed the water out with both hands until I could see again.

Now, *this* was different. There were still trees, bushes, and ferns every which way I looked, but there was also a stream now, nestled in between two mossy banks just up ahead and centered at the edge of my vision. It was a new sight and a new element, something dramatically different from the teeming flora, and I was immediately compelled to get closer to it.

While I'd been in more of a dazed stupor than a genuine panic wandering aimlessly through this strange environment, the water still served as a helpful reminder that somewhere nearby, there was a bridge built over that water. If I followed the stream, I'd eventually stumble upon the bridge, and that would of course bring me right back to familiar territory and to the road I'd left behind.

Thoughts of the bridge and the road reminded me that there was also still a blue car not too far away, and that sitting in that car was my mother, who, by this point, had to be getting worried about me. While I had no clear sense of time or how long I'd been gone for, I imagined she must be getting anxious now if she wasn't already before.

If her concerns intensified to the point where she decided to come look for me herself, what would happen if she crossed the bridge and realized I wasn't there? The only thing worse than being lost by myself would be getting two of us lost at the same time and in different places, particularly in this weather.

I couldn't risk it. My mother had been brave, gracious, and accommodating to bring me all the way out here in a massive thunderstorm so I could search for answers on my own. It wasn't fair to put her in harm's way, too, just so I could potentially have the instant gratification of discovering those truths here and now.

She was right, after all; we could always come back another day at another time. The tree would still be there, wherever it was hiding. It would be easier to find it on a warmer, less rainy day, anyway.

All I had to do now was follow the stream back to the road, the car, and my mother.

I had to take special care not to slip as I delicately picked my way down the bank. The grass was particularly slick here, coated with a thin film of rainwater runoff that visibly trickled in waves all the way down until it leveled off and joined the moving current of the stream.

It helped to turn my feet sideways, taking one step down at a time and leaning my torso back slightly so as to counterbalance my own weight. The process was slow-going, and by the time I reached the flatter ground beside the stream, my legs were sore and quivering beneath the wet, matted denim.

Quick glances to my left and right gave me little certainty as to which way I should head. Again, I surprised myself at just how lost I'd become in such a short time. Yes, I'd been searching the trees for a while, but it still felt embarrassing to be so thoroughly perplexed. There was nothing but more greenery and more rain in both directions.

On further examination, however, the path to my left seemed to move gradually uphill against the current of the stream. My sense of direction was unreliable, but something in my gut told me to find higher ground, so I set off to follow that blind intuition.

Strange creatures moved just below the surface of the creek on my right. It was hard to see them underneath the constant battering of raindrops on water, but when I stopped and bent down to get a closer look, there they were all the same: small, black, slimy-looking things, some sort of cross between a fish and an insect. Most moved with the current of the stream in groups, but occasionally, I'd come across a loner going its own way, seemingly oblivious to the swirling torrent surrounding it.

The sight made me smile for some queer reason. More than once, I squatted down to cup the water in my hands and try to help the rogue creature along its way, but the little guy was always faster than me and would dart away in a shimmery flash.

"I'm not going to hurt you."

As if they could understand me. Now I was talking to animals; it appeared I was totally losing my grip on reality out here in the elements.

I realized it was time to pick up the pace and refocus on the task at hand. With one last look at my bizarre aquatic friends, I pushed myself back up to standing and started to traipse forward again.

The vegetation above me grew thicker as the path along the stream bank climbed and twisted. Raindrops had a harder time finding their way down through the knotted woods and leafy moss, to the point where it almost began to feel like I was just walking through a wet mist rather than a full-blown thunderstorm. The continuous sound of precipitation colliding with the branches above was the only real indication I had that it was still raining as hard as it was.

There was something up ahead on the side of the water, right at the edge where the creek met the grass. Even from this far back, it was visibly out of place, a large mass of white and dirty grey against what was otherwise a uniform green background.

This felt like an even more egregious crime than the cigarette butts, beer cans, and other assorted pieces of trash I'd encountered before. At least all of those had been scattered on the man-made roadway. Still not a valid excuse, but better than whatever this gross anomaly was doing out in the middle of pure, unadulterated nature.

As I moved closer, though, the hairs on the back

of my neck and arms began to stand on end. Something was wrong. My brain searched for a logical explanation for the shape looming just up ahead, flipping rapidly through suggestion after suggestion, none of which made much sense or felt believable.

Bits of pale beige peeked out from beneath the folds of fabric, and then I froze in my tracks when I saw what was unmistakably human hair.

Chapter Eight

It was a girl. There was no longer any sense denying it.

The pale beige was the color of her skin beneath a soiled and soggy dress that may have been white once upon a time, but was now caked in mud and loose clumps of algae.

What looked like an arm was bent at an angle and motionless further up the side of the bank, along with a tangled mess of brown-black hair that covered her head and made it impossible to tell where her face was.

She was half-submerged in the creek, the water flowing freely around what looked like her mid-thigh, though I couldn't be sure in all the bundled mass of cloth that wrapped and floated around her.

To the best of my knowledge, I had never seen a dead body before. It was a strangely serene feeling, standing there looking at another human being lying there motionless, accepting the fact that this person was no longer alive.

Even those burgeoning feelings of fear and panic when I'd first seen the form seemed far away now, a distant memory in the face of cold, hard truth. This person was dead, and there was nothing I could do to save them.

So, what now? What was I supposed to do? Run the opposite way in horror? Cry for help?

It seemed ludicrous to believe there was a protocol for this type of situation or a proper procedure to follow that everyone knew but me. I had to make up my mind how I was going to handle everything, and I had to do it fairly quickly; I couldn't just stand here frozen in shock with a dead body in the middle of a rainstorm.

Tentatively, I moved a bit toward the mass on the ground. Whether I wanted to get a closer look or not, this was still the way I had decided to come in order to find my way back to the road. I'd made up my mind to follow this stream, and there were no guarantees that turning around and going the opposite direction, as far away from this body as I could, would do me any better.

Turning around at this point could get me even further lost in the woods, and now the scenery had an entirely different shade of severity to it, given what I'd just stumbled across. Morbidly, I wondered how long it might take my own body to succumb to a similar fate as the girl's, assuming I didn't find my way back soon.

But now I was making assumptions. What proof did I have that she'd died of natural causes, drowning, fatigue, hypothermia, exposure, or something of the like? Her death could have come from something far more sinister. What if she was murdered, and the killer hid her body out here?

Worse yet—what if she'd been killed right here?

Again, my feet came to a sudden standstill. If that possibility existed, then it was just as possible that whoever did this to her could still be nearby.

My heart thumped faster in my chest. Slowly, I allowed my eyes to rove the landscape around me, straining intently to pick up on any unexpected movement. My ears pricked for the sound of approaching footsteps or the telltale snap of a twig.

It was no use, though; the storm made surveillance utterly impractical. If someone or something was stalking me from the brush on either bank, there was nothing I could do to prepare myself or stop an ambush. I would just have to hope and pray that my cold, waterlogged, still-rusty legs would work long enough to give me a fighting chance at running away.

Standing here, waiting for a possible attack from a potentially nonexistent assailant, was stupid, though, and even in this insane and unimaginable situation, I knew it would do me no good to do nothing.

So again, I prodded myself forward, closing the negative space between me and the girl until her body was just a foot or so in front of my soggy sneakers. Steeling my courage, I knelt down into a slow crouch until my tailbone floated just above my heels.

Almost immediately, I regretted the position, as the muscles in my upper thighs and calves quivered once, then gave way to gravity, collapsing my whole body forward until my knees came to rest about an inch deep in the mud.

For half a horrific heartbeat, I thought I might actually topple over onto the body, but at the last second, I steadied my torso and regained my balance.

I'd gone from breathing in rapid, shallow bursts, to forgetting to breathe entirely. Now that I was on the ground mere inches from the body, my breath was sticking in the back of my throat like some kind of thick, gooey paste. Consciously, I willed myself to swallow it down, hoping to break the dam through sheer force and drive the stagnant, humid air down into the belly of my lungs.

The effort made me gag and sputter into a short, choking cough. It shook my chest cavity from the inside out until my eyes watered and spittle formed on my lips. Through the bleary wetness of this spasm in the storm, I somehow managed to see a wrinkled fold in the girl's dress twitch... and then I wasn't choking anymore.

My eyes trained on the exact spot I'd seen movement. Maybe it was only a hallucination brought on by the coughing fit, something like seeing stars when you're out of breath, or your eyesight going black when the blood rushes up to your head too fast. Obviously, that made the most sense, and it's what I wanted to believe.

But kneeling there in the mud and the rain, watching and waiting for further proof, I knew deep down that what I'd seen was real and unmistakable. It was subtle, no doubt—not much more than a quick flinch, like what I'd seen a horse's tail do to a gnat on one of my nature shows—but it was still motion where none had before existed. I stared at the dress and wondered to myself just what I would do if and when it moved again.

Equal parts impatience and curiosity mixed together to form courage. Slightly shaking, I extended my right hand toward the fabric until the tips of my fingers brushed lightly against the edge of the material. It felt cold and wet to the touch, but there was no physical reaction to the contact.

I pressed my hand further forward until my fingers met something sturdier beneath the clothing, something that definitely seemed like flesh, bone, or muscle. Feeling braver still, I gave the mass a small but concerted nudge. The body moved, but only as a reaction to the pressure I exerted; when I took my hand away, it was still once more.

Maybe it would help if I had a better idea just what I was looking at. The shape in front of me was still barely recognizable as a human being; I'd only assumed it was a girl because of the long hair and the dress. The only clearly discernible feature was the pale, white arm stretched out on the bank to my left, so I decided to grab an area of cloth beneath the hair that could conceivably be a shoulder opposite that arm.

Gently, I pulled the area toward me until the mass began to shift underneath the heavy fabric, and with a little extra effort, the momentum carried it over until a second arm spilled out onto the ground. The hair rotated on an axis, and just like that, a face was finally visible beneath the dirty curls.

It was indeed a girl. Her eyes were closed and her lips were milky grey and slightly agape, but the eyelashes, cheekbones, and overall composition of her face was decidedly female. She looked young, perhaps in her mid to late teens, though it was hard to tell, given the dirt and grime that obscured her features.

Something about the face felt familiar to me from the moment it was revealed, like I'd seen it before. It wasn't necessarily a sensation of déjà vu, so much as a kind of easy recognition, the way a person might feel seeing a famous actor or television personality passing by on the street.

If I'd seen this girl before though, I wasn't sure where it would have possibly been. Perhaps on the sidewalks of downtown Lenoir while exploring with my mother one day?

Or could it be that I knew this girl from school or from my past, and for the first time since coming out of my coma, I was actually remembering something concrete from before 'the accident'?

The second possibility was the more exciting one, but it was still just that: a possibility. And now that her face was finally visible, it all but confirmed what I had suspected from the beginning: she was truly dead, and therefore she wouldn't be able to provide me with any further clarity or insight as to whether we ever knew each other in some capacity.

Maybe it was because of the dress twitch, or maybe it was just because I wanted her alive so she could tell me what she knew; but for whatever reason, I placed my palm above her chest just below the collarbone, to feel for the telltale indication of life that I knew wasn't there.

Everything stopped; the driving rain, the wind howling through the trees, the stream rushing by, my own body and mind and breath, my feelings and thoughts.

Everything stopped in that instant, because there it was, soft and faint and impossible, but a heartbeat all the same. It couldn't be happening, and yet it was, a tiny little contraption still functioning against all odds in a form that showed no other outward signs of life.

I kept my hand pressed firmly against her sternum and questioned my own certainty. The miserable weather had dulled my senses, after all, and my brain was anything but sharp these days. I even switched hands just to make sure it wasn't some weird personal anomaly in my hand that was giving me a false reading, but my other hand felt it too: a weak but present palpitation.

It wasn't a dead body after all. If she had a heartbeat, it meant she was still alive; and if that was the case, something needed to be done.

As cold and wet as I was, at least half my body wasn't underwater. I reached both hands under her armpits and attempted to slide her further up the bank and out of the stream, but she was surprisingly heavier than I thought she'd be, considering her diminutive form. The soiled and soggy dress wrapped around her legs and torso probably weighed her down even more, but there was nothing I could do about that.

For a second, I wondered if removing it would make things any easier. But that notion made me understandably uncomfortable, and I made up my mind to do it only if absolutely necessary, and as a last resort.

Instead, I decided to stand up and get better leverage by pulling her up the bank, rather than just pushing her up it from my kneeling position. It wasn't easy, but it was definitely less difficult this way, and about thirty seconds later I managed to drag her completely up on land and out of the water.

What now, though? Getting her out of the creek was a step in the right direction, but there was still no hope of getting her warm or dry as long as we remained in the forest. Somehow, I needed to find a way to get her back to the car, where at the very least, she'd be out of the rain and under the vents of hot air.

But how could I get her there? I still wasn't sure if I was even headed in the right direction, and even if by some miracle I was, how could I possibly hope to transport her? It had taken most of my strength just to pull her body a few feet out of the water. I couldn't drag her all the way back to the road, and the idea of carrying her in my arms all the way there seemed even more impossible, given my unreliable muscles and all-around fatigue.

What other options did I have though? I could try to forge on ahead by myself, find the road and my car, and then bring my mother back to help me carry her to safety.

I looked down at the girl. Her face was unchanged—still ghastly white with eyes closed and lips slightly apart. She did look more serene now, nestled angelically atop the wet grass.

My stomach twisted into knots. Even though I'd discovered her all alone out here, the idea of leaving her alone again just didn't feel right. She was too unprotected, too vulnerable in this state.

A strange thought crossed my mind. Was this what I looked like in the immediate aftermath of my accident? Seemingly dead by most accounts, still and unresponsive, save for the near-imperceptible flicker of a hidden heart that just plain refused to give up? Was this what it looked like to be on death's doorstep, unconscious and drifting tenuously between one realm and the next?

No, I couldn't abandon her like this. Just the idea of it made me sick. I had to try and carry her, though, because dragging her behind me like a corpse was even more unconscionable than leaving her behind.

I shook my arms out at my sides, wiggled my fingers, and alternated lifting my knees up in front of my hips as high as they could go, limbering up as best I could in preparation for what I had to do. Whether I'd even be able to pick the girl up off the ground remained unclear, but if I somehow was able to do it, I needed to be as prepared as humanly possible to carry our combined weight forward along a slippery uphill journey.

After a couple deep breaths, I knelt down at her side and maneuvered one arm below her knees and the other under her back, until I was holding her body snugly against my own. Bracing myself to stand up again, I glanced down to take one last look at what I was doing… and nearly had a heart attack when I saw two luminous green orbs staring back up at me.

Chapter Nine

Moisture pooled at the corners of her eyes until little tributaries of saltwater leaked out and joined the raindrops on her reddening cheeks. Her chest shuddered as air rushed in and out at erratic speeds through the gaping cavities of her mouth and nostrils. From beneath the twisted layers of clothing, she stretched a trembling hand up through the air until five ice-cold fingers gently grazed the side of my jaw. The physical contact triggered more tears, but of a different sort, and now her breath steadied as a warm and mysterious smile spread across her face like the sunrise.

"Daniel."

The word gurgled out from her throat, and the sound of it seemed to surprise the girl just as much as it did me.

"Daniel… it's me."

I shook my head slowly in stunned disbelief, struggling to comprehend what was happening, and what she was saying to me.

"Daniel… I found you."

She wasn't talking sense. Undoubtedly, she was as confused as I'd been when I first came to in an unfamiliar environment and encountered a series of strange people I didn't recognize.

Perhaps she saw the confusion written across my face. Her eyebrows furrowed, her expression grew serious, and she reached up a second hand to the other side of my face, so that it was now framed between her fingers.

"Daniel, it's me. It's Kirsa."

Again, I shook my head slowly. I *wanted* her words to mean something, to unlock something on my end, for her sake as much as my own. But there was nothing I could give her.

"It's okay. You're going to be okay."

It's exactly what the nurse had said to me in the hospital, so it seemed like the appropriate thing to say in this situation, too. Even if I couldn't give her what she wanted, I could at least try to calm her down and reassure her that everything would be all right.

The girl tightened her grip around my face until it felt like she was trying to pull me down toward her, all the while keeping her eyes locked on mine. I was struck by just how cold her fingers felt on my skin, and it served as a sharp reminder that I needed to get her out of the rain and into the warm, dry safety of my car.

"We have to get you out of here. Do you think you can walk?"

More face-clutching and questing-looks.

"Don't you recognize me?"

Her voice broke a bit as she finished the question.

Should I lie? If it was the only way to get her to follow me out of the woods, maybe I had no other choice.

"I do. I recognize you. We need to get you out of this storm, though. Do you want to come with me?"

103

Her reply was surprisingly quick. "No. I want you to come with me."

It seemed like we were saying the same thing, just in different ways, so I nodded my head between her hands.

"Don't worry. We'll go together."

She smiled, and again, it was like a ray of vivid sunshine bursting through the clouds.

"Okay."

I smiled back at her, grateful that we were finally getting somewhere.

"Do you think you can walk?"

"If you want me to, I will."

For the first time since they'd opened, her eyes left mine as she looked down at her body. A second or two passed in relative silence; the only sound came from the steady rainfall bouncing off leaves and the stream beside us.

The girl let out a soft grunt and relaxed her grip on my face. Her hands fell through the air until they landed on her chest, roved down along her stomach, and then finally spread out around the contours of her upper legs beneath the soggy canvas of her dress.

After they had maneuvered around the majority of her midsection, they made their way back up her body until at last, her fingers found her face. Like two explorers, they tracked up across her chin, ears, and hairline, before descending down along her eyebrows, nose, cheeks, and finally to her mouth. There, they were met by a quickening channel of breath passing through chattering teeth. Her shallow ribcage visibly puffed in and out, in and out, faster and faster as her eyes grew wide and wild with terror.

"I—I don't—I—I—uh…"

They were more gasping, sputtering, guttural sounds than discernible words, and they spilled out from her fluttering jaw with reckless abandon as I tried to understand what was happening in front of me. The girl's entire body shook violently now as she fumbled her fingers around the top of her face, all the while striving in vain to articulate whatever horrors she was suddenly overrun by.

"Who—I—oh… oh… Daniel?"

She jerked her head back to look up at me with an expression of pure helpless desperation. And before I could say or do something to try and quell the seizure, her eyelids fluttered shut, and her body slumped loosely in my arms.

For one terrible moment, I thought she might actually be dead this time. Thankfully, I could still feel her breathing slowly yet steadily against me, so that was a welcome relief. I had absolutely no idea what prompted her sudden frenzy and fit. At the same time, I was grateful she'd at least passed out before she could do any physical damage to herself, or to me.

Theatrics aside, I now found myself in the same situation I'd been in before she woke up: holding an unconscious body I wasn't certain I could lift off the ground, and hoping to carry it through a forest to a road I wasn't sure was even up ahead. On top of it all, my muscles were starting to cramp up again from being in the same uncomfortable position for too long.

I let out a heavy sigh, stared down at the limp figure in front of me, and wondered how I'd managed to stumble into this bizarre predicament. It was enough trouble just trying to take care of myself. Now here I was entrusted with another human being's welfare, too, whether I wanted the responsibility or not.

My ears pricked at a new sound, something different from the general ambient noise of rain and occasional thunder that I'd grown accustomed to. It came from somewhere up ahead, further along the stream. I strained my attention toward it, waiting to see if I'd hear it again, or if it was just my imagination playing tricks on me.

But there it was again, and this time it was even louder and clearer than before. It sounded like a voice. Like a woman's voice, in fact, and it was definitely coming from up ahead. Though it was difficult to determine what was being called out over the chaos of the storm, I thought it sounded a lot like someone yelling "David."

I wiggled my arms out from under the girl's body and stumbled up the grassy bank to higher ground, where maybe I'd have a clearer view to see who or what was coming up ahead.

It was a short but strenuous climb, made harder by legs and feet that were now in open rebellion against my will. By the end, I was clawing my way to the top on my hands and knees like an animal, but my efforts were rewarded with the welcome sight of a familiar figure picking her way through the trees up ahead.

"Mom!"

Her head snapped in my direction, and even from a distance, I could see the look of immense relief wash over her face.

"David!"

She broke into a jog, and I tried my best to do the same, careful not to trip over fallen branches and other obstacles on the forest floor.

When we finally closed the gap between us, I flung myself into her arms, and she wrapped me in them and pulled me into a fierce and smothering hug.

How I felt in this moment must have been similar to what her and my father felt when they first saw me awake in the hospital and rushed to my bedside: just absolute, overpowering joy.

"Davey, where have you been?"

She spoke into my wet hair as she kissed the top of my head frantically, squeezing and rocking me, and rubbing her hands on my shoulders and the back of my neck.

"You're soaking wet. Are you all right? You must be freezing!"

"I'm okay, Mom."

She was probably just as wet and cold as I was. The human contact already made me feel a bit warmer, and neither one of us seemed in a great rush to break it. Time stood still as we huddled together, shivering and grateful for each other's presence.

"I'm okay."

"Come on, let's get out of here. The car's just up ahead."

She broke the embrace, took my hand, and turned around to start walking, but my thoughts traveled back to the girl in the white dress lying at the bottom of the creek bank.

As much as I wanted nothing more in the world than to be back in the welcoming shelter of the cozy vehicle with the chance to sit down in a leather seat and turn the heat on full blast, that girl needed me still, and I couldn't fail her. Gently, I resisted my mother's force tugging me forward, until she finally noticed and turned her head back around.

"I need to show you something."

She gave me a confused look.

"Is it where you had your accident? Because I've seen that enough already; I don't need to see it again…"

"No, it's something else."

Now I was the one leading her by the hand, back the way I'd come, down toward the gully and the streambed. We didn't have to go far before we were at the edge of the bank, and I knew she saw the girl when I heard her gasp behind me.

"Oh, my God."

My mother stopped dead in her tracks and freed her hand so it could cover her gaping mouth. The color drained from her face as she stared without blinking at the sight before her.

"Is… is she?"

The unspoken final word in her question was obvious.

"No."

Unless something catastrophic had happened in the past five or ten minutes since I'd left her side, the girl was still alive, despite all visual evidence to the contrary. But who knew what kind of internal injuries or illness she might still be struggling with; the longer she remained out here, the worse off she might be.

"We need to help her."

My mother reached down to touch her pants pocket.

"My phone's in the car. We need to call 911."

"But we can't leave her here."

That much was clear to me. I didn't trust the idea of going all the way back to the car to call for help. Sure, it made sense, but it also involved leaving the girl alone again out here by herself; a thought that was simply unbearable to me. She was too vulnerable, too unprotected.

There was only one thing we could do.

"Will you help me carry her?"

Before my mother could answer, I started lowering myself down the hillock and moving toward the girl.

Since waking up in the hospital, my day-to-day existence had been marred by constant feelings of doubt and uncertainty.

This was the polar opposite, this new motivation driving me forward. It was pure, primal instinct, and deep in the marrow of my bones, I *knew* that what I was doing was right.

Thankfully, my mother didn't try to argue. She was close behind as we slowly approached the girl together. I circled round and knelt down near her head, surmising it might be easier for me to carry her by the shoulders and for my mother to carry her legs.

There was a strange look on my mother's face as she gazed down at the person splayed out on the ground below her.

"This is the girl that's missing."

She said it to herself as much as she said it to me.

"The girl on the news this morning. I think that's her."

I hadn't made the connection myself, but immediately, I knew she was right. It helped explain the uncanny familiarity I'd experienced earlier when I'd remembered the girl's face without knowing how or why. She was the girl they'd shown on the television set as I was eating breakfast, right before my mother turned it off so we could talk about what to do with our day.

"Are you ready?"

She knelt down across from me and gingerly scooped the girl's legs. We stood up at the same time, and I was surprised at just how light she was, now that there were two of us sharing her weight.

Actually, the hardest part of carrying her was trying not to fall on the wet grass, especially along stretches made more treacherous by shifting mud or broken tree branches. There were a couple close calls where I'd start to stumble, only to catch my balance at the last possible second, regain my equilibrium, and then carry on once again, cautious as ever.

Each time it happened, I found myself instinctively tightening my grip on the girl and locking eyes on her form, just to make sure she didn't slip out and hit the ground or get hurt by my clumsiness. My mother, for her part, was patient with me and my occasional missteps, each time suggesting we stop and rest as long as I needed before trekking on.

It was a slow and tiresome process. After what felt like forever, I saw the outline of a bridge materialize through the fog and rain ahead, and I knew we were finally getting close. We scaled the last slope that brought us fully level with the road, and I let out a deep sigh of relief as the soles of my shoes at long last made contact with pavement.

Part of me would have been content to lie down right then and there on the asphalt, happy to just get out of the woods and on mapped terrain again.

But the girl kept me going, staggering on toward the blue car that waited for us up ahead.

"Here, set her down real quick."

We lowered the girl carefully down to the ground as my mother dug the car keys out of her pocket and unlocked the vehicle. As soon as I heard the click, my fingers were on the handle of the back door, and I pulled it all the way open to make loading her in as easy as possible.

My mother took charge of the situation.

"Go around to the other side; I'm going to pass her in to you."

I followed her instructions, climbing in from the opposite door and sliding across the backseat to receive the girl. My mother lifted her up by the shoulders and slid her upper body toward me, and together we eased her in as carefully as we could, until her legs and feet were safely inside and free of the door. I ended up cradling her head in my lap with both hands still tucked under her arms.

When my mother saw that her cargo was secure, she shut both rear passenger doors and stepped into the driver's seat, switched on the ignition, and spun the temperature dials on the control panel to their maximum output.

A torrent of glorious hot air came rushing back to smack me in the face. I closed my eyes and leaned back in the seat, losing myself to the dry heat as it wrapped me in an invisible embrace.

Blissfully, my mind drifted away, surfing on a new current of warmth and tranquility that knew nothing of the rigorous trials I'd left behind. Only the weight of the girl's head in my lap kept me tethered to reality, and

I remembered then that all of us weren't in the clear just yet.

"Is she okay?"

The question severed the mini-trance I'd been in since letting the heat envelop me. I met my mother's gaze in the reflection of the rearview mirror, and then looked down at the person we'd rescued together from the forest. She was still pale, cold, and wet, but she was breathing, and that was all that really mattered.

I nodded slowly and turned my attention toward drying her off as best I could, using the car's interior to free my own hands of moisture so that I could wipe away the rain from where it speckled her skin. Largely, it was an ineffective exercise, but it felt good to take action, nonetheless. Between the air vents and the friction of my hands on her body, maybe she'd regain a little color and show some signs of life again.

The car's windows had all fogged over in the time we'd spent since crawling inside, so it took another few minutes for the clouded haze to recede back to the edges of the glass, allowing the world outside to become visible again. With the windshield clear, my mother moved the gearshift and lurched the car into motion, turning it about-face until we were headed back in the direction we'd come from earlier.

I wasn't sure where exactly we were headed. Maybe a police station? Or, more likely, a hospital? We hadn't discussed the next step of what we were doing, but maybe we didn't need to. My mother's focus was on the road, and she seemed to be driving with a quiet confidence and speed that suggested she knew exactly where she was going and what she was doing.

Whether that was true or not, who knew. There

wasn't much I could do in the backseat anyway. I still didn't know enough about the area or the world I lived in to offer up tangible advice; the best I could do was keep my attention on revivifying the unconscious girl resting in my arms.

If only I had a blanket or a fresh set of clothes I could give her. My denim jean jacket, light blue when I'd grabbed it from my closet, was now a deep shade of indigo after absorbing so much rain. It wasn't ideal, but perhaps the weight of it would provide some kind of comfort; anything had to be an upgrade over the little white dress, a garment that even if dry didn't look particularly cozy.

I undid the buttons on the front of the jacket, peeled it off my torso, and draped it across her, spreading the material out to cover as much surface area as possible. In the end, I was able to stretch it out from her neck all the way down to her hips, and I tucked it in around her the way I imagined a mother would swaddle a newborn baby.

Two ivory legs still protruded from the torn hem of her dress, and even from the other side of the backseat, I could make out visible goosebumps all over them. My wool pullover wasn't much drier than the jacket, but at least it could also serve as an extra layer of covering, so I took it off and nestled it around her lower half until that too was wrapped sufficiently.

Losing not one but two layers of my own clothing would have sounded suicidal half an hour ago, but it was actually kind of nice exposing more of my naked skin to the steady flow of air streaming from the front. Clenching my fingers in toward my wrists left me satisfied with the improvement in my blood circulation, so much so that I decided I could share some of that body heat with my fellow passenger.

I rubbed my palms back and forth against one another, then placed my hands alongside her face, and willed the kinetic energy to flow into her. The physical arrangement was reminiscent of the way she'd grasped my face between her hands in our initial encounter, and the parallel resonated with me.

As we continued our drive back toward civilization, I was vaguely aware of my mother's voice speaking on the phone. For the most part, though, it was all background noise to me, as indistinct and nondescript as the marginal sights outside my window that whizzed past without impact. On the ride here, that world had commanded my rapt attention; now, it was relegated to little more than scenic dressing, a general green periphery that only further framed the arrow of my focus—which was *her*.

Every halting breath she took, every minor twitch of a shuttered eyelid, every strand of dark hair still wet and stuck to the smooth alabaster surface of her forehead or cheek… it all piqued my curiosity and begged further investigation.

Who was this girl? How did she end up alone and unconscious in a creek? Why did she act like she knew me, even though she called me by another name? And what had caused her to panic and pass out again?

I had so many questions for her, and yet I knew there was a very tangible possibility that none of them would ever get answered. After we delivered her to the doctors, the police, her family, or whomever, what would I be to her? A local hero who was in the right place at the right time to make a potentially life-saving discovery, but still, ultimately, a stranger.

In the brief time she was conscious, she'd been every bit as confused as I had been waking up in the hospital. I couldn't imagine what my reaction would have been if some weird teenager had been waiting by my bedside to prod me with a thousand separate questions when I first came to that day.

But the odd part was that she *hadn't* treated me like a weird teenager she didn't know. From the moment she opened her eyes, there was a strong sense of recognition there. Whereas I had stared dumbly at the two human beings who created and then raised me for the past seventeen years, she had looked at me like we'd known each other our whole lives. It was a surreal impression to be on the receiving end of, and I felt guilty I couldn't reciprocate the feeling.

At some point, the car slowed to a gradual stop. I peered out my window to realize we were parked in front of what looked like a hospital or some kind of medical building. Briefly, I imagined Dr. Frye or Loretta Jean the nurse coming out to intercept us, but then I remembered that hospital was all the way out in Charlotte, and we were definitely still in Lenoir.

"Stay with her."

My mother said it as she stepped out into the rain. She left the door ajar and ran around the hood of the car and past the sliding double doors into the lobby.

I watched her form disappear behind the tinted glass, and when she reappeared again, she was joined by two young men in hospital scrubs towing a wheeled stretcher between them. She opened the rear passenger door wide enough to allow them to gently extract the girl from the backseat and from my lap, easing her out and up until she was securely fastened.

Then they were rolling her back through the automatic doors and out of sight. Just like that, the doors closed again, and my mother and I were left alone in the parking lot.

Chapter Ten

I wasn't sure what was supposed to happen next. So much of my concentration over the past few hours had been channeled into singular tasks: revisiting the site of my crash, finding my way out of the forest, rescuing the mysterious girl in the water.

Now that there was time to breathe again and take stock of all that had happened, I didn't know what I was supposed to do or say. I looked up at my mother from inside the car, hoping to take a cue from her, but she was staring blankly at the double doors, evidently lost in thought.

"What did they say?"

My words appeared to startle her, as if she'd forgotten I was there. She also seemed to remember she was still standing outside in the sprinkling rain, because she reached an arm up to cover her head, loped around to her side of the car, and quickly got back inside. With the door shut behind her, she took a moment to wipe beads of water off her face and neck.

"What did who say?"

"The doctors."

She glanced up at me in the rear-view mirror.

"I just told them what happened. That we found

her alone out there and unconscious."

"Did they say it's the missing girl?"

She shook her head.

"I mentioned the news report to them and said I thought it might be the same girl. They told me they'd contact the police as soon as she's admitted. They probably want to make sure she's okay first and foremost."

"Do you think she is? Okay, I mean?"

Again, my mother shook her head.

"I don't know. I wish I knew more. I think it's a good thing that we got her here when we did. It's also a good sign that she's breathing normally. They probably just need to run some tests to make sure everything else is okay, too."

She must have seen the worry stenciled across my face, because she turned in her seat and put a hand on my knee.

"I'm sure she's fine, Davey. She's in great hands. I have all the faith in the world in doctors, and I think you know why."

She gave me a soft, meaningful smile, and rubbed my cheek with her thumb.

Something stirred inside me.

"So, what do we do now? Do we wait with her until her family gets here?"

"I don't know what we do now, exactly. I have to go back in and give them my contact information, just as the person who brought her here, but I don't know if that means I have to stay until the police get here to fill out a report, or how it works. How are you feeling, though? I can call Dad and have him pick you up if you want; you must be exhausted."

Now it was my turn to shake my head.

"No, I want to stay here. I'm the one who found her anyway, so I should probably be here too, just in case they have questions for me."

"Are you sure? If you're not feeling up to it…"

"No, I am. I want to stay."

I pulled the door shut to accentuate my conviction. It was enough to mollify my mother, who nodded, put the car in motion, and guided us to an open spot in the parking lot. She cut the engine, and together, we jogged through the light rain to the cover of the hospital entrance overhang and then darted in through the doors.

My mother made her way right up to the check-in desk, where either a nurse or a receptionist was waiting for her with a clipboard of paperwork to fill out. We found a couple of empty chairs in the corner of the small lobby and had a seat.

There were maybe a dozen other people in the waiting area. Some read magazines, some watched a small television mounted in the corner, and some spoke quietly amongst themselves. Nobody seemed to pay me much mind, but I did catch a few of them casting curious glances toward my mother. No doubt her dramatic entrance, coupled with the young girl getting wheeled in on a stretcher, had turned some heads.

It wasn't long before the hospital lobby became a bit more crowded with the arrival of a pair of uniformed police officers. After a brief chat with the woman at the front desk, they split up—one briskly followed her out of sight down a corridor, while the other came over to speak with me and my mother.

We each took a turn recounting the events that led to the girl's discovery, and for the most part, the officer just stood and listened to us, inserting the occasional question or request for further details.

When he was satisfied with the information he'd gleaned, the officer thanked us both politely, gave my mother his card, and departed toward the same hallway his colleague had disappeared down.

Once again, the lobby was relatively calm and quiet, with only the low murmur of the television set serving as gentle background noise.

"Davey?"

My mother broke in with a soft nudge of my shoulder.

"Are you ready? He said we can go now if we'd like."

I still didn't want to go. Somehow, in the brief time we'd spent together beside that creek in the forest, something had changed in me. Anybody could have found her; or, more frighteningly, nobody could have found her at all.

But neither of those things had happened. I was the one who found her, and though the officer had called my discovery "amazing" and described the girl as "very, very lucky," all of those words failed to properly convey the significance of what had transpired out there.

It was more than just finding a missing girl—it was how she acted when she woke up. The way she looked at me, touched me, talked to me… that's what I couldn't stop thinking about now, and why the idea of leaving her felt incomprehensible.

I'd never experienced that kind of magnetism, that

all-pervasive, sublime, fundamental intuition that, for one moment, I was exactly where I was supposed to be.

How could I leave all that behind now and walk away, when there was still so much left to discover?

"Maybe we should stay until her parents get here. Just in case they want to know what happened, too."

"I don't think they need us for that, babe. That's why the police are here."

"But what if they want to hear more? Shouldn't we stick around just in case?"

My mother gave me a pitying look.

"When Dad and I got the call that you were awake, nothing in the world was more important to us than getting to Charlotte as fast as we could. I guarantee you that this girl's parents have been through hell since she went missing. All they want to do right now is see her again and hold her in their arms."

There was no disputing my mother's logic. I wanted to tell her about the strange, almost psychic connection I felt with the girl, but what good would it do? If I couldn't understand or articulate that sensation in my own head, how could I explain it to another person out loud?

"I don't want to go."

Vainly, I tried to come up with a decent justification. But all I had left was my desire, plain and simple as it was, and so I spoke bluntly and truthfully from my soul.

"I want to stay here."

The look on her face was sympathetic but puzzled.

"I understand if you're worried about her, Davey, but what do you want us to do? We have to trust the doctors now to take care of her. There's not really anything left for us to do."

"You can leave if you want. I just want to stay here a little longer. Just in case…"

My voice trailed off, but in my head, I completed the sentence.

Just in case she wakes up again and asks for me.

Even if she didn't know me or know my name, I was sure that I'd been a comfort to her. And there was something poignant and powerful shared between us in that brief encounter she'd been conscious for. Admittedly, I couldn't begin to describe or understand it, but I'd *felt* it all the same. Maybe if I waited long enough for her to wake up again, we'd get another chance to interact and mine the depths of our mysterious connection.

"I'm not going to leave you here by yourself, Davey."

My mother sighed, pulled her phone out from her pocket, and stood up slowly.

"If you're sure you want to stay, we can stay a little longer, at least until Dad gets off work, I suppose. I'm going to call and let him know, though, just so he doesn't worry."

She started to move toward the sliding lobby doors, then turned her head back in my direction.

"You're sure this is what you want to do?"

"I'm sure."

She clearly didn't share my conviction, but my mother nodded her acceptance all the same before stepping out through the doors to call my father and inform him of our plans.

I was mildly curious as to how she planned to

explain my decision, and also curious as to how he would react to it. Did she step outside so as not to disturb the other people in the waiting room, or did she step outside because she didn't want me to hear what she really thought of us staying here?

Whatever her reason, the conversation didn't last longer than five minutes or so. Soon, she was right back in the chair beside me, only this time, she was armed with a couple magazines from the rack beside the check-in desk.

"So, what's the plan? Are we waiting for anything in particular, or just waiting until her parents get here, or what?"

"I'm not sure. I just want to stay a little longer, if that's okay."

She chuckled and opened one of the magazines in her lap.

"Well, you're not really giving me much of a choice, are you?"

She started to read, then looked up at me again.

"We can stay until Dad's off work, okay? Then I think we should meet up with him at home. We can always come back, you know."

Maybe she was waiting for a response, perhaps for me to acknowledge that she'd established a firm cut-off time for this momentary sojourn. But my attention had already drifted elsewhere.

Specifically, it had gone beyond the glass barricade of the hospital entrance and out to the large red truck that came squealing to a halt in front of it. No sooner had the vehicle stopped than two passengers came hurtling out of it, a man and a woman, sprinting the short distance through the light rain and into the lobby.

It was hard to tell whether their faces were wet with tears, rain, or some combination of the two, but both of them looked wildly about until their eyes trained on the short woman standing behind the reception counter. As one, they moved toward her.

The nurse seemed to expect their arrival, and without so much as a word, she glided out from behind her station to intercept them.

"Where is she?"

The man barked out the question, not just to the nurse, but seemingly to the whole lobby of people.

"Follow me."

The nurse spun on her heel and led them briskly down a corridor and out of sight, leaving behind a pregnant hush in the small hospital waiting area.

Once again, the only real sound came from the TV in the corner, but after a minute or two, conversation resumed around us, only this time in animated whispers and punctuated with brief glances in the direction the three people had gone.

My mother articulated what many of them no doubt were discussing amongst themselves.

"They must be the parents."

She took a deep breath, shifted in her wooden chair, and gently placed a hand on my shoulder.

"I remember that feeling all too well."

We sat like that for a while in silence, looking at the empty space of the hallway across the foyer, lost in our own separate thoughts and reflections.

At some point, her hand left my shoulder and found its way back to the pages of her magazine. Different doctors or nurses emerged from the hallway intermittently, reading names from clipboards they carried and escorting their selections off to unseen examination rooms.

The mood in the lobby remained tense and expectant, even more so than I imagined most hospital lobbies inherently were. Surely, most of these individuals had come in today for a routine check-up or physical; they probably had no idea they'd bear witness to so much drama and intrigue.

Maybe an hour or so had passed before I realized my mother and I were the only two people left in the lobby besides the receptionist. The sun hadn't made much of an appearance all day with the constant storm, but it was still obvious from the dimming light outside that dusk was fast upon us. Soon, my father would be calling to inform us he was leaving work, and then I'd finally have to surrender and head home.

Our impending departure was inevitable, but that didn't make it any easier to come to terms with. I still didn't know what exactly I was hoping to have happen. I just knew that leaving now would feel like a defeat, like somehow, I was abandoning the girl all over again to a terrible fate.

"Are you Daniel?"

The doctor materialized out of nowhere and now loomed up above us. He asked the question softly enough, but it startled me all the same, and my mother appeared similarly taken aback by his sudden presence.

"I'm... David?"

Maybe he was looking for someone else. But who? We were the only ones left in the lobby.

"Are you the one who found her, though? Out by Lower Creek?"

I nodded once, and the doctor looked relieved.

"Do you mind coming with me? She's asking for you."

My mother interjected.

"Who?"

"Jessica, the girl you brought here."

Jessica. That was unexpected. I didn't quite remember the name the girl gave me when she first woke up, but it definitely wasn't Jessica.

The confusion was contagious; my mother clearly wasn't satisfied with his response.

"What do you mean she's asking for us?"

The doctor smiled thinly and scratched the back of his head.

"Actually, she's just asking for him, for the young man who first came across her."

He shrugged then, and his demeanor turned apologetic, embarrassed even, as he addressed my mother directly.

"Normally, a situation like this is strictly friends and family, and I know the police said that neither one of you know her personally, but she's awake now, and she's insisting that she sees him."

He turned back to me.

"This isn't really my place, but you're sure you don't know her from somewhere? Not from school, or from your neighborhood, or from a party or something? She keeps saying she only wants to talk to you."

Again, he quickly became contrite.

"It could just be shock, the hysterics and all, after everything she's been through. But then, when the nurse said you were still waiting out here, I figured it couldn't hurt to at least ask."

My heart beat faster. None of it made sense, but it was a monumental relief all the same. The girl was awake, and what was more, she was asking for me. As a matter of fact, she was *only* asking for me!

Maybe they were right after all—maybe we did know each other from somewhere. And if we could talk, if we could just have a minute to really talk without any more seizures or rainstorms or mistaken cases of identity, maybe, just maybe, she could shed some light on my past, and on the person I'd been before my accident.

Maybe the universe brought us together so that we could help each other out in our respective hours of need. First, I rescued her, and now, it was her turn to rescue me.

"I'll see her."

This must have been why I couldn't bring myself to leave the hospital; why I couldn't just drive home with my mother and trust that everything would work itself out on its own.

There was a reason I'd felt utterly compelled to remain in the lobby and wait, even without any real sense of what I was waiting for. It had all been for this, for this moment right now. The realization was staggering—and frightening—but I'd made it this far, and now it was time to go a little further.

Chapter Eleven

I stood up slowly, rubbing the pins and needles out of two legs that had long since fallen asleep while sitting in the chair. At least my clothes were dry now, and while most of my body ached and throbbed with a dull pain, that all-pervasive cold wet feeling had finally gone away.

"David."

The doctor and I had just started to move off in the direction of the hallway when I heard my mother say my name behind me. I waited to see what more she had to say, but she just gave me a concerned look instead.

For my part, I didn't really know what to say either, so I just sent her back my most reassuring expression of confidence, then followed the man in the white lab coat down the bright corridor and past a string of closed wooden doors on either side. We turned a corner down another hallway, and up ahead, I saw that one of the doors on the left was open, with a fuzzy halo of white, fluorescent light spilling out onto the tile.

Our pace slowed as we reached the portal. The doctor stopped in the doorway to face me and gestured wordlessly to come inside, and as I rounded into the small space, I was struck by just how similar the room was to the one I'd occupied myself at Carolinas Medical Center.

There, in the center of it against the opposite wall, was a hospital bed flanked on both sides by the man and woman who'd arrived in the red pickup truck.

And between them, dwarfed amongst a bundled mass of sheets and blankets, was the girl, translucent and fragile as before, and still with those incandescent jewel-green eyes that glinted and sparkled as they caught sight of me.

There, too, was that gigantic smile again, that splitting, radiant expression of unbridled joy that transformed the rest of her face into one big beaming mask of refulgent adulation.

I didn't feel worthy of such a reception; hot blood flowed up under the surface of my skin as self-consciousness set in and the blush overtook me.

"Daniel."

Her voice was breathless, reverential, even. She was still confused about my name, but at least she recognized me. That was a good sign, and proof perhaps that there hadn't been any setbacks since her recent bout of unconsciousness.

Just as you can only stare directly at the sun for so long before your eyes start to water, I had to divert my attention elsewhere, at least for a few seconds to regroup and compose myself.

My focus shifted to the woman perched on the edge of the hospital bed. She was bent over the small figure, her face buried in the girl's midsection, and I saw her body tremoring with stifled sobs. Either she didn't hear me come in, or she didn't care, because either way, she was entirely fixated on the person in the bed; the girl I assumed was probably her daughter.

Conversely, the man was immediately aware of my presence. He stood tall and towering on the opposite side of the bed with his back against the window. Clearly, the girl had gotten her eyes from her father, if that was indeed their relationship; his eyes were smaller and surrounded by narrow wrinkle lines, but the bright, verdant green was unmistakably the same. Freckles dotted his nose, neck, and cheekbones, and tufts of grey-blonde hair poked out from beneath the brim of a sweat-stained cap he wore low over his forehead.

"Are you Daniel?"

They were the exact same words the doctor had used, but they couldn't have sounded more different. Whereas the former's voice was tentative, unassuming, and polite, this man spoke with an aggressive, gruff staccato. He also had an accent I'd only heard occasionally on television and in the streets of Lenoir before; one that was apparently fairly common in North Carolina, according to my parents.

His voice also had an accusatory tone to it that made me feel as if I'd committed some heinous mortal crime against him, even though we'd never met. Needless to say, it was unpleasant to be on the receiving end of it, and now I felt self-conscious in an entirely different sort of way.

"I'm David."

The man didn't blink.

"You're the one who found my daughter, though? That's you?"

I reminded myself it wasn't a trick question, even if

it sounded like it, coming from this hulking figure. There was no reason to hide from the truth; if anything, I was a hero and a lifesaver, and he owed me thanks for discovering his daughter near-dead in the wilderness. The thoughts emboldened me enough to take another step further into the room.

"Yes, I found her."

"I found you."

The girl's voice trickled out from the pillows at the top of her bed, and the way she said it was like she was gently correcting me. Magically, it lifted some of the tension in the room, catching the man off guard and rousing the woman's head up from the hospital linens. Her face gleamed with tears, and for the first time, she seemed to register my existence.

In a clumsy rush, she scrambled to her feet and charged across the room at me. I didn't have time to prepare myself, only managing to take half a defensive step backward before she crashed into me in a tidal wave of raw emotion.

"Oh, God, thank you! Thank you, thank you, *thank God!*"

She squeezed me harder and harder, swaying back and forth in a rollicking motion that kept me precariously off-balance, but wondrously still secure in her tightening embrace.

"It's okay."

Feebly, I tried my best to get the words out, but they were muffled in the scratchy wool of her sweater, and ultimately drowned out by the heaving exclamations of gratitude that poured freely from her mouth.

When at last she regained some control over her

motor functions, the woman pulled back to take a long, penetrating look at me.

"How old are you? Are you one of Jessica's classmates?"

"I don't think so. I haven't been in school for a while."

"How did you find her? Were you—"

"What do you mean?"

The man interrupted the woman abruptly.

"What do you mean you haven't been in school for a while? You can't be more than fifteen."

"I-I'm seventeen."

There wasn't much certainty in my voice, but considering all the memory problems I struggled with, how could there be? My body, still trapped firmly between the woman's outstretched arms, squirmed under the man's gaze.

"I haven't been in school because... because I was in an accident."

"What kind of an accident?"

His questioning was relentless.

"Jim!"

The woman's rebuke came swiftly out of nowhere, and was accompanied by a curt sideways snap of her head in his general direction, before it swiveled back around to face me once again.

"It doesn't matter. We're just so incredibly thankful you found her, that you found our daughter."

"I found him!"

The girl was emphatic in her declaration, so much so that she sat bolt upright in bed.

"I found *you*, Daniel... and now, *we need to go back!*"

"It's okay, baby..."

The woman released me and cooed tenderly as she returned to her daughter's side.

"He says his name is David, I think... is that right?"

I nodded affirmation as she lowered herself down gently onto the mattress and placed a hand alongside the girl's face.

"David, this is Jessica... my Jessica. Thank God David was out there today."

The girl twisted slightly under her touch.

"Daniel, come here!"

She then reached out a thin, pale arm in my direction.

"Come here... *please.*"

I looked nervously over at her father, seeking permission to get any closer, but the man was stoic and unreadable. His wife seized the opportunity to chime in, again trying her best to soothe the girl, who was growing increasingly restless.

"Jessica, this is David, honey. He's the boy who saved you."

Sinews in Jessica's arm strained against her skin as she reached for me, as if maybe with just a bit more effort, she could pull me over with her mind. Her eyes were wider now, and I saw as much white in them as I did green. There was panic there, too, a glazed intensity and fervor that hadn't existed before.

"Daniel... Daniel, please!"

Her voice shuddered with pain, and I could see that she was starting to cry.

"Daniel, it's me! It's Kirsa!"

The doctor had remained respectfully in the background up until this point, but now he sprung instinctively into action, gliding over to the electronic instruments and making a few quick adjustments that didn't go unnoticed by the girl's father.

"He needs to go. He's gettin' her worked up."

"Jessica… Jessica, honey, it's okay, baby…"

But the more her mother tried to calm her down, the more the girl fought back, writhing and struggling against the constraints around her.

"Daniel! Daniel, please—please help me!"

She tried to wrestle her legs out from under the sheets while simultaneously slapping her mother's hands and arms away from her. The scene was quickly devolving into a frenzied mania, increasingly violent and out of control.

Sensing his wife's inability to contain her, Jessica's father came quickly to the other side of the bed and placed two large hands on her shoulders, leaning his weight down to pin her in place.

"*Let go of me!* Daniel, please—*help me!*"

But there was nothing I could do except stand there, frozen in shock, terror, and guilt.

Veins exploded at the side of the man's neck, splotchy and red, as he bellowed a command at the doctor.

"Do something!"

Even with two full-grown adults exercising everything in their power to keep her still, the girl was a blur of motion and sound, shrieking and howling and convulsing as if she were on fire.

With a lithe, cool deftness, the medicine man retrieved a small object from a cabinet drawer, approached his patient, used one hand to hold her arm steady, and with the other, slid the needle into her skin and compressed the plunger smoothly with his thumb.

The girl let out a heartbroken whimper but didn't so much as flinch.

"Daniel."

Three bodies draped across her, and she only had eyes for me.

"*Daniel…*"

Her lashes fluttered and the lids grew heavy as her body slowly surrendered against her will to the injection, sliding limply down into the bedcovers until the back of her head crumpled into the pillow. The final bit of movement came from her lips, working in spite of everything else to try and form the word she'd been repeating over and over, one last time, to no avail.

An eerie silence descended on the room now that its centerpiece had been subdued. Jessica's father eased himself off of her, and there were dark purple marks forming on her body where his hands had been. He must have noticed me noticing them, because he came around the foot of the bed to block my vantage point and addressed me head-on.

"You'll understand if we want our privacy right now."

I suddenly felt very foolish, the one person in the room who didn't really have a reason to be there. Sure, I was the one who found her and who brought her here, and yes, she had supposedly asked to see me.

But then again, she had asked to see Daniel, not David. And all I'd really done was upset her to the point where she had to be sedated.

Worse still, this was now the second time I'd been directly or indirectly responsible for the girl's seizures. It was getting harder and harder to justify my desire to stay close to her. Maybe it was time to think less about what I wanted, and more about what was best for her and for her family.

"I'm so sorry."

And I meant it. I said it for the man, the woman, and the doctor; but most of all, I said it for the one person who couldn't hear it.

There was nothing left for me to do but leave. So that's what I did, walking briskly from the room without so much as a look back or a word of goodbye.

Chapter Twelve

Halfway down the second hallway, I heard footsteps approaching quickly from behind. Instantly, my brain conjured up a vision of the girl's father chasing me down for a retaliatory attack; it was a scenario that was far too easy to accept as plausible rather than fantastical.

Thankfully, my fears were dispelled when I caught sight of the white lab coat and scrubs that adorned the doctor.

"I apologize for how that happened back there. She just kept demanding that she see you, and at the time, it seemed like it was the only way to get her to calm down without administering an anesthetic. I had no idea it'd have the opposite effect."

He walked me out the remaining hallway distance until we arrived in the front lobby. The nurse or receptionist from before, I still wasn't sure which she was, had disappeared, replaced by a young man dressed in similar medical attire. He briefly looked up as we first approached, but then returned his focus to the paperwork in front of him.

The only other person in the waiting area was my mother, who sat with her eyes closed and her head tilted back against the cream-colored wall, the magazine still spread open in her lap.

"Again, I'm sorry I helped put you in that situation."

I was only vaguely aware of the doctor's presence at my side. Something about the tableau of the empty hospital lobby and my mother dozing off by herself in the corner, lonely and forgotten, made me feel even more guilty and downtrodden than before. My curiosity was only natural after everything I'd been through, but perhaps I'd taken it too far. Investigating life's mysteries was one thing; doing it at the expense of those around me was quite another.

"Mr. and Mrs. Silverton are obviously going through a lot right now, but I know how grateful they must be for all that you've done for them and for Jessica. Usually, it just takes people a little time to process all that's happened, and for the shock of it all to wear off some. But I'm sure they'll reach out once everything calms down a bit. Take care until then."

The doctor gave me one last apologetic smile, nodded his chin, and then turned on his heel and walked away.

Alone again, I shambled over to my mother and gave her a light tap on the arm. It wasn't enough to wake her, so I gave her a second tap, this one a little firmer, and she came to with a start.

"Hey, Davey. How'd it go?"

It was a difficult question to answer.

"It was fine. I met her parents."

"What did they say?"

The girl's parents had said quite a few things.

However, it was what her father hadn't said that

was truly concerning. The rampant hostility he'd displayed in such a short window of time was bizarre and unfounded. I had no idea why he'd treated me with such overt suspicion and disdain, but if his intention was to unsettle me, he'd succeeded. Minutes earlier, I'd dreaded the prospect of leaving the hospital; now, I couldn't get away fast enough.

"They thanked me for finding her. And for bringing her here. They said to thank you, too."

I tacked on the last bit hurriedly, glancing back toward the hallway to the patient rooms. Any second now, I expected to see him emerging from around the corner: tall, angry, and full of violence.

"Has Dad called you yet?"

She studied my expression carefully, and I was sure she still had dozens of questions she wanted to ask. But the mention of my father reminded her of the purse she'd left neglected underneath her chair, and she reached down to pull it forward, dig her phone out from inside, and check the screen.

"Dang it."

She tossed the magazine over onto the empty seat beside her and stood up.

"We've got to go. You ready?"

"Yeah, I'm ready. Let's go."

The rain had finally stopped, though the night air outside was still cold and thick with moisture. Together, my mother and I moved briskly across the slick asphalt and over to the car, again wasting no time in starting up the engine and turning the heat vents on high.

Our headlights swept across the red pickup truck as we drove past the lobby entrance and out onto the main road, and I couldn't stop myself from taking one last look back at the row of glowing white windows along the side of the building. Which of those was her room? I thought maybe I'd be able to recognize it, or at least spot some telltale shadows moving within one of the squares of light, but there was nothing obvious or familiar there; at least not from this distance.

After a quick call to my father letting him know we were on our way home, my mother picked back up on her line of questioning, prompting me for more details about what had happened in the girl's hospital room. I recounted the whole episode, from first meeting her parents, all the way through being asked to leave after the girl's emotional meltdown, only leaving out the bit about her father's unexplained animosity toward me. There was no point in sharing that unless I understood it myself.

Dinner was ready and waiting for us at home, and so was my father. Already upset that he'd had to return to work today and miss out on time with us, he bemoaned the fact he wasn't there to help me locate the tree I'd crashed into and promised that he'd take me there himself whenever I wanted him to.

With unapologetic, enthusiastic curiosity, he also bombarded me with questions about the girl I'd discovered by the creek. Of particular interest to him was how I'd managed to revive her, and how my mother and I managed to reunite in the forest.

The three of us sat at the kitchen table long after we were all finished eating, reflecting on the day's events and all that had happened. I poked at the cold clumps of mashed potatoes on my plate without really looking at them; yet another one of my favorite foods that I now found borderline inedible, but had tried valiantly to enjoy for the sake of my parents—particularly my father, the dutiful cook.

Thankfully, I could blame my lack of appetite on fatigue from all I'd experienced, and no one disputed the notion, even though secretly, I was famished. I'd made midnight excursions to the pantry before, and over time, I'd even discovered which foods agreed with my taste buds and which ones did not. It wasn't a problem if I wanted to sneak back to the kitchen for sustenance later once my parents went to bed.

Usually, we'd relocate to the living room to watch evening television together after dinner and the dishes were done, but tonight was different. My father refused to let us help gather or wash the dirty plates, even though he'd cooked the whole meal for us, instead suggesting we go relax in the other room. When it was clear he wouldn't be deterred, my mother relented to his wishes, but not his suggestion, instead asking if it would be okay for her to go to bed. Obviously, no one had any objections, and my father reassured her that he was close behind, as soon as he was done cleaning up in the kitchen.

I lied and told him I was also exhausted and ready for bed. Once again, he professed his willingness to take me back to find the tree, or to see the girl in the hospital, or really, just to accompany me wherever I might want to go. I thanked him, hugged him, and wished him goodnight, before climbing the stairs to my bedroom and shutting the door behind me.

Alone for the first time in hours, I collapsed on top of my bed and stared up at the ceiling. Finally at rest, my body shuddered and gave in to gravity and the soft caress of the mattress and bedcovers beneath me.

It would have been all too easy to fully surrender myself to sleep if not for my mind, which still churned energetically as images and sensations from the day replayed themselves at frenetic speed. The film inside my brain danced wildly between thoughts and feelings, all out of order and randomly occurring, but all of them centered around the two encounters I'd had with Jessica.

Jessica… Silverton. That was the family name the doctor had given her parents.

It was a pretty name to think and say aloud, and I tested it with my mouth the same way the girl had formed my name in hers—though it hadn't been my name, not really. Close, but unmistakably different: Daniel and David. Both two syllable words, both beginning with the letter D. It was forgivable that a person in her condition would get them confused.

Then again, she'd called me Daniel before I'd introduced myself as David, and there was no rational explanation for that. There wasn't a rational explanation for much of what happened today.

Would I see her again? Even if she asked for me, would they allow it?

From the very beginning, Mr. Silverton seemed to want me as far away from her as possible, and even Mrs. Silverton and the doctor couldn't deny the correlation between my presence and her fit. Maybe in time, their opinions would change, perhaps after she showed signs of progress in her recovery. After all, it had to be encouraging that they let me see her at all; if she was physically injured, ill, or in any kind of life-threatening danger, the doctor never would have allowed me into her room in the first place.

More likely than not, it was just too much, too soon, both mentally and emotionally. With the proper amount of care and rehabilitation, there might come a time in the not-too-distant future when it'd be permissible for us to see each other again. And maybe, just maybe, that meeting would prove as insightful as I suspected it could be, if indeed this girl knew something about me like she claimed to.

It wasn't an unrealistic notion at all, though there was no telling how long it'd be before a conversation like that could conceivably take place. Even if her mood and mind stabilized quickly in the coming days, there was always the threat of relapse, particularly with how I'd affected her just by my presence alone.

I wasn't sure when it happened exactly, but somewhere along the line, I must have fallen asleep, because the beige textured ceiling I'd been looking at for so long now was gone, replaced instead by a glittering black sea of stars.

Maybe I was seeing through the walls and up past the roof of our house into the night sky—but no, it wasn't quite the sky at all. Whatever it was moved and undulated with a lazy rhythm, alive in a way I knew was impossible for something as wide and vast as the sky.

It wasn't until I smelled it that I recognized the sea, inky black and stirring with steady, magnificent waves that swelled all around me, but never broke. The stars were logically a reflection on the surface, then; yet somehow, I knew that also wasn't true.

Thousands upon thousands of them sparkled up at me from deep beneath the dark water, and in the pale glow they gave off, I could make out rippling silhouettes of mysterious finned animals and moving shapes I'd never seen before. The stars dimmed altogether until the sea was black and invisible, and now I was afraid, knowing the world below me teemed with aquatic alien life I could no longer see.

I became aware of my body, and to my immense relief, my viewpoint changed, so that my feet were now on solid ground, and I was taking in the ocean vista from a distance, standing at the edge of a high cliff looking down at everything I'd just seen.

Now, from the relative safety of this new perch, I found myself conflicted: longing to be closer to the water, so that maybe I could glimpse the stars twinkling out from the depths again, but also terrified of what that proximity entailed with so many creatures swimming just below.

Don't be afraid.

The voice came suddenly from the darkness, soft and familiar and kind. I looked around, but there was no one there. I stood alone at the edge of the universe, but now in every direction there was ocean, and the cliff underneath me was gone, replaced by a tall, slippery rock jutting out from the rising water.

Panic seeped in as the waves rolled higher and higher, lapping at my feet, and still there was no sign of stars. If only I had their illumination around me again, then I'd be able to better prepare myself for whatever challenges or dangers the tide brought with it.

I'm here for you now.

My eyes darted around in a futile attempt to pinpoint the source of the voice. The world spun with me, then against me, then started rotating on its own at random, and I began to feel nauseous.

A particularly violent change in direction caused my foot to slip, and with a thud, my body slipped out from under me, the rock melted into the sea; and I was floating then, whether I wanted to or not, adrift in an eternal wash of black.

The fear of what swam around and below me was still palpable, but so was a new feeling, a curious sensation of familiarity and nostalgia, almost as if I'd been in this situation before.

If that was true and I had been here before, then there was a comfort in knowing I'd survived it once and presumably could do so again. The gulf might feel endless, but that was just a false impression, a sensory tactic meant to incite panic or despair; when in truth I knew that this, too, would pass.

Already the ocean was changing again into something different than water, something lighter and less defined.

You remember this.

I did. I did remember this—this void, this loss of time, space, function, and form. This absence of identity, this negative of reality, of wakefulness, of consciousness.

I'd been here before; for how long, I wasn't sure. But it was undeniably something I'd experienced. More importantly, it was something I'd come out of, emerging on the other end confused and changed, but emerging all the same. And if I could do it once, I could do it again.

You will. We both will. Together.

Chapter Thirteen

———————————

A week ago, I never would have dreamt this scenario possible. Yet here we were all the same, all three of us driving together.

As much as the timing of the call had surprised my parents, what *really* surprised me most was that it came at all.

Neither me nor my father had been home when the phone rang; he was at work, and I was at a session with Dr. Eiding, recounting more of what had happened by the creek and detailing my recurring dreams of late. She was as fascinated by the dreams as she was by my inability to quantify them in concrete language, and we had spent the better part of our two weekly sessions analyzing what 'the void' was and what it might represent.

My father had picked me up on his evening commute from work after the second session, and we were both equally taken aback when we arrived home and learned that my mother had just gotten off the phone with Mrs. Silverton, and that we were all invited over for dinner at their house Friday night.

The invitation couldn't possibly have come from Mr. Silverton; that I was sure of. How his wife even managed to invite us over at all was crazy to think about, considering how much I knew he disliked me.

I'd spent most of my week trying unsuccessfully to put thoughts of the girl out of my head, knowing that another interaction with her might be impossible after the way I'd upset her in the hospital. Her father blamed me for that—he'd said it out loud to my face—and I had no doubt he probably also held me responsible for her disappearance in the first place.

It must have taken an extraordinary effort by Mrs. Silverton, and most likely by Jessica herself, to finally convince him to allow me anywhere near his daughter again.

All that ultimately mattered, though, was that the call was made, the invitation was offered, and it was accepted. And now, against all the odds in the world, it appeared I was about to see the girl once again.

My father slowed the car as we approached a cross street, peering forward to try and read the sign hanging from the traffic light.

"What's that say? Is that Morningside Lane?"

I couldn't blame him; it wasn't completely dark outside, but night was fast approaching, and the dark green hue of the marker didn't make it any easier to read in the twilight. We had to pull all the way up to the street before any of us could decipher the name printed in small white letters.

"Morningside. This must be it."

He turned the wheel right as we coasted slowly down the residential street.

"What's the address again?"

My mother had it written down on a piece of paper from the stationery she kept in the kitchen.

"Eleven seventy."

She looked out the passenger window at the houses that passed by, and after a second or two, found what she was searching for.

"It should be on this side of the street. That's eleven sixty-two... eleven sixty-four... I think it's that one up ahead with the porch swing."

I saw the house she was referring to, and I also saw a familiar sight parked outside it.

"That's it. I recognize the red pickup truck."

There was light coming from a number of windows inside the house, as well as from an iron lantern perched atop a matching grey-black mailbox at the end of the driveway. Four shiny reflective numerals indicated the address we'd been instructed to come to.

My father angled our car close to the curb so that my mother would be able to step right out onto the walkway that connected the sidewalk with the front porch. Then he turned the key in the ignition, the interior lights came on, the doors unlocked, and it was time to get out. My mother retrieved an expensive bottle of red wine from the floor near her seat. We'd stopped at a package store along the way to purchase it, and she'd since commented several times that she hoped the Silvertons would like it.

Together, we made our way up the path through their yard and toward the porch. I found myself hypnotized by the wooden swing that swayed gently in the evening breeze, letting out the faintest creak as it moved back and forth on rusted chain-link supports.

That feeling of weightlessness; that's why I wanted to sit on it, I realized. It reminded me of being suspended in mid-air, mid-water, or mid-whatever-it-was that I kept experiencing in my dreams.

The porch swing would have to wait though, at least until after dinner, if I was lucky—and if Mr. Silverton didn't throw us all out of his house the second I triggered some kind of horrible reaction in his daughter. There were an alarming number of 'ifs' I'd considered on the drive over here, and very few of these imagined scenarios ended well for me or my family.

But there was nothing I could say to warn my parents or to prepare them for whatever happened once we found ourselves inside. I knew nothing about what caused the girl's episodes, nor did I know how Mr. Silverton would treat me, now that I was no longer an intruder but a guest in his home. There was only one way to find out, so I climbed the porch steps behind my parents and kept my eyes locked on the front door as my father rang the bell.

We waited in silence for about ten seconds. Then I heard the click of the lock being turned on the other side, and the door swung inward to reveal the form of Mrs. Silverton standing in the entryway.

She appeared far more composed now than she had the first time I met her, which was understandable, given the extreme circumstances of that day. Honestly, she probably looked a good ten years younger without the tears and wrinkles of anguish written all over her face, and it put me more at ease to see her like this: warm, smiling, and vivacious in a casual yet elegant denim jean dress.

"Hi there! Hi! Oh, I'm so happy you all could make it."

She couldn't quite decide who she wanted to greet

first, so she just bounced forward and slung her arms loosely around all three of us at once. It was awkward, but certainly heartfelt.

"Sorry... I'm a hugger!"

"No, that's okay!" My mother had no problem with the physical contact. "We're huggers, too."

I wondered to myself if that was actually true— were we huggers? I'd never really noticed before, but I supposed my parents did hug me and hug each other a lot. Maybe we were huggers, too.

"You must be Steven, nice to meet you. I'm Katherine, but please call me Kate, if your wife hasn't told you that already... *Jim, they're here!*"

She bellowed the summons out to her husband, then refocused her attention, this time on me.

"How are you Dan—*David*. David! I'm sorry, I want to call you Daniel still; it's Jessica's doing, not mine. But she's better about it now, so don't worry!"

She was quick to add that last bit in, clasping my hands between hers and nodding emphatically before turning her head to holler out again.

"Jim!"

I heard Jim Silverton coming long before I saw him, his arrival foreshadowed by steady, thunderous footsteps descending the wooden staircase behind his wife.

Just as Kate Silverton looked like an entirely different person than the haggard creature I'd met at the hospital, so, too, did her husband. His tattered hat was gone, and his face was freshly shaven—I could see even more of his freckles now that the silver whiskers were all gone. Perhaps he'd just finished getting ready in the bathroom, because there were little red splotches on the skin of his cheeks and along his throat. Regardless, it looked like he'd made a real effort to clean himself up, going so far as to slick his hair over and sport clean khaki slacks, a denim button-up shirt, and polished leather boots.

"How y'all doin'?"

If he felt any pressure to hurry up and get downstairs, he sure didn't show it. His voice was an easy drawl, friendly yet reserved—the exact opposite of what it'd been a week ago.

"Jim Silverton."

He stuck out his right hand toward my father, who took it and shook it vigorously.

"Steven Abbott. Nice to meet you, Jim. You remember my wife, Ellen, and my son, David."

Jim nodded amiably to my mother and then moved quickly over to me, zeroing in with his gaze and stabbing his hand out into the shrinking space between us. I placed my hand in his and was immediately taken aback at just how firm his grip was. The bones in my knuckles actually cracked as he looked me level in the eyes.

"Good to see you again, *David.*"

Mrs. Silverton took a few steps toward the staircase and tilted her head up at the landing near the top.

"Jessica, honey! They're here!"

The woman had a talent for projecting her voice when she needed to; it wouldn't have surprised me if you could hear it all the way outside on the street corner. All five of us followed her gaze up the stairs, waiting with hushed anticipation for the arrival of the one person responsible for this gathering.

151

Right on cue, she materialized on the landing.

It was strange to see her standing upright, and even stranger to see her walking at all. The girl still looked pale and delicate from this distance, but not quite as fragile and sickly as she'd been in the hospital bed hooked up to all those tubes and machines. Her hair was redder than I remembered, a lighter auburn color than what it had been when it was wet. She had her father's freckles, and she certainly had his eyes—those hadn't changed a bit, still wide as saucers and an otherworldly shade of green.

And just as they'd done by the creek and in the hospital, they locked on me immediately, and then that brilliant smile followed just as fast.

The world around me suddenly wasn't important anymore, and it all faded and fell away until I was no longer aware of anything else but her. I couldn't think thoughts or move any part of my body; all I could do was see her seeing me, and for some reason, it was all I'd ever wanted or needed in my whole life.

"You ready, honey?"

Mrs. Silverton asked the question gently, as if speaking too loudly might frighten her daughter away.

"Jessica?"

The girl blinked, momentarily breaking our wordless trance of an exchange, and swiveled her moon-eyes onto her mother. There was a pause where she seemed to consider what to do or say; her eyebrows furrowed together in concentration, like she was trying hard to remember something important she'd forgotten. Then her face relaxed again, she sent a different smile to her mother than the one she had given me, and with one hand sliding lightly down the guardrail, she glided down the steps until she joined us in the foyer of their home.

Up close I realized she was a bit taller than I'd given her credit for; the crown of her head came about flush with my chin. She was still the shortest person in the room, but standing firmly on her own two feet and bathed in the soft, golden glow of the overhead light, she looked stronger and healthier than she had before.

Now that she was closer to me, I felt a strange sort of energy coming off her; a psychic heat that emanated effortlessly from her body. It was unlike anything I'd ever felt, and there was no simple way to describe it. It felt almost as if there were invisible ropes pulling us closer together; like millions of tiny, microscopic particles circulated back and forth between us, exploding with electricity and splashing into the pores of our skin, soaking in our truest essence, and then detaching once again to float back to the place they came from, deposit their ionic charge, and begin the cycle anew. There was a living, breathing world growing there between us, even without any words or action. I could taste it—and I wanted more.

"Jessica, this is Mr. and Mrs. Abbott... David's parents. Mrs. Abbott is obviously the one who drove you all the way to the hospital."

The girl's father put a hand on her shoulder. It brought back memories of him holding her down in the hospital bed as she thrashed around, and of the deep purple bruises along her upper arms where his fingers had been. The marks were still there just below her shoulders, although they were fainter now, and had turned about as green as they were purple.

"Thank you." Her voice was light, girlish, and

offered softly in my mother's direction. "Thank you for what you did for me."

There was a momentary silence where no one knew if she was done speaking. Jessica herself seemed on the verge of saying something more, her lips slightly askew and her chest rising with quick, shallow intakes of breath.

Sensing a potential opening, my mother decided to venture out a reply.

"You're welcome."

She fidgeted with the wine bottle in her hands.

"I'm just happy that we were in the right place at the right time, and that you're home safe now."

Jessica's mother put a hand on her other shoulder, so that she was now flanked on both sides by her parents.

"We are, too. It was nothing short of a miracle, you and David going out there and finding her the way you did. I have no doubt in my mind that God led you to her."

"David knew where he would find me."

I wasn't sure which was stranger: the girl finally calling me David for the first time or the cryptic nature of her statement. As if her words weren't enough, she accompanied them with a knowing smile that was as conspiratorial as it was mysterious.

No one knew how to respond this time. I noticed that while my parents and Mrs. Silverton were focused on Jessica and trying to interpret the meaning of what she'd just said, Mr. Silverton had returned his attention back to me. And there, to my immense dismay, was the same familiar, penetrating, suspicious glare he'd seared into me the day we'd met.

I racked my brain for something to say in my own defense, for anything that might help dispel the sudden cloud of tension that formed around us.

But what was there to say? Would it help or hinder the situation if I told everyone the truth—that I was only out there in the woods because I was hoping I'd find a tree I crashed into three months ago? The same one that put me in a coma, wiped clean my memories, and basically deprived me of an identity I so desperately wanted to recover?

It was a lot to process, especially for me. Who knew how they'd take it, or if they'd even believe me; though I had a strong hunch Jim Silverton probably would not.

His wife came to the rescue.

"I'm sure we all have a lot we want to talk about. I, for one, think we should do it over dinner, though, which should be just about ready now. Ellen, do you mind if we open that bottle of wine? Thank you, by the way, for bringing it! You really didn't have to do that; you've already done so much!"

My mother passed the bottle over to her.

"I hope you both like red. It's a Petite Sirah the clerk at the store said is pretty popular. I sometimes have a little port after dinner, but I'm not really the biggest wine drinker... so hopefully, it's good."

"Oh, I'm sure it's perfect! Jim won't have any because he's married to his Heinekens, but I'll try anything once. We're eating in the dining room, but do y'all want to wash up first? Jessica, honey, can you show the Abbotts where the bathroom is while I get everyone something to drink?"

In a blur, Kate Silverton moved off, bottle in hand,

down a hallway and toward what I presumed to be the kitchen.

Jessica stared blankly after her as if awaiting further instruction. It soon became apparent that she either hadn't heard her mother's request, or she simply didn't know where she was supposed to lead us.

If it was indeed the latter, my heart broke for her. I understood all too well that feeling of being lost and of not knowing how to give people the reaction they wanted of you.

"Come on, Jess… we'll take them together."

Despite his tough, masculine exterior, I detected a hint of concern in Mr. Silverton's hard-set eyes, and there was a slight crack in his voice when he said his daughter's name. Clearing his throat unassumingly, he piloted her around and beckoned for us to follow them down a different hallway.

Along the way, I took in all the objects and decorations mounted along the plain beige walls. Here and there were small paintings or pieces of wood fastened together in the shape of a cross, but overwhelmingly, the walls were dominated by family photos of the Silvertons throughout the years. Most seemed to be staged in a studio with a uniformly-colored background, but occasionally, I came across an image that was taken more candidly outside somewhere in a scenic or exotic location.

"You have a beautiful family."

My father said it to Mr. Silverton as he took in the hallway sights alongside me, the two of us waiting our turn outside the bathroom. Inside, Jessica and my mother stood at twin sinks, washing their hands in silence.

Mr. Silverton had his thumbs hooked in his belt straps and his weight propped up against the doorframe. He tried to look casual, but was doing a poor job of concealing his obvious discomfort at being left alone with us. His head had been lowered and fixated on his boots, but now he jerked his chin up, followed my father's gaze to the photos on the wall, and nodded slowly.

"Yep. What can I say? I'm blessed. Very blessed."

He reached out and carefully straightened a picture on the wall that didn't really need straightening.

"So… Katie tells me you work for the city. Is that right?"

My father switched places with my mother, rinsing his hands under the water while addressing Jim Silverton's reflection in the mirror above the sink.

"I do. I'm a city planner."

The polite conversation continued between them, three adults negotiating one another amidst an unfamiliar and uncomfortable social setting.

Once again, though, I wasn't really seeing or hearing what happened around me. Jessica finished washing her hands and drying them on the small dark green towel that hung limply from a brass ring on the side of the counter.

Now, she turned around and took a step toward me, closing the small distance left between us, and curled the corner of her mouth up slightly in a challenging expression that stopped my heart.

"Are you ready?"

Three little words, innocuous and upbeat.

But there was another meaning there, I was sure of it, only thinly disguised as an invitation to approach the bathroom sink she'd just vacated.

She was trying to tell me something, trying to communicate some hidden message. But I had no idea what it was she wanted me to understand.

I felt the raw force of her intention, pure and powerful, radiating into me, compelling every cell in my body to know her and to comprehend the blazing truth she needed to impress onto me.

"Are you going to wash up, Davey?"

My mother momentarily broke the spell, and I maneuvered my way past the human energy vortex and over to the sink to wash my hands with soap and water. I looked up at the reflection in the glass to see if she was still standing there behind me, but she was gone, along with the rest of the adults.

Chapter Fourteen

When I was done toweling off, I followed their voices down the remainder of the hallway until it spilled out into the dining room. It was a moderately-sized space, tastefully decorated with four rippling cream-colored curtains that swept out on either side of two large windows in the far wall.

During the daytime, the windows probably allowed in a good amount of natural light. Since it was dark outside, the chandelier hanging overhead provided most of the illumination that was needed; the rest came from a bouquet of tall, spindly wax candles flickering gently at the center of a long wooden table.

Six identical place settings were arranged meticulously along the edge of the table, spaced evenly apart to correspond with six dark wooden chairs. My parents occupied the two chairs on the side of the table furthest from where I stood, facing me with their backs against the windows.

Mrs. Silverton hovered above my mother with the open wine bottle in one hand and her own full glass in the other, watching to see what her guest's reaction would be. My mother tilted the glass up to her lips and tasted the wine she'd brought with us, hesitated for a moment, and then beamed with satisfaction and relief that she hadn't chosen poorly. Mrs. Silverton squealed with delight before sampling her own glass and adding her approval as she sat down to my left at one end of the table.

Directly across from her to my right sat Mr. Silverton. He looked far too big for the chair he was in; his torso was bent and wedged up against one of the chair's wooden arms, and he gripped the other chair arm like he was bracing himself for impact, his knuckles white and prominent against the skin. His other hand transported a green beer bottle to and from his mouth, and I was amazed at just how quickly the liquid inside disappeared every time he brought the beverage back to rest.

Wedged between him and my father was a small square table in the corner of the room, and on top of it there were at least four or five different food dishes, none of which looked familiar to me.

Dinner was shaping up to be quite the adventure.

As was quickly becoming a trend, the real focal point of the scene was the one person whose face I couldn't see: the girl seated to my left with her back to me. Of course, the only spot left at the table was the vacant chair right next to her. I gathered up my courage and sat down at the dinner table, trying my best to stay calm and collected despite the building inferno inside me.

What little empty space existed between us seemed to shrink rapidly, the very air in the room compressing and pushing us closer together until I could have sworn her arm was touching mine. It was already too much; I had to check and see for myself, just to make sure I was actually hallucinating.

I stole a glance downward out of the corner of my eye and was genuinely shocked at the distance still between us. We were near to each other, sure, but not anywhere as close as my feverish brain led me to believe, and definitely not touching.

So, why did it feel like she was practically sitting in my lap?

The distinct ring of metal on glass focused everyone's attention on Mr. Silverton. He patiently waited until the conversation in the room was fully extinguished, gave the neck of his beer bottle one final rap with his knife, and then set it down and cleared his throat.

"I don't mean to interrupt anyone, but I'm sure I'm not the only one here who's hungry, and I don't want this delicious meal to get cold. So, let's say grace."

He dipped his chin toward his chest, as did his wife and my parents. I lowered my head, too, and clasped my hands together between my legs, as I'd learned was only proper. But again, from my periphery, I caught a glimpse of the girl to my left. Her head was unbowed, and her hands were flat against her thighs.

"Bless us, oh Lord, and these thy gifts which we are about to receive from thy bounty through Christ our Lord. Amen."

It was a different prayer than the ones I was used to my father giving at home. His always seemed to change night after night, recycling and repeating certain themes or keywords, but for the most part, varying in length and content. This was more of a monotone recitation, but it must have been somewhat common and well-known, because my parents knew all the words too and joined the Silvertons in saying them out loud in unison.

After they all finished with "amen," the heads came back up, and Mr. Silverton twisted around in his chair to grab the supper items. One by one, he fixed up his own plate with a hefty portion and then passed the serving plate or bowl over to my father.

Slowly, the components of the meal made their way around the table from person to person, and as I watched the food travel, I began to nervously wonder what the exchange would be like when it came time for Jessica to hand me the first dish. It was such an innocent transaction, passing a plate of meat, vegetables, or whatever the food was; but so far, there had been no such thing as a simple or meaningless interaction between me and this girl. Every second of every single exchange between us was pure electricity.

"I'm so happy y'all could join us tonight."

Kate Silverton poured herself another glass of wine before turning to receive a bowl from my mother of what looked like mashed potatoes. Oh, how I hoped they weren't actually mashed potatoes; I *hated* mashed potatoes.

"Jessica has been asking after you just about every day, Dan—*David*."

She winced as she corrected her mistake, taking a little pause before continuing on.

"I'm sorry, hun; I promise I'll have it down by the end of the night!" She laughed and took a healthy swig of wine. "But she *has* been asking to see you, so we figured it was high time to invite y'all over."

"We're happy we could make it."

My mother held her wine glass out toward Mrs.

Silverton, who lightly tapped her own glass against it, and both women drank.

"This is all absolutely delicious, by the way, Kate."

Always reliable to bring a big appetite, my father somehow had consumed at least a quarter of the food on his plate already, even as I still waited for the first dish to make its way over to me.

"I usually play chef in our *casa*, but I'm thinking you could give me quite a few pointers on how I might up my game. This is fantastic."

"Hey, you."

The words were spoken softly so that only I could hear them. She waited for me to turn and see her, then outstretched the bowl in her hands as an offering.

I took it from her carefully, hoping she couldn't see how badly I was shaking, as I set it down on the table and scooped the bare minimum of potatoes onto my plate.

"Thank you."

Given how fast my mouth had dried up, I was surprised I could speak anything at all. Carrying on a conversation—and for that matter, just eating food— was beginning to feel like an impossible endeavor. Unlike my father, my appetite was long, long gone. There was no room in my stomach for anything other than the knot that kept growing larger and larger by the second.

I tried to focus on what I was doing and not on how I was feeling. Above all, I tried not to focus on her. It wasn't easy; already I sensed she was ready to pass me another item, so I picked up the bowl of potatoes in a hurry, anxious to pass it on to her father and get this whole rotation thing finished already.

163

He was ready for me, pinching the dish between his thumb and forefinger and then swinging it back behind him onto the square serving table in the corner.

"Not to monopolize the dinner conversation, but if y'all are anything like us, I'm sure you've got plenty of questions that have been keeping you up at night."

He reached forward to grab a small glass shaker and began flurrying salt all over his plate.

"My wife is fond of reminding me that sometimes when I think I'm just being curious and asking someone a few friendly questions, it comes across like I'm interrogating that person, or... what's the word you use, Katie?"

"Badgering."

"*Badgering* that person. Which is certainly never my intention."

Satisfied with the service it provided, he returned the salt shaker to the table.

"But as a wise man once said: my wife is always right. So, in the interest of avoiding *badgering* anyone here, I'll start off by filling y'all in on how my daughter ended up alone in the woods that day. And then maybe, if he wants, David can fill me in on how he came to find her, and how the two of them even know each other in the first place.

"Or maybe if he doesn't want to, then that's fine, too. Like I said, I'm not here to badger anyone. I just feel like there's a helluva lot to talk about, and for better or worse, my normally bubbly daughter has not been particularly talkative since she came home. So maybe tonight's the night to change all that, now that we're finally here together. Sound good?"

Maybe he really was trying to sound friendly and

jumpstart some easy dinner conversation, but the resulting mood in the room felt anything but light or cordial. Both my parents appeared anxious, like perhaps they were suddenly afraid they'd been implicated in some kind of crime or conspiracy. Even Kate Silverton looked concerned; maybe she sensed the real threat her husband posed in sabotaging their roles as gracious and appreciative hosts for the evening.

Since my return from the hospital, my father had become something of an expert at defusing tension during awkward moments. Recognizing this as one of them, he gallantly sallied forth with a cheerful response.

"Sure, Jim. As long as nobody feels pressured to say something they're not comfortable with, I don't see any harm in it."

He directed most of what he said to me, but I noticed he cast a couple quick glances in Jessica's direction as well.

It was enough of an affirmation for Jim Silverton.

"Absolutely. No one has to say anything at all, whether they're comfortable or not. I just feel like you're nice people, and since you're the ones who found my girl, you're entitled to some sort of explanation."

He folded his hands together in front of him and gazed over at Jessica thoughtfully.

"Maybe you've heard by now, or maybe you haven't, but when you folks found her down by the creek, Jessica had already been missing for over twenty-four hours. She wasn't at breakfast on Thursday morning, and when we found out she wasn't at school either, we had no choice but to call the police and report her as a missing person. Katie and I spent most of that day at the station, and then we were out looking for her that night. We didn't stop until the call finally came in from the hospital the next day letting us know she'd just been checked in."

His focus roved to his wife at the other end of the table.

"I don't want to speak for Kate, but I can honestly tell you that those twenty-four hours were the longest of my life. The thoughts that run through your head, the way your brain just keeps going down those dark paths, wondering what if, trying not to think about the stories you see on TV and in the news; it's every parent's worst nightmare, losing their child.

"And you know what the hardest part of it all was for me? The thought that it may have been my fault, that I may have been responsible for what happened."

He looked back toward Jessica.

"You see, we had a fight the night before she went missing. Nothing too serious or crazy, just the kind of stupid argument that dads get into with their teenage daughters from time to time. And I know they say never go to bed angry. But that night, Jessica and I—we both went to bed angry. Only difference was that I was there the next morning, and she wasn't."

He adjusted his body in the chair, arching his back and reaching for what little was left in his beer bottle with a heavy sigh.

"I blame myself. Every parent blames themselves in that situation. You're the parent and they're the child. That's how it is and how it's always supposed to be, no matter how old that kid gets or how much they think they've got the whole world figured out. It's a parent's job to teach you to stand up and face your problems head-on, and that running away from them won't get you anywhere in life; except maybe killed, and then there's no point to any of it, is there?"

He finished the last of the beer and placed the empty bottle on the serving table behind him.

"Anyway, that's the long and the short of it. I don't know if Kate wants to add anything, or Jessica?"

Kate was quick to seize the opportunity.

"I just want to say again how eternally grateful we are for what you did for us as a family. Life is full of ups and downs, but the most important thing of all is that you see it through to the bitter end, and that you do it together—that's why God gives us a family in the first place. And we have your family to thank for keeping ours intact."

She reached over and clasped her daughter's hand in hers.

"Jessica, honey, do you want to say anything? You don't have to, of course; we know you've been through so much already."

With everyone's attention squarely on her, the youngest Silverton bore an expression of embarrassed astonishment, as if she hadn't really been listening, and now she found herself forced to comment on all that was said. Her lower lip trembled, and I saw the muscles around her jaw tighten and flex as she processed the situation and realized that she was at the crux of it now, whether she wanted to be or not.

Again, I felt a tremendous outpouring of empathy for her, registering in this kindred spirit that familiar rush of panic and terror at disappointing those around you.

Something grabbed at my left thigh. I almost

yelped out in surprise, but before I could let out a noise, I felt five fingers dig into the flesh there through my jeans.

Without looking over, I knew that it was her, and that she was clutching onto me because she was afraid. She didn't know what to do or what to say, and though her mother held her other hand in an obvious gesture of comfort and encouragement, it either wasn't enough for her, or it wasn't what she really wanted or needed.

She needed me. I could feel it in the way she held onto me now for dear life, like now that she had me, she'd never let me go again.

Shaking, I laid my hand on top of hers and held my breath, praying to every force in the universe that it was the right move to make, and that she'd accept my touch.

I felt the energy again, so hot it felt cold, tingling and vibrating furiously between the thin layers of paper-skin that separated our bones and our blood, rushing a million miles a minute.

Her grip loosened, and for one terrible second, I thought she was pulling back and away from me. But then her wrist rolled upward and her fingers found the blank spaces between mine, and now she was holding my hand just as fiercely as she'd held my leg.

Somewhere in the midst of it all, I'd completely forgotten how to breathe.

"My mom and dad are right."

She started off soft and slow, the sentiments falling out of her like little drops of water when it first starts to rain. As she went on, her voice grew brighter and more confident, drawing power from the strength I tried to will into her body through mine.

"Family is the most important, precious thing, no matter where you are or where you come from. I would do anything for my family, for those I love. Absolutely anything. And the thought of losing my family... I could never let that happen. I know that now, better than I ever have before."

Kate Silverton sniffled and detached herself from her daughter, freeing both hands to preemptively wipe away the glistening from her eyes.

"We'd do anything for you, too, baby. You're never going to lose us."

She gave Jessica a meaningful smile, then looked at me and at my parents, and with a jolt, sprang back into host-mode.

"Whew! Sorry, sometimes I can't help myself. Ellen, can I pour you some more of your wine? I feel like I'm hogging it all to myself... it's just too darn good!"

Before my mother could object, her glass was filling up again.

"Katie, since you're up, do you mind grabbing me another one?"

Jim tilted his head back toward the empty green bottle behind him.

"Anyone else need a refill? Or how about seconds? I can get the train going again."

He didn't stop to wait for an answer, loading up his plate directly from the table before offering up a bowl of creamed corn to my father, who accepted it with excitement.

Mrs. Silverton disappeared down the hallway to fetch her husband another beer while the rest of us rotated the food around a second time, with my mother serving both herself and Kate while she was in the kitchen. When both their plates were filled, she passed the dish across the table to Jessica, who had to break off our hidden embrace to receive it.

Long after our hands were physically separated, the sensation of contact remained there like a dull ache. And now, there was an additional thrill every time our fingers intentionally grazed against one another's as we moved a plate or pot between us.

Far and away, this was the most exciting meal of my life, and it had absolutely nothing to do with what I ate or drank.

Once all the dishes made their way back to the square table in the corner, everyone's drinks were refreshed, and Kate sat down again, I decided it was finally my turn to talk. Jessica's heartfelt speech, succinct but moving, emboldened me to share a bit of my own history. If she could allow herself to be so vulnerable and to speak from such a place of naked truth, then I needed to find the courage to do the same, no matter what kind of reaction I received from Jim Silverton or from anyone else.

I waited nervously for the right moment, for a natural lull in the conversation that I could take advantage of. My father was finishing up an anecdote from his job between mouthfuls of food, laboring to communicate the humor of the tale while acknowledging "you really had to be there" to fully grasp its hilarity. Recognizing he'd gotten everything he could from the story, he shrugged and laughed to himself, before gulping down the rest of his water glass.

"Mr. Silverton…" My voice cracked. I hoped no

one heard it, even though I was sure they all had. "You said earlier that you wanted to know what I was doing out there in the woods when I found your daughter.

"Now, this might sound a little crazy or... or weird, or something, but I was only out there because I was looking for something... for this tree, for this specific place where I had an accident a few months ago. I was driving home from school, and it was raining outside, and I guess I must have lost control of the car or something and crashed into this tree, because it put me in a coma."

I heard Mrs. Silverton audibly gasp to my left, but her husband's face was unchanged.

"I don't really remember much of what happened before the coma, honestly. All I remember is waking up in the hospital. I've been through all sorts of tests, and I'm still going through physical therapy, as well as seeing a psychiatrist who tries to help with some of my memory loss. But all this is to say that I asked my mother to take me out to where it happened last Friday in the hopes that maybe being there again would free something up inside my head, or help me remember something from before it all went dark, I guess.

"I just... I couldn't find the spot where it happened. Or, maybe I did, but I didn't even recognize it; I don't know. And then I got lost for a while. And that's when I found your daughter... when I found Jessica lying at the edge of the water. I didn't know what to do, or if she was even alive, but I knew I couldn't just leave here there."

I had a quick internal debate on whether to mention any details surrounding our initial verbal interaction in the forest, but decided it was probably

171

safer to omit this section of the narrative for now.

"I thought about trying to carry her out myself, but honestly, I was still so lost, it wouldn't have done either one of us much good. Thankfully though, it was around that time that my mother found us, and together, we were able to get her back to the car and drive her to the hospital; and you all know the rest of it from there."

I'd mentally prepared myself for a slew of possible reactions from Mr. Silverton, all of which were negative.

What I hadn't accounted for was what he gave me now: no reaction at all. He just stared blankly back at me with the same expression he'd had since I first started talking.

Maybe he was expecting more from my story? Had Jessica filled him in on the exchange that happened when she first woke up? Even if she had, there was nothing said between us that made much sense to me, and certainly nothing shocking or worth hiding on my part.

I couldn't possibly interpret what he wanted from me still, so I decided to gauge the reactions of the other listeners around the dining table. My father had heard the whole story secondhand a week ago, and of course my mother herself had been a prominent player in the saga from start to finish, so neither one of them were of major interest to me now. Mrs. Silverton still looked as I imagined she had when I heard her gasp aloud: somewhere between shell-shocked, amazed, and sympathetic.

Jessica's reaction was the one that really interested me the most, and it completely caught me off guard. I figured she'd be intrigued to learn the details surrounding her rescue and all that occurred while she was drifting in and out of consciousness. The way her body was tilted and zeroed in on me seemed to confirm that I was right, that she had hung on my every word and soaked it all in like an eager sponge.

But what I didn't understand was the look of bleak devastation on her face. She looked at me like I'd just told her matter-of-factly that she only had days to live.

Sure, I had suffered, and so had she. But here we both were now: alive, revived, and for the most part, no worse for wear. To the best of my knowledge, I'd relayed my account of the car crash and ensuing coma without any melodramatic wallowing or self-pity, and the ending was a happy one.

Nevertheless, her reaction now was mystifying. Even if she was the most empathic human being on the planet, it was still a bizarre, puzzling response.

"Thank you for sharing all of that, David."

Mr. Silverton leaned far on his forearms over the table, close enough to me that I could see all the tiny brown age spots mixed in with the freckles around his eyes and forehead.

"It sounds like you've been through a lot. You and Jess both have. I'm just glad you picked the day you did to go on your little nature trek down memory lane."

He raised his eyebrows, grunted out half a laugh, and took a quick sip of his beer.

"Last couple questions; then I promise we can all adjourn to the living room, where I know my wife wants us to gather while she puts away the dishes and gets dessert ready."

He winked at my father before levelling his gaze on

me again.

"Like I said, I know my daughter's been through a helluva lot over the last week, and the doctor told us there might be some... side effects... as she gets better. But I gotta tell you: she talks about you *aaaall* the time these days, asking when she's gonna see you again, when can you come over, yadda yadda yadda...

"But here's the thing: until last Friday, *I'd never even heard of you before.* Jessica's never mentioned you, and Kate told me the other day that you don't even go to the same school as her. So, what's the big secret? You two meet at a football game, or go on a blind date, or what? I just want to know, as a father, what the relationship here is. And not because I'm mad or anything; hell, I'm thankful. I should *still* be shaking the hand of the young man who saved my daughter's life. I just oughta know what name I should call that man first, don't you think?"

I couldn't argue with anything he said. Even if the incisive tenor of his voice made his questions sound more like demands than requests, nothing he asked of me was out of line or unreasonable.

At the same time, it didn't make answering him any easier. I'd had good reason for stumbling upon Jessica in the wilderness, and if sharing that reason didn't fully satisfy him, well, that wasn't my problem. At least I'd told the truth.

What I didn't have was any shred of explanation for why she called me Daniel instead of David, or why she acted as if we knew each other so intimately. Maybe if we'd been allowed to spend more time together in the hospital, something would have come up organically in conversation that revealed what our

174

relationship was. Unfortunately, that possibility was snuffed out the second I got thrown out of her room.

So, what could I say? I looked across the table to my mother for aid. She didn't know any more than I did, so I'm not sure what kind of assistance I expected to get from her. But wasn't this what mothers were supposed to do—be there for their children? She opened her mouth as if she might try to proffer something helpful, but before anything came out, she was interrupted by a voice to my left.

"It's my fault."

Once again, all eyes centered on Jessica Silverton.

"I didn't want to say anything earlier because I was embarrassed; but the truth is, I thought he was someone else. David, that is. I don't know why—if it was just me being out there so long, I was delirious, I thought I recognized him, thought he was someone I knew from school, a stupid crush of mine… I think my head was playing tricks on me, making me believe it was him who came for me, who rescued me. And now, of course, I just feel so stupid, like I've wasted everyone's time. I was afraid to tell the truth… but I have to, so… I'm sorry."

Why did I suddenly feel decimated on the inside? Her confession was the last missing piece in the puzzle. Not only did it put an end to the Daniel versus David mystery, it also exonerated me from her father's inquisition. I should have felt relief, satisfaction, closure; but all I felt was profound disappointment, and something else…

Was it jealousy? Jealousy, and maybe dismay: dismay that all of what she'd given me, the overwhelming intensity of her attention and affection, had all been one big mistake. She'd meant it for someone else, some stupid kid at her school whose name also started with a D and had two syllables in it. Some kid who probably looked a bit like me and talked a bit like me, but wasn't me.

"You didn't waste anyone's time, Jessica."

Now my mother found her voice.

"We've gone through what you're going through right now; we're still going through it. You have nothing to apologize for. I hope you know that."

The mood at the table was somber as everyone processed Jessica's revelation in their own way. I wondered if I was expected to say something else; to accept her apology, or reassure her like my mother had, for mistaking my identity.

The moment became awkward once again, and this time, I looked across the table to my father, wordlessly imploring him to work his verbal magic and dissipate the tension. He caught my gaze and smiled back at me, but didn't pick up on the hint.

Instead, it was Jim Silverton that finally severed the silence.

"Well... I guess that explains it, then."

He stretched and pushed his plate away along the tabletop.

"Curious to learn more about who this real Daniel is, but I suppose we can save that for another night; don't want to bore the Abbotts or embarrass my daughter. Y'all save any room for dessert?"

Mention of dessert elicited various responses from around the room: my mother groaned apprehensively, my father smacked his lips, and Kate bounced up to her feet and began gathering our plates. Maybe I was only imagining it, but the Silverton family matriarch seemed to move with an astonishing new sense of speed, purpose, and cheerfulness—almost as if she was absolutely elated we'd all made it through dinner unscathed.

Both of my parents offered to help her clear the table, but she would have none of it, shushing and swatting them away while whirling about the room like a tornado.

"Like Jim said earlier, please go make yourselves comfortable in the living room. This will only take me a few minutes—leave it, Ellen, please!—and then I hope you did save a little room still, because I have a pecan pie that I'll warm up a bit while I load the dishes. I thought it might be nice to have dessert in there and light a fire in the fireplace; it's just cozier like that, don't you think? And, please, bring the wine with you."

That was the one thing she allowed us to do.

Jim gave her a light kiss on the cheek as she bent over to pick up his plate, then stood up and gestured for us to follow him.

"There's no arguing with her; Lord knows I've tried. Better to just give her what she wants and go peacefully."

He led us off down the hallway and into a cavernous living room with high vaulted ceilings, a long L-shaped couch, and two leather armchairs, all of which surrounded a white stone fireplace at the base of a chimney.

Halfway up the chimney stones hung another family portrait. This one featured an infant Jessica nestled inside a wooden wheelbarrow, with Kate and Jim on either side of it, resting an arm on each handle.

Both her parents were smiling and facing the picture-taker, while baby Jessica was either laughing, crying, or screaming—I couldn't be sure.

Mr. Silverton produced a long match from a box at the corner of the flue, and after a couple attempts, managed to light it and guide the flame to a wad of crumpled-up newspapers beneath the logs that served as kindling. Before long, it grew into a modest but crackling fire. He took a step back to admire his handiwork, then turned around and seemed surprised we were all just standing there watching him.

"Y'all can sit down and get comfortable. I'm just gonna check on Katie real quick and grab another beer. Maybe a couple more chairs, too. Anyone need something to drink?"

The question was solely directed at my parents, who both politely declined as they settled down onto the couch. Mr. Silverton rubbed his palms together, held them out toward the fire for a second, and then strode off in the direction of the kitchen.

I turned to Jessica, waiting to see where she wanted to sit before making a decision myself. There was still a little space left at the other end of the couch, but it probably was only wide enough for one person. Surely, she'd take one of the two empty armchairs; and if she did, should I take the other one, or sit down on the couch beside my parents? Where were her parents going to sit if I took the armchair? Mr. Silverton mentioned grabbing more chairs on his way back, so did it matter if I chose the armchair and left the couch space open? Was one choice more appropriate than the other?

"Mr. and Mrs. Abbott, would it be okay with you if

David and I talked outside for a while? There are just a few things I want to ask him. Maybe he might be able to help me understand what's going on better, you know, with the memory stuff, and what I can do to get my head straight."

My parents looked about as surprised as I was by the request. Considering the way Jessica's prior revelation had knocked the emotional wind out of me, this time, she caught me unawares in a completely new way.

I also sincerely doubted I'd be able to provide her with any real help or insight into her situation. After all, I still barely understood my own.

Despite all that, there was no denying the appeal of spending some private time one-on-one with her outside. Her presence had a powerful, physiological impact on me. It made my heart race and my palms sweat, and it was a thrilling, energizing sensation. I was quickly finding myself somewhat addicted to it, and I tried hard not to wonder whether Jessica felt the same way when she was around this Daniel figure from her school—because the idea still made me jealous, and a little sad, too.

"It's certainly all right with us."

My father draped an arm around my mother and shifted further back into the sofa cushions.

"Just don't stay out there too long. I'll try to save you both some pecan pie, but I can't make any promises. Mrs. Abbott has a terrible, terrible sweet tooth."

She gave him a playful whack on the stomach in retaliation.

"Okay. I'll try not to keep him long."

Jessica smiled at them, then turned to face me. She was close enough that I could see the reflection of the fireplace flames dancing in the emerald rings of her eyes. It was absolutely hypnotizing.

"Are you ready?"

Lost in a trance, I nodded dumbly and followed her outside.

Chapter Fifteen

Jessica closed the front door behind us softly and moved to sit down on one end of the suspended wooden porch bench.

I'd longed to test out the swing when we first arrived, and now it looked like I might finally get my chance. Even better, I'd be trying it out with a girl... and this specific girl, to be exact. Best yet, it was just the two of us.

I sat down next to her and allowed my inertia to glide us backward on the iron chains connected to the roof. With a faint, tired, metallic groan, the bench swung forward again slowly, then backward, and now we were moving gently through the air, propelled by gravity, our weight, and the occasional extra push from my foot.

Jessica didn't seem to be enjoying the ride quite as much as I was. She chewed on her lower lip and twisted her hands together in her lap, looking anxious. I felt guilty then, afraid that my desire to set the swing in motion may have somehow upset her.

"We can stop if you want to."

My voice cracked again, and I was sure my cheeks flushed with embarrassment in reaction. Sheepishly, I lifted both feet up off the ground and tucked them underneath me on the bench.

"I'm sorry. I just don't think I've ever been on one of these before."

The corners of her mouth twisted upward as her expression morphed into a look that bordered on pity.

"Yes, you have."

Her eyes shone with a quiet intensity, and suddenly, her voice sounded deeper, older to me.

I wondered if perhaps I hadn't heard her right.

"What did you say?"

Both of us were very still now. The only movement came from the wood below and the metal above us, creaking and shifting as the swing came to a gradual stop.

She didn't blink.

"We have a swing just like this. At home."

That didn't make much sense. She *was* home, and this *was* her swing. It certainly wasn't mine.

Was she having a mental episode again? Dr. Eiding had a word for this; she called it 'amnesia'. According to the therapist, it was perfectly normal for a recovering coma patient to suffer the occasional bout of amnesia.

Jessica hadn't been in a coma, but she had exhibited plenty of signs of forgetfulness and confusion since first waking up in the forest. Was this what she meant then, when she asked me to accompany her outside and help with her memory problems? Because if so, there was nothing I could do for her.

"Jessica…" I had to try and be delicate with her, respectful in my correction. It was important that I treat her with the same level of patience Dr. Eiding always had for me; otherwise, I'd risk accidentally offending her. "This *is* your home and your swing."

She shook her head slowly.

"No." Her voice was almost a whisper. "No, it's not."

She leaned forward and took my hands in hers, holding onto me with the same desperate strength she'd shown at the dinner table, as if letting go even for a second might prove fatal for the both of us.

"I need you to believe me... to at least keep an open mind, okay? Promise me that you will."

Her grip tightened even further.

I was beginning to lose feeling in my hands, the circulation of blood flow cut off in the blue-green veins that ran just below the skin, yet I didn't dare break away from her now or cry out in pain, not with her holding onto me for dear life and waiting with bated breath for my response.

"Okay. I will."

As if I had much choice. Still, I had to admit that she'd thoroughly piqued my curiosity. Even if all she had to share was more nonsense, it meant I could still sit here with her, hold her hands, and be the compassionate listener she wanted me to be.

"What do you remember from before your coma?"

I wasn't expecting her to shift the conversation over to me so quickly.

"Um... well, I honestly don't remember a whole lot. That's why I said I wanted to go back to the crash site, and why I'm seeing a psychiatrist. She's trying to help with my memory."

"You don't need to go back to the crash site or see

a psychiatrist. The reason you can't recall any memories from before the coma is because they're not really your memories... they're someone else's."

I had to repeat her words in my head a few times before they fully registered an impression. She still wasn't making much sense, but the conviction in her voice and face was starting to unnerve me.

"What do you mean?"

"Exactly what I just said. You're trying to remember a life you've never led before, with a body and a brain that don't belong to you."

My instincts kicked in. I tried to squirm away from her, but she wouldn't let me go. Instead, she scooted even closer to me on the bench, begging me with her eyes to listen to all that she had to say.

"I know it's a lot to take in, Daniel—" She was calling me by the wrong name again... "—but you have to trust me, and trust yourself! There's a reason why nothing about this life feels right to you; why you can't find the answers you're looking for, no matter how hard you keep trying. And there's a reason why we're here now, the two of us, together again. It's not an accident that we found each other out there in the rain. That's not just random luck or coincidence."

She paused for a second to smile.

"You think you're the one who found me, who rescued me and saved my life. But *I* found *you*, Daniel. And you're not supposed to be here. Neither of us is supposed to be here. This boy and this girl, this isn't *us*; these aren't who we really are, who we're supposed to be and who we've always been. We have another existence waiting for us... and now it's time to go back."

The girl was completely insane.

I'd expected our interaction to be tense and even potentially awkward, given the extreme conditions of our first meeting and all the exciting confusion that had since followed. But this was outrageous and impossible to comprehend.

Maybe I was foolish and naïve for thinking I could have a normal relationship, never mind just a normal conversation, with a person I pulled back from the brink of death. I didn't really even want it to be normal between us.

But I wanted to at least be able to learn more about each other through basic human dialogue. Even if our relationship was doomed to stay platonic or never advance beyond the labels of 'the rescued' and 'the rescuer', I had hoped we were capable of having a simple conversation where she didn't still think I was someone else.

And here she was suggesting we *both* were someone else.

So, what could I say to her? She needed professional care; someone like Dr. Eiding, who could sit down with her and patiently help her navigate through the various quagmires of her own unreliable brain. I was neither qualified nor mentally stable enough myself to offer any real kind of support, insight, or healing.

The sound of the front door opening behind us came as a welcome respite. Kate Silverton poked her head out from around the big wooden rectangle and took us in.

I was immediately aware of what it must have looked like: Jessica and I huddled close together on the swing with our hands interlocked, so I broke free of her grasp and tried my best not to look suspicious.

Undoubtedly, the situation would have unfolded very differently if it'd been Jim Silverton at the door, but his wife pretended not to notice anything unusual about our positioning.

"You two doing all right out here? I've got warm pecan pie ready inside."

I swung my feet back down to the ground, grateful for an excuse to avoid formulating a response to Jessica's fantastical ramblings. Just as I was about to stand up, though, I felt her hand again, this time clamped firmly down on my knee, holding me in place.

"We're okay! Can we just talk a little bit longer? Then, I promise we'll come inside."

I don't know which surprised me more—the boldness of her openly touching my leg in front of her parent, or the way she casually decided to speak for the both of us.

Her mother looked surprised as well, but she didn't protest.

"Sure, honey. Just don't catch cold."

Mrs. Silverton rubbed her upper arms and disappeared slowly back inside, closing the door behind her.

Before I could open my mouth to protest, Jessica was speaking again. Her mother's interruption seemed to remind her that there were still other people nearby who were very conscious of us, even if we weren't of them. She spoke quicker now and with heightened intention, aware that at any minute, someone could appear again on the porch and put an end to our conversation.

"Listen to me. I know this all sounds crazy to you. I can see it in your face; the way you're looking at me right now. It's the same way that 'my parents' have looked at me every single day since I got here, especially the way they look at me when I talk about you, or when I ask them to let me see you. I've tried to leave so many times, to sneak out to come find you myself, but he keeps the doors locked, and he watches me all the time.

"Daniel—that's right, Daniel, not David. Daniel is your real name. I know you know it. Just like I know you know me—Kirsa, not Jessica. You feel it, too; the connection between us, the love that's there. That's not an accident, and it's not imagined. It's real. It's always been real, from the second we first met—and I'm not talking about when the boy and the girl met in the forest.

"I'm talking about the man I met at the beach, far, far away. The man who saw me stringing together a seashell necklace and then asked me who I was making it for. The man who asked me what my name was, and when I told him, bet me that if he could spell it right on the first try, I would go on a date with him sometime. And even though you spelled it wrong three times before you finally got it right, I still let you take me out. Do you remember that?"

Everything felt tingly around and inside of me. She wove a deep spell; the more I listened, the more I wanted to believe. What she said flew in the face of reason, logic, and common sense. She'd shrugged off my identity and then her own, the way a person might shed a jacket and hang it on a hook, disassociating from herself coolly and calmly mid-sentence like it was common practice.

And yet there was nothing pedestrian about what she was saying or the way she said it. Every word was carefully selected, every thought articulated to achieve maximum effect.

Many, many times, my parents had sought to communicate something of importance to me, some staple of my pre-coma personality that I could tell meant more to them than it apparently did to me. I'd always dreaded disappointing them. Over time, I'd learned to try and fake some shred of recollection for their sake, if only to avoid witnessing the desperation and anguish that came from them realizing I couldn't be the same person they wanted me to be.

This seemed like it could be a similar situation. Except, for whatever reason, it felt just the tiniest bit different. Wisps and threads of meaning flickered at the edges of my mind, hinting at something greater and potentially more promising that was just beyond the scope of my understanding. But maybe their very presence was enough.

After all, whenever someone in my life tried to jog a specific memory—whether it was my mother, my father, Dr. Eiding, or anyone else—nothing ever happened. I'd try and focus on their suggestion, on piecing together some part or parcel, waiting for the lights to turn back on and the familiarity to rush in as I rediscovered a fragment of my past.

It never happened, though, and I was always left with the difficult choice of whether to upset someone else with the sad truth or upset myself with a manufactured lie.

This was not entirely different from all those

disappointing moments. I was still left waiting for that signature breakthrough, that soul-shaking, earth-shattering catharsis I knew would one day come, when the dam would burst and the floodwaters of revelation would come rushing through—when I'd be normal again and complete, made whole by all that I'd lost since my accident.

As much as I wanted that moment to be right now, it wasn't meant to be. There was no monumental breakthrough, no climactic explosion of knowledge and truth and significance.

And yet, there was still *something* there. Something that was different; something that scratched lightly on the other side of the locked door in my brain. Fragments of light, color, feeling; they were hard to latch onto, moving fast, coming and going and slipping from my concentration before I could take a firm hold of any of them.

But when they were there, even for the briefest of seconds, there was something familiar there, even if it was faint. There was something factual that made me wonder if they were more than just the fever dreams of a beautiful girl I knew nothing about, yet still felt strangely connected to.

Daniel. Kirsa. Beach. Seashells. Necklace. Salt. Ocean. Sunshine. Laughter. Children.

Some of them were clearly-defined images—static like a photograph, but detailed and complex—before they fluttered away into nothingness again.

Others were alive and seemed to change within themselves, miniature movies like what I'd seen late at night on my television screen. But even those disappeared as quickly as they came.

And then some of them were nothing more than a vague impression or the thinnest hint of a feeling, like a flash of joy or a pang of nostalgia for something I couldn't remember. Some seemed linked to words she'd given me, names and images and concepts, while others arrived unbidden and without any clear sense of inspiration or birthplace... namely, the sound of childlike laughter. That one came up again and again, and every time it felt more real, like it was actually happening right here and right now, until finally, I couldn't help myself. I whipped my head over my shoulder, convinced I'd find a little boy or a little girl there, laughing as they ran along the sand.

But I found only darkness staring back at me, kept at bay by the pale glow of the sentry porch light above us. It reminded me where I was again: sitting on a wooden swing, looking out into the night, and losing myself in fantasy and imagination.

And I remembered that I wasn't alone. I turned back to find the girl I knew as Jessica, but who called herself Kirsa, watching me closely. Maybe she'd been doing that this whole time, studying and observing my reactions, and I just hadn't noticed her.

I tried to steady myself and stem the random percussive string of thoughts that went bouncing in and out of my consciousness like skipping stones along a glassy lake surface. It was time to focus back in on reality. If I didn't maintain a firm hold on that, on what I knew was true, solid, and substantial, I risked following this girl down a rabbit-hole that only led to make-believe at best and madness at worst.

"I don't know what you're talking about."

It pained me to say the words, but she left me no

other choice.

"I won't deny that I feel connected to you somehow, even though I don't think we've ever met. You're... important... to me. And I'd like to continue to get to know you better, if that's okay with you."

Now, for the hard part.

"But it's not fair to you or to me if I just sit here and go along with everything you're saying. I know you've been through a lot, and maybe you're confused... Maybe the right thing to do to pretend that I agree with everything you're saying, and maybe that's what a person is supposed to do in this situation.

"But I just know that I'd be upset if our roles were reversed and you helped me believe in something that wasn't real, and I've already lied enough to other people. So, I'm sorry, but maybe you've got the wrong guy. Maybe all this is meant for the guy from your school, the real Daniel. Maybe that's who you need to talk to."

The girl tilted her head to one side.

"There is no guy at school. Or, if there is, I don't know who he is, and he doesn't mean anything to me. Because *this* isn't really *me*. Daniel..."

She paused to take a deep breath. For someone saying such sensational things, it amazed me how incredibly earnest, calm, and sincere she came across.

"When I say that we don't belong here, I mean that *literally*. These aren't our bodies, our brains, or our lives. I know it's hard to believe, but you and I... we exist together in a separate dimension, a parallel universe, of sorts. What matters, though, is that it's ours; we have a life there, something we've built together and shared, and it's real and it's ours. This

191

world? This world isn't ours. This isn't who we are, Daniel. This is something that happened by mistake, because we're not supposed to be here.

"In our world, in our real world, we've been married for fifty-five years. We've raised four beautiful children, who've given us six amazing grandchildren: three boys and three girls. We've lived in the same house now for thirty-four years. It's the same house where you used to go on vacation as a kid during the summers with your family growing up. Even when you were little, you used to say that you were going to live in that house all the time one day, and you were right.

"It's right by the beach. You can hear the waves crashing up on the shore late at night. Before you bought it, you told me that we needed to spend the rest of our lives by the sea, because it would remind me every day of how we first met, and keep the image fresh in my mind of just how handsome you were back then, even though I still think you're very handsome now."

She smiled and leaned forward to take hold of my hands again, and I was powerless to resist her.

"There is one crazy coincidence, I suppose, between this universe and the one we left behind. In the real world, in our life together, you *did* have an accident, and it *did* put you in a coma. But what you need to understand is that it wasn't a car crash. That may have been what happened to this boy that you're *in* now, but it's not what happened to *you*.

"You were out walking, not far from our house at all, and you had a stroke. When you didn't come home, I went out looking for you. When I finally found you,

you were alive but unresponsive. The doctors told me you were in a coma, and that you probably would never make a full recovery, even if your vital signs remained stable. I didn't know what to do.

"Days went by, and then weeks. Eventually, the doctors told me we might be better off to just let you go. Even the kids wondered if maybe it was finally time, if maybe I was just holding on to you for myself, and not because it was the best thing for you."

Her eyes were wet and her lips trembled. She paused a second to regain her composure.

"So, I decided it was time. I would do what I had to do, no matter how much I didn't want to do it. And then…"

She swallowed hard.

"And then, the night before I was going to do it, I had a dream. But it was different somehow, more real and visceral than any kind of dream I'd ever had before. And you were in it, and I knew that you were lost somehow. You were floating out in space, or the afterlife, or… I don't know where you were, but I knew that you were stuck there. And I could see you there, even though I couldn't physically touch you. I didn't know what to do. So finally, I just decided to try and call out to you, to see if you could hear me.

"And you did! You heard me. I knew that you heard me somehow, even if we weren't actually there together; you could tell that I was there with you. That's when I knew that you were out there somewhere.

"Sure, I woke up the next morning, and your body was still next to me on the bed, and you were still in a coma. But I knew then that it wasn't time to give up on you. I knew that your soul, your spirit, your consciousness, was out there somewhere; and more importantly, I knew then that I could find it. And maybe if I could find it, if I could find you, the *real* you, then maybe I could bring you back.

"That's what led to my idea. The doctors didn't like it, and the kids downright hated it. They begged me not to do it, saying it wouldn't work; but I had faith. It was my idea and ultimately my decision, so it was an easy one for me to make.

"With a little help from our doctors, and a lot of help from the wonders of medicine, they put me into an induced coma. I went out looking for you, and I swore to myself that I wouldn't come back until I'd found you. Across stars and moons and galaxies, through time and space, light and dark and everything in between, I scoured infinite realms of the universe until finally, I found you here."

Chapter Sixteen

It was a gorgeous story. Exquisitely detailed, vibrant with imagery and full of imagination. Occasionally, she'd struggled to contain her emotions, but for the most part, she'd been simple and straightforward in the delivery of her speech, seldom breaking eye contact or pausing to gather her thoughts.

What could I possibly say to her now? I'd already laid out my position, informing her in no uncertain terms that as much as I might want to humor her or go along with this sprawling fantasy for her sake, I was not going to do it tonight.

Everyone else in my life was capable of functioning in a constant state of flux—an unfortunate byproduct of daily engagement with a seventeen-year-old still trying to find his bearings between what felt right and what was *supposed* to feel right.

This girl had shown me nothing to even remotely suggest that she was mature or stable enough to live in that same blurred universe of change and contradiction. Encouraging her might seem like the harmless, even benevolent thing to do right now, but down the road, I knew all too well there could be consequences.

Who knew what sort of shape I'd be in today if my parents and doctors had allowed my infantile brain to wander unchecked in the immediate aftermath of waking up from my coma? There was a reason for post-traumatic therapy; physical, mental, and emotional. There had to be. Otherwise, you risked further confusion, damage, and self-harm, as I'd always been led to believe.

Still… she didn't seem like a lunatic.

Sure, all this talk of parallel universes and traveling through dreams sounded like the rantings and ravings of someone who'd lost their touch completely with reality. Not to mention what she'd said about our children and grandchildren. If Jim Silverton had walked out and overheard his daughter fantasizing about having children with me, I probably wouldn't even be alive right now.

But there were other elements from her account that had an uncanny familiarity to them; so much so, that I couldn't just write them off as utter nonsense.

Her description of discovering me suspended in a void of nothingness—that was one of the few clear memories I had about my coma. Granted, I wasn't positive it was even a real memory; it may have been a dream, a hallucination caused by drugs, or it may have been nothing at all. The more time I'd spent awake, the more I'd begun to doubt the veracity of any thoughts, feelings, or experiences linked to my comatose state, including ones that occurred immediately after coming to in the hospital.

That said, it had become somewhat of a recurring dream and vision for me to find myself weightlessly floating or spinning in that same vortex space, over and over again.

I'd ended up there in my dreams late at night on the same day I discovered the girl in the forest, and pretty much every night after that as well. I couldn't remember if all my dreams were spent like that, but seeing as I never remembered anything else the next morning, it had to be the dominant through-line in my psyche these days.

She was right about the voice, too. Sometimes, it would only come once; other times, it would speak to me more often. Certain words and themes were repeated more frequently, but the three phrases I heard most were variations of "it's okay," "don't be afraid," and "I'm here for you now."

I was sure that the voice in these visions was different from the voice of the girl I sat next to now, though. Whereas Jessica sounded like she ought to, a girl in high school, the voice in 'the void' sounded older. There was a soothing quality to it as well, earthy and kind and rich, like spiced wine. The voice always seemed to know the exact moment when the terror set in for me that I'd be stuck there for all eternity. Right at that point of bleakest hopelessness, it would vibrate into my soul out of nowhere; and magically, I'd find calmness and serenity, assured once again that nothing is forever.

If I wanted to believe her for a second—and that was still a gargantuan 'if'—I supposed her story might actually corroborate the difference between these two voices. Assuming Jessica was actually an older woman in another universe parallel to this one, then the voice I heard at night could conceivably belong to her, to Kirsa.

But if that were true, then wouldn't that mean that I was old, as well? She hadn't shied away from her depiction of the two of us as grandparents living together in a seaside house with a large, extended family. Everything about it was idyllic, sure, and probably an ideal scenario for many middle-aged or elderly individuals. The appeal wasn't lost on me, either, but neither was the obvious downside that came with it: age.

In this alternate reality, I was a much, much older man. I couldn't remember exactly how old she said I was, but she did say that we'd been married for fifty-five years, which meant I was probably somewhere between seventy and ninety.

She also was pretty clear that my health was failing. I'd suffered a serious stroke that left me comatose.

Why would I want to return to any of that if I had the choice to stay here; alive, awake, and relatively healthy, with my whole life ahead of me at seventeen?

Enough, though. I was getting ahead of myself. None of this really mattered unless it was even possible in the first place.

I couldn't deny that there were chunks of her story that felt eerily plausible. But the more I let go of my snap judgments and opened up to the possibility that she could be telling the truth, the more I realized that I needed proof.

Too much had already happened between us for me to write off everything she said as insanity. I'd already felt an instant and overwhelming bond with this person I knew nothing about, and everything she'd said confirmed that the feeling was both mutual and unimagined. Who was I to call her crazy or deny the possibility, however remote, that she was telling the truth, and that we *were* actually lost voyagers from another dimension?

Maybe I wasn't supposed to be here. I wasn't supposed to be alive after my car crashed into the side of a tree. I wasn't supposed to be awake after slipping into a coma for almost two months. When I woke up in that hospital bed, Dr. Frye called it a miracle. I remembered him using that word specifically: *miracle.*

She looked nervous, sitting still as a statue, waiting for me to say something.

I felt it, too: the immense importance of how I chose to respond, knowing full well that whatever I decided to say would dramatically affect not only her life, but my own life as well.

From the moment I first saw her, small, limp, and lifeless at the edge of the creek, it was clear that our relationship could never be anything other than extraordinary. So much of my life since then had revolved around her, and on figuring out *why* she meant so much to me.

I guess I owed it to myself to go a little further.

"If… if all of this is true… then why am I here? How did my spirit, or consciousness, or whatever… end up in this body?"

She shook her head slowly from side to side.

"I don't know. I wish I knew, Daniel, believe me. In the beginning, not long after you fell, I started reading a lot. First, it was all science stuff: health books, studies on comas, brain damage, strokes…

"Then, after you appeared in my dreams that first time, everything changed. I started reading everything I could find on altered states of consciousness, astral projection, string theory, the multiverse, you name it. The more I read, the more it began to make sense to me.

"You weren't dead at all, you were just having an out-of-body experience. I thought it was only a matter of time before you came back, but every night, it got a little bit harder to find you in my dreams. And every time I did, you were a little less yourself than you were the night before. Until finally, one time, you weren't there at all.

"At first, I thought you might have died, but no; your body, your brain, it was all still just as it had been. I waited to see if you'd come back, but you never did. So finally, I decided to take matters into my own hands, like I said before."

She smiled at me.

"Listen. I don't know who David Abbott is or where he is. I don't know if his spirit got lost somewhere, too; maybe it's something that happens more than we think it does. But I think somewhere along the way, while you were having your grand metaphysical adventure, you crossed over into this realm by accident. You stumbled into this young boy's body and his life, and naturally, when you woke up, you just assumed that it was yours. I can't explain why it happened or how it happened, just like I can't fully explain how I found you or why it had to be through this girl, Jessica Silverton."

She leaned in so close I could feel her breath on my face.

"But these are empty *vessels*, Daniel. They're not our responsibility. And the longer we stay in them, the harder it'll be for us to get back, and the harder it'll be for these kids—wherever they might be—to get back as well."

It was all very convincing, but I still needed proof. Without it, everything she said was just a fairytale, rooted in a believable premise and peppered with kernels of truth, but ultimately made myth by brazenly defying all laws of reason and common sense.

"How do I know this is real? How do I know any of this is possible?"

The girl chewed on her lower lip, furrowed her brow, and was silent for a while. Her jade eyes gleamed in the soft porch light as she tried to work out a solution.

When the breakthrough finally came, her entire face lit up with it.

"Let me come to you tonight, in our dreams, like I always have. That way, you'll know that it's really me, and that everything I'm saying is true."

Her plan was flawed.

"What if I just dream about you anyway, though? Especially now, since I'll be thinking about it, and expecting it when I go to sleep. How will I be able to tell if we're sharing the same dream, or if I'm just having my own personal dream that you're in or the voice is in?"

This time around, the solution came much faster for her.

"What if I tell you something, say something specific to you? Like I tell you to meet me later in a specific place, somewhere you would never normally be, somewhere obscure, and at an exact time. And then, if we both show up to the same place and at the same time, you'll know that it's not just a dream or a coincidence. You'll know that it was actually me who came here for you, and you'll see for yourself that everything I've said is possible. And then we can go back."

It wasn't a bad idea. There was a very good chance that she would have ended up in my dreams regardless of whether she intended to be there or not. If she had shown up, there'd be no telling if it was actually her breaking into my consciousness from the outside or just my own brain projecting her within itself.

But if she gave me specific instructions on when and where to meet up in person, and we actually somehow both arrived in concert with one another, then she'd have to be telling the truth.

I supposed there was still a one-in-a-million chance that even if it worked, it could be a coincidence. Especially if we ended up meeting in a place like in front of one of our houses, one of our schools, the hospital I'd taken her to, or a similarly familiar location we both had a history with.

But even then, it was a long shot we'd arrive at the exact same time. Besides, she'd already promised that she would choose an obscure location, somewhere I'd never normally be. If everything went according to her plan, I'd have pretty indisputable proof that she wasn't just making all this up.

When and if that happened, then everything I thought I knew about the world, and my place in it, would shatter into a million pieces. But I couldn't let myself go there just yet. It was too much to consider, the notion of forsaking this life to instead catapult my consciousness across unknown expanses of time and space into a tangent universe, and all on the promise of a stranger that there was something waiting for me on the other side... and that *that something* was worth returning to.

My thoughts wandered away from me long enough to make the silence between us noticeable. I remembered that she was still waiting on me, still waiting for a verbal declaration on my part as to whether I'd participate in this experiment of hers.

There was a beautiful vulnerability about her, the way her body angled into mine, her face just inches from my own. I could see plain as day a variety of emotions as they coursed through her: anticipation, excitement, apprehension, doubt, hopefulness...

Putting her mind at ease was the noble thing to do. But selfishly, I wanted to linger in this moment as long as I could, enchanted and enraptured as I was by such a dazzling display.

The front door opened again behind us. And this time, it *was* Jim Silverton who appeared from the other side.

Chapter Seventeen

———————◆———————

Instinctively, I recoiled from his daughter, prying my hands free and sliding away to create some space between us. I tried to do it all quickly yet subtly at the same time, but it was pointless; his face darkened as he took stock of our close proximity. The veins bulged along his temples and red splotches formed along the skin under his neck. His jaw tightened as he folded his arms in front of his chest, glowering down upon us, and reeking of disapproval and the threat of retribution. I slid a little further until my hip was pressed hard against the side of the bench, as intent now on getting away from him as I was from his daughter.

"You've been out here long enough."

It was unclear exactly to whom he was speaking; maybe it was directed at both of us. All of his neck was now red, white, and purple, visible even in the dim glow of the porch light. I was surprised he could get any words out at all, considering how clenched his teeth were.

"Come on inside now. We're done with dessert. David, your folks are getting ready to take off."

He made it clear he wasn't going to move until we

both complied with his orders, holding his position in rigid silence as we got up off the bench and shuffled through the entryway. I half-expected him to throttle me as I scuttled around him, but thankfully, he allowed me to pass by in peace.

Still, I jumped a bit when he slammed the door shut behind us. It felt like a greater relief than it should have when we were back safely in the living room and in the presence of other adults.

He was right, though—it seemed we had missed dessert. All that remained of Kate Silverton's pecan pie was a large empty plate on the coffee table that was covered in crumbs, flanked by four smaller dirty plates, forks, and napkins. Off to the side, two unused plates were stacked atop one another, along with two clean forks.

My father saw what I was looking at and misinterpreted the fear I'd entered into the room with as disappointment that the pie was all gone.

"Well, son, we waited and waited as long as we could, but I told you we couldn't make any promises."

Kate Silverton rushed over to me.

"Are you still hungry, David? I think I might have some brownies left in the pantry... or there's ice cream, too?"

I held up one hand and placed another on my stomach.

"I'm still full from dinner, but thank you, Mrs. Silverton."

She grabbed me by the shoulders and held me at arms' length.

"Are you sure? Normally, I would never allow a dinner guest to leave my home without dessert. I tried to ration out the pie as best I could, but these two fellas both have such hearty appetites. Can I at least fix you a hot fudge brownie sundae or something?"

As good as that sounded, I didn't relish the prospect of staying in Mr. Silverton's company any longer than I needed to at this point. And more importantly, the sooner we left and went home, the sooner I'd be able to go to sleep and test out the girl's dream theory.

"I appreciate it, but I'll pass. Thank you, though."

Mrs. Silverton looked genuinely crestfallen by my answer, but she pulled me into a warm hug all the same.

"All right. Well, listen, I think y'all are taking off, but we need to do this again sometime, okay? It was just so wonderful finally getting together."

My parents got to their feet and offered one last time to help with any dishes that needed cleaning, but Mrs. Silverton would hear none of it. All she wanted was a good long hug goodbye from each of us, as well as a solemn promise that we'd return again for another dinner date, and sooner rather than later. My mother agreed, but only under the condition that we host the next event, and my father suggested that he would grill for us if the weather cooperated and we could all eat outside on our back patio.

While Mrs. Silverton doled out hugs, her husband dealt firm handshakes with his free arm. The other arm was draped around Jessica's shoulder, pinning her close to his side in a cozy paternal fashion that looked neither natural nor comfortable for either of them. I couldn't tell if he was intentionally trying to squeeze me harder now or if his grip was just that intense. Either way, it was painful.

"Take care of yourself, David. Good luck with all the therapy."

"Thanks."

It didn't matter if he was sincere or not. All that mattered was that I locked eyes just long enough with his daughter to watch her mouth the word "tonight." I gave her a quick nod to show I'd understood.

"Goodnight... Jessica."

"See you soon."

It sounded like a promise.

The Silvertons walked us out as far as their front porch and waited as we made our way down the path through their yard and out to our car on the street. All three of them were still standing there together when I opened the rear passenger door to get in.

By the time I'd lowered myself inside, closed the door, and fastened the seatbelt across my body, however, Jim and Jessica Silverton were gone. Only Kate remained in view, still waving good-naturedly, as we started up the engine and drove off into the night.

Initially, conversation within the car focused on making sure my father knew where he was going and had us on the right road home. Once we were in familiar territory, though, my mother spun around in her seat to face me.

"You and Jessica sure talked for a long time outside. Anything interesting?"

I felt a little sheepish.

"What do you mean?"

"I don't know. I guess I was just curious what had you both talking for so long. You don't have to tell me, though."

She pivoted back around in her seat.

Putting myself in her position, I understood why she'd be curious. One minute, Jessica was confessing she mistook me for someone at her school; the next minute, she was asking my parents if it was okay to speak to me in private outside.

We'd also probably been out there much longer than I thought. Even though there was no chance they would ever suspect the bizarre true nature of our conversation, everything surrounding the detour to the porch could understandably invoke some intrigue.

"She just wanted to know more about what it's been like for me, getting back to normal after 'the accident' and all. I think... I think she's been pretty confused since we found her out there."

I hesitated before continuing.

"And I think she just wanted someone to talk to for a while, other than her parents. Someone her own age. I think she's spent a lot of time with them the past week, and a lot of time inside that house. Maybe she just needed some fresh air."

It wasn't a great explanation, but it worked. No one asked any further questions about Jessica, and conversation between my parents drifted to more benign topics, like their reactions to what we'd had for dinner.

By the time we pulled into our driveway, everyone seemed to be half-asleep already, myself included. There was nothing like riding in a warm car through the midnight-blue wilderness of the evening to get me drowsy. More often than not these days, I'd fall asleep somewhere along the drive, long before we reached our final destination. My mother or father would have to gently rouse me from the backseat, letting me know we'd arrived, and that it was time to get out.

I stayed awake throughout this particular nocturnal trip, even though it wasn't easy, mainly because I didn't want to risk the girl coming to me in a semi-lucid state with my parents in the car.

And also, if I was being honest with myself, I stayed awake because I was excited. Whether or not this experiment worked, I longed for something in my life to get excited about again. Physical therapy and psychiatric appointments may have been what I needed right now, but neither were what I wanted.

What did I want? I knew the answer immediately, even if it embarrassed me slightly to admit it to myself.

I wanted Jessica... or I wanted Kirsa. I didn't know who she was, what she was, or where she came from. Maybe she was telling the truth about all this alternate universe stuff, or maybe she was completely deranged. Either way, I found myself inexplicably drawn to her in a way I hadn't felt about anyone since waking up from my coma.

When I closed my eyes, I could see her face hovering there in front of me. I could hear her voice echoing around inside my head, entreating me to listen to her, believe in her, follow her wherever she might lead me. Whether or not her plan worked didn't matter, because either way, I knew it meant I'd be seeing her again.

Right now, that was all that mattered.

I hugged and kissed my parents both goodnight once we were back inside our house. Vaguely, I thought I heard my father say something about taking a family trip into Charlotte tomorrow. I murmured that it sounded like a good idea, though I'd have to come up with a decent excuse not to go if Jessica or Kirsa or whoever she was actually succeeded in making contact with me. But I could handle that situation when and if I needed to; this was all still very much hypothetical.

A new thought crossed my mind: what if she was already trying to reach me? We hadn't had a chance to discuss the logistics of this plan, like when we'd both go to bed, for example. If she was already asleep and trying to contact me, how long would she wait for me before giving up?

Or what if she dreamt that she saw me, but it wasn't actually me? What if it was just some figment of her subconscious that she conjured up because she wanted to, and she gave her instructions to this imagined apparition, instead of to the real thing, the real me?

The potential for miscommunication, for this whole theory to falter and fall through before it even got started, was frighteningly real to me all of a sudden. I hurried up to my room, flipped the lights off, and dove under the covers of my bed.

Of course, the maddening thing about sleep is that you can never truly control it. If you're thirsty, you can fix that instantly by drinking some water. The same could be said for eating food if you're hungry or lying down if you're tired.

But falling asleep was a more delicate, complicated ritual. The more you try to force yourself into slumber, the more awake and alert you inevitably feel.

Now more than ever, I needed to sleep, but the more I wished it upon myself, the more it resisted me. I needed a distraction, something to take my thoughts off the task at hand.

So, I decided I'd reflect back on everything that had happened over the course of the night, from the moment I first saw the girl appear at the top of the staircase like an angel, all the way through dinner, our secret physical contact beneath the dining room table, and most importantly, through everything we'd shared together while we were alone outside on the porch swing.

In my mind's eye, I replayed it all, savoring the nuances and details of my recollection, now that time was infinite and every moment belonged to me. I thought about her freckles, how much I liked them, and how I hadn't given them nearly as much mental attention as they deserved, and how they seemed to... to all be different... but still all together... at the same time...

Darkness came flooding in as it always did, empty and silent as ever.

There were moments when I realized I may have been dreaming; but more often than not, I was along for the ride, caught up in a jumbled sequence of experiences and feelings that seldom were connected or made much sense.

Storylines flowed together, and my role in them was ever-changing.

One second, I was a first-person protagonist living it all in real-time. And then in the next, I was a silent spectator outside myself, watching events unfold without any control over them.

I relived segments from dinner at the Silverton house. Jim was larger than life: a great, monstrous caricature of himself, perpetually red-faced and looming over me as I tried to keep my head down and focus on my plate. The food in front of me was all mush, brown and cold and slimy like a rotten banana, but I could feel his fingers on the back of my skull, pushing me closer and closer to it as Kate urged me to eat from the background.

I tried to ask my parents to intervene and spare me from this torture, but there was no one else at the table now, just me and Jim Silverton. His wife's voice was gone, too, and now that I found myself totally abandoned, I decided there was no point in resisting anymore. Relaxing my muscles meant giving over to his power; so, with a sad detachment, I relented and relinquished, closed my eyes, held my breath, and felt my face press into the slop until my whole head submerged in it.

Sooner or later, I'd need to breathe again. Already, my lungs were starting to burn within my chest.

Fear crept in that if I opened my mouth or nostrils to try and suck in air, I'd suck in the sludge instead and choke on it. What was the alternative, though? Either way, I was probably going to suffocate.

I held out as long as I could, until my ribcage trembled and it felt like I might burst from the inside under all the pressure. At last, I opened my eyes, inhaled deeply, let out a bloodcurdling scream, and sat straight up in bed.

Was I awake now? It sure seemed like it.

Sitting and sweating beneath the bedsheets, I tried to make out specific details of my surroundings, but everything was dark and amorphous inside my bedroom.

Had I screamed just in my dream alone, or had the

scream carried over to my waking life as well? I glanced over at where I knew my bedroom door was supposed to be and noticed a soft light spilling in from beneath the crack at the floor.

Either my parents were still awake or I'd just woken them up with my scream. Trembling, I waited for someone to arrive to check on me, but nobody came. My ears strained against the silence to try and detect the sounds of approaching footsteps, but everything stayed quiet all around me.

Where were they? I struggled to my feet, padded clumsily across the floor, and wrenched open my bedroom door, then went stumbling down the dimly-lit hallway toward the closed bedroom door and away from the swelling cry of alarm rising up inside me.

But when I opened their door and cautiously flipped on the light, it wasn't what it was supposed to be at all. The walls were a different color than what I knew they should be; and the bed was a different size and shape, and it wasn't in the right place. I didn't recognize the desk in the corner or the dresser centered against the opposite wall. Other things were missing, too, like their wall-mounted television and the large walk-in closet they shared. None of it was there.

And neither were my parents. Maybe they were downstairs in the living room or eating dinner in the kitchen.

I raced downstairs to check both places, but these areas were different, too, than what I knew them to be from my house. The layout, the furniture, the decorations—everything was unfamiliar, and I began worrying that I was either trapped, or trespassing, or both.

Eventually, the only option I had left was to return to my own bedroom, since it was the only place I somewhat recognized—even if it meant finding something terrible there waiting for me.

I turned to start my way back up the staircase, but it was gone. The space darkened around me until everything was gone, and the strange interior of the house faded away into a blanket of black.

Immediately, I longed for it to come back, even though I had no idea where it was or what, if anything, it meant to me. At least it possessed a shape and a substance, with defined edges, borders, and boundaries.

This new place, this wasn't a place at all; and yet, I recognized it. A dawning familiarity came with it, and even a kind of smug satisfaction when I predicted that soon gravity itself would cease to hold me down.

I looked down at the floor, and sure enough, there was nothing there now but empty space. My feet floated out behind me, dragging me upside-down in a slow revolution around an imaginary axis, until with gentle concentration, I slowed my body down.

Maybe I couldn't stop myself from ending up here, but at least I could steady myself into a calm, cool surrender. At this point, anything was better than the frenzied terror and abject hopelessness that usually accompanied 'the void'.

There you are.

It was the voice; the same one that had been there in the beginning, the first few times I found myself here. There was no specific origin behind it; at least not any that I could discern. For all I knew, the voice only existed within the confines of my own head. What mattered really was that it was unmistakable, and that I understood it.

Are you ready?

"Yes."

I thought the word and said it at the same time. But when it came out from my throat, it sounded different than I expected. It was like someone else was speaking for me, or speaking with me at the same time, like two voices layered on top of each other. Now I was curious if it would happen again.

"Yes. I'm ready."

Ready for what, though? Distracted as I was by the strange, distorted acoustics of my speech, I'd forgotten just what I was agreeing to in the first place. I twisted on myself from side to side, glancing about as though maybe I'd refresh my memory with something I found there.

But I'd also forgotten that there was nothing around me to see. Like a tiny sliver of sunlight poking above the horizon at daybreak, panic started to seep in. Where was I again? How did I get here, and more importantly, how was I supposed to get out? There had been something, something brief but hopeful, that had happened not too long ago... or was it forever ago already?

I couldn't remember. Why couldn't I remember anything?

Do you remember me?

That was it! That voice! The familiar voice again, sounding out from everywhere and nowhere all at once. That was what I'd found comforting, and now it was what I needed to latch onto and keep front and center at the nucleus of my mind. Because if I didn't, if

I let it slip away again into the inky darkness, I'd be lost.

What had she asked, though? She'd asked if I remembered her. That was a difficult question, impossible to answer in this state. How could I remember her if I couldn't remember myself even, or where I was now? It wasn't fair for her to ask me that, or to expect so much of me right now. I wasn't sure whether I felt more angry or shameful at where her question left me, but it left me without an answer all the same.

You will. You'll remember me tonight.

"Tonight?"

What did that mean? Was it night right now?

The world around me shifted and swayed as tiny pinpricks of light in the distance rapidly took shape, growing and glowing brighter as meaning formed around them. My brain started associating now, filling in the blank spaces with information.

Those lights were stars… that's what they were. Stars were something familiar, something I knew something about. They only came out at night, and she'd said "tonight." That meant something, too…

You're slipping back. Hold onto me.

The voice was fainter now. I still understood what she was saying, and I could sense a newfound urgency behind the words, but it was harder for me to focus on them than it had been before. Whereas earlier I'd had nothing around me *but* the voice, now I had a legitimate lifeline that was carrying me back to what could only be reality.

I felt my brain humming and buzzing along as one deduction led to another: stars were visible at night, which followed day, which followed night again… which meant each could be expected to repeat, as in a cycle or a circle or a progression… any one of which illustrated the basic concept and law that I knew as *time*. Maybe not in this place, but at least in some place, time was a real thing.

So, what was the difference between the two? Discover that, and I'd have my way out.

The only way out is with me, tonight, at the top of Ayeli Rock. I'll be waiting.

Some of what she said made sense to me, and some of it did not. More than anything else, though, I was beginning to fully unlock the meaning behind that word "tonight." That was the key, I knew it had to be; tonight meant night, but why was that so important? What happens at night?

More lights were appearing now, but they were a different color than the stars, a weird mix of orange and beige and white.

Streetlights. My lips formed the word as it came to me. Streetlights at night, lighting up.

Roads. Forests. Trees. Buildings.

Word upon word, concept after concept, they all came rushing back to display themselves in front of me, reminders of a physical world ruled by time and gravity and space, a world I'd left behind at night.

Ayeli Rock. Come find me there when you wake up.

When I wake up… a world at night…

Sleeping! I was sleeping… and I was dreaming…

Wake up.

Chapter Eighteen

With a wrenching gasp, I opened my eyes, inhaled deeply, and sat up straight in bed.

It seemed that I was awake this time; *actually* awake.

But I still needed to be sure. I needed to confirm I wasn't still dreaming.

For some reason, I decided the best plan was to squeeze my eyes shut repeatedly, as if the effort alone might be enough to snap me awake.

Unsurprisingly, nothing happened. I don't know what I was expecting to happen; it was more muscle memory than anything, though I couldn't recall why it felt like an appropriate tactic to try right now.

I pinched the skin on both arms to see if that would do something. Though I felt pain both times, none of the scenery changed around me.

Now for the big one...

Slowly, cautiously, I made my way over to where I thought there was a switch on the wall. Blindly, I extended my fingers to the spot, found a little plastic knob, and flicked on the overhead light.

Right away, I recognized the various accoutrements of my bedroom, which at least provided me some level of normalcy. I turned my bedroom door handle and looked out both directions down the hallway.

Even in the dark, I could see the layout was how I remembered it: my parents' room at one end and the staircase at the other. None of this confirmed that I was definitely, unquestionably awake, but at least my surroundings made logical sense and weren't moving or changing in some kind of bizarre dreamlike fashion. That was a start.

If this was actually reality, then that meant I had just woken up from dreaming.

And if that were true, then it also meant that the girl had made contact with me while I slept, exactly as she promised she would.

Well... I was getting ahead of myself again. The voice was the only thing that made contact with me, and I still didn't know for sure that it even belonged to Jessica... or Kirsa.

And even if it did, there still existed a strong possibility that the message delivered didn't actually come from her, but was instead a manufactured wish fulfillment on the part of my subconscious.

Of course, there was only one way to find out, to prove once and for all that the girl's story was true and not just some delusion of fancy. On her front porch, she insisted she'd find me in my dreams and give me instructions for when and where to meet her.

The voice seemingly had done just that: "come find me when you wake up."

Clearly, the time she intended was right now, if I was indeed truly awake. And where did she want me to meet her?

Ayeli Rock.

I'd never heard of such a place; or if I ever had, I'd long since forgotten. I couldn't recall my parents ever mentioning it to me, and as far as I knew, I'd never seen any signs for it while traveling around town, either. It was a weird name, and I mumbled the words aloud a couple times just to hear myself say them.

Surely, I would have remembered something with such a strange name. Then again, Jessica had also told me she'd pick a place that was foreign to me, somewhere neither one of us had any ties or connections to. Presumably, this Ayeli Rock was in keeping with that portion of the plan as well.

Where was it, though? I needed to start moving if I wanted to meet her there. She hadn't mentioned a specific time, only to come meet her when I woke up, and that meant now. There had to be some way for me to find out where this place was…

I paced around my bedroom in circles, thinking hard and looking around randomly at the objects that surrounded me, hoping something might trigger a bout of inspiration.

And then, it came to me.

I rushed over to my bed and kneeled down at the side of it, stuck my head below the mattress, and started rummaging around in hopes of finding the object I was searching for. It had been days since I'd last seen it or held it in my hands, but last I remembered, I'd stuffed it under my bed with a whole host of other discarded items I hadn't found a use for.

My fingers found something cold, smooth, and slippery, and the proportions were promising enough for me to slide it out into full view.

The folded map of Lenoir, North Carolina, the

same one my father had left for me as a gift, intending that I study and reacquaint myself with my hometown. None of the words, colors, or shapes had meant anything to me back then, but maybe they would come in handy now. Maybe somewhere on one of the laminated rectangles I'd find the words 'Ayeli Rock' printed neatly, and that would be a huge head start.

It took some time and concentration, but eventually, I found the words I was looking for layered in small black letters at the edge of a light green feature. The legend at the corner of the map told me the green represented a mountain range. If that was accurate, did it mean she expected me to trek up a mountain in the middle of the night to meet her? Because that was a ludicrous proposition.

How was I supposed to climb a mountain in the dark? I couldn't climb a mountain in the daylight. My legs threatened to give out on me just climbing up the stairs sometimes; I couldn't imagine what would happen to them going up a mountain.

Further problematizing the scenario was the distance on the map I traced between Ayeli Rock and the street I lived on. While it didn't seem particularly far—less than half the length between the knuckles of my pinkie finger—I had no concept of the scale on the map. There was a written chart underneath the corner legend that presumably gave a conversion rate, but the units didn't mean much to me. They were just more words I didn't comprehend, and obviously, I couldn't ask my parents for help. Never mind the time of night; they would *never* let me go out on an expedition like this based solely off a dream I had.

Was this crazy enough to give up on? That was the

only question I needed to ask myself now.

Because if the answer was yes, then the best course of action was to go back to sleep, chalk up all this talk of dimension-traveling and alternate realities as nonsense, and hope that in time, Jessica would regain enough of her faculties to make a normal relationship possible. Even that might be a long shot, though I couldn't deny a strong desire to maintain her presence in my life in whatever capacity I could keep her.

If the answer was no, however, if I didn't want to wake up from the dream just yet, if I was willing to venture even further into the unknown in the lunatic hope that maybe there was a one in a trillion chance that she was actually right about all of this, and I'd find her standing there in the cold night air, waiting for me on top of Ayeli Rock; and if I really wanted proof that we weren't both insane, that the powerful feeling I got around this person wasn't just a mirage, but was real and absolute and limitless... then I needed to get a jacket and a flashlight from my closet, and I needed to get them quick.

Armed against the night with another layer of warm clothing, the town map, and a flashlight that I made sure was operational, I was as ready as I was going to get. After a deep breath, I flipped off my bedroom light and crept quietly down the stairs to the front door. Gently, I unlocked the deadbolt, pushed the door ajar ever so slightly, and slithered outside, making sure it closed behind me just as softly.

It was a good thing I brought my jacket. The temperature outside had cooled significantly, and there was a much stronger wind than there had been back at the Silvertons' house. A tinge of moisture was also in the air, just enough that I could notice it, but it wasn't a problem unless it turned to rain. One cold thunderstorm was enough for me, especially since I found myself once again adventuring outdoors into uncharted territory.

This time, I had a map, though. Whether or not I made it all in one piece to Ayeli Rock, at least I knew I wouldn't be getting lost along the way. Every time I came to a major road crossing, I'd check the map to make sure I was still going the right direction.

And so far, it hadn't led me astray. There were even a few landmarks, mostly city buildings and historic locations that were listed on the map alongside the gridlines, and sure enough, I'd come across them right around the same time I expected to.

So far, so good. The guide in my hands was proving indispensable. My father would be proud of me, though I'd never be able to tell him why and how I used his gift.

I'd learned that Lenoir wasn't necessarily a huge town, but it still shocked me just how empty and quiet everything was this time of night. Understandably, most normal people were at home asleep in their beds. But it was still a little eerie to walk alone down so many streets I'd only ever seen in daylight.

Every now and then, a solitary car would pass by, and my heart would beat a little bit faster as the headlights swept across my body. I wondered what I looked like and what the drivers might think of me.

Would they deem me suspicious? If a policeman happened to drive past, would he pull over and question me? And if that happened, what could I possibly say in my own defense?

Nothing, really. The prospect of such an encounter chilled me almost as much as the wind did, so I picked up my pace to get out of the downtown area as quickly as I could.

Gradually, the space between streetlights got longer as the scenery became more and more rural. The paved sidewalk soon ended altogether, leaving me to hug the edge of the road between the asphalt and the grass.

When the line of streetlights ended completely, I pulled the flashlight out of my jacket pocket and turned it on. The bright white beam was crucial—both for reading the map and for avoiding obstacles and trip hazards as they appeared before my feet.

Sometimes, I'd hear a twig snap or the screech of a bird in the forest on my right, and the flashlight came in handy for those moments, too. Every time I flung the light in the direction of a sound that startled me, I expected to illuminate a wild animal, a dangerous person, or maybe even a hideous monster. And every time, I found nothing there, just swaying branches or rustling leaves on a bush.

I couldn't decide which idea I preferred less: actually seeing what I was hearing or never seeing anything at all. Finally, I resolved to just focus more intently on the map and on what was immediately in my physical path, rather than let my imagination run wild over what unseen creatures could be stalking me in the dark.

My breathing became ragged as the road sloped further up a steady incline. Yes, it made walking harder, but it also meant I was getting closer to the foothills of the mountains on my map.

Out here, there were fewer crossroads that could serve as checkpoints. More than anything, I just had to keep following the line I was on, higher and higher, until I came across a sign or marker that indicated Ayeli Rock was nearby.

At that point, I'd then have to abandon the safety and security of the paved road and truly venture into the wilderness. All I hoped was that there was at least a dirt trail for me to follow. Heading into the woods at night was scary enough with a path; I couldn't imagine doing so without one.

Walking alone, relatively out in the middle of nowhere, afforded me plenty of time with my own thoughts. Soon, I started reflecting on why I was even out here in the first place and vacillating on whether or not I'd made the right decision.

Part of me consistently wanted to turn around and go back, especially as the hike grew more strenuous and the world around me grew more frightening. The rational part of my brain kept piping up the further along I went, questioning the wisdom of this expedition and wondering what the consequences might be if I failed.

Best-case scenario, assuming I found Ayeli Rock and the girl waiting for me atop it, meant second-guessing everything I thought I knew about the world and my life in it.

Worst-case scenario, I could die falling off a cliff in the dark somewhere along the way.

Most likely scenario? I make it to Ayeli Rock and don't find anybody there at all.

And then what? Where could I go from there? Back to therapy sessions with my doctors and memory exercises with my parents? Back to school and reacquainting old friends and teachers? Back to facing imminent decisions about college and my future, whether or not I could even remember any of my past?

All I could really do was take one moment at a time. Right now, that meant putting one foot in front of the other and continuing along this path until I either found Ayeli Rock or decided to turn around and go home.

Just as the latter option began to feel like it might be the correct one, the beam of my flashlight came across a little wooden trail marker up ahead, right at the edge where the road met the forest. As I got closer to it, two words became visible along with an arrow below them that pointed off into the trees. I didn't need confirmation from the map in my hands, because I already knew what the sign said before I could read it: Ayeli Rock.

My legs slowed and stopped moving altogether as I came face-to-face with the signpost I'd come all this way to find. This was it: my last chance to turn back if I still wanted to.

A quick sweep of my flashlight revealed there was indeed a dirt path leading off into the woods, so at least I'd have some kind of trail to follow if I wanted to keep going. But more than likely, I'd be doing so without any help from my map, electric lights, smooth pavement, or any of the other conveniences of civilization I'd had with me up to this point. Whatever mysteries and possibilities waited for me up ahead, I'd be seeking them with my flashlight and my own resolve, and not much else.

But after coming all this way, there was really no

point in turning back around, not when I was finally this close. After a little stretch of both my legs, I folded up the map, tucked it in the back pocket of my pants, and set out on the dirt trail.

It was a taxing climb right from the start. Not only was the trail at a significantly steeper slope than the road leading up to it, the path was also littered with natural obstructions. Jutting rocks, fallen branches, hidden cracks and crevices in the ground itself... Whatever slim hopes I'd harbored that the ascent might actually be easier than expected were soon forgotten.

Thankfully, the flashlight allowed me to carefully pick my way up without completely tripping or stumbling flat. But even with the added visibility, my progress was slow and laborious. I had to stop frequently to rest and catch my breath, and the further along I got, the more my legs threatened to give out on me.

Complicating matters even further, the higher I went, the harder it was to see. At first, I thought the haze in my flashlight beam was just dust kicked up by my feet or by the wind. As I climbed higher, though, the haze grew until it was a thick fog—cold, wet, and dangerously opaque. It pressed in all around me until I could feel it even on the skin under my clothes, coating my body from head to toe in a dull chill I couldn't shake off, no matter how fast I tried to move.

Obstacles along the trail magically popped out of the fog at the last possible second, and it took all my focus and concentration to swerve around them while still maintaining my balance. The air itself was thinner up here, and it made my lungs burn with every inhalation. There was never enough oxygen to take in, and whatever meager amount I managed to suck in was quickly expended just keeping my legs moving and my body upright.

Sooner or later, I was going to lose this battle. I had no idea how far ahead the summit was. I didn't even know for sure that there was a summit, or if the girl intended to meet me there specifically. She'd only given me the name of this place, and there was nothing on that first signpost or on my map to clue me in on anything else.

I was fairly confident that at least I was generally in the right area. There were no other 'Ayeli Rock' names on the map, and it was such a unique moniker.

This had to be the right way. I just needed to keep moving, keep breathing, and keep following the trail up as far as it went, until I either found the girl, reached an impasse, or fainted from exertion. And preferably the first option over the second two.

I wondered how long I'd been climbing for. Truthfully, I hadn't had much concept of time since waking up and deciding to set out on this journey. Whatever normal ability I had to process time and distance felt damaged, perhaps irreparably, by the purgatory I kept falling into during my recurring dreams.

That, combined with my all-around physical and mental fatigue, made it impossible to think straight. The pale light of my flashlight beam, diffused and distorted by the heavy fog, played tricks on my eyes, manifesting strange hallucinations that I struggled to dodge and shrink away from, only to realize too late that they were all imaginary to begin with.

One such apparition came in the form of a human being. But I saw this one coming, so I waved my arm out in front of me to dispel the illusion as I kept trudging forward. Only this time, I made contact, unmistakably striking solid flesh and bone.

When I stopped to see what I hit, I saw green eyes staring back at me, and there she was. A couple seconds passed in silence as I debated whether or not this, too, was some kind of mirage, but when she smiled and spoke out loud, I knew it was really her.

"Hello, Daniel."

Chapter Nineteen

My knees buckled, and I started to fall, only half-attempting to stick out a hand to brace myself against the impact.

The girl reached out, though, and grabbed me before I hit the ground. With surprising strength, she managed to steady me on my feet and hold me up as my vision swam in and out. Maybe I was going to faint after all… and maybe that wouldn't be such a bad thing. I'd probably wake up on the other side, as if from a dream, back in my own bed, in my own room, in my own house, in my own life.

Right now, that seemed like the easiest thing to do. All I had to do was give myself over and surrender to these crippling waves of shock.

Staying awake, staying in this moment with her, felt like it might be powerful and painful enough to fracture my fragile mind completely. And if that happened, there'd be no recovery. I'd be lost to the coma again; except this time, there'd be no coming out of it.

"Shh, it's all right. I've got you now."

She was right; she did have me now, both literally and figuratively.

There was no longer any sense in questioning the merits of what she'd told me on the front porch after dinner. However outlandish and improbable her claims had been, in this singular moment, she'd proven that they were possible—all of it was possible.

Somehow, someway, she was capable of finding me in my dreams, of entering the deepest realm of my own subconscious, making contact, and instructing me to meet her here and now at a place that meant nothing to me.

And here we both were, in the present, in the physical, conscious world, as impossible and illogical as that was to believe.

Still, my brain fought against it, writhing and wrenching away from the truth as it desperately searched for a more reasonable explanation.

"Am I dreaming?"

It was all I had left.

"No, Daniel, this is real. Well, not entirely real... This is someone's version of real, but not yours. Not ours."

She felt real enough with her arms wrapped around me. Especially with the world spinning in lopsided, dizzying circles, her solid presence was an anchor, and it kept pulling me back from the brink of hysteria. There was a sturdiness to her touch, as small as she was, and I felt genuinely supported by her; like even if I fell totally apart right now, she'd still be standing here, letting me lean on her as tempests raged inside my head.

"How... how did you do this?"

I struggled to get the words out over the sound of my own breathing. If I wasn't going to pass out, then I needed to try and calm down. This state of hyperventilation and panic was too painful to maintain for very long.

"How did you find me, Jessica?"

"Kirsa." The correction was soft but firm. "Like I said before, Daniel, I don't know how exactly I found you. Just like I don't know how you found your way here, into this world and into this boy's life."

She put a hand under my chin and gently tilted my head up to face her.

"But what I do know is that we don't belong here, you and I. And we need to go back."

What could I possibly say to her? I wanted to believe her, to say yes. Seeing the look on her face, hearing her speak with such ringing conviction, even just the way she said that name—my name, according to her—it was all so overpowering, so intoxicating.

She said this was real, at least someone's version of real, but everything about it felt wondrous and dreamlike, as nebulous and undefined as the living fog that clouded in around us.

"Back to where?"

She paused to consider my question before replying.

"Home."

The word was so simple, yet so exceedingly complex.

"We need to go home."

As if it were that easy.

"I—I don't know what that means."

And that was the truth. Just like I'd predicted, finding the girl all the way up here was both a blessing and a curse.

On the one hand, it meant neither one of us was crazy for feeling such a strong, immediate connection with one another, and trusting that connection over common sense and practicality.

On the other hand, it essentially eradicated the fledgling life I'd worked so hard to reconstruct in the wake of my accident.

Not only did it call into serious question all my relationships, my beliefs, the fundamental truths of my life, it called into question my very being, and opened up the existential door to infinite possibilities, not a single one of which was easy to digest.

"Maybe we should sit down for a second."

Slowly, she guided us both downward until we were seated on the ground across from one another, touching knees and holding hands in the dark. If not for the dim glow cast off from the flashlight set down between us, the fog would have rendered her face as invisible to me as it had the moon and stars above us.

Thankfully, the battery-powered device provided just enough light for us to see one another. I could even make out some of her freckles now; the very ones I'd fallen asleep thinking about earlier that same night.

She leaned forward slightly, squeezing my hands tight and warm within hers.

"Do you want to know how you asked me to marry you?"

The girl must have seen the look of surprise on my face, because she didn't wait long for an answer.

"We weren't much older than these kids are now. We'd only been dating for a couple of years, but both of us knew that it was more a matter of 'when' than 'if'. I remember you taking me out to dinner at a fancy restaurant once, and you were so nervous the whole time. You kept wiping sweat off your forehead with a napkin and looking around like you were afraid someone was out to get you. I thought for sure you were going to ask me that night, and that's why you were being so nervous; but do you remember why you were acting that way?"

All of this was unfamiliar to me. I tried to concentrate on the details of what she'd said so far, hoping something might come back to me. But it was futile, so I shook my head no.

She looked crestfallen only for a second before quickly composing herself with a smile and continuing on with the story.

"Turns out you weren't nervous because you were thinking of proposing. You realized after we'd already ordered our entrees that you'd left all your money at home that night!"

She couldn't stop herself from giggling a bit now. Her face was even more beautiful when she laughed.

"So, there you were, trying to enjoy a lavish, four-course meal, wondering how in the world you were going to break it to me that I'd have to pay for everything at the end of dessert. And here I was, trying to prepare myself to be asked the biggest question in a person's life. Then, at the end of the night, you look over at me, lean across the table, take a deep breath... and ask if I mind picking up the check!"

She wiped tears from the corners of her eyes as she gave in to her laughter.

"I'm sorry... I know I said I was going to tell how you proposed, but I can never get enough of that story, it gets me every time! They're always kind of connected for me, those stories. I'm sorry, I'm sorry… I'll get it together."

There was something contagious about the way she couldn't stop laughing and crying. It was so earnest, so vulnerable and real. Even if I didn't remember participating in the narrative myself, I found myself smiling and sharing in her amusement. I genuinely wanted her to keep talking so I could learn more from her—and learn more about this life she claimed we'd lived together.

"What's the story? Of the proposal. Of how I asked you… to marry me?"

It felt odd stringing those words together out loud, since somewhere in the back of my mind we were still just two teenagers sitting in the dark on top of a cliff playing make-believe. Though somewhere else in my mind, maybe we were not.

She seemed happy that I asked her that question, and her laughter subsided naturally into an expression of pleased reflection.

"You'd brought me to your family's beach house on a number of occasions, always when it got too hot outside to stay in the city. I knew how much you loved it there, right from the start, and I loved it, too. A lot of my earliest memories of us took place up there. Spending all day down by the water, lying out in the sun, just talking for hours about what we wanted to do with our lives.

"There's something magical about the beach. It feels somehow… eternal. From the moment the sun is up and the day has started, until the moment it dips back below the horizon and the sky changes into a thousand different colors, everything just moves so slowly, drawn out forever by those endless waves crashing upon the sand, never tiring, never stopping.

"After a while, it came to mean as much to me as it always had to you, and I think you sensed that. So, one particular time, you asked me to come away with you for the weekend, and of course I said yes, like I always did. But then, right as we got there, you told me you got called in to work, and you couldn't get out of it; you'd have to head into the city, and you wouldn't be back till the next morning at the earliest."

She paused to take a breath.

"I remember thinking that was odd, because in all the time I'd known you, you'd never had to leave the beach house early for work. But you told me there was nothing you could do to get out of it. So, you wrapped your arms around me, kissed my forehead, and told me to enjoy a little 'me time' until you got back. And—I'll never forget this—as you were walking out, you casually suggested that maybe I should take a walk right after sunset down to the dock, because you'd read something about a natural phenomenon that might happen down in the water around that time of night and that time of year. Do you remember that?"

The question may have been rhetorical, but it didn't make it any less awkward for me. I listened intently to every word she said, recreating the story detail-by-detail in my head as she shared it with me.

But still, it was all reactionary. As much as she and I may have both wanted my memory to spring into action and fill in the rest of the narrative gaps with my own recollection of events, it just wasn't happening; at least, not yet.

When I didn't speak up, she continued.

"So, later that evening, about an hour or so after you'd gone, I decided to take your advice and have a walk down to the dock to watch the sunset. And all this time, I'm focusing my attention on how beautiful the sky is. Then, suddenly, I happen to look down at the water, and I see that some of the waves are glowing, literally *glowing*, this brilliant light blue shade I've never seen before. And as I'm walking along, pretty much dumbfounded by what I'm seeing, all of a sudden I come upon the dock... and that's when I noticed it for the first time."

She paused again to reminisce, soaking in the memories as she relayed them to me.

"On every single individual plank of wood along the dock, there was a candle lit up at either end. And then, next to the candles, on every single board, was a photograph of us. Some of them were more serious than others; but as I walked out along the pier and studied them, I was taken back to the time in our relationship that was captured in that one individual moment of time, preserved forever in a candid snapshot, a physical history of our time together. Birthdays, holidays, road trips, game nights; some of the images were of important milestones, and some were as basic and everyday as they come.

"I remember seeing a photo of us taken by one of my friends, and in this particular photo, you and me are just lying on a couch together, asleep. It's probably my favorite photograph of us. You know what the remarkable thing about it is? We're both totally asleep in it, but we're also holding hands, and not just side-by-side. We're facing each other, completely unconscious, our faces just barely separated, and my right hand is in your left hand, and your right hand is in my left hand. Our legs are intertwined, too, at the bottom of the couch. I remember that from the image. It's always stuck there in my mind; I don't think I'll ever forget it.

"Anyway, as I walked out along this dock, trying to decide which was crazier—all these extremely personal photographs pinned up along the way or the magical alien creatures lighting up around me beneath the waves—I realized there was a person up ahead that I couldn't quite make out in the dark from far away. As I got closer, it looked more and more like you, even though I knew that couldn't be, because I'd watched you drive away for work earlier that day.

"But then, once I was completely out on the dock, surrounded by candles, photographs, and this crazy bioluminescent sea-life, I realized that it was you after all. You were waiting for me all along, and you'd planned this whole sequence of events, up until the very moment you took a knee and asked me if I would marry you.

"I remember that day like it was yesterday. The night sky, the glowing waves, the way it felt to have you hold me in your arms as the ocean wind whipped around us."

She gave my hands a light squeeze, and her face was complete and utter adulation.

"I still have trouble believing how you did it all; the planning that must have gone into it, and the way it all worked out so perfectly, like something straight out of a fairytale. You suggested ahead of time that I walk down to that particular spot, and you knew that those tiny little ocean creatures would be there in the waves. The whole experience was pure magic. Just the most magical night of my life."

She reveled in it a few more seconds, then sat back to take in my reaction.

"So... thank you for that. As always. You continue to be the most romantic person I've ever had the pleasure of meeting."

And then, she winked mischievously at me.

"Don't you forget that I've met plenty. I was wined and dined by the best of them before I met you. But I think I made the right choice."

I was speechless. What could I say after all that? It was a picturesque story, and she'd done an exceptional job of painting out the events with her words, crafting a detailed visual tale that played out in my mind's eye exactly as she described it to me.

What it hadn't done, however, was jumpstart any memories or moments of recognition.

I wanted to believe I was capable of such ingenuity and romance—who wouldn't?—but it still felt like she was talking about a stranger the whole time, rather than recounting a history she'd shared with me so many years ago.

Maybe she could sense my confusion, or see it written there across my face, as I struggled to make her memories my own.

"What about our family? Can I tell you a little bit about them?"

She waited for me to give her an affirmation, and after seeing me nod my head yes, she leaned back a little bit and closed her eyes. I watched her nostrils flare as she breathed in the cool, foggy air, and I couldn't help feeling a bit envious imagining the rich, vivid memories she cycled through right now along the narrative of her past.

When she finally did speak, she did so softly, and with her eyes still closed, concentrating on the intricate minutiae of everything she wanted to convey to me.

"Our oldest daughter, Rosemary, she's a chef. Which makes perfect sense, because she's always loved being in the kitchen. Even as a toddler, she'd sit up on the countertops with us, watching us stir in sauces, mix ingredients together, frost the tops of sugar cookies.

"That's always been your thing, the two of you, making sugar cookies. And eating them, too, for that matter. You both have such a sweet tooth.

"Jacqueline is our second-oldest, and she's basically a carbon copy of you, even though she'd never admit it out loud. She works at the same company you worked at, and she lives just five minutes away from where we live, in a cute little house with her wife Isabelle. They have four children, just like we have.

"Jacquie reads the same books you read, listens to the same music you listen to, she doesn't eat meat because you don't eat meat, and she sleeps with her socks on at night because her feet get cold, just like you.

"And then, of course, there are the twins, Martin and Ivy, who couldn't be more similar genetically but more different personality-wise.

"Martin came out first, and he immediately proceeded to throw up all over everything and everyone in the hospital room that day. Marty's been a messy person ever since, but we love him for it. His wife, Shara, might be the only being I've ever met who's even more unorganized than he is, but they're perfect together in their own weird little way, and they've even managed to bring up two fairly normal kids.

"Martin's like you, too, in that he's romantic. He manages a furniture store and works long hours, but that still doesn't stop him from writing poems for Shara whenever he can, even if he's got terrible handwriting and can't spell to save his life.

"Ivy's just the opposite. When she came out five minutes after her brother, she was already in a tizzy over what a mess he'd made for her to arrive into. She kept waving her small pink little hands in the air, crying and screaming and squirming, and the only thing that finally got her to stop and calm down was when you tried singing to her.

"Now, I love you, Daniel, but you're not necessarily the greatest singer that ever lived. I tell you what, though, you worked some magic that day. And it's been a tradition ever since; you sing to Ivy on her birthday. Even if she's on the other side of the world, as she often is, you still find a way to sing to her on her birthday. It's just one of those things that always happens."

She opened her eyes again to take me in. I could see the tiny milky-grey dot of the flashlight bulb reflecting off her irises, and I could also see where emotion glassed over them.

"Daniel." Her voice wavered as she peered across at me. "When I went under, her birthday was just around the corner. All she wants for it is to hear her daddy sing to her again. I really think that if we do this now, if we leave together and find a way back, we can make it there in time for her to get her wish."

241

Chapter Twenty

Why couldn't this all just be easy?

If everything she said to me—from the second I first met her in the forest, all the way up until this moment right now—if all of it made crystal-clear sense to me, everything would be so much easier. There'd be no mental struggle, no turmoil or uncertainty over whether everything she said was true.

By virtue of us both showing up at the same time in the same place, I'd come to at least accept the bizarre, impossible phenomenon that this girl was capable of contacting me in a dream state.

But was that enough to validate everything else she claimed about our life together in an alternate universe?

What she was sharing with me tonight was incredibly powerful and undeniably heartfelt on her end. I had no doubt that the people and the places she denoted in these stories were real for her, and that all these vivid moments and memories had actually happened for her, too.

There was nothing dissembling in the way she described all of it, no shred of artifice or ounce of manufactured construction on her part. Every detail came forth freely and fully-realized, flowing out from the wellspring of her experience as only one's true life story could.

The problem was that none of it felt that way for me. It didn't necessarily come across as inconceivable or unlikely; if it had, it'd be all the easier to dismiss the whole thing as someone else's reality. Then, the hardest part would be just telling the girl that maybe she had the wrong guy after all.

Understandably, that would be a difficult conversation to have, and the idea of disappointing her and harpooning our relationship as she believed it to be was not a pleasant thought, even if it was the right thing to do. Unenviable as that path would have been, at least I'd be armed with the belief of knowing it had to be done, for her sake more than anything.

But I couldn't go down that road, either, because everything she said *wasn't* hard for me to believe in. On the contrary, I routinely found myself moved by her account of our courtship, our engagement, our children, and all the other details of our supposed life together.

Even if none of it cut through the haze and struck me to the core of my being as real, definitive proof of my own identity, it all sounded so idyllic and so conceptually attainable that I *wanted* it to be my life.

I didn't know if I'd ever seen the ocean before, or if David Abbott had, in the seventeen years he or I had been alive for. But the way she talked about it: the blue rolling waves, the color of the sky above, the sea life, the sun and the smells and the sound…

All of it just felt right somehow. The way I imagined it, listening to her describe it all, I could see myself falling in love with such a place, and even wanting to live there for most of my life.

Other fragments of her story also resonated with me in peculiar ways I hadn't expected and couldn't fully explain.

I liked the idea of taking walks along a coastline. It was also strangely easy to imagine myself working in a big city but retiring further out in nature, away from the urban sprawl. Potentially, that explained the curiosity and affinity I'd had for the North Carolina wilderness I'd seen outside my car window on so many trips through town.

My parents—or David Abbott's parents—swore I loved certain foods that I now hated, whereas Jessica or Kirsa's account of my preference for sweets and vegetarianism felt more in keeping with my actual taste buds.

Even the names of the children she said we'd raised together: Rosemary, Jacqueline, Martin, Ivy… I liked the sound of all of those names, and though I'd never considered it before, I could easily envision myself either suggesting or agreeing to any one of them for a newborn baby.

Where did all of this leave me, then? The life she described had never felt more possible and accurate, but it was still just a feeling after all, and not anything definitive or indisputable. Nothing she'd said or done had been the magic key that unlocked the truth of my past.

Yes, I could imagine myself living in her world. But she wasn't asking me to simply fantasize with her about a potential future for Jessica and David—she was asking me to abandon all I knew so we could become Kirsa and Daniel.

"Let me ask you this: how do you plan to get back? If all of this is real, and we have lives waiting for us— bodies waiting for us on the other side, I mean—then what do we do? How do we get back there?"

I didn't need to make a decision; at least, not yet. But obviously, if I did even want to entertain the possibility that all of it was true, I needed to know what her plan was. Ultimately, whether I believed her or not didn't matter, unless she had a concrete plan for how we could return to the lives we'd left behind in her story.

"I've been thinking about that a lot. Honestly, after I found you that day in the woods, I haven't really thought about much else."

She furrowed her brows in concentration.

"I'll admit I'm not an expert on this. There's really no clear-cut procedure we can follow. This is all purely from the realm of experimentation and theory; and even in our universe, astral projection and ideas of interdimensional traveling aren't exactly commonplace. It was a struggle to find doctors that were open-minded enough to even consider putting me in an induced coma to begin with."

The girl tightened her grip on my hands.

"I've come up with three separate potential scenarios, although I don't know if any of them will work, of course.

"The easiest way we could go back is the same way I got you to come here tonight: by meeting up with you in our dreams. If it's possible for us to find each other while we're asleep, then maybe it's also possible to cross back over completely while we're asleep. That would be the simplest way to do it, I think; but like I said, I don't know if it'll work, or how exactly we're supposed to do it.

"The other two ways aren't as easy. One option would be to somehow put ourselves under, back into a coma or a state of intentional unconsciousness through medicine, like what I did to get here. I don't know what kind of drugs are out there in this world, or what the prevailing opinion about such a procedure is with the doctors, but that would be the second option. Find a way together to go even deeper than sleep, and suspend our consciousness indefinitely while we travel back to where we belong.

"And then, the last option I thought of... This is only as a last resort, I suppose, but I have to say it all the same, because I still don't really know what's possible and what's not... But a complete fracture from this world, a clean break, might also be enough to send us back to where we belong... if you know what I mean.

"Obviously, it's not the top choice, especially considering the possibility that the real Jessica and David might still be out there somewhere in the aether trying to get back to these bodies, and we don't want to ruin that for them if we don't have to.

"But it's still worth considering, at least as an option. As scary as the idea is, death might be the quickest way to split from these physical vessels and return back to the ones that actually belong to us, because it would force our consciousness out of these bodies for good."

She wasn't lying—it *was* a frightening idea to consider, absolutely. It was easy to agree with her rationale in terms of the choices she'd considered available to us, and which ones were the most and least desirable. If we could simply lie down right here, right now, drift off into a deep sleep, and somewhere along the way, find ourselves waking up in the world she described so vividly, then that would be the optimal way to go.

Anything beyond that either required drugs I didn't know how to procure and couldn't begin to understand, or required me to sacrifice myself to a certain death and an uncertain fate. Neither of those options were appealing, so the choice was all too clear.

Did I want to make a choice at all, though?

Technically, I had a fourth option, which was to do nothing at all and just carry on with my life as I currently knew it. Sure, it was imperfect, and I still knew less about my seventeen years of existence as David Abbott than I was supposed to.

But there was time for me to fix that, and plenty of hope and support from the people in my life that I could do just that. I had my mother and my father, my doctors, and my therapist.

There were others, too: friends, relatives, classmates, teachers, mentors, neighbors, and people I still hadn't seen since waking up from my coma. Any number of them might be instrumental in helping to resuscitate my past and shape my future.

And then, of course, there was this girl sitting in front of me, calmly asking me to follow her across the universe so we could finish out our lives together.

Every moment we spent together was sublime. Everything that happened between us was miraculous. Since waking up from my coma, very little had made sense to me or felt familiar. Yet here I was with a stranger that claimed to be from another universe, and never before had so much in my life suddenly felt so right.

She was waiting for me still, in every aspect of the word.

What was the worst that could happen anyway, especially if we tried the easiest option?

Assuming it worked, and we actually woke up as an elderly couple in an alternate dimension, then we'd be right where we were meant to be. If everything went according to plan and we found ourselves in another miracle, then it meant I'd made the right choice by trusting her and trusting my intuition.

And if it didn't work, then we'd wake up the exact same way as we were when we fell asleep, and the only loss would be time.

"Let's do it. I don't see any harm in trying the first option at least."

She squeezed my hands and let out a girlish squeal of excitement. And then, without warning, she suddenly rocked herself forward onto her knees, pulled me in closer to her, and pressed her lips against mine as our faces met in a kiss.

I didn't have time to think, but my body thought for me, responding to her organically as my eyes closed, my arms wrapped around her back, and all the rest of me fell ever deeper into her embrace.

It was, in a word, effortless. The kiss was a complete surrender, a merging of our bodies that made me completely lose track of time and space and everything else but her.

When we finally did break apart, I found myself yearning for more, frozen in place with my eyes closed and my lips still tingling. It was as if she'd physically left her mark on me, imprinting some of herself on my senses so that I still felt her, tasted her, smelled her, even though there was physical space between us once again.

I savored the sensation of the phantom contact, afraid that if I so much as moved a muscle, it would lift off from me and disappear into the fog.

"Are you ready?"

The sound of Kirsa's voice gently dispelled the effect, bringing me back to the present moment and the situation at hand. Even in the hazy darkness, I could see her face was flushed and her breathing was erratic and accelerated. She appeared just as overcome with rapture by our kiss as I was, but there was also an eager determination in her expression and in her tone that bordered on impatience.

"Are you ready to try?"

I was surprised.

"Now?"

It hadn't even occurred to me that we might try to dream-walk together right here tonight. Falling asleep together in the dark, in the fog, on a deserted mountain trail... it just didn't seem like a good idea, and definitely not a safe one.

Also, if we tried to go back now, I wouldn't have a chance to say goodbye to my parents, or to make any sort of peace with the fact that I was about to leave this world and this life all behind.

Did I need to do any of that, though?

I kept having to remind myself that if this plan actually worked, it meant none of this was mine to begin with. No matter what my relationships were with these other people, or what I felt about or for them, none of it was truly authentic—at least, not if the girl was right about all this. Everything I'd experienced as David Abbott was only real if she was wrong. If she was right, then it was all just a masquerade, a game of imitation I'd played as I unwittingly pretended that this existence was my own.

"If you're ready."

She stroked my hands with her thumbs soothingly, but I could tell she was having a hard time containing her own enthusiasm. Clearly, the desire to resume her life as Kirsa far outweighed any attachments she harbored for the trappings of her life as Jessica, if any existed at all.

I wondered if she felt anything for her parents—for Jessica's parents, rather? Probably not for Jim, but maybe for Kate? Was there anything there, or had her parents always been just another obstacle she needed to circumvent on her path back to me?

There was just enough doubt, combined with uncertainty and apprehension, to taint what had otherwise been a transcendent encounter. Most of me still believed in the girl and in the mysterious power of the bond we shared, enough so that I didn't resist her when she started to guide us both down slowly onto our backs. Logically, I knew there was no real harm in trying, and instinctually, I trusted her on a deeper level that I couldn't fully explain or comprehend. But there was still just the smallest part of me that trembled on the inside and dared to wonder if I was making the right choice.

"I'll be here with you the whole time. We'll do it together."

Kirsa whispered the words into my ear, and I tried my best to relax, now that we were both lying side-by-side in the dirt with our fingers and our feet interlocked. Already, she seemed much calmer and more composed than she'd been in the immediate aftermath of our kiss.

I did my best to synchronize my breathing with hers, letting the air move in and out, slowly, deliberately. Above us, there was nothing to see; the fog was even thicker now than it had been before, so I decided to close my eyes and concentrate solely on my breathing.

"There's nothing to be afraid of. I'm here with you. I'll always be here with you."

My brain raced feverishly around in a thousand different directions at once, caroming between thoughts and feelings as I frantically tried to consider all the possible angles of what we were doing. But listening to her speak words of comfort to me, feeling her presence at my side, even just the sound of her voice, all of it served as the perfect antidote to the poison of my nerves.

Somewhere in the midst of my breathing, I must have relaxed long enough to drift into sleep.

Chapter Twenty-One

I wasn't sure how long I slept for, but I woke up shivering.

The fog had dissipated significantly, paving the way for a few particularly bold stars to pierce their way through the grey-black blanket overhead. I tilted my head from side to side and wiggled my toes to see if it felt like I was truly awake or if I was still dreaming. Discerning the difference was getting harder and harder to do these days.

As far as I could tell, I was awake. I was also cold, I was wet, and most importantly, I was still here.

And by 'here', I meant in North Carolina, in David Abbott's body, my body, or whatever I wanted to call it all.

Kirsa still slept soundly on the ground beside me, eyes closed and lips slightly agape, her chest rising and falling with the steady pace of slumber.

She looked so peaceful that I didn't dare wake her. I wondered if she was dreaming, and if so, what were her dreams about? Was she traveling back without me to the life she'd left behind? What if she didn't wake up at all; or worse, what if she woke up and had no memory of any of this?

If it was possible for Kirsa to depart this body, then it was equally possible for the real Jessica to return to it. And if that happened, what would I do? I would mean nothing to that person, and she'd probably shrink away from me in fear, wondering who I was and why we were alone together out in the middle of nowhere at night.

This line of questioning was as endless as it was pointless. There was no telling what was happening right now or what I was expected to do. The only thing I knew for sure was that for whatever reason, I hadn't been able to cross over with her while we were both asleep. That much I was certain of.

It didn't necessarily mean I wouldn't be able to do so at a future date. Perhaps if I laid back down and managed to fall asleep again, maybe I'd hear that voice—her real voice, I guess it was—calling out to me. Maybe I'd find myself in her company, or at least in a place that felt familiar to me from my previous dreams, where conceivably something magical or important could happen. Then at least there'd be something to strive for, something I could latch onto and work at exploring, until I either found myself in Kirsa's dimension or I didn't.

One way or another, I'd finally have an answer to the question of who I was. Then, it would simply be a matter of deciding whether I liked that answer or not.

After a good deal of internal debate, I ended up reclining back on the ground and curling up next to her to try and fall asleep again. If she did wake up as the *real* Jessica Silverton with no idea of who I was, she'd probably scream and thrash at me, but that was a risk I was willing to take just to share in some of her body heat. My teeth chattered, and all my muscles shivered as I tried to focus on something other than how cold and wet I felt.

I realized then that there actually *was* some potential for harm if this plan didn't work out. After all, Jessica had been wheeled into a hospital on a stretcher after I found her vulnerable and exposed to conditions not altogether different from these.

While it had been raining heavily that day—and, so far, the moisture hadn't amounted to more than a clammy fog tonight—it did feel substantially colder right now than it had the day of the storm. If I couldn't fall asleep quickly, or find her in my dreams once I did, I worried about what might happen to us the longer we stayed out here.

In the end, nature made the decision for me. As cold as I was, it would have taken a minor miracle to succumb to unconsciousness, even with the added heat of Kirsa's body pressed against mine.

When I felt the first couple raindrops splash against my skin, I knew it was time for us both to get up and get moving. There was nothing stopping us from trying this plan again; unless, of course, we both froze to death before we got a second chance.

She still looked so serene and angelic lying there that it pained me to wake her up at all. Fleetingly, I remembered that there was a chance the person I'd be waking wouldn't recognize me, so I did my best to mentally prepare myself for whatever kind of reaction I might receive. When I was as ready as I was going to get, I lightly grabbed her shoulder and shook her a few times, until her eyes opened and she saw me.

Her face contorted into a flurry of complex

expressions as her mind processed what was happening, but the one that I recognized first was disappointment.

"It didn't work."

Especially now that it was starting to rain, I couldn't help but think back on the parallels between this setting and the one I'd first met her in. In both instances, we were outside in the wilderness, and I'd been kneeling over her when she woke up both times. Except the first time, her reaction was one of blissful excitement and profound relief as she saw me, while this time around, it couldn't be more dissimilar.

It occurred to me that she neither hoped for nor expected to see a seventeen-year-old boy when she woke up from her dreams. She wanted Daniel, not David, and I actually felt genuinely sorry to disappoint her.

"We've got to go. It's starting to rain."

She gave me a look that let me know she couldn't have cared less.

"It doesn't matter. We've been through a lot worse than a little water falling from the sky."

As if on cue, the rain intensified, and I saw a distant flash of lightning streak across the clouds. Seconds later, the thunder followed, and now the wind was beginning to pick up again, too.

It was my turn to take control of the situation physically. Whether she wanted to move or not, I grabbed her hands and gently hoisted her up to her feet.

"I believe you; and we can try again. But not if we get struck by lightning or washed off the side of a cliff before we ever get the chance."

I tried to smile at her, to help her understand that I wasn't giving up on our plan, just postponing it temporarily. It was hard to pull off a smile, though, with the rain and wind whipping all around us, so I wasn't sure if I really conveyed the proper kind of assurance I hoped to impress on her.

"Come on, let's get out of here."

I pointed my flashlight back down the trail I came up, and noticed the dirt was already transforming into a glistening mud. It was only going to get wetter and slicker the longer we stayed up here, which meant the trek down would be even more difficult and dangerous than it had been on the way up. We had to start moving before it got any worse.

"Where are we going to go?"

She practically had to yell just so I could hear her question over the sound of the rain and thunder. I took her by the hand and started to lead her carefully down as we talked, making sure to keep the flashlight trained on the ground in front of our feet so we wouldn't trip on anything that suddenly popped out of the darkness.

"I'll take you home. Do you think you can remember how to get us there?"

She jerked back on my hand forcefully, and for a second, I thought she saw something up ahead that startled her. But there was nothing to see besides more mud, rocks, and grass. I turned back around and lifted the light up a bit so I could make out her face more clearly; now, she was the one who was smiling.

"That's exactly what I'm trying to do, Daniel. I'm trying to get us back home, if you'll let me."

I took a step closer to her. Even more than before, she reminded me of what she'd looked like when I found her that day at the edge of the forest creek. Her skin was pale and almost bluish, and her hair was wet and wild and untamed, with rebellious strands stuck at odd angles across her forehead, cheeks, and neck.

Seeing her like this a second time, there was no denying how close to death she must have been when I first found her out there. Whatever our true relationship was, I couldn't in good conscience allow her to put herself in harm's way, no matter how much she protested.

"I *will* let you, I promise. I want to go back with you, back to our lives together." I shouted the words out above the quickening storm. "Just, please... do this for me now. Please! Come back with me, back to my house—back to David's house, okay? Please... Kirsa... I don't want to lose you."

It may have started out as a desperate attempt to coerce her into following me. But by the end, it was a heartfelt plea, and one I truly meant with every ounce of blood in my body.

She held my gaze for a long, meaningful moment as she considered what she wanted to do. Finally, she dipped her chin into a quick, shivering nod.

"Okay. Let's go."

And together, we started to shuffle our way back down Ayeli Rock, relying on each other for balance and stability as we descended the slippery path.

The way down took much, much longer than the way up. We took no chances along the journey, moving slowly and stopping to rest whenever one of us needed to take a quick break. The entire descent was made in silence; even if we'd wanted to talk, it would have been near-impossible to hear each other over the thunderstorm.

It was a lengthy, physical ordeal, and more than once, I thought my legs might give out on me entirely.

But every time it seemed I might collapse, suddenly she'd be there for me, pulling my arm over her shoulder and helping to support my weight, as if she could read my mind and sense when I needed her the most.

At long last, we reached the bottom of the trail where the dirt path met the paved road. I asked Kirsa if she needed more time to rest or recover, but she shook her head, insisted she was fine, and instead asked me if I needed more time to physically regroup. Inspired by her tenacity and seemingly endless endurance, I told her I wanted to carry on, and so we kept moving.

The street seemed a tad brighter now than it had before. Maybe it was the glow of my flashlight diffusing through the rain, or maybe it was closer to dawn than I thought it was. If it was the latter, we needed to move fast if we wanted to have any hope of making it back to my house before my parents got up. My mother, in particular, was an early riser; I knew she went on her morning jogs not long after daybreak.

What would she do or say if she caught us sneaking into the house? I'd been so focused on convincing Kirsa to get off Ayeli Rock that I hadn't really considered the potential ramifications of my offer.

Inviting a girl over to my house would have been a big deal to begin with—especially a girl I'd only recently met and under such bizarre and critical circumstances.

Inviting a girl to come over to my house before

sunrise, after already sneaking out and spending a whole night with her at a deserted location? That sounded even worse in my head. I couldn't begin to fathom how my parents would react.

These mounting concerns provided plenty of motivation for me to maintain a brisk pace, and thankfully, Kirsa didn't have any trouble matching me stride for stride. Before long, the tall metal streetlights reappeared on both sides of the road. Then came the first few outlying structures of civilization, and then more and more buildings sprung up, until we were moving rapidly through Lenoir.

All the while, I kept checking the sky as we walked, hoping and praying that the colors stayed predominantly grey and black without displaying any telltale hints of the blue or white that I knew signaled morning.

Occasionally, I pulled out my map of the town just to make sure we were still on the right track, but overall, I was pleased with how well I remembered the passage I'd made earlier that night. It helped too that the further along we got, the more the rain began to let up; it was barely more than a drizzle when we finally reached the street I lived on.

There was no turning back now. If there'd been a time to second-guess this decision, it would have been back while we were moving through town. We could have split up and gone our separate ways, or I could have accompanied her back to the Silvertons' house and then excused myself to come home alone.

It didn't really matter, though, because I hadn't done any of that. I'd suggested she come back to my house, or my parents' house, or David's parents' house—it was all still too confusing to make any definitive conclusions—and she'd accepted that proposal, so here we were. Whatever happened next, we were in it together, for better or worse.

Moving with all the careful stealth and quiet concentration of a burglar, I eased the front door open just a crack and took a look inside.

Everything was dark. That didn't mean we were in the clear, but it was at least a better sight to behold than two angry adults waiting up for my return.

I whispered a quick word of caution to Kirsa, and she murmured back that she understood. Gently, I closed the door behind us and slid the lock back into place, then I took her by the hand and led her lightly up the stairs to my bedroom.

The last order of business was closing the door to my room, and once that was done, I waited for a couple seconds on the other side of it with my ear pressed up against the wood, listening for anything that might mean they'd heard us.

If they had, it didn't sound like they were doing anything about it. There were no creaks, no footsteps, no voices coming down the hall. We needed to be extremely quiet still, but at least for the time being, it seemed we'd escaped detection. I decided to play it safe and leave the overhead light off, turning on my closet light instead so that we could see each other.

Kirsa was huddled in the corner of my room by the bookshelf, her arms hugged tightly around her body as she visibly trembled. Despite how cold, wet, and miserable she must have been, she was still smiling back at me, like she was just happy we were breathing the same air. I was thoroughly chilled to the bone myself, but seeing her like that made me smile too, and already I felt a bit warmer.

"Let me get you some dry clothes."

She had done such a spectacular job supporting me when I needed her most during our treacherous mountain descent. It was my turn now to take care of her and make sure she didn't end up back in the hospital again.

I rifled through the clothes in my closet until I found the warmest, thickest, most comfortable-looking pieces, then laid them all out on top of my bed.

"Choose whichever ones you want, and I'll take whatever's left. You can change out here, and I'll change in my closet, with the door shut, of course. I would go to the bathroom, but it's further down the hall, pretty close to my parents' room."

She didn't seem too picky, spending only a second or two examining the options before selecting a baggy pair of sweatpants, a long-sleeve t-shirt, and a wool pullover. I scooped up the rest of the garments and carried them back into the closet, making sure the door shut with a soft click behind me.

As I peeled off my wet clothes and used some of the dry ones to towel off, I realized that by shutting the closet door, I'd essentially cut off her light source and left her to change in the dark. My hand went to the knob to open it again, but then I paused, contemplating how embarrassing it would be if she thought I was trying to spy on her as she undressed.

After a quick inner debate as to which of the two evils were lesser, I decided the best course of action was to keep the door shut unless she specifically asked me to open it. Hurriedly, I finished drying myself off and then bundling up in several layers of clothing.

I was on the carpeted closet floor pulling a second pair of socks up over my ankles when the door opened without me. There, standing on the other side in a sliver of light, was Kirsa, already looking healthier in dry clothes, but still noticeably shaking a bit.

"Daniel, is it okay if I get into bed?"

I could tell it was a bizarre question for her to ask, although probably not for the most obvious reason. After all, by Kirsa's own account, the two of us were already trespassing in these bodies; maybe she felt just as out of place being in a stranger's bedroom.

"I mean, this bed that's here?"

"Yeah… yes, of course."

Framing the context of the situation in my mind didn't make it any less awkward to experience.

"Um… do—do you mind if I get in, too? I mean, I can sleep on the floor, too, I really don't mind. Whatever's most comfortable for you…"

Whatever insecurity she may have felt, all it took for Kirsa to rediscover that trademark tenacious resolve was the suggestion of creating space between us. Before I'd even finished speaking, she had me by the hand and was dragging me toward the bed.

"Of course not! We've been sleeping together for over fifty years. I think, in all that time, I've made you sleep on the couch maybe twice, and both times for good reason."

She chuckled to herself as we snuggled in beneath the covers.

Even if we had been doing this for decades, right now, it felt like the very first time, and my heart was exploding out of my chest. Surely, Kirsa could hear it racing along, too. I could even hear it over the sound of her whispered voice and through all the layers of sheets and blankets.

"I didn't travel across whole galaxies of time and space just so I could sleep in the same room as you." Her face was only a hair's breadth away from mine. "I came all this way because I'm not ready for *this* to stop yet…" She pressed a hand against my thumping chest. "Not unless mine does, too. And I mean our real ones, by the way. Although it's nice to know I can still do this to you, even here, like this. You've always done it to me." She took my hand and pressed it against her chest. Her heart was beating just as fast. "More than anything else, trust this feeling. Trust *us*. This—this is real."

Chapter Twenty-Two

The knocking was soft at first, so it was easy to ignore, more background noise in a cacophony of sounds and images that only make sense to the dreamer. Steadily, it became more prominent, though, until it was altogether impossible to shut out any longer.

That was when the fantasy world split asunder. All of a sudden, I was staring up at a plain white ceiling, there was a girl's face cradled in my shoulder, and the knocking came again from the bedroom door off to my side.

Before I fully understood where I was, who I was with, or what was even happening, the door swung open to reveal my mother standing in the hallway. She let out a loud gasp and covered her mouth with one hand as she caught sight of the girl still sleeping beside me.

Instinctively, I jerked my shoulder away from Kirsa to try and create some distance between us, but it was too late. My mother's face turned bright red, and for a second, I didn't know if she was going to cry or scream. She turned to look at something below and behind her, and when she whipped her head back around, I could see the veins popping up from her neck as she wrestled her emotions.

"You need to get dressed and come downstairs *right now*. Both of you!"

I'd never heard my mother sound like that before; not that I could remember, at least. It was a tone that left no room for argument or rebuttal; just a stern command that necessitated immediate action.

And it worked. I tossed the covers off, partly to show her that we were both fully-dressed underneath them, but mainly to show her that I was eager to comply. My legs were still half-asleep, so I gave them each a quick shake before rolling over and out of bed.

Kirsa must have felt my weight leave the mattress, or else all the commotion finally got to her, because she cracked open her eyelids and stretched her arms out lazily. I watched her face as she became more aware of where she was, first taking in the room, then the woman standing in the doorway, and finally coming back around to me. The reality of the situation set in, and her lips parted as she let out a little sigh. When she spoke, her voice was soft, sullen, and heartbroken.

"It didn't work."

I knew what she meant by it. My mother, of course, did not; but she was the one who answered the girl all the same.

"Your parents are downstairs, Jessica."

The news sent shockwaves through my body. Jim Silverton was in my house?! I couldn't believe it. Just the idea of him lurking downstairs was horrific, and what did he know already? Did he know she was up here with me?

I'd seen his volatility up close and personal before,

but this dynamic was altogether different. If he thought or knew that his teenage daughter had just spent the night with me, there was a legitimate chance he might actually murder me.

It wasn't hard to imagine that scenario unfolding at all, and I wondered what would happen if it did. Would my parents protect me? *Could* they even protect me against him?

I turned to look at Kirsa, expecting to find her similarly disturbed by this revelation. Her face welled up with emotion, but it wasn't necessarily fear or concern that I saw there. It was profound, abject disappointment, and I knew right away where it came from.

For her, all that mattered was that our plan had once again failed. We'd fallen asleep as close to one another as physically possible, our minds and spirits completely in sync, and yet we'd woken up the same as we were the night before. Kirsa didn't care about her parents or my parents; and why should she? The only thing she cared about in this world was getting us both out of this world. So far, it was proving an impossible feat to accomplish.

"I wouldn't keep them waiting."

My mother glanced at each of us before retreating from the doorway and out of sight. I could hear her talking above the sound of her own footsteps as she descended back down the staircase to the front door. What could she possibly say to the Silvertons in this situation?

I felt sorry for her then, forced into the unenviable task of being the bearer of bad news. It wasn't her fault that Kirsa had turned up here; it was my idea, my suggestion all along. And as surprised as she must have been to find the Silvertons on her doorstep, she must have been downright shocked to find their daughter asleep upstairs with me.

"We have to go down."

I didn't want to leave my mother alone out there any longer than I had to. As soon as Jim Silverton learned the truth of his daughter's whereabouts, there was no telling what he was capable of.

"It'll only get worse the longer we stay up here."

Kirsa tilted her head at me quizzically.

"What do you mean? You know it doesn't matter."

I took half a step toward her before reconsidering and taking a couple steps back. This wasn't the time for an intimate debate. Any second now, I expected to hear pounding footsteps coming down the hallway and see a red-faced giant barreling into my bedroom.

And at that point, it'd be too late. There'd be nowhere for us to go, unless we wanted to try climbing out my bedroom window and onto the shingles of the roof outside. Knowing the state of my physical coordination, I'd probably slip, fall, and plummet to my death.

At least then I'd know for sure that Kirsa was right if I discovered myself to be an old man on the other side...

"I know it doesn't matter, and that if we're not actually these kids, then who cares that we just spent the night together. But I still don't want to leave her alone down there. I care about her, and I don't want her to get hurt."

Kirsa nodded her understanding, although she still didn't seem too concerned by our predicament. Her mind was obviously elsewhere.

"We need to find another way to get back, Daniel. It's not working while we're sleeping."

"It won't work at all if your father kills us before we get another chance."

"He's not my father."

She gave me a sly smile.

"And actually, that *might* work."

Absolutely not. If and when we were forced to try option three, the death route, it would not be at the hands of Jim Silverton, that much I was sure of. There had to be another way.

What day was it? Ever since I'd met Kirsa in the forest, whatever meager sense of normalcy or routine I'd previously established for myself had gone completely by the wayside. Days and nights blurred together, especially as the line between conscious and unconscious grew ever fuzzier.

I was fairly confident I had therapy scheduled today with Dr. Eiding. It felt like it had been quite some time since our last session, and if I was right, then maybe she'd be the perfect person to talk to about all of this.

The psychiatrist had reminded me throughout numerous sessions that everything we discussed was confidential. Could she be trusted with something as delicate as this? Would she believe any of it? And, if she did, would she help us?

"I think I'm seeing someone today who helps me with my memory. She asks me about my dreams all the time, and she might be able to help us. I don't know if she'll do it, she might think we're crazy, but it's worth trying, at least."

I shrugged.

"She's a doctor, too, so if nothing else, maybe she can get us some of the pills that we need—"

"*—to induce a coma!*"

Kirsa interrupted me excitedly, bouncing up and down on the balls of her feet. For the first time this morning, her face exploded into that radiant, infectious smile I'd grown to know and love. Her unbridled enthusiasm was enough to make me excited, if not altogether optimistic, about what could happen with Dr. Eiding.

All those good feelings went flying out the window when I heard footsteps thundering down the hallway. I turned to face the sound and took a few steps back, placing myself squarely between Kirsa and the door. Truthfully, I wasn't sure what I hoped to accomplish—hide her or shield her?—but either way, I knew I couldn't possibly succeed. Still, I did it all the same, simply because I had to.

In he came—just as ruddy, sweaty, and wrathful as expected, his eyes lancing through us and then sweeping across the bed, trying to compute whether the worst of his fears had been realized. His lower jaw twitched and twisted as he gnashed his teeth and licked at his sun-chapped lips wildly, and I could only wonder what terrible thoughts and impulses he fought for control over.

Kate Silverton appeared at his side and immediately put a hand on his arm. Jim Silverton recoiled as if her hand was on fire, but she kept it there firmly and wrapped her fingers around his bicep.

"*Jim.* Not here. Not now."

The words were only for him, and they worked just

long enough to freeze him momentarily in his own bubbling prison of rage. When she was satisfied with his condition, Mrs. Silverton turned and walked deliberately over to her daughter and took her by the hand, without so much as an acknowledgment of my existence.

"Come on, Jessica. We're going home."

Kirsa opened her mouth to argue, but before she could get anything out, her mother placed a finger on her lips and yanked her toward the doorway.

"*Now.*"

It was uncomfortable to watch, but I didn't know what I could do to help. Mrs. Silverton used all her brute force to practically drag Kirsa out of my bedroom, ignoring her daughter's stammering pleas as easily as she ignored my presence.

When the two women disappeared around the corner of the doorframe, I heard Kirsa let out what sounded like a squeal of pain.

I couldn't help myself; I took a few quick steps forward to help her…

…and then stopped dead in my tracks as Mr. Silverton leveled his gaze on me.

He didn't need to say anything; I knew exactly what he was thinking about doing to me, and it sent shivers down my spine. In my bones, I knew that this was it; this was my last moment, whether I liked it or not, because without a doubt, he was going to kill me.

Slowly, Jim raised a clenched fist, the knuckles bare and white and bony, and then pointed one thick, quivering finger straight between my eyes like a spear.

"So, help me, God…"

He struggled to contain himself. The veins in his

neck pumped blood as little beads of sweat trickled down his freckled temples.

"Don't talk to her. Don't look at her. Don't touch her. Ever again. Or, so help me, God, I'll kill you."

He let the message fully sink in. I knew that if he could have it his way, he'd kill me right now where I stood.

Finally, when he couldn't repress his urges any longer, he turned away from me and moved shakily out the doorway. I heard his boots stomp down the stairs, and waited until there was relative quiet again before daring to walk out into the hallway to assess the scene.

From where I was standing, I could see out the foyer window to the front yard and to the sidewalk that led all the way to the street where the familiar red pickup truck was parked. I saw Jim Silverton move around the front to get in the driver's seat, and I saw Kate Silverton's profile sitting in the passenger seat. Although I couldn't see Kirsa, I assumed she was somewhere inside the cabin of the truck. The engine started, the tires screeched, and seconds later, the vehicle disappeared from view.

"Well?"

The voice startled me. I turned to my right and saw my mother standing with her back flat against the wall, her arms crossed in front of her chest, and a look of severe disappointment on her face.

"What happened?"

There was so much I could say to her, but doing so would only cause more harm than good. I'd already made up my mind that I couldn't discuss any of this with my parents. It would be too hurtful if they believed me, even though they probably never would.

271

More likely, they'd think me insane, and forbid me from spending any more time with Kirsa; though there was a pretty decent chance of that happening now anyway, in light of this morning's discovery.

"Nothing happened."

She gave me a withering glare.

"Honestly. We went out for a walk last night, just around town, not too far, and then when it got cold and rainy, we came back here and fell asleep. That's it, though. I told her she could spend the night because her house was far away and it was late. I'm sorry, I know I should have asked you guys first."

"You went out for a walk last night? At what time?"

I had no idea.

"I don't know, honestly; it was late, though, I'll admit. After dinner, obviously."

"Obviously." She scowled. "So, you snuck out in the middle of the night, went God-knows-where with Jessica, and then brought her back here to your room to spend the night?"

I swallowed and looked down at my feet.

"It sounds bad when you say it that way…"

"It sounds bad no matter which way you say it. Do you know how much of an idiot I felt like when Jessica's parents showed up at the front door, worried sick, and asked if by some crazy chance she was here? I told them no, of course, because that was crazy, you would never do something like that, but yes, all right, I'd check just to make sure.

"And then, afterward, I had to come back downstairs like a fool, and tell them that yes, as a matter of fact, their teenage daughter *was* here after all, asleep upstairs with my teenage son. Do you know what that makes me feel like? Do you?"

I blushed with shame and kept my gaze downward. It was impossible to look her in the eye right now.

My mother's voice wavered.

"What kind of mother does that make me, to not know something like that?"

She waited long enough to make me wonder if the question was rhetorical.

"Help me understand all this, please, Davey, because I'm having a really hard time. This just isn't like you, sneaking out, keeping secrets. You don't even know this girl. You just met her.

"And I know you've been through a lot, and so has she; but what about me? What about Dad? What about the Silvertons, who just went through hell thinking their daughter was missing or kidnapped or killed; only to get her back, and then to have her disappear again with the person who found her? Have you thought about any of this?"

Truthfully, I had not. I could see how from her perspective, none of my actions made much sense, and none of them could be justified, because they all directly or indirectly hurt the people that should have mattered the most to me.

The problem was, of course, that Kirsa mattered the most to me of all those people.

Whether or not it made sense, whether or not any of it was possible, the one thing I knew unequivocally, the only thing I knew unequivocally since my brain started knowing things again when I woke up in the hospital that night, was that I loved her.

Jessica or Kirsa, girl or woman, this world or the

next one, fate had brought us together. And I wasn't going to let anything stand in the way of that now.

Although I did need to find a way to explain this to my mother without *really* explaining it.

"I know it's hard to understand, and I know I messed up. Believe me, I would never intentionally do anything to hurt you or Dad. And I don't want to upset the Silvertons, either; I know they've been through a lot."

Mid-sentence, I had an idea. I wasn't sure if it would work, but if there was ever a time to try it, the time was right now.

"The thing is—and I didn't want to say this last night in the car, because I didn't want to get your hopes up—but something happened with me. While I was outside on the porch with Kir—with Jessica after dinner, I was trying to talk to her about my recovery and all the sessions I've had with Dr. Eiding, and something happened.

"Some of my memories came back; not all of them, obviously. But for the first time, it felt like something unlocked in my brain, and I had something to work with. I don't know what it is about her; maybe just because she's also recently experienced trauma? I'm not sure. All I know is that stuff started to come back, so I got excited and wanted to keep talking to her, but then her dad brought us back in, and dessert was over, and we had to go. So, I'm sorry, I really am, but I just couldn't wait to see her again. And I'm glad I did. Even in the small amount of time we spent together on our walk, more stuff started to come back."

And now, for the finishing touch…

"But I'm worried now that I won't be able to see her again, not after what happened, knowing how strict Mr. Silverton is. I totally get it, too. I'd be upset if it were me, and my daughter went missing.

"I just… I don't know what to do or who I can talk to about it now. Don't get me wrong, you and Dad are great listeners, and you've been there for me every step of the way. But I feel like if I can't talk to Jessica, then I need to talk to Dr. Eiding. Just because she knows me, and she's guided me along the recovery process so well. She can approach everything with her experience and her professional knowledge on it all. But I don't know when my next appointment is…?"

My mother listened carefully to what I had to say, and by the time I was done, she looked just a tad more excited and a tad less angry. There was still a decent amount of trepidation in her face, though, like she wasn't quite sure how optimistic she should allow herself to be.

"What kind of memories came back? What happened?"

I thought about the beach house, the fake engagement story, the *real* engagement story, the accounts of our children, their spouses, *their* children, our lives; no, none of those memories could be shared.

"It's hard to explain. It's like flashes, or wisps, of memories, that come back strongly and then are hard to hold onto, like they're slippery or something. But they're real. I really think they are, at least. It's different than anything that's happened for me before, anything that's come up for me. It feels like I'm onto something for the first time. And I want to try and see if I can go further, or find a way to hold onto them and really

275

absorb it and think about it, just so I know it's real and lasting. I don't want it to go away as soon as I fall asleep again or think about something else."

She nodded her head thoughtfully and smiled.

"Well... I'm happy for you, Davey. I still don't see what Jessica Silverton has to do with any of it, but I guess at the end of the day, I'm just happy that you feel like you may have had a breakthrough. That's the most important thing to me."

Her face became serious once again.

"Just promise me that you'll ask next time you feel like inviting a girl over for a slumber party. I know you're almost eighteen and that you're pretty much all grown up now, but you're not in college yet, okay? You're still my baby boy for as long as you live in this house; you're still my baby boy even if you don't live in this house one day, actually. That never changes. You got it?"

I smiled back at her, though I felt a little melancholic.

Choosing Kirsa and our alternate life meant forsaking my life here as I knew it, and that also meant turning my back on my mother and on our developing relationship. Even if Kirsa was right about everything, and this woman wasn't actually my mother, it didn't lessen any of the love for me that I saw plain as day in her eyes right now.

For the first time, I considered what might happen to my parents if we were successful in transitioning out of these bodies and they remained unoccupied after we left. If David Abbott's true consciousness was lost somewhere out in the infinite reaches of the universe, or even stuck inside some other person—and perhaps without any knowledge that it's not meant to be there—then there was a legitimate possibility that my exit would leave this boy altogether empty of a soul.

Whether that resulted in another coma, death, or something equally terrible but unfathomable, there was no way of knowing. But I did know that any of those scenarios would be devastating for my parents. For David Abbott's parents, that is.

And perhaps I needed to factor that in and consider some of the other consequences and casualties of my actions. Because whatever I decided to do would dramatically affect the lives of more people than just Kirsa and myself.

My mother was still waiting.

"I need to hear a 'Yes, Mom, I'll always be your baby boy,' before I let you off the hook."

I tried hard to ignore the lump in my throat. No matter what changed, I still hated lying to these loving people who called themselves my parents.

"Yes, Mom, I'll always be your baby boy."

Maybe she heard the emotion in my voice, or maybe she saw it in my face, because she stepped forward and pulled me into a tight hug.

"Aww… that's what I wanted to hear. Thank you."

We both savored the embrace for a few powerful seconds, and then she pulled back to observe me again at arm's length.

""So. Dr. Eiding. Do you want me to call her and see if she's around at all today? Maybe she has some extra time or an opening she can see you in. I don't know what her schedule's like on Saturdays, but it can't hurt to ask at least. Dad got called into work today unexpectedly anyway, so we've got some time on our hands."

"That would be great!"

The psychiatrist had never mentioned what days her work week consisted of. As a doctor, though, it seemed only natural that she'd make herself available in the event of an emergency or a major crisis with one of her patients.

Granted, this was neither an emergency nor a crisis. But perhaps a breakthrough could justify an impromptu session as well? I seemed to remember her mentioning once upon a time that I was free to contact her in the event of a significant change. If so, this development, even though it was fake, certainly qualified.

And I was right. No sooner had my mother disappeared down the stairs to make the phone call than she was returning back up them again, and with news that Dr. Eiding would see me in an hour.

Apparently, she was also thrilled to hear I'd had a breakthrough, couldn't wait to learn all about it, and urged me to write down anything now that I feared I might forget in my dream journal.

There were really only two matters I wanted to discuss with Dr. Eiding, neither one of which I could possibly forget. I dug out the dream journal from beneath my bed all the same, more to satisfy my mother than anything else, and scribbled down a few random musings and doodles. If pretending to jot down notes helped sell this routine to my mother, then it was worth it. Besides, it did make the time go by faster.

Conversely, the car ride to Dr. Eiding's house seemed to stretch on for an eternity. Part of it was just me being excited and anxious to get there, but part of it was also having to duck and weave around my mother's constant line of questioning.

I couldn't blame her for being curious, and obviously the only reason she kept peppering me for more details and information was because she cared. She was also no doubt excited at the prospect that if memories and mental associations were coming back to me, then maybe I'd start behaving more like the person I was before my coma.

It was the promise of progress, really the first significant sign of it since they'd brought me home. She was understandably energized at what might come of it.

I had nothing to give her, though, except more lies and vague redirections. She wanted to know what Jessica had said outside on the porch that triggered my memories, what those memories were, what it felt like to have pieces of my past restored, what we talked about on our night hike, what I planned to discuss with Dr. Eiding, and seemingly hundreds of other inquiries.

If my replies were too cryptic or unsatisfactory, she let me know and pressed me further, at which point, I'd feign a headache, rub the skin between my eyes, or basically do anything I could to try and avoid giving a decent answer. I was a terrible liar—I'd struggled for weeks now trying to appease my parents—and coming up with anything too specific was risky, considering I was aware just how well she knew me and knew who I was supposed to be.

My hand was on the door lever as soon as she put the car in park outside the familiar white house. It was somewhat disorienting seeing Dr. Eiding's home at this time of day, because our sessions were always in the late afternoon, when the sunlight turned the white wooden panels of her house a rosy amber color with shades of pink. It was much earlier in the day now, with the sun on the opposite side of the sky, and the entire exterior of the house looked different to me.

I waited impatiently for my mother to get out of the car and join me on the sidewalk before I started walking briskly toward the front door.

Chapter Twenty-Three

———————◆———————

Per usual, Dr. Eiding came as a package deal with her two big dogs, neither one of which wanted to be restrained when company came over. Both sniffed and licked at me and my mother, and they fought against Dr. Eiding to move closer to us, even as she tried to talk them down and pull them back by the collars around their necks.

"*Hey*! Hey, you two, come on now! Get back! Get back now, let them come inside. Hi, David! Hi, Ellen! How are you two doing—*get back now!* I'm sorry... let me put them outside real quick, it'll just be a minute. Make yourselves at home. So happy you called! How exciting—*come on now, you two...* let's go outside! Outside now, come on!"

We wandered into her living room as she led the two animals to the back door. Even though we were a bit early, it was clear she'd been expecting us; the television was on, the coffee table by the couch displayed a plate of cookies and a glass of sweet tea, and a small fire burned in the fireplace. We heard Dr. Eiding talking to us from the other room before she returned a couple of seconds later without the dogs.

"I wasn't sure if you planned on staying or not,

Ellen, but if you are, I left the remote next to the plate in here so you could watch whatever you like. There's a whole pitcher of tea in the fridge if you want more, and you'd better believe there are more cookies in the pantry, too, if you're hungry."

My mother put one hand over her stomach and held her other palm up in protest.

"Ohhh, no; I can't do any more of your cookies. Don't get me wrong, they're delicious, but that's the problem! I told Davey just the other day that I think I've gained ten pounds since we started coming to see you."

Dr. Eiding laughed and swatted the air dismissively.

"Nonsense! It's all in your head. Chocolate chip cookies are good for the mind, body, and the soul."

She winked.

"Probably more so the mind and the soul than the body, but two out of three isn't bad now, is it?"

My mother sat down on the sofa, crossed one leg over her knee, and stared at the plate of cookies apprehensively.

"This is going to be a real test of my willpower. Hopefully, the next time you see me, this plate still has eight cookies on it. Anything less means I've failed."

The psychiatrist laughed again.

"If there are still eight cookies there when we come back down, I'm going to be personally offended. So please, eat up. And as always, feel free to mosey around and make yourself comfortable. *Mi casa es su casa.*"

She turned to face me and clapped her hands together.

"Well. Shall we? I'm sure you have a lot to talk about, and I for one could not be more excited to hear all about it. Lead the way!"

We climbed up the creaky steps to her office and took our normal spots in the room. She pulled out her yellow notepad and a pen, then gestured toward the dream journal I had tucked beneath one arm.

"Has that been helpful for you?"

I nodded dumbly, hoping she wouldn't ask to see anything inside it.

"It's been great. Thank you for suggesting it."

"Of course. I'm happy it's working."

She shifted her weight around in the chair until she found a comfortable position, took a deep sigh, and smiled over at me.

"Well, David, my time is yours. Tell me what's been going on for you lately. Some major developments, I've been told, is that right?"

There was no point in carrying on the pretense any further.

"Um, yes and no. There *have* been some major developments, but not necessarily the ones my mother may have told you about over the phone."

I waited to see what kind of reaction I would get, expecting anything from anger to confusion to disappointment, or something in between.

Her face was unchanged for the most part, though. She scratched the back of her head with the capped end of her pen and blinked.

"Go on, David. You can talk about whatever you want to, you know that."

Soon, we'd find out if she really meant that.

"I met a girl."

This time, her face did change slightly, registering amused surprise. I noticed it before continuing on.

"It's the same girl I told you about, actually; the one I rescued after I found her alone and unconscious out in the woods. It's kind of a long story, and I know we only have an hour. But what's important to understand is that at first, I had no idea who this girl was and neither did my parents. We go to different schools, and we've supposedly never crossed paths or seen each other a day in our lives before this moment.

"And yet, when she woke up, she started calling me by another name and repeating over and over again that she'd found me, and now we could go back home together. Before we had a chance to really talk that long, she passed out, but after my mother and I took her to the hospital, she asked for me, and it was more of the same. She just kept looking at me and talking to me like we were old friends…"

I hesitated a moment while I found my courage and tried not to blush.

"Actually, more like we were lovers, like we've been together, for a very long time. Every time she started talking to me though, she'd get too worked up and then she'd pass out. But afterward, she asked her parents every day if she could see me, until finally they invited my whole family over for dinner last night, and after we ate, the two of us went outside by ourselves to talk, and…"

Everything up to this point had been relatively easy. After all, the memories were still fresh, and they were all true. Now was where the story really got interesting, and where I'd have to pay extra close attention to Dr. Eiding's reactions.

Whether or not she believed any of this would determine how much help she could actually provide to me and Kirsa. If at any juncture it became obvious that she didn't believe me, or didn't think any of this possible, then there was no point in continuing on this session or wasting anyone's time.

I really, really, hoped that wouldn't be the case, though, because the genial psychiatrist sitting across from me represented our best—and perhaps, our only—chance at realizing the second option Kirsa outlined in her plan to get us back to our world.

"I guess… let me just get right to the point. This may sound crazy, and I understand if your initial reaction is not to believe me or to think that I'm crazy, or she's crazy, or we're both crazy—"

"Let me stop you right there, just so I can put that fear out of your head for good, okay? Nothing you say is going to make me think you're crazy. So, don't you worry about that. You can actually drop that word from your vocabulary completely while you're in here."

Easy for her to say when she doesn't know what's coming.

Still, it was encouraging to hear her interject so swiftly on my behalf. And so far, she seemed to be about as open-minded as I could have possibly hoped for. I needed someone in her position now with a very open, non-judgmental mind.

"Thanks. I appreciate you saying that. Because honestly, I don't know who else to go to about this."

I could feel perspiration gathering in all the folds and creases of my skin underneath my clothes. The room felt substantially hotter than I remembered it being when I first walked in.

285

"I guess what I want to ask you, Dr. Eiding, is if you believe it's possible for our souls to detach from our bodies? Because the girl I'm telling you about, she came to me in my dreams last night. And it wasn't just in my own head, because in my dreams she told me when and where to meet her, and when I woke up and went to the place she told me to go to, *she was there.* She was right there at the right time, waiting for me."

The psychiatrist had been furiously taking notes on her yellow pad of paper, but now she paused to glance up at me. She looked surprised, but not incredulous. I decided I may as well go on and test the limits of her capacity for reason.

"There's more; a lot more, actually. She says that we're both from an alternate dimension, a parallel universe to this one. And that the only reason we're here is because I had a stroke in our real world, and somehow, my consciousness or soul or whatever it is got lost and ended up here in this boy—ended up here as David Abbott. She says she followed me here—in the real world, her name is Kirsa—but she followed me here until she found me, waking up in the body of the girl that I came across in the woods.

"And I know all of that sounds crazy—sorry, I know you said not to use that word—but it actually makes a lot of sense. I don't remember anything from before my coma, because those aren't my memories in the first place, they're David's. The reason I haven't been able to go back to being the kid I was before the accident is because I *never was* that kid to begin with.

"Everything she's told me so far, it all just... *feels* right. It's the only part of my life that's really felt right since I woke up in a strange hospital in a body I didn't recognize. The way she talks about us, the real us, and our lives on the other side, it just makes sense. It explains everything. And it's why... it's why we have to go back.

"Not just so we can be together, the two of us, as we really are. But so we can be with our children, and our children's children. And so everything else can start making sense again, too. I can really start *living* again, living my real life, a life I know is mine, that I'm not constantly trying to pretend is mine or understand or be the person that other people want me to be.

"That's not me. This isn't me. She knows me. Kirsa knows me. She's the only one who really, truly knows me; even I don't know me, not yet. But I know that she does. So, I have to follow her. And we have to find a way to go back. So... will you help us?"

Dr. Eiding sat stock-still in her chair. Only her mouth moved as it chewed on the end of her pen. Finally, she cleared her throat.

"Help you with what?"

"Help us find a way to travel back. I know it's crazy—sorry again for that—but we got here somehow, so there must be a way to get back. We tried doing it in our sleep, because we know we can communicate that way, but I don't think it's deep or powerful enough to let us fully cross over. Maybe there's something you could do, something you could give us, like the drugs a doctor gives to put someone in a coma manually. That's how Kirsa got here and how she found me, so it's probably the best way for us to get back."

Dr. Eiding cleared her throat again, set the pen and paper down on the desk, and rubbed her thumb in circles between her eyebrows.

"David, I have to stop you again. I'm so sorry."

She looked down at her notes, as if whatever she wanted to say next might be written there on a cue card.

"I can't help you with this, with any of this, if you're asking me to intentionally put you in harm's way. That's something I just can't do."

I shook my head. She must have misunderstood me, or else she'd just glossed over everything without really hearing it for what it was.

"I'm not asking you to harm me; I'm asking you to help me. To help us both get back to where we're meant to be."

She sighed and massaged her forehead.

"Listen... I want to make a few things very clear to you right now, David, and it's important that you hear me out."

She paused to make sure she had my full attention before folding her hands together on top of her notepad.

"When I say I can't help you, I want you to know that it's not because I think you're crazy, or because I don't believe you. I've been in psychiatry all my adult life, almost forty years now, and I've seen and heard pretty much everything under the sun. Moreover, I've been a Christian my entire life, I read the Bible nightly, and I believe with all my heart that science and study can only take us so far, and then the rest is the divine, the miraculous.

"All this is to say that I'm not going to sit here, judge you, and tell you that it's impossible for two people to communicate with one another in their sleep.

I'm also not about to refute the idea that parallel universes exist, or that you or this girl Kirsa could actually be from one of them. There are smarter people out there than me that have given those ideas more time, thought, and attention.

"So, I'd encourage you to do some research on your own, or visit your local library to see what you might find there. Because I'll admit, it's a little outside my wheelhouse as a mental health practitioner. Which is not to say, again, that I don't believe you. I'm just not the most qualified person to speak on such things, so I'd be remiss in my job if I gave you false information or bad advice.

"What I can give you is, as always, an open ear and an open mind. That includes a promise to never judge you, call you crazy, or violate your trust by divulging anything you choose to share with me during our talks.

"There is one big caveat to that last part, though, which is that I am legally and morally obligated to intercede if I believe you pose a threat to either yourself or to someone else. That's important to understand, and it's why I can't in good conscience entertain talk about ingesting any substances that could harm you or harm another individual. Does that make sense?"

Her explanation was detailed and surely well-intentioned. Every bit of it made sense, and I understood exactly where she was coming from.

Unfortunately, I also understood that she wasn't going to help me; at least, not the way I wanted her to. We could sit up here in her office and talk about my interactions with Kirsa all day, but if she wasn't going to give me the drugs we needed to go comatose, then what was the point? She was right; I was better off checking out a library to find more information there.

"It does. I understand."

It was hard to mask the tremendous disappointment I felt. Suddenly, I didn't want to be here anymore, shut up in a hot little room with someone I knew couldn't help me, couldn't *really* help me get what I want. The longer I stayed up here, the more time I was wasting, time I could be using to figure out another way to be with Kirsa.

"Dr. Eiding, is it okay if we end our session right there for today? It's just... it's a lot to process. I'd appreciate having some time to think it all over before I see you again on Monday."

She looked surprised by something I said.

"Am I seeing you again on Monday? I thought we were switching to once a week on Saturdays with you going back to school."

I stared back at her blankly.

"What?"

"Isn't that the plan? Of course, I'm happy to still see you on Monday night, if you'd like. We can set something special up like we did today. I'll just need to check my schedule first."

She smiled warmly and pulled out her planner from a drawer in the desk.

"Would you like me to see what I have open, or do you want to maybe talk with your parents first and then give me a call? What do you think?"

The shock was quickly surpassed by anger as I fully considered what she'd casually revealed to me. I couldn't believe it. How could they possibly do this to me? How could they make a decision this significant without so much as even asking my opinion on it first? It was completely unfair, and it invalidated everything they'd always said about not rushing my recovery or forcing me to do anything I wasn't ready for.

"David?"

I forgot where I was for a second, I was so wrapped up in the seething sense of betrayal. The psychiatrist still waited patiently for an answer.

"I'll talk to them, to my parents, first, and then we'll call."

The room was spinning. I needed to get up off the chair before I passed out. Jerkily, I stood up and started to stagger over toward the door.

"David—"

"*What?*"

I didn't intend to snap at the kindly psychiatrist like that, and right away, I felt a little guilty for exploding. But I couldn't help it. I felt like a caged animal, like a dog backed into a corner. Really, my animosity was meant for my mother and father, but I also didn't appreciate being detained like this, especially since there was nothing Dr. Eiding could do for me anymore.

If she was surprised or hurt by my outburst, she hid it well. Calmly, she pushed her chair back and stood up from her desk, and her tone was still as pleasant and polite as it always was.

"I know it must feel sometimes like you're alone in this, like no one else really understands what you're going through, what you've been through, and where you want to be headed. But let me fill you in on a little secret that only us old folks know: *everybody else feels the exact same way.* It's part of what makes us human, and it's honestly the main reason why my job exists in the first place. I've had the pleasure and privilege of getting to know hundreds of different people over the course of my lifetime, and every single one of them—myself included, for that matter—has had the same struggle. Sure, it comes and goes, and some are luckier than others.

"But let me tell you something now, David: you're one of the lucky ones. It might not feel like it now, but I promise you: one day, many, many years from now, you're going to look back and realize just how lucky you were to have parents who love and care for you, to have friends who stuck with you through thick and thin, and to have been blessed with a healthy body, mind, heart, and spirit, all of which are uniquely yours and no one else's.

"Sure, you've had more than your fair share of hardship. But I'd strongly urge you not to give up or despair. Don't get angry with the world, with yourself, or with the people that love you. And, most importantly, I'd urge you not to do anything rash or impulsive; at least not without truly considering all the ramifications of your actions.

"I could be wrong, but I'm pretty sure we all only have one life to live. And you've got a great one ahead of you, David. Please don't lose sight of the fact that you've been given a rare second chance at all the infinite, brilliant possibilities that this life of yours has in store."

It was hard to ignore the immediate impact her speech had on me, both mentally and emotionally. I was still upset with my parents, but the uncontrollable rage I'd felt mere moments ago was contained more or less to a simmering boil now.

And from a mental standpoint, she'd put forth a compelling counterargument to totally discarding this life without at least considering what it had to offer.

"Can I walk you out?"

The woman's hospitality was endless, and it made me all the sorrier for lashing out at her. I nodded and gave her a half-appreciative, half-apologetic smile, and together we went down the stairs and back to her living room.

My mother wasn't expecting to see us so soon, but Dr. Eiding covered for me beautifully. Without missing a beat, she explained that we'd both agreed I needed a little more time to sort things out on my own before we started plumbing the depths of my newfound memories together.

As if that weren't already enough, she waved my mother's purse away and insisted that this session was 'on the house' because of how short it was. She refused to argue over her decision, and when it was finally clear that her stubbornness would win out, she bid us both goodbye and reminded me to call if I really needed her again.

The whole time, too, she kept insisting she'd see me again soon, and then she waved as we got in our car and drove away.

I let my mother ask all of her questions, and dutifully I tried to give her sufficient answers while inwardly I contemplated how best to bring up the subject of my return to school. Seeing how excited she was to learn more about my session didn't make it any easier to confront her.

I had to remember that even if she was being

sweet and supportive right now, she and my father had still secretly betrayed me. When there was finally a lull in her line of questioning and I sensed an opening, I took it.

"You know what the most interesting part of my conversation with Dr. Eiding was?"

My mother glanced over at me before returning her eyes to the road.

"What?"

"When she told me that we wouldn't be meeting on Monday because I'm going back to school. That was news to me."

I watched the blood drain slowly from her face and the muscles in her cheeks tighten. She didn't dare look over at me now, but after several seconds of uncomfortable silence, she managed to find her voice again.

"It's not set in stone, Davey; it's just something that came up naturally in conversation a week or so ago. We were talking to Dr. Eiding about how well you've been doing and how your doctors think you're ready for the next step, and she just asked us if that next step was school. I asked if she thought that was a good idea, and she said yes.

"So, yes, it's something Dad and I have talked about. But obviously, it depends most of all on you, and whether or not you think you're ready to go back. No one's going to force you before you're ready."

She turned a dial on the instrument panel to lower the heat.

"The plan was to talk about it at dinner tonight as a family. We wanted to discuss it while we're all together, which I'd still like to do, if you're open to it.

Again, I'm sorry if all this caught you off guard. Nothing is set in stone, and Dad and I aren't going to make you do anything you're not ready for."

The rest of the car ride home passed in relative quiet as each of us sat alone with our thoughts. She turned to ask me if I was upset with her at one point, and I shook my head no.

Truthfully, I hadn't made up my mind whether I was still angry or not. I could understand where my parents were coming from, and their intentions were noble enough.

Also, I believed her when she said she just wanted what was best for me. Maybe it was even kind of flattering that she and my father thought I was ready. So, too, did my physical and mental therapists. They all thought I was fit and capable enough to return to school.

It still stung that they'd had those discussions without me, but I supposed it wasn't completely unheard of for parents to have private conversations with their child's doctors, even if I was closer to being an adult than a child.

Chapter Twenty-Four

By the time my father came home from work later that evening, I'd spent most of my Saturday either sleeping or daydreaming about my future. Kirsa and I had been out late—and of course, we'd also been woken up early—so I wasn't surprised when the fatigue came on strong and I finally surrendered to a nap in my bedroom.

Several times, I'd woken up and wondered whether I'd just been dreaming; and, if so, I wondered if Kirsa had been there in the dream somewhere, too, waiting to connect with me and pull me through to the other side of the universe.

If she was, it never worked. Because sure enough, I'd wake up again, alone in the same room I fell asleep in, and none the wiser.

This process went on for some time, drifting in and out of consciousness, hoping all along that somehow I'd find her, or at least find some guidance on what I needed to do next.

Dinner with my parents only further muddled my thinking. My father must have been warned ahead of time that I was on to them. His attitude toward me was overly friendly and enthusiastic, as if he was trying above all else to put me at ease and let me know we were all on the same team. Multiple times, he referenced how much stronger and healthier I looked, and both my parents marveled at my 'increased appetite' and 'heightened mental dexterity'.

Of course, I felt pretty much the same as I always had. But then I remembered that as far as they knew, I had recently experienced a major memory breakthrough. I probably needed to play that part up a bit, especially if I wanted to maintain any hopes of somehow seeing Kirsa again.

Predictably, she was at the epicenter of most of our dinner conversation. My father alternated wolfing down mouthfuls of spaghetti and asking me questions about 'Jessica' and why she, of all people, was so instrumental in my recent discoveries and revelations.

Conspicuously absent from all conversation was any mention of the fact that she'd spent the previous night sleeping in my bed with me. I kept expecting the topic to come up, and I'd prepared myself for it as best I could.

But thankfully, it never came. Maybe my parents were too scared to bring it up or to chastise me on it, for fear they'd only alienate me further, especially since I'd just learned about their school plan.

By the time we finished eating, I was exhausted again from making up so many stories about my memory floodgates opening and the leaps of progress I'd made in my recovery. It was careful, conscientious work, selling the idea to my parents while making sure I never contradicted myself at the same time. I talked about my breakthroughs so much that after a while, even I began to believe them.

Honestly, I also couldn't deny the satisfaction it gave me to see my parents' reactions up close, and to watch how unabashedly proud and ebullient they were to hear my good news. At one point toward the end of the meal, I looked over at my father just in time to see him wipe the corner of his eye with his napkin. Maybe he was embarrassed that I'd seen him, but more than anything, he just looked so incandescently *happy*—happy, and thankful that at long last, his son was coming back to him.

The stories I told might have been fake, but my parents' reactions to them were all too real. Soon, I felt guilty carrying on with the ruse. No matter what our real relationships to each other were, they didn't deserve this kind of false hope.

To make myself feel better, I decided to change the subject and take the conversation to the uncomfortable terrain we'd all been avoiding since we first sat down at the table.

"So. Am I going back to school on Monday or not?"

As much as we all knew this part of the night was coming, it didn't make it any easier to bring it up. My parents glanced at each other, perhaps wondering who would take lead on their argument.

After a long swig of his light beer, my father abruptly pushed his chair back from the table and stood up.

"You know what? Let's go for a drive." He clapped his hands together with excitement and smiled across the table at me. "You up for that, David?"

I was fairly taken aback. For her part, my mother looked just as surprised as I was, like she had no idea either where he was going with this. Evidently, a post-supper drive had not been part of their plans.

My father sauntered over to retrieve a set of car keys from the kitchen countertop, and when he returned, he had his jacket on and was carrying mine under his other arm. He looped around behind my mother's chair and placed his hands on her shoulders.

"You don't mind, do you, Ellen? I promise we'll be quick."

Still in a daze, she barely shook her head, and he took it as permission to leave. My father kissed her on the cheek, tossed me my coat, and started walking toward the front door and the driveway.

"Come on, David. Let's talk in the car."

I'd learned to appreciate these random flights of fancy my father was given to from time to time. My mother had made the comment to me before in private that she thought they kept him young. She also admitted she found his impulsiveness highly attractive, and that it was one of the many reasons she'd fallen in love with him when they first started dating.

There was nothing for me to do except put the jacket on and follow him outside. I gave my mother a little shrug as I excused myself from the dinner table. She shrugged back, further confirming that my father had ventured off-script. I buttoned up my coat and walked out of the house, closing the front door behind me.

When I turned and started heading for the driveway, I saw my father waiting next to Mitsu... except he was standing on the wrong side.

I froze in my tracks, utterly confused, but reached up just in time to catch the silver keys he gently tossed through the air to me.

"Mitsu's your car. How about you drive?"

He didn't wait for me to answer, popping open the passenger door and stepping inside.

Now, this... *this* was completely unexpected. Of all the ways the conversation and the night might have gone, this was definitely nowhere near anything I'd anticipated happening. Never before had either one of my parents suggested that I drive this car, or any other car. The last time I'd been behind the wheel, I knew and they knew, was the night of 'the accident'.

Suddenly, the impact of the moment hit me, and I realized the seriousness of what my father was doing. I turned to look back at the house, wondering if my mother was watching us, and if so, what she'd think of what was occurring. There was no way she'd approve of this particular whim of my father's. It was too dangerous, and too much, too soon, I was sure of it. Going back to school was one thing. But driving the same car that put me in a coma?

Timidly, I opened the driver's side door and lowered my frame into the seat, still very unsure of the situation.

Maybe it was all just a test, some sort of bizarre simulation my father had dreamt up to gauge my confidence at this point in my recovery. Perhaps he just wanted to see if I actually thought myself capable of driving again, and whether or not I put the keys in the ignition would determine if I passed or failed. Maybe it was his way of assessing for himself whether anything I'd said at dinner was true.

We sat there inside the car long enough for the cabin lights to fade to black. My father shivered a bit and gestured toward my seatbelt.

"Well, buckle up and let's get going. It's too cold to just sit here without the heater on."

"Where are we going?"

He blew warm air into his cupped palms and rubbed them together.

"I don't know. Wherever you want to go. It's your car."

He clicked his own seatbelt into place.

"I don't have to be back at work until Tuesday, since I worked today, and you may or may not be going to school Monday, so we've got plenty of time if you want to take a little road trip."

I whipped my head over to see if he was serious.

He seemed like he was. His expression was outwardly hardened and stern, with just a glint of mischief in his eyes. Then, he relaxed and looked back out through the windshield with a grin.

"Or, maybe we can just take it around the block for starters. Probably don't want Mom to worry, and I don't feel like sleeping on the couch tonight, anyway."

It was a relief knowing that he was only kidding around with me about the road trip. I began to think that maybe this whole episode was a joke, and maybe he didn't expect me to drive anywhere at all. But then he nodded toward the ignition.

"Start 'er up, son."

"I—I don't know how…"

"Yes, you do." It was a statement of fact, not an argument. "I know you do." His tone became gentler. "It's just like riding a bike; it'll come right back to you."

Except I wasn't sure if I knew how to ride a bike, either.

I'd been in the car enough times with my parents to remember what they did to start it up at least, so nervously I put the key in the ignition hole and turned it to the right. The engine roared to life, and my father immediately reached forward to turn the heat on.

"Now, put it in reverse and back down the driveway. Use your rear-view mirror and take it nice and slow. But don't be afraid to give it a little gas, and remember: your brake is always right there if you need it."

My palms were sweating as I did my best to follow his instructions, working my feet and hands in concert to put the car in motion. It helped to reflect back on what I'd seen my parents do while driving, and I erred on the side of extreme caution, braking frequently and sometimes jerking the car to a complete stop if I ever felt we were going too fast. I kept the speed low, much lower than I knew I needed to even in our residential neighborhood, and tightened my grip on the wheel any time we passed by other cars parked along the sides of the street.

Thankfully, it was late enough already that we rarely saw another moving car, and when we did, my father was quick to reassure me that I had everything under control. We'd pass one another safely in silence, even as I held my breath.

Amazingly, the more I did it, the more natural the driving became. As I grew more comfortable behind the wheel, I eased up on the brake and even allowed my speed to pick up a bit as we glided down some of the longer streets that had fewer cars parked along the edges.

My father had been remarkably calm and hands-off

from the very beginning, but as we continued to drive around and my confidence ballooned, he relaxed his guidance even further, until finally, he just sat back and let me do it on my own.

As focused and intentioned as I was on my driving, my brain was buzzing as it tried to process the meaning behind all that was happening. Sure, it was positively exhilarating to be driving a car. But it was also incredibly confusing. Was this knowledge coming back to me because I'd driven many times before as David, or as Daniel?

Kirsa had never mentioned cars or driving while describing our alternate universe, though that didn't necessarily mean they didn't exist there, too. From the limited conversations we'd had together, she'd always painted a picture of a world that felt very similar to this one, so it wasn't out of the question that I'd know how to drive in both realities.

But what if I didn't know in the other world, in her world? Would that mean she was wrong, that she was making all this up and that she was actually crazy, and I was crazy for believing her? Was this proof somehow that maybe I really was David Abbott after all, and that everything my parents and my doctors said about me was true?

Maybe they were right; maybe it would just take time, energy, and effort on my part to fully rediscover my identity as it was before the accident. Perhaps it was perfectly natural for me to feel as lost and disconnected as I felt. Not because I was living someone else's life, but because I'd suffered a major brain injury and had been in a coma for two months.

And yet, the one thing I kept coming back to was

her: Kirsa. I could explain everything else if I tried hard enough, but how could I explain the way I felt about her, and about how she'd magically appeared out of thin air in my life and then instantly become the most important part of it?

How could I explain the inexplicable miracles she'd already involved me in? Or what about the connection I felt, not just with her, but also with a world that I knew even less about than the one I currently inhabited?

There was no rational explanation for any of that.

"David…"

I'd been swimming in my own thoughts so long I'd completely forgotten where I was, what I was doing, and who I was with. The car was idling at a stop sign, so I spun the steering wheel slowly to the right and turned us onto a new road.

In the white glow of the headlights, I recognized a few houses that looked familiar to me, and suddenly, I realized we were back on our own street.

"Pull over here to the side real quick. I want to talk to you before we get home."

Gently, I nosed the car up along the curb. We were maybe six houses down from our own. I wasn't sure whether he wanted me to turn the ignition off or not, so I just sat back in my seat after I put the gear lever in park and awaited further instruction.

My father combed a hand through his beard and looked over at me. For the first time all night, he seemed a little nervous and unsure of himself.

"Listen. I'd be lying if I said I don't want you to go back to school on Monday. And it's not because I'm trying to rush your recovery, or because of college or your future, or because I want you out of the house. Far from it. Nothing would make me happier than to have you with us here at home, forever."

He fidgeted in his seat uncomfortably.

"I have a confession to make, and I'm not proud of it. But you're old enough and mature enough to understand it, I think. Or, I hope, at least.

"When we got the call about your accident, and then found out about the coma, that was the worst thing I possibly could have imagined happening as a parent, outside of you getting killed or dying from your injuries, of course. Having to come to grips with the very real possibility that you might never wake up, that you'd maybe spend the rest of your life like that, it's just something you can't really fathom or accept, even when it's real, and it's actually happening to you."

He gave me a sad smile.

"And then, when you woke up, against all the odds and everything the doctors said, that was unbelievable. It was a miracle, one hundred percent, and truly right up there with marrying your mom and the day you were born as one of the most blissful moments of my life. I think you know all that.

"But what you don't know, and what I'm ashamed to say out loud right now, is that as happy and as grateful as I am to have you back again, there's a little part of me—an ugly, evil, selfish part of me—that's sad. And it's sad because I know that I'm not going to be able to keep you now, as much as I want to, as much as Mom and I want to keep you here with us safe and sound at home.

"Life in a coma, frozen like that, isn't a real life at all. But you would have been here with us, and we could have held onto you and taken care of you, and we'd never have to let you go if we didn't want to.

"I'm not saying it would have been right for you or for us, but it would have been a possibility. And it disgusts me to hear myself say that out loud, and I hope you can forgive me for even thinking something like that.

"It just hurts; it hurts so bad to imagine what it'll be like when you go off to school somewhere. To imagine what it'll be like, coming home from work and you're not here every night, doing your homework, or eating dinner with us, or practicing your trumpet upstairs in your room. I still see you as a boy, running through sprinklers in the backyard, calling out for me in the middle of the night if you have a bad dream or need me to put rubbing alcohol on your achy legs.

"I know it's all a part of life, growing up. And from the moment you have a kid, from the first moment you were born, and I laid eyes on you, there was a clock ticking. I knew there'd be a time when you didn't need me to tuck you in at night anymore, or pack your lunches in the morning for school, or teach you—for the second time now—how to drive a car. Yes, I knew all that, but it still doesn't make any of it any easier when it actually happens to you."

This time, he made no effort to conceal the fact that he was crying.

"If I had it my way, buddy, you'd stay at home with us forever. But I know that's not what's best for you. And just like it would have been selfish of me to keep you on life support forever if you never woke up from your coma, it would be selfish of me now not to speak my mind and tell you just how ready I think you are. For school Monday, sure, if *you* think you're ready for it. But also for everything else that comes with being an adult."

He wiped away some tears, sniffled his nose, and pointed at the steering wheel.

"I mean, just look at you. You're out here driving again already. Your memories are coming back. Next thing I know, you're going to be growing a beard, majoring in astrobiology or something crazy, and telling me I'm going to be a grandfather—*after* you and Jessica get married, that is."

He was laughing more than crying by the time he was finished.

I had to smile a bit myself as I tried to imagine what I'd look like with a beard. And even though I had no idea what astrobiology was, I still understood the meaning behind everything he was saying and appreciated it all the same.

"We should get back before your mom calls the cops. I guarantee you I'm going to be in enough trouble as it is."

He was partially right, as his wife was absolutely aghast when the car pulled up in the driveway and I was the one who stepped out on the driver's side.

But as shocked and initially angry as she was at the risk we'd both taken without her knowledge or consent, those feelings quickly gave way to curiosity and then excitement. Just as my father had eagerly grilled me for details during dinner, my mother now wanted to know every single thing she'd missed out on during our drive. I did my best to satisfy her, recounting the nervous thrills of the whole process from start to finish.

Out of respect for my father, I elected to leave out everything he said to me at the end of our little excursion. Surely, she knew how he felt anyway. But it still just didn't feel right for me to repeat everything he'd said to me in confidence.

Collectively, we agreed to postpone any further talk of my education until the morning. Both of my parents thought 'sleeping on it' sounded like a good idea.

I wasn't so sure. In my mind, I stood as good a chance of waking up a different person in another universe as I did of finding any clarity on my school decision.

I laid awake in bed a long time, staring up through the darkness at the ceiling, wondering what was real and what was not, and wondering just what exactly I was supposed to do about any of it.

More than anything else, I wondered why this couldn't have all been easier. If I'd woken up in a miserable life with wretched parents and no discernible future, or alone and in pain in some horrific world I despised, then leaving it all behind to follow Kirsa into the unknown would have been simple.

Similarly, if I'd never stumbled upon her that day in the forest, sat outside with her after dinner on her parents' porch, followed her up to Ayeli Rock, and then invited her to spend the night with me, maybe I'd already be back at school, catching up on what I'd missed, preparing for college, hanging out with friends, and basically picking up the pieces of my life where I left off. And I'd have no concept of what I might be missing out on, because I'd have no concept of any other life but my own, and no concept of Kirsa *or* of

Jessica Silverton.

Was that what I really wanted though?

It absolutely would have been easier. But now that I knew what it felt like to be around her, to talk to her, to listen to her, to touch her or be touched by her, or even just to sit in silence with her, could I imagine what my life would be like without any of that? Without *her*?

If I chose to obey Jim Silverton and to move forward without Kirsa, to truly commit myself entirely to living *this* life as David Abbott, would I regret it? Would I always wonder what might have been? Or, would I get over it in time, moving on to other things, other people, and perhaps even other love?

Chapter Twenty-Five

———⟨⟩———

Morning came before I realized I'd even fallen asleep.

The sunrise peeking in my bedroom window dashed any hopes I'd held onto that maybe this time she'd find me in my sleep, explain everything so it all finally made perfect sense, and lead me back to an idyllic world where I could have everything: her, my parents, my children, my grandchildren, my youth, my wisdom, my future, my past, and my present. My life as Daniel and my life as David, all without sacrificing anything or being asked to make a choice.

It was a fairytale thought, and it was impossible—though if anyone was capable of proving the impossible possible, it was Kirsa.

But she hadn't come for me, so it didn't matter. There had been no vivid dreams, no insights or instructions. Not even the familiar voice, the woman's voice that came to me in 'the void' when I needed it most.

None of it had happened, so now there was nothing else to do but get up and start the day, and as David, not as Daniel.

And honestly, it got a little easier to do that with

every hour that passed. A glass of cold water and a heaping plate of my father's made-from-scratch blueberry pancakes, drenched in melted butter and maple syrup, was a welcome diversion from my own brain.

When my parents suggested a post-breakfast 'power walk' around the neighborhood to burn off some of the pancake calories, I not only joined them, I found myself relishing the exercise and the brisk air against my skin as I sweat. Maybe it was all in my head, but I could have sworn the trembling in my legs was the smallest it had ever been, and I'd never felt stronger or more confident in my muscles and in my body.

After our walk, we each showered and freshened up, then went into town for a late lunch. Again, I surprised myself with my appetite for food, my appetite for conversation, and even my appetite for change. I boldly ordered a dish I could barely pronounce out loud, and I loved it from the very first bite.

Normally, my parents were responsible for driving the conversation during meals, but today, I just couldn't stop talking. Mostly, I asked questions about Lenoir, about my high school, and about my father's job and the building he worked in every day.

After we finished eating and paid the check, he asked me if I had any interest in seeing his office for myself, since we were already downtown.

It was as if he'd offered to take a child to a candy store. I followed him like a shadow up and down the hallways of the building, pestering him with questions about anything and everything we came across.

It was Sunday, so the offices were all empty, but

that just made it even more fun for me somehow. Wandering around a strange new environment and seeing it completely uninhabited, my imagination went wild, conjuring up images of the coworkers he described and the various tasks they went about over the course of a work week.

My mother trailed close behind, giggling at the jokes my father randomly worked into the information he shared with me. Clearly, she had a keen sense of the people he worked with and the jobs they all maintained, and I enjoyed her reactions to his running commentary as much as I enjoyed the commentary itself.

It was her idea to visit my school next. She warned me ahead of time that we might not be able to get in—similar to my father's work, school wasn't in session on Sunday—but we still were able to see a lot of the property just from walking around outside. They gave me a tour around the exterior of the building, stopping now and then to cup their hands against darkened windows and encouraging me to look inside.

Here was my old chemistry classroom; I'd liked that teacher, Mrs. Vayner, because she had a unique way of conveying her passion to her students.

And here was the band hall, a large cavern of a room with many chairs and instruments. I spent tons and tons of time in there, both in class and after school during practice. Before my accident, I was 'first chair', which meant I got to sit at the head of the row of trumpet players; a real honor, apparently, and something they were both very proud of me for.

There, of course, was the football field where our marching band practiced and where we performed during halftime for all the home games.

The sun was a goldenrod color and hung low in the sky when we finally started meandering our way back to the car. I wasn't sure exactly how much time we'd spent at West Caldwell High School, but my parents had given me as thorough of a tour as they possibly could have without actually having access inside.

While nothing they said triggered any flashbacks or uncovered any buried memories, it was still fascinating to hear them both describe in detail my history as a WCHS student, as well as their own history as WCHS parents.

Year by year, they recounted my progression up until the accident, at which point, they abruptly turned around in time and started to work backward, regaling me with stories from my middle school and elementary school days as we drove back home.

We prepared dinner as a family—my father, as the self-pronounced head chef and 'culinary mastermind', doled out cooking tasks accordingly—and continued the reminiscing as we worked, as we ate, and then afterward as we washed dishes and cleaned up.

When we were done, we moved into the living room. My father lit a fire in the fireplace for us and then went back into the kitchen to pour a glass of port for his wife. On the couch, my mother and I got comfortable beneath a shared blanket and waited for my father to return before picking back up with our conversation.

She finished telling a story she'd started while we were loading the dishwasher: a humorous one that involved me as a five-year-old playing and being tossed around in a public pool with my uncle, her brother.

The climax of the story hinged on the fact that, unbeknownst to my uncle, I'd eaten too much pizza before swimming and had something of an upset stomach, which, of course, translated to me projectile-vomiting all over him and some of the other unfortunate kids and adults who'd been nearby at the time.

I let the story come to a close and waited for the laughter to subside before announcing the decision I'd already made several hours prior.

"I think I want to go to school tomorrow."

There was a moment or two of silence as they both regarded me. My father smiled slightly from his armchair, and my mother put a hand on top of my knee.

"Really?"

She sounded both hopeful and surprised.

"You sure it's what you want to do?"

I rested my hand on top of hers.

"I think I'm ready. At least, I can give it a try."

"That's all anybody can ask for. Give it a shot, and if it doesn't feel right, or it feels like it's too soon, you don't have to go back again until you're ready."

My father leaned forward in his chair and rested his elbows on his knees.

"Mom's right. We can go in early, all of us, if you're okay with it, just to talk to the counselor and explain where you're at. Let her know that you're trying it out and easing back into things. And if, like Mom said, it gets too overwhelming or too stressful at any point, you can call home, and we'll come pick you up right away."

It was as if I'd inadvertently created a friendly competition between my parents to see which of them could put me more at ease. Now, it was my mother's turn again.

"Don't worry about the time you've missed, either. Make-up schoolwork, essays, tests, SAT prep, all of that can come in time. Tomorrow's just about getting your feet wet again. Seeing your teachers, catching up with your friends, reacquainting with that whole environment. That's what tomorrow's all about, okay?"

I nodded my understanding and tried not to look intimidated by some of the words she'd rattled off. I knew that essays and tests weren't things to get excited about, and though I was less sure what SAT prep was, it didn't sound like a good thing, either.

My father slapped his knees, stood up, stretched, and yawned loudly.

"Sounds like we've got a big day ahead of us tomorrow, then. I might get up early and get the car washed. Want to make sure you return in style, of course."

He turned to my mother.

"Would you like another glass before I go?"

She rolled her eyes at him and stood up herself.

"Because getting the car washed is what's really important. And no, I'm fine, thank you."

She kissed me on the cheek, picked up her empty wine glass, and started to walk off toward the kitchen.

"Davey, I love you, and I'm happy for you, and I promise I'm not still mad about you and your father's secret adventure last night, but I just want to lay the law down now—"

She sent an arrow of a glare at her husband.

"—for *both* of you, that more practice is required behind the wheel before you start driving yourself to school. I just want that to be made perfectly clear now, to avoid any *uncomfortable confusion* later on down the road."

Even as she disappeared into the kitchen, it was obvious who she was really talking to. My father dramatically grimaced and pulled at his shirt collar, winked at me, then reached over and tousled my hair lightly.

"Proud of you, son. I know it's a big decision. Sleep well and see you in the morning. Love you, pal."

He turned a metal knob at the side of the fireplace and ascended the stairs. Left alone momentarily, I watched, mesmerized, as the fire died down behind the glass until there was nothing left but a tiny blue flame in the corner under the brown-black logs.

"You going to bed, too?"

My mother broke the spell. I turned to see her standing at the foot of the stairs waiting for me.

"Can't sleep in tomorrow, so you shouldn't stay up too late."

I folded the blanket up into a neat pile on the cushion beside me, stood up, and crossed to join her on the stairs.

"No, I'm coming too."

Together, we climbed up the stairwell until we reached my bedroom doorway, where she turned to kiss me goodnight.

"You're going to do great tomorrow, I know it. Sleep well, Davey. I love you so, so much."

She gave me one last hug then slipped into her bedroom and quietly shut the door behind her. I could already hear the faint sound of my father snoring from inside the other room, and I marveled at how quickly the man could fall asleep when he wanted to.

Frankly, it was a trait I wish he would have passed down to me. Because for the second straight night, I found myself tossing and turning, unable to slip away into sleep with all the whirring of my mind.

A lot of the thoughts centered around the day's events: revisiting moments, locations, feelings, and memories in the infinite blank space behind my eyelids. It was also difficult to relax with the steady rise of anxiety gurgling up inside my chest. I figured it must have been a direct result of the growing insecurity I felt concerning my return to school.

When and if I did fall asleep, I found myself thrust into spiraling nightmares I couldn't control. Some were populated with hostile classmates who either criticized or outright ignored me. Others featured looming teachers who asked questions in a language I couldn't comprehend and then punished me when I couldn't answer them.

The worst of all were the visions I found myself completely alone in, running or falling down endless labyrinthine corridors without any hope of escape, abandoned by my parents, abandoned by everyone.

Something else was there, too, though. I could hear it scratching its claws on the glass around me.

Fear set in as I spun wildly in every direction, and the blurred maze walls of the school spun with me, obscuring whatever new threat approached. It was getting louder and louder, till the scratching was more like violent pounding on the sides of my skull, pummeling the soft matter of my brain into a fine grey sawdust of blood and bone.

My eyes opened, and in rushed the night all at once.

To my horror, I heard the sound again; only this time, I knew that it was real. Steady, awful beating came against the darkened glass of my windowpane.

As much as I didn't want to, I had to look. And even in the pitch-black, I saw a clear outline of some shadowy mass pressed up against the window. Whatever it was saw me seeing it, and the sound started up again outside: measured, incessant knocking that wouldn't go away.

If it kept up like this, it would only be a matter of time until my parents heard it, too, and came in to investigate. And while having the extra backup would be great if the strange form proved to be a monster or an intruder, I was beginning to mull another possible explanation for its identity. If I was right, the last thing I needed was for my parents to wake up.

Without any further hesitation, I gathered up my courage, got out of bed, and walked over to the window.

The face I saw on the other side confirmed my suspicions. There, crouched between a crooked tree branch and the sloping shingled roof of our house, was Kirsa, her pale white face framed between two small hands pressed up against the glass.

Chapter Twenty-Six

As quietly as I could, I unlatched the window at the bottom and slid it up and open until it was wide enough for her to crawl through. Once she was fully inside, I carefully closed it behind her, turned, and found myself immediately enveloped within her arms.

"I've missed you." She breathed the words into my ear as she planted quick kisses all over my cheek and throat. "Where have you been?"

Her very presence was like a jolt of electricity fired through my nervous system. The hairs on the back of my neck stood on end as waves of pleasure rippled up and down my spine. She was intoxicating and invigorating; I had to keep my wits about me and keep both of us in check, or we'd be discovered instantly.

"What do you mean?"

I hoped she might take a cue from my concerted effort to whisper and pick up on the fact that we needed to be quiet if we didn't want to wake my parents. Admittedly, however, she'd shown little concern in the past for anything, or anyone, besides the two of us.

She did understand me now, though, and her voice became hushed, though no less intense or passionate.

"I've been looking for you in my dreams, but I couldn't find you. I had to break out so I could come here and see you myself, like this."

"I haven't been able to find you, either."

It was true, but I still felt guilty for some reason. The thought of her all alone, locked away in some room in the Silvertons' house, desperately willing herself to fall asleep so she could try again to make contact with me; and all the while, unbeknownst to her, I was out and about seeing the town and making plans for a future that maybe wasn't mine to plan for.

All of it made me feel ashamed, and I wondered if it was possible that she knew or suspected some of what had happened. After all, she'd already proven she could access my mind if she really wanted to.

"Did you see your doctor?"

I stared blankly back at her.

"What doctor?"

Even in the dark, I noticed her expression change subtly. There was a growing level of alarm there, maybe even suspicion.

"The one you said you'd see yesterday. The one who could give us the drugs."

It felt like it'd been ages since my impromptu session with Dr. Eiding. Now I remembered. Before her parents dragged her away, I'd promised Kirsa I would ask the therapist to help us procure the medication we needed to induce a shared coma.

And Dr. Eiding, of course, had summarily denied my request on the grounds of morality, before sending me off with a rousing speech on why I had a great life and a promising future ahead of me, as well as a warning that I'd regret it if I threw those things away.

Could I share any of that with Kirsa, though?

"She... she said she can't do it. She's not allowed to."

"Not allowed to what?"

"She's not allowed to give us anything that could cause self-harm."

"But did you tell her everything, though? Did you tell her that we're not really these people, so we wouldn't really be hurting ourselves? That we'd only be doing it so we could go back to our real lives and our real selves?"

"I told her all that, yes."

"And, what? She didn't believe you?"

"No, she said she believed me. It just... it's still not enough reason for her to do it. Even if she wanted to, I don't think she could. She's probably not the right kind of doctor anyway."

Kirsa may have lowered her voice, but the emotion in it was higher than before.

"So, what do we do now? Getting back together in our dreams isn't working. Do you have another doctor you see who you could ask? Or is there some place you could buy the drugs, maybe?"

I shook my head.

"I think it would just be more of the same, because honestly, I don't know if any doctor is going to understand. Dr. Eiding's the only one I think would believe me in the first place, and she immediately said she wouldn't do it. And I don't know anything about what we would need to do it ourselves, or where we'd find any of it."

"Then we have to try option three. It's the only other way."

321

The air in the room suddenly felt very still and heavy. Whatever currents of electric energy passed between us came to a freezing halt as I swallowed the implication of what she suggested.

"You mean… kill ourselves?"

Just saying it out loud tied my stomach up in knots.

Kirsa stayed gentle but firm.

"Don't think of it that way. These aren't 'ourselves', remember? So, we wouldn't be killing ourselves at all. We'd just be setting ourselves free, so we could return to our actual bodies and our actual lives."

"But what about these bodies and these lives? If we destroyed them, what would happen to their lost souls, wherever they are out there? They wouldn't be able to come back then, right?"

Kirsa thought for a second before answering.

"I don't know." She lifted her shoulders and let out a long sigh. "I honestly don't know enough about how all this works, but I guess that makes sense."

Again, she paused for a couple seconds.

"I don't know where they are, or if they're coming back, or if we do this, if that means they can't come back. And I don't even know for sure that doing this will get us back. I just think that we should try. Everything we know so far about how we moved between these realms, it all revolves around separating consciousness from the body.

"You had a stroke and then a coma; this boy had a car accident and then a coma. I was artificially put into a coma; and this girl, for all we know, she was already dead when you found her, drowned or frozen to death. So, how do we know that death is lasting, or that

322

releasing from these bodies means that no one else can come back to them? I did it once already. The only thing we really know is that our first two plans didn't work, and maybe that's because we need a stronger way to sever the ties that keep us here.

"Daniel, we have two empty bodies waiting for us on the other side, and the longer we stay here, the less time we have with them. That, I know for sure."

She made a convincing argument, even if it wasn't enough to fully persuade me. But something she'd said there at the very end gave rise to a new thought in my mind, a possible alternative that was a whole lot safer and more certain than option three.

And, most importantly, it still allowed us to be together.

"What if we stay?"

Kirsa didn't seem to understand.

"What?"

"What if we stay?"

It was such a simple, beautiful solution, that it actually amazed me I hadn't thought of it earlier. This was the answer to all our problems, the perfect compromise that enabled me to have everything I wanted without the risk of losing anything at all.

"You said it yourself: the longer we stay here, the less time we have there. Think about it. We're both old in the other universe. It sounds like we've lived long, full lives together. But who knows how much time we have left? Especially if I just had a stroke!

"If we stay here, we not only stay together, we stay *young* together. We get the opportunity to spend a whole entire lifetime together again. Isn't that what everybody wants? And we can have it. We don't have to do anything, either, because the hard part's done already. You did it when you found me."

My imagination took another massive quantum leap.

"Kirsa... do you realize, *we could do this forever.* We could live forever essentially, the two of us, moving from body to body, life to life, world to world, forever, if we wanted to. And we wouldn't be stealing anyone else's life; we'd only do it with kids who are already gone, like Jessica. We could have a whole second life together as Daniel and Kirsa *through* David and Jessica.

"And when we're older, we could learn more and practice more, and prepare ourselves to one day do it all over again. You said you've done this before and that you searched through all these galaxies and worlds before you found me here, so you could teach me how to do it. We could do it together, and live forever that way.

"And think, just think about everything we could learn along the way with all that time, all that knowledge and adventure and experience. All the places we could visit in the world, maybe even other worlds, alien worlds, or places beyond our own dimensions. We'd be masters of space and time, proprietors of our own existence, and we'd have each other every step of the way. We'd never have to stop, and why would we ever want to?"

Kirsa regarded me carefully, deliberately, in deep silence before responding.

"Because Rosemary, Jacqueline, Martin, and Ivy. Because Isabelle and because Shara. Because Robert, John, Jeanette, Mike, Lily, and Kenneth. Because they're your family. They're our family; our real family.

Because they love us, and they're still waiting for us to come back. Because as scary as death is, without it, I'm not sure that life has the same meaning. And, frankly, because I'm not convinced we *can* do this forever, even if we wanted to, which I don't."

She took both my hands in hers.

"Finding you was the hardest thing I've ever had to do. Finding our way back together might be even harder. But we have to try."

"What if it doesn't work? What if we do it and we end up somewhere else again, somewhere wrong; and what if we're not together?"

"Then I'll find you again."

"Or what if we do it and that's it? What if we die, like actually die, and end up in the afterlife?"

Her confidence was unshakeable.

"Then at least we'll have each other, and at least we'll know we died trying to get back to the people that love us."

"But what if we die and that's that? There's no afterlife, no continued consciousness, just nothing. What then?"

She smiled mysteriously.

"I don't think that's what will happen, and I know you don't really think that, either. But I suppose it's just a risk you have to be willing to take. I am. Are you?"

"I'm not sure."

It was how I truly felt. But as soon as I said it out loud, I wished I hadn't.

Her smile faded away like the last bit of sunlight vanishing below the horizon, and for the first real time that I could remember, Kirsa looked afraid.

Throughout everything, all the physical, mental,

and emotional duress, she had maintained that indefatigable spirit of hopefulness. Bright, optimistic, almost childlike at times.

Now, all of a sudden, there were worry lines drawn along the cracks and crevices of her face, and in the dusky space of night between us, she finally looked a bit like a tired, troubled old woman.

"Well, I hope you decide soon, Daniel. I've been with you every step of the way for nearly sixty years now. But I don't think I can come with you this time if you do decide to stay here.

"I risked everything to come find you. Don't get me wrong, I'll risk it all again to bring you back. Because that's what love is. Maybe if it was just you and me still, and I didn't know all that I know now, and have all that I have now… who knows, maybe I'd want to stay here, too. But that's not the way it is, so I know what I have to do. And I know you do, too."

She dug her fingers into her pocket, pulled out a folded piece of paper, and handed it to me.

"As much as I want to stay the night with you, I know you well enough to see when you need to be alone. So, I'll leave you this as a little extra something to think about in the morning when you wake up. For now, though, I suppose… I suppose you should just sleep on everything."

She gave a bitter laugh.

"Maybe this time, one of the kids or the grandkids will be sleeping, too, and you'll have a new visitor in your dreams, and that'll be enough proof for you."

Kirsa moved toward the window and went to open it.

Instinctively, I rushed over and pulled her into a

hug. She responded, hugging me back just as hard. I couldn't see her crying, but I could hear it, and I felt her body quivering against my own as she tried to control it.

My heart split right then and there. I could have said a million different things; I wanted to say a million different things.

But nothing came out. Just silence.

Finally, she broke from the embrace, lifted up the window, and crawled back out into the cold dark night. I stood there shivering as the wind whistled by me, wallowing in my guilt and my shame, and watched her slide without a sound along the roof, down the side of the house, and then completely out of sight.

Long after she was gone, I stood still like a statue in the open window, staring out into the bleak gulf of a future just as murky and unknowable as the past.

I don't remember whether I fell asleep standing up, or if at some point, I toppled over onto my bed or maybe even the floor. But sleep did come at last, although not as I'd hoped it would, with any new answers or indisputable truths.

Instead, sleep came armed with dreams that mocked me and aggrandized my soul's confusion, playing out alternative sequences of events that changed depending on the choices I made in them.

The worst of all was the most realistic one, which picked right back up with Kirsa handing me the folded piece of paper and moving despondently toward the window.

Only this time, in this version, I used words as well as action. I found my tongue in time, and everything I said was right and true and what she needed to hear.

"I don't need proof. This is enough for me. You're enough for me."

I tried to kiss her tears away as fast as she could make them.

"I'm sorry, I'm sorry for saying that before. I didn't mean it. Of course I'm sure. I'm sure of this. I'm sure of us. I know I love you, and that's enough. That's all I need."

My lips found hers, and then we were both crying and kissing and breathing together as one.

"Just tell me what I need to do. Tell me how we're going to do this."

She pulled back slightly and stared at me with wonderment, then laughed.

And she was Kirsa all over again, beautiful and radiant and transcendent and perfect. She was mine and I was hers, and we were going to do this. We were going to find a way back to our family, back to our world, back to our lives... and we were going to do it all together.

Chapter Twenty-Seven

And then, I woke up.

Hovering above my head was a familiar face, but it didn't belong to Kirsa. My mother gently pulled the blankets down from under my chin.

"Davey, honey, it's time to get up."

I groggily scanned the room, though I wasn't exactly what I was looking for.

The window was closed and locked. Nowhere did I see a folded piece of paper in my immediate vicinity— not tangled in my sheets, not crumpled in my pajama pocket, not down on the floor or up on my bookshelf.

I sat up in bed and checked the carpet for muddy footprints, dirt, or any physical sign that she had been there, but there was nothing. It was as if the whole thing hadn't even happened.

A terrifying notion took hold of me: what if that were true? I was almost positive that she had visited me in the night, and that we had carried on a long and serious conversation about what we were going to do.

I was less positive about how that conversation had resolved. Did we end up agreeing on a tangible plan for how to execute option three, or was the situation still unsettled, mired by the doubt and uncertainty that plagued me even now? Had the night ended with passionate kisses and professions of love, or had it ended in turmoil and a solemn hug that maybe meant goodbye?

As was so often the case, there were no concrete boundary lines I could reference to separate facts from fiction and dreams from reality. I was doomed, perhaps eternally, to rely upon a bent and broken mind I neither trusted nor fully understood.

"Dad's got breakfast going downstairs. You want to shower and come down when you're ready?"

Numbly, I mumbled some sort of response and swung my legs over the edge of the bed. She kissed the top of my head and gave me some privacy as I stood up and tried to get my brain and body functioning again.

School. That's what was happening right now; I was supposed to be getting ready for school. After spending the better part of yesterday with my parents, I'd agreed that perhaps I was in fact ready to return to high school. At the very least, I'd been willing to give it a try and see what happened.

Even the hot water and steam from my shower couldn't help me shake off the bleary daze of the night before. I tried to replay the events in my mind, searching for minute details or telltale signs that certain moments had definitively, absolutely, positively occurred... but they simply didn't exist.

After I toweled off and returned to my room to get dressed, I even got down on my hands and knees to scour the carpet for clues that might confirm Kirsa's visit. I searched under my bed, between the sheets and blankets, under my pillows, inside the pillowcases, in between all the books and photographs on my bookshelves.

I even looked in places like my closet, my bathroom, even my parents' bedroom, thinking that perhaps there was some crazy chance I wasn't fully remembering all the action and settings of our encounter.

Everywhere I looked, though, I was disappointed. It was all exactly as it should have been. The only proof I had of our entire interaction was in my head, and I knew that wasn't enough.

It wasn't long before my parents quickly picked up on my mood at the breakfast table. My father served me a couple leftover blueberry pancakes with a side of fresh fruit and a glass of water, took one look at my facial expression, and offered to make me something else or pour me a bowl of Fruit Loops. I reassured him that the breakfast was perfectly fine and started eating, but then it was my mother's turn to chime in.

"Are you okay? We don't have to do this if you're not ready."

I chewed a couple banana slices thoughtfully and swallowed before answering.

"I'm okay."

She didn't appear convinced.

"Sorry. Just tired."

My father laughed as he joined us at the table with his own plate.

"Not used to getting up this early, huh? Welcome to the grind, son. School, work, it's all one big happy party."

I faked a smile in his direction and then focused back on eating. The rest of the breakfast conversation faded into the background until it sounded like muffled voices speaking underwater.

I wasn't sure how long I'd been staring glassy-eyed at the streaky, syrupy residue on my empty plate when I saw my mother's hands take it off the table in front of me. Moments later, something new was set in its place: a dirty, hunter green backpack I'd never seen before.

"Remember this guy?"

My mother unzipped the top pouch and opened it so I could take a look inside. Multicolored folders, sheaves of pure white paper, textbooks with words printed on the sides that I didn't recognize; there was all kinds of stuff crammed within its recesses.

"I wasn't sure what you'd need. Probably none of it today. But I grabbed it all just to be safe."

As she rifled through the contents, I recognized at least one item, even though it didn't really belong: the map of Lenoir my father gave me.

"Most of it was buried underneath your bed. I wasn't sure what was school-related and what wasn't, but I tested the pack myself and didn't think it was all that heavy. I don't know, though. You try it and tell me what you think."

I stood up and allowed her to help me thread my arms through the straps until it rested squarely on the flat of my upper back. She zipped the pouches closed behind me, took a step back, and admired the finished product.

My father walked over and slid his arm around her waist. Both of them looked a little misty-eyed as they regarded me.

"How does it feel?"

My fingertips traced the strange material of the straps and tested the tension they held, pulling the cords back and forth, experimenting with the way the whole system adjusted the weight placement behind me. For some reason, I felt a little foolish, standing there with both of them gawking at me as I attempted to acclimate myself to the backpack.

"I'll get used to it."

It was the best I could come up with under the circumstances.

My father glanced at his wristwatch.

"We should get going."

He grabbed keys from the kitchen counter, my mother flipped off some of the overhead lights, and the three of us made our way out the front door and to the vehicle outside. Mitsu shone in the bright morning sunlight, bluer and newer-looking than I'd ever seen the car look before.

"Not so bad, huh? Told you I'd clean her up for you."

Again, I faked an appreciative smile. It felt like that conversation about the car getting washed had happened years and years ago. So much had changed since then.

And yet, at the same time, I realized maybe nothing had changed at all. It just felt that way to me; and that feeling was probably a mirage.

We listened to my mother's favorite smooth jazz station on the radio as we started the drive over to West Caldwell High School. I watched the color of the sky change outside my window from the backseat: pinkish white to muted yellow, then creamy blue-grey spotted with dark swirling clouds. It seemed like the threat of rain was always there above us, day or night, waiting for the opportune moment to spill over and wash everything away to start anew.

The closer we got to the school, the more activity I noticed outside the moving car. Our speed slowed as the narrow streets congested with other vehicles, including large yellow buses filled with the faces of people who looked to be about my age, maybe younger, all barely visible through small, dark-tinted windows carved up along their sides. Some of the floating heads were laughing or smiling with one another, while others stared gloomily straight ahead or sideways out the glass.

I wondered if I was supposed to know any of these people, and I wondered if they could see me like I could see them. If so, I wondered if they recognized me. And if they could, what would they say? Would they be excited or surprised to see me for the first time in months? Were there people on that bus who presumed me dead? Or perhaps lost forever to a coma, fated to confinement in a lonely hospital room down in Charlotte?

My pulse quickened as we made the turn into the school parking lot and found an open space close to the entrance. Suddenly, I wished to be anywhere else but here. I'd made a mistake thinking that I was ready for this, and I wanted to turn back around and go home.

Maybe it wasn't too late. Maybe if I spoke up now and expressed how genuinely terrified I'd become over the last few minutes, my parents would take pity on me and drive me back to the familiar sanctuary of our house.

Thoughts of Kirsa sprung unbidden to the forefront of my mind. Where was she right now? Was she locked away in the Silvertons' house, or had her parents forced her to return to school as well?

Maybe she was sitting in the back seat of that red pickup truck on the other side of town, staring out the window ominously at a strange school and its even stranger inhabitants, suffering from the same tremendous panic I was now locked in the bowels of.

I hoped she wasn't. While the idea of us having a shared experience from a distance was romantic, I didn't wish this hysteria on anyone, especially not the person I loved.

It only got worse the closer in we got. My parents did a commendable job trying to keep the mood light and upbeat, pointing out various sights that may have once been of interest to me but that failed to distract or occupy my attention now.

For my father, it was commenting on some of the 'cooler' cars we passed as we approached the mammoth brick building up ahead, or regaling us with his predictions of how my school's football team might do.

My mother also played the role of prognosticator, theorizing which of my friends and teachers would react to my return a certain way.

I held my breath as my parents opened the great big glass doors to the school's entrance and steeled myself to receive all these various reactions from hundreds of people all at once, just as my mother had foretold.

Surprisingly, however, our arrival went largely unnoticed, drowned out perhaps in the mundanity and routine of people going about their daily business. I thought I saw a few curious glances here and there, a few heads turn or whispers shared between inquisitive faces, but for the most part, we made our way undisturbed to the lobby of offices adjacent to the front doors.

It occurred to me that my parents must have called ahead at some point to let the school officials know I was coming, either yesterday or earlier this morning, because nobody reacted the way I thought they would. I'd imagined jaws dropping, things falling to the floor out of people's hands, maybe even tears or dramatic exultations as people I didn't remember rushed to greet and embrace me.

But none of it happened that way. Instead, every person we encountered smiled kindly, politely shook me by the hand or grasped me by the shoulder, and repeated some variation of how happy they were to see me again. Several adults awkwardly introduced themselves to me, and I realized after the first couple interactions that it was only awkward because I was supposed to know them already.

As bizarre as it all was for me, it must have been weird for them as well, pretending to meet me for the first time when they'd known me for years. Maybe they'd all been instructed by a doctor or a school counselor, or maybe even by my parents, on what was the proper way to try and engage me. If that was the case, while I appreciated their intention, the end result made me feel even more like an outsider than I already knew I was.

The guidance counselor was the worst of all. She kept holding and patting my hand in the most patronizing manner, reassuring me over and over again how quickly I'd get back in the swing of things, without even realizing that by doing so, she only made me feel further behind.

She spoke as much as to my parents as she did to me. Several times, it felt like I wasn't even in the room at all, the way she discussed me with them. She concluded our meeting by passing my mother an enormous bundle of papers she'd gathered behind her desk.

At the top of the stack was a bright yellow note with 'David Abbott' scribbled across it. She must have mistaken my distress and detachment as a direct reaction to the schoolwork, because she quickly chimed in that there was "no rush" for me to complete everything I'd missed out on, "just whenever you get around to it would be fine."

All I could think about was how much I wished I was with Kirsa again, somewhere far away from here in a quiet, peaceful place. Safe, warm, and dreaming together beneath the heavy layers of my bedding. Curled up side-by-side at the top of a starlit mountain. Suspended in the gentle evening breeze on a wooden porch swing. Cradling her head in my lap in the backseat of a car. Witnessing her wake up and see me for the first time and say my name—my real name—as cold rain fell around us on that grassy streambank, lost together somewhere deep in the lush heart of the forest.

Anywhere with her was where I wanted to be.

A long, metallic bell sound came from the ceiling. With another uncomfortable pat of my hand, the counselor informed us that it was time to go.

We all stood up and walked back to the corridor outside the offices. The area was less populated now, with only a few stragglers quickening their pace as they rushed off to where they needed to be.

Graciously, the counselor assured my parents that she herself would escort me to my first class: AP Calculus with Mr. Gulbroyle. Every one of those words sounded wrong to me. She then stepped to the side, folded her fingers together, and gazed off at nothing in particular, ostensibly in an attempt to give us some space so we could say our goodbyes.

Each of my parents took a turn pulling me in close for a hug as well as sharing some parting words of wisdom and comfort. I only half heard what they were saying to me. My brain was spinning around faster and faster, and with every second that passed, I found myself precariously closer to either throwing up or having a full-fledged panic attack. Maybe even both at the same time.

Wouldn't that make for a memorable first impression if I suddenly started screaming, vomiting, crying, and foaming at the mouth like a crazy person, right here in the lobby of my own high school. How would people react? Would they drag me away to a hospital or send me straight to a psychiatric ward?

More kisses, more hugs, more hollow assurances that I was going to do great, even as I splintered and crumbled into a thousand pieces inside.

One last wistful look over the shoulder. One last wave from the other side of the glass doors. And then they were gone, their backs turned to me, getting smaller and smaller as they moved off together, hand in hand, and receded from view in the parking lot.

It wasn't their fault. I kept telling myself that there was no way they could have known how bad it was, and how it all seeped in so quickly and mercilessly.

If anything, it fell on me. I should have cried out for help, found my voice in time to let them know that I'd changed my mind, I'd made a terrible mistake, and I needed to get out of here now.

But I hadn't done those things in time, and now they were gone, too, leaving me alone with this trusted adviser that I did not trust.

Chapter Twenty-Eight

"Come on, David. Let's get you where you need to be."

I needed to be with Kirsa. I needed to be as far away from here as possible. And I needed to be there now. That's where I needed to be.

But I let the woman guide me by the shoulder into motion, and we were walking together down the hallway, past rows of doors, cabinets, lockers, bulletin boards, and other people. Some moved in our direction, some moved against us.

Again, I noticed that sometimes people noticed me, while other times, it felt as if they purposefully avoided making eye contact at all. Maybe I was only imagining all of it, but the tension felt very real every time. The closer we got to wherever she was taking me, the more the pressure built up inside my body and my mind.

The counselor finally brought us to a halt outside a closed wooden door.

"Are you ready?"

Even if I'd been able to answer her, it wouldn't have mattered. She turned the knob and opened it, stepped inside first, and placed a hand on my shoulder as I stood frozen in the doorway.

An ocean of faces peered up and into me as the room fell silent.

A portly little man stood in front of them all, his fingers writing something on a wall-mounted whiteboard with a red marker. He turned as they all turned, and seemed surprised at first, but then maybe just a bit delighted. His smile was warm and friendly enough. He looked like he wanted to say something, but the counselor beat him to it.

"Sorry for the interruption, everyone. But today's a very special day, because we've got a very special student making his long-awaited return to WCHS this morning. Let's all give a very special, very warm, very Warrior-like welcome to Mr. David Abbott here."

The classroom swelled with the sound of palms clapping together enthusiastically. A few voices whooped or cried out "yeah!" or "yay!", and the small older man up front walked over and took my hand in his, shaking it up and down. I could barely hear him mumble out a stilted introduction over all the commotion.

"Good to see you again, David. We're just thrilled to have you back."

The counselor still had me by the shoulder.

"David, you remember Mr. Gulbroyle."

It was not a question.

Mr. Gulbroyle nodded as if she was speaking to him and not to me. And maybe she was.

"You've still got a spot waiting for you right where you normally like to sit."

He pointed to a desk toward the back-left corner of the room, sandwiched between two other occupied desks. The sound of hand-clapping was long gone by now. I could feel all the pairs of eyes glued to me, watching to see what I would do next. Whispers came from the corners of the classroom, hushed voices as they uttered secrets about me or jeered about my strange history.

Of course they would think me strange. I didn't belong here anymore, and they must have known that by now, or else picked up on it from the second I walked in all dazed and bewildered.

"Here, David. Let's get you where you need to be."

Why did she keep saying that? Like she knew anything about where I wanted to be? As if she knew anything at all about me?

Nevertheless, I didn't resist her as she propelled me past the rows of watching strangers to the empty desk at the very back. Dumbly, I slid into the chair, and the counselor helped tug my backpack off and set it down beside me on the floor. Then, it was time for another pat of my shoulder and another sympathetic smile.

"There, now. That's better. You're all set."

Proud of her accomplishments, the woman strode back up through the classroom and nodded amiably at Mr. Gulbroyle as she made her way to the open door.

"Sorry again for the interruption. They're all yours."

And with one last benevolent grin in my direction, she exited and closed the door behind her.

Only a few people watched her go. The rest still had their heads pivoted back in my direction.

Even Mr. Gulbroyle seemed at a loss for how to proceed. He glanced back and forth between me and the doorway, as if he expected the counselor to return and instruct him on what to do next. Finally, he capped the marker in his hand, set it down on a tray beneath the whiteboard, and opened up his frame to address the entire class.

"Now, I'm sure we all have a lot we'd like to say to David in terms of welcoming him back. But let's try to remember that we also still have a job to do, and right now, that's learning more about vertical, horizontal, and oblique asymptotes. I'm sure you can all find time to catch up at lunch, during passing periods, or after school. Provided you're up for it, of course, David."

The teacher didn't appear fully-satisfied with his own remarks, but apparently, he'd ran out of things to say. So, he cleared his throat loudly, spun on his heel to retrieve the red marker, and picked right back up where'd he left off on the board. His hand flew across the shiny surface, fiercely stringing together a random string of letters, numbers, and shapes for all of us to see.

The teacher's breathy, halting narration of what it was he was doing might have made sense to the others, but it was pure gibberish to me. He alternated facing us to make a point and turning his back on us to write some more. Every time he did the latter, I noticed at least one or two of the students sneaking peeks back in my direction.

There was no escaping all of it. The room began to pitch and heave around me like how that black sea of stars did in my dreams from time to time, and I felt crippling waves of nausea ripple up and down from my belly as sweat pooled at the corners of my temples and under my armpits.

343

Something needed to change. I couldn't take it much longer, sitting here in this strange world pretending to care about things I couldn't even begin to understand, with all of their faces turning one at a time to stare at me and gawk like I was some kind of freak. More sweat, faster heartbeat, more sickness threatening to spill up and over. I had to get away from this... had to get away from all of this...

The metal chair legs shrieked as I pushed them back away from the desk across the floor. By the time I'd picked my backpack off the floor and pulled my body up to standing, every human being in the classroom was staring at me, including the teacher.

"Are you all right, David?"

Mr. Gulbroyle looked more terrified than actually concerned. My mind whirled and flailed around inside my skull, desperately searching for the magic words that could put an end to this anguish. Somehow, I knew that saying this had all been a major mistake and that I simply wanted to leave just wouldn't be enough.

"I—I have to go to the bathroom."

It wasn't entirely untrue; all my innards felt like bursting.

Someone not far behind me giggled. Mr. Gulbroyle turned a lighter shade of the color marker in his hand, and for the second time in as many minutes, he seemed utterly at a loss for how to react. We stood facing each other in brutal silence for a few seconds before he remembered something hanging on the wall behind him.

"Oh. Oh... of course."

He spun back around and handed me the object he'd retrieved: a rectangular piece of wood about the size of my forearm with the symbols 'RM. 135' carved into the side. I stared blankly down at this new object he'd given me, wondering what in the world I was supposed to do with it.

He blinked his beady little eyes and adjusted the frames of his glasses further up the bridge of his nose.

"That's your hall pass."

Still, neither one of us moved. He sniffled a bit and tried to smile at me, but I could see he was just as uncomfortable as I was in the situation.

"You need to keep it with you to use the bathroom."

That made no sense to me. But there was less sense in arguing with him. Clearly, this was some standard high school custom I just didn't remember. But if carrying a random stick in my hand meant I could get out of the classroom faster, I was all for it. The door was only a few steps away now; if I moved quickly, maybe I'd make it out in time before anyone called out or tried to stop me.

"David!"

He stopped me just in time; I already had one hand on the knob. How effectively could I run with these legs? Maybe I was about to find out. Slowly, I brought my chin around to face the soft-spoken calculus teacher who'd called out my name.

"Do you... do you want to leave your backpack here?"

He squeaked the question out meekly.

Defensively, my hands went up to the straps at my shoulders and pulled to tighten them. I wasn't sure why I'd grabbed it, but now that I had it with me, I didn't want to let it go. Setting it back down would take too much time, and it would mean I'd have to walk back there again to the desk, past all the faces and eyes and mouths and looks, and I couldn't do that again. I had to keep moving.

"I'm fine."

The words splatted out as I wrenched the handle and swung the heavy wooden door outward. And then, I was flying down the hall; past all the other doors and windows, past the signs and lockers and cabinets, the tiled walls and everything else around me, all of it one big blur, streaking by in my periphery as I honed in on the exit.

Animal instinct propelled me forward along twisting hallways and around corner after corner, gliding through amorphous scenery like I had so many times before in the mazes of my dreams.

The thought struck me that all of that had prepared me for all of this. It was impossible, sure. But then again, so was so much else that had happened. All of the good stuff had been reasonably impossible, and it had happened all the same because of her. I imagined just up ahead around every turn that I might find her waiting for me, waiting to take me by the hand and guide us both far away from here.

Thick, silver bars dissected the double doors of the school lobby entrance up ahead, threatening to block me in and break my charge. I gathered up all my energy and momentum and threw my body against the gates like a battering ram, and with a magnificent crash, the bars gave way and the doors flung open on their hinges to daylight.

Just like that, I was free again. Free of the school, free of the kids, free of all of it, the good and the bad.

There was no time to think of anyone specific I'd left behind; there was only time to think of one person, and to find her before it was too late.

The map! Of course; I needed the map.

It hadn't been an accident after all that my mother included it with all the other superfluous belongings she had tucked in my backpack this morning. She had no idea what she was doing at the time, but fate must have known I'd need it now. Everything happened for a reason, and all those reasons were finally beginning to shape my destiny.

I couldn't remember the name of the street the Silvertons lived on. Maybe if I read some of the words along the little black lines that crisscrossed all over town, something would jumpstart my memory. The map had brought me to her once before. I knew it could do it again.

Hurriedly, I threw both the 'hall pass' and my backpack on the ground, opened the zipper on the bag, and started rooting through the jumbled contents, searching with my eyes and fingers for the familiar plastic folds.

Everything else was meaningless; books, papers, pamphlets, pencils, pens… Words like 'Calculus', 'European History', 'Physics'; it was all so unimportant. Although I had to admit, a textbook on local geography would prove quite useful right about now.

I finally found the map sandwiched between two of the thicker books I carried. As soon as I had it in my hands, I wasted no time in pulling it loose and spreading it flat along the ground.

Something small and white fluttered out from inside the map, swept airborne with a sudden gust of wind. I had to react quickly to reach out and snag it before it blew away. Secure within my clenched fist, I brought it back in front of me to see just what it was.

Naturally, I assumed it was some random bit of homework that got lodged there by mistake, trapped within the map's creases while my mother shoveled everything in this morning.

Right away, I realized I was wrong. The size of the paper, the color of it, the way it was folded neatly, even the dull shadow of the dark, inky handwriting, scarcely visible inside. All of it was immediately familiar to me.

Familiar, and also impossible, once again. Because she'd handed it to me, and I hadn't put it under my bed. I certainly hadn't placed it inside a map of Lenoir, or inside a backpack I never knew I had. Up until this point, I hadn't been convinced she'd even visited me at all last night, let alone given me the note.

But here it was, physical proof, right here in my hands. Trembling and out of breath, I smoothed it out against the moist grass and read what was written there. The note was simple, succinct, and printed in small black letters:

D.R.,
Trust this feeling. Trust us. Trust me to bring you back to you.
You know where you'll find me.
-K.R.

I read it over several times. The two sets of initials must have related to her and me—Kirsa and Daniel, though I wasn't sure what the R stood for. I couldn't remember if she'd given me our family surname before in conversation.

What did she mean by the rest of it, though? I did trust her. And I trusted the feeling I had now, more than anything I'd trusted in my life as I knew it.

But how was I supposed to know where I'd find her? Was she locked away in the Silvertons' house, or had they forced her to go back to school today?

Or, worst of all, was she somewhere else entirely, trying unsuccessfully to communicate her location to me through our subconscious? Maybe she'd visited me twice last night, once in 'real life' and once in our dreams. What if the second time she'd given me the location of where she'd be, and I'd either missed it or forgotten it after waking up?

I reread the note again and again, trying to decipher a hidden meaning between the lines or find any kind of clue that would help me continue onward.

Eventually, I'd be forced to make a decision one way or another. I'd already been absent longer than any normal person would need to use the bathroom. Soon, I expected someone would get suspicious, either Mr. Gulbroyle or some other school official. Then it would only be a matter of time until they tracked me down out here. I needed to figure out where I was headed and put some distance between me and the school as quickly as I could.

Furtively, I stole a glance over my shoulder just to make sure no one was approaching from behind. Everything seemed quiet, still, unthreatening.

Good. I needed to calm myself, to try and center my focus and relax for a second. Maybe then, the answer I was searching for would come to me instead.

Slowly, methodically, I closed my eyes and steadied

my breathing. I let the air flow in and out through the nostrils of my nose, while keeping my lips pressed together and my jaw relaxed.

Gradually, the slowdown of my lungs caused a ripple effect across the rest of my body. My heartbeat fell into a gentle rhythm, my muscles lengthened and softened, and my brain smoothed over, until what once was raging chaos became a tranquil peace.

When I was ready, I opened my eyes again. With fresh perspective, I then considered the objects strewn out on the ground before me.

Some cosmic magnet directed my pupils, not to the note, but to the map below it. That's when I saw the little area shaded light green, right next to where she'd written on the note the words 'You know where you'll find me.'

Of course.

It was no accident finding the note folded up inside the map.

Just like it was no accident that the two documents aligned perfectly to draw my attention to the mountain range, and to the name of a point that now had great relevance to the two of us.

I knew where she was now and where I needed to go. With the map in hand, I even had all the tools I needed to find her.

And so, I started running. I left the backpack and the hall pass behind without so much as a second thought, because I didn't need them where I was going. Soon enough, I wouldn't need the town map, either. Not once I got to Ayeli Rock.

My feet soared across the pavement, and I basked in the marvelous sensation of pushing my body to its extremes. Gone were the fears and concerns of what might happen if my muscles failed me. It was as if all I needed to stay upright and keep moving in perfect fluid harmony was the sheer power of my intention.

This is what it must feel like to have body and brain in sync finally, working together to make the perfect machine. It was only a pity that it took me this long to test my own limits. But at least I would have this one chance to do so, before surrendering up this body forever.

I passed by all manner of plants, animals, humans, cars, and buildings. Mere backdrops along the path I blazed to my final destination. When I was tired, sweaty, and out of breath, I'd slow down to a jog or a brisk walk, but only for a minute or two. Then I was off and running again, reignited and reinvigorated by the purpose that thumped like a drum inside me.

The closer I got, the more energy I seemed to find. Every time, it surprised me a bit just how much strength and endurance I possessed now that I actively needed both.

Somehow, I barely needed the map's direction, making turns and lightning-fast decisions without a breath of hesitation, and always finding my instincts rewarded by ending up on the right path.

This was what I was meant to do. Ayeli Rock, towering up ahead above the tree line, but getting closer and closer by the second, was where I was meant to be. Kirsa was who I was meant to be with. And Daniel was who I was meant to become.

My thighs convulsed and throbbed as I stumbled my way past the wooden signpost at the side of the road and up the inclined dirt path. The forest surrounding me looked different in the light of day than it had that foggy night; it was brighter, livelier, and less intimidating now. If I had more time, it would have been nice to stop and take it all in, to really appreciate it and immerse myself in the grand scope of it all.

But I had no idea how much time I had, so I could not stop. Not now, not when I was finally this close. I refused to stop moving, willing my burning legs onward as I focused my attention on my feet. The ground below them was rocky and uneven; not as troublesome as it had been in the misty darkness, but still quite a challenge even in direct sunlight.

If I could just make it to the top, I knew deep down that she'd still be there. She was waiting for me.

It was the only explanation for how I could do any of this at all. If she was gone already, if I was too late, I would have been lost long ago. I never would have left the school, discovered the note and the map, or found the agility and determination to get all the way here.

The scenery grew increasingly familiar. I rounded an edge along the trail and allowed myself a quick sideways glance through the trees, and the view alone took my breath away. My legs had brought me much higher than I'd imagined.

Far, far below me, I glimpsed a winding grey path cut its way through an endless expanse of green. Was that really the road I'd come here on? The occasional spots of color moving along it must have been cars. It was all so tiny, so distant now.

I turned back ahead to face forward and realized I was there.

The path leveled out into a flat, open clearing that

looked out over the surrounding foliage, and there were manmade wooden barricades set up all around the cliff edges. Beneath the rickety fence, the earth simply ended and fell away where I could no longer see it, presumably into a steep drop all the way down to the forest floor below.

A large wooden sign sprouted out of the dirt at the opposite end of the summit across from me. Standing in front of it was Kirsa.

Chapter Twenty-Nine

Even though I *knew* she would be here, it still amazed me to see her.

Once again, she made the impossible ordinary without making it mundane, and I approached her slowly in a spellbound, reverential trance.

From the very beginning, she represented a magnificent paradox: a soulmate wrapped inside a stranger.

I didn't know which I wanted more: to rush up, throw myself on her, and catapult headlong into our future together; or to slow down, elongate every step, and simmer in the frozen majesty of the moment.

She kept her back to me the whole time, but it didn't matter. Just as I knew she would be here waiting for me, I knew she knew when I would come to her.

And she knew that I had finally arrived— physically, mentally, and spiritually—even as I glided to a stop right behind her and let the map fall from my hand to the ground, its purpose complete.

"I knew you'd come." She didn't need to say it, but she said it anyway, savoring every word that she spoke. "You found my note?"

I held it aloft like an offering. The paper was

crumpled and moist from the sweat of my palm, but otherwise intact.

"What does the R stand for?"

She turned her head around to face me, and her eyes danced in the sunlight.

"Rain."

Of course, that's what it was.

Kirsa Rain. It was a gorgeous, one-of-a-kind name. I loved it the second I added it all together in my mind.

Kirsa and Daniel Rain. It just *sounded* right.

Kirsa Rain brought her attention back to the sign in front of her.

"Do you know what this is?"

She traced her fingertips lightly along the board's indentations.

"It's all about how Ayeli Rock got its name. The word comes from the Cherokee, the native inhabitants of this land originally. In English, 'ayeli' roughly means 'between' or 'coming to center'. Isn't that perfect for us?"

She turned her head to face me again and smiled.

"This is where it's supposed to happen. Can you feel it, too?"

I nodded, mesmerized by everything.

Kirsa's incandescent smile melted into something a little more serious. Gently, she took both of my hands in hers and moved a step toward me, shortening what little distance was left between us.

Right on cue, the invisible psychic heat flared up again, swirling around our bodies and mixing our essences together into an electric soup of energy. The exact feeling was indescribable, but the closest word I could think of was *sublime*. She positively glowed in front of me.

"Are you sure about this?"

Every fiber of my being screamed out in answer.

"Yes."

She smiled again as the breeze picked up and blew around us. Kirsa closed her eyes a second, her face a portrait of pleasure, as she savored what it felt like to have the wind whisper through her auburn hair.

"My one and only regret is that I didn't take the time to enjoy this world and all it has to offer."

Kirsa opened her eyes again and drank in the view from our perch.

"I don't blame you for getting lost here, Daniel. You really did pick a beautiful place."

I followed her gaze outward, and for the first time in a long time, I reflected on all that I had here.

I thought about North Carolina's sprawling magical forests, rivers, and mountains, and all the teeming wondrous wildlife that lived within, and realized I was giving it all up.

I thought about all the countless other places on this planet I hadn't been, filled with different kinds of people, different languages, different customs, and realized I was giving it all up.

I thought about my age right now in this moment, and how I had years, probably even several decades, still ahead of me; all rife with endless possibility, a million different futures dictated only by the limits of my imagination, and realized I was giving it all up.

I thought about my body, and how I'd only scratched the surface of what it was capable of, like running all the way here without surrender, and realized I was giving it all up.

I thought about my mind—about David's mind, rather—and the treasure trove of memories, secrets, idiosyncrasies, and fantasies that needed preservation, and realized I was giving it all up.

More than anything though, I thought about my parents.

Even if they were only David's parents, they'd showered me with patience, care, and selfless love. The kind of love that's unique between parent and child, a love without question or judgment or fatigue. They'd given all of that and more to me, because I'd given them the greatest gift of all: a second chance with their only child.

And how did I intend to repay them? By potentially snuffing out that second chance forever.

"Are you ready?"

What an odd question. How could anyone ever truly be ready for anything? You could prepare yourself for something as best you could and set up your own expectations. But the future by its nature was as impossible to be ready for as it was to predict. All any of us could do was make decisions that hopefully we could live with—or, in my case, die with.

I couldn't think about that now, though; any of that. I'd had as much time as anyone deserved to weigh out my choices and consider what I might lose either way.

With a calm, sober acceptance, I realized that there was no right or wrong choice, only choice itself. And ultimately, that choice came down to either a life without Kirsa or a death and then maybe, just maybe, life again with her.

Spelled out that way, the choice was easy.

"I'm ready."

As we climbed over to the other side of the wooden barricade, I had another revelation: no matter how at peace my soul was with this decision, my body and my nervous system definitely were not.

Sweat formed in places I didn't think possible as the human instinct for self-preservation kicked in. My breathing and my pulse accelerated, my muscles cramped, and my eyes watered, all physical manifestations of a fearful, logical brain that was in full-blown rebellion against my psyche.

If she was in any way shaken, Kirsa hid it well. She scooted forward until the toes of her shoes jutted out over the edge.

I steeled my courage and followed her lead, sliding my sneakers up until the balls of my feet teetered dangerously on the loose gravel. Though I didn't need to look down to know how far the drop was, I did it anyway, giving in to my own morbid curiosity.

Far, far, *far* below us, I could see the unforgiving ground. At least it looked relatively flat, like we wouldn't hit any jagged rocks or boulders on the way down. Not that it mattered much, anyway; a fall from this height had to be as painful as it was fatal.

Maybe Kirsa really could read my mind, because she took my hand and spoke softly to me.

"Some people say you die from a heart attack before your body ever hits the ground. I don't know if that's true, but it sounds a little bit better, don't you think?"

I nodded and tried to laugh. My body shivered all over from head to toe. No matter how much I tried to concentrate on why we were doing this and on who we were doing it for, I couldn't stop my muscles from shaking.

Kirsa squeezed my hand tighter.

"Hey, you."

She waited for me to raise my eyes up from the ground and look at her.

"Hey. I love you, okay? No matter what."

Carefully, she leaned in and kissed me on the lips.

While it wasn't enough to completely dispel the terror and physical paralysis, it was amazing just how much it affected me internally. Kissing her felt like submerging my head beneath a pool of warm, dark water. It gave me goosebumps all over my skin, but it also made me feel safer somehow, protected like a baby inside its mother's womb.

After allowing me to absorb some of her remarkable calm, we broke the kiss and opened our eyes to each other. There, in all its glory, was that inimitable mysterious smile, like she alone knew the secret to the meaning of life, but she was toying with the idea of sharing it with me, and only me.

"It's a leap of faith. That's all it is, right? You know that."

I nodded again and tried to maintain my tenuous hold on whatever semblance of peace she'd given me. Whatever happened next, I decided I wouldn't look down again.

"Look at me, Daniel."

I looked at her and took a deep breath.

"Let's go home."

And then, everything happened so fast.

One last random thought.

One last fleeting desire to stay.

359

One last memory of the woman I called Mom, laughing and eating cookies.

One last memory of the man I called Dad, telling a corny joke over dinner.

One last look at the girl, the person her parents called Jessica Silverton.

One last look at the boy, the reflection in her eyes, called David Abbott.

And one last brief, beautiful feeling of flying or falling through the sky.

Chapter Thirty

The first things I remembered were the flowers, bunched closely together, maybe half a dozen of them, stuck out from a thin, glass vase. They were vibrant and tall, with long, shiny green stems, rings of bright yellow petals, and fuzzy black centers. I couldn't stop staring at them and wondering why and how I knew them as intimately as I did.

What did I have in my hands? The material was familiar to me—thick, heavy, warm, and old. It felt like…

… my wool blanket. Of course; I slept with it every night. It was draped over my body even now like a protective cocoon, swaddling me in place. I stirred my muscles beneath it, flexing the ache of sleep off each of them one by one.

Why was I so sore? What had I done yesterday to overexert myself? My joints ached and creaked, resisting my brain's instruction for them to move. It felt like some of the bits and pieces of me had completely rusted through overnight. Maybe I was going to need a little more help to get back in the swing of things.

Lucky for me, I knew I hadn't slept alone in

decades. In over fifty years of marriage, my wife had banished me to the couch maybe twice—and both times, for good reason. Unless my physical condition was in some way tied to bad behavior, she was probably lying right next to me, and most likely still fast asleep. She had to be, actually, because I could feel the weight of another person at my side.

Slowly, and with more than a few heavy grunts and sighs, I rolled myself over to face her. I always hated waking her up—she often looked her most beautiful as she slept—but I was confident she'd forgive me after she heard just how sore and confused I was.

To my immense surprise, she was actually already awake. Her eyes were wide open, and she breathed harder and faster than I knew she normally did while slumbering.

Right away, I knew that something was wrong. Trails of dried tears lined her weathered cheeks, and her lips moved frantically, mouthing words without making any sound. Seeing me see her for the first time only seemed to make it worse as she choked on her breath and coughed a few times.

I stretched out a hand to her chest to try and comfort her, but she jerked back from my touch and looked at me with red and watery eyes. There was a profound fear in them unlike anything I'd ever noticed before, as if she'd experienced some unimaginable horror that even now refused to let her go.

"Kirsa…"

My voice sounded a little weird to me, hoarser than it normally was, even for the morning.

"Kirsa… what's wrong?"

Slowly, something changed in her. The muscles

around her mouth and jaw began to relax and her expression softened dramatically. Fresh tears welled up in the corners of her eyes, and with trembling, age-speckled hands, she reached over to touch my face.

"You... you remember me?"

Normally, I would have laughed at the absurdity of that question, coming from her, of all people. But her strange reactions had shaken me. What exactly was going on right now?

Desperately, she asked again.

"You know who I am? Who I really am?"

Her fingers felt cold on my cheeks. I brought my own hands up and placed them on top of hers to warm them, hoping this time she wouldn't recoil from my touch. Thankfully, she did not. If anything, the physical contact seemed to steady her, and I could feel her relax a bit more beneath and beside me.

"Of course I do. You're my Kirsa. Who else would you be?"

She stared back at me like she was still searching for something, so I decided to press her a bit.

"What's going on?"

Again, her lips moved of their own accord as she struggled to find her voice or the right words that she wanted to say. My wife appeared just as disoriented as I was. The only difference was that she also seemed terribly afraid of something, and I wasn't sure of what.

"I need to ask you something, something crazy. But humor me, okay?"

I nodded sympathetically and stroked the backs of her hands.

"Anything. You know you can ask me anything."

She didn't blink.

"Do you know what your name is?"

This time I couldn't help but laugh, although I quickly suppressed it. Nothing in her face suggested she was joking. Concerned as I was, I gave her what she wanted.

"Daniel. My name is Daniel." Maybe she'd let me get away with a teeny-tiny smile. "Is that the right answer?"

Kirsa regarded me for a long, careful moment. And then, she ambushed me all at once, pulling my face into hers for a deep, tearful kiss. I responded in kind, grateful for this kind of reaction as opposed to the one I'd received from her earlier when she'd shrunk away from me like I was a stranger.

I tried to pull away for air after a few seconds, but she wouldn't let me go, weaving her arms around my neck and pressing her body firmly into mine beneath all the sheets and blankets.

Normally, I would have been overjoyed at eliciting this kind of greeting in the morning, but it was hard to take my mind off how bizarre everything was today. As if my own mysterious weariness and patchwork memory weren't enough to contend with, Kirsa was acting like a completely different person—or like I was a completely different person. I couldn't be sure which one was more accurate.

When at last she finally allowed us a moment to catch our breath, I seized my opportunity.

"What's going on? Why are you acting so funny?"

Her shin butted up against my shin. The pain was double what it should have been, but at least it served as a reminder.

"And why do I feel like I just fell off a cliff?"

Now it was her turn to laugh, and my turn to squash it with a vacant stare. She looked like she expected me to laugh, too, but I didn't understand what was so funny.

"Do you remember that, too?"

There was a soft plea in the way she asked the question. I knew her well enough to understand that it would have been easier for me to just answer "yes," even if the real answer was "no."

I licked my lips and sighed, thinking hard. At least now maybe we could get somewhere.

"The last thing I remember…"

My voice trailed off as my brain did the same.

I don't know why I thought it would be so simple, because it certainly wasn't. The terrible truth was I had no idea what the last thing was I remembered. My eyes swept around our bedroom, searching for clues that might help me.

And then I saw them: the flowers.

Of course; the last things I remembered were the flowers.

And then it all started to trickle back for me.

"The flowers."

I pointed at the vase with my index finger and nodded, confident I was finally onto something here.

"I remember now. I went out for a walk."

The cliffs, the sunshine. The waves of the sea below, and the salt wind blowing through my hair.

"I went out for a walk to pick you flowers. Your favorite kind, the wildflowers that only grow out here. The ones you've always loved the most."

Kirsa stared at me intently, waiting.

"Do you remember what happened, Daniel? What

happened on your way back?"

I racked my brain for answers, but it was like trying to retrace footsteps in a heavy snowfall. When I couldn't come up with anything, she continued on carefully in a soft whisper.

"You never made it back, Daniel."

More images flashed through my mind, none of which made sense. Giant, hissing petals falling all around me, steam and sticky paste, popping sounds… and silence. And then, after the silence, darkness. A void of nothingness. *The* void.

"You had an accident. You had a stroke."

So, that was it. That was the great big mystery, the reason why there was a giant crater in the center of my memory. It probably also explained all the aches and pains I felt right now.

"All right, then."

I digested the information quickly. Frankly, I was even a bit proud of the way I processed it all without flinching. I'd suffered a stroke while out on a walk picking wildflowers for my wife. All that really mattered was that I had survived.

And so far, my mind seemed fairly sharp. I'd passed the initial tests of remembering who I was and who she was. Everything else would surely come back as well, if any of it was even gone to begin with.

"So, I had a stroke. I understand that."

I ran my fingers along her lips, still wet from our kiss.

"I'll take it easy, and I'll do whatever I need to do to get back in the swing of things. Don't worry. I'll take it slow if you want me to. But you've got to admit, it's encouraging that I know who you are and that I know who I am. I feel like I'm off to a pretty good start for an old guy that just had a stroke. What do you think?"

She smiled at me and kissed each finger of my hand, one at a time, before going back again.

"I think you're right. And I think you're doing a great job." Kirsa levelled her gaze back on me, and I could see the seriousness there again. "I could be wrong, but I think Jacqueline and Isabelle might be here right now with the kids. Ivy, too. I don't know what day it is for sure, but there's even a chance that today might actually be Ivy's birthday."

My heart swelled within my chest.

"Then that means she's in for a treat! Aren't people supposed to slur their words after a stroke? Personally, I don't think I've ever sounded better. Maybe a little hoarse, but nothing a saltwater gargle can't fix."

To drive the point home, I started dramatically reciting scales the way an opera singer might do as a warm-up. My joke had the desired effect: Kirsa tried to maintain a straight face as long as she could, but eventually, I wore her down into a tired smile, and then even a rollicking giggle. That was all I needed. I reached out and played my fingers along the sides of her stomach, going for the surefire tickle spots that I knew she loved and hated at the same time.

Laughing and convulsing, she fought me off; first playfully, then with a little more vigor and sternness. When I finally gave up and allowed her to pin my hands together within hers, she gave me a look that let me know she wasn't done with me yet.

"There's one last thing I need to know, and then you can go sing 'Happy Birthday' to Ivy until you're blue in the face, okay?"

I smiled slyly back at her.

"*If* today is even her birthday, after all. I'm recovering from a stroke. What's your excuse for forgetting what day it is, old woman?"

Kirsa was not amused.

"I'm serious, Daniel. This is important."

She waited until I fully extinguished the smile from my face before continuing.

"I'm only going to ask you this once. If it doesn't make any sense to you, then I want you to forget I ever asked you, okay?"

She must have noticed the corners of my mouth threatening a playful smile again.

"I'm serious, Daniel. One last question. Then I'll leave you in peace so you can collect yourself, and I'll go see what day it is and which of our offspring or grand-offspring might be running around out there. Deal?"

I nodded my head, relishing the admonishment in the way only a married man of many years can do.

"Deal."

She needed to sit up in bed for this one. I decided maybe it was best if I did the same, although doing so wasn't as easy as she made it look. The vertebrae in my spine signaled right away that they would have preferred it better if I never moved again.

Something about that thought, random and inconsequential as it was, stuck firmly at the front of my mind for a second. The image of my own body lying still in a bed forever, alive but immobile... it registered something in me, a shadow of a memory that I couldn't quite place.

Kirsa raised her eyebrows, leaned forward, and asked her question.

"David Abbott and Jessica Silverton. Do either of those names mean anything to you?"

I paused, pretended to think, and then gave her my best roguish grin.

"No. Should they? I feel like I'm being interviewed by a detective or something."

She held my gaze for a meaningful moment, studying and scrutinizing my reaction, before breaking into a smile herself and then a full-fledged laugh. Suddenly, she was Kirsa again. Kirsa as I always remembered her: playful, exuberant, adventurous, youthful, and fun-loving. A person very different from the person I'd woken up next to.

Then again, was I one to talk? I thought I was doing a terrific job picking right back up where I'd left off before this stroke thing happened, but I guess I couldn't really be sure. The best way to judge my normalcy was by gauging Kirsa's reactions to what I said and did, as she knew me even better than I knew myself; and her reactions had been anything but ordinary.

Granted, I had no idea how long I'd been out for, and we were bound to have some bizarre interactions after such a significant health scare. I was just grateful to have my mental faculties seemingly working normally. Everything else would return in time.

Kirsa stood up from the bed and stretched. I noticed she was a little wobbly on her feet, and she had to lean on the corner of the headboard to find her balance. I reached out a helping hand in her direction, but she batted it away good-naturedly.

"Oh, I'm fine, I'm fine."

She turned and flashed me an enigmatic smile.

"Maybe you're not the only one who feels like they fell off a cliff, huh?"

Slowly, stiffly, she made her way to a large window and drew back the curtains to peer outside.

"Yep, just as I suspected."

She clucked her tongue and turned her face in my direction.

"You, my flower-picking adventurer, have some people outside who I know would just be absolutely stunned, thrilled, and overjoyed to see you right now. Are you ready?"

Again, there was a flash of something that came and went inside my head, an indecipherable but undeniably visceral reaction I couldn't control. I wasn't sure what it was or where it came from. All I knew was that it felt triggered by the last thing Kirsa had said to me—the question of "are you ready?"—as simple and benign as those three words were together.

"I'm right behind you. Just need a second to get the old machine back in business, and then I'll be good to go."

"Do you want me to wait for you?"

I flexed my feet beneath the bedcovers and massaged my thighs with my knuckles.

"No, don't bother. I'm sure you've waited for me long enough."

When I looked up from my legs again, she was still there, silently watching me beside the window.

"What?"

Kirsa shook free whatever thought was in her head and started shuffling toward the door.

"No, nothing."

She turned the knob and was halfway out before she stopped and stared at me again.

"Hey, you."

I grinned at her.

"Hey, me what?"

"I love you. More than you'll ever know."

"I love you, too. More than you'll ever know, either." She started to walk away as I called out after her. "Not that it'll stop me from trying!"

I heard her laugh girlishly out in the hallway before she re-emerged seconds later in the doorway. Kirsa slid one hand up along the wooden frame and leaned so that her temple rested on her arm. The pose was effortlessly flattering; even in our golden years, both well past the physical peaks of our existence, there was something timeless, ageless, and flirtatious in the way she stood and looked at me right now.

"Thank you."

"For what?"

"For trusting me; for trusting me to bring you back."

I wanted to ask her what she meant by that. But before I had the chance, she was gone. I heard her footsteps recede down the hall, and not long after that, the noise of a screen door opening and then swinging shut.

Soon, I imagined there might be other noises as well: sounds of excitement, delight, and surprise, as she broke the news to the rest of our family that I was awake and presumably recovered. When that happened, I didn't want them to see me like this: weak, feeble, and smelling like an old man who'd spent far too much time in one set of pajamas, albeit through no fault of his own.

Gingerly, I lowered the pads of my feet to the floor beside our bed, reached up in the air with both my arms, and stretched from side to side. Hundreds of kinks and knots roared in protest along my body as I did so, but I gritted my teeth through the pain and brought myself slowly up to standing, using the bed's headboard for support as I'd seen Kirsa do moments earlier.

Something caught my eye beneath the flowers on my nightstand. There, beneath the bottom of the vase, was a small white piece of paper, folded neatly along the edges, but showing some outward signs of wear and tear. I lifted the flower vase up off the paper and set it to the side.

Now that it was fully uncovered, I could just barely make out a few printed letters of someone's writing from inside the note, though I didn't recognize the penmanship. Whose handwriting was that? I reached out to take hold of it and was surprised to see my fingers trembling as I did.

Before I could touch it, though, I heard a child's voice let out a shrill scream in the distance, followed by a cry that sounded a whole lot like "Grandpa!"

My curiosity got the better of me. I let it carry me over to the window, where I parted the curtains to get a better look and take in my family for myself.

Maybe the reflection of the sunrays bouncing off the ocean was too bright and blinding. Or maybe my eyes just weren't as good as I remembered them being.

Either way, I couldn't really see much of anything from the window, so I pulled the curtains shut, grabbed a bathrobe from my closet, and put it on. I cinched the cord of the robe tight around my waist and eyed the piece of paper on the nightstand one last time, making a mental note to remember to read it later. Then, I walked through the bedroom doorway, down the hall, and out the screen door at the other end.

Somewhere up ahead in the glittering interplay of sunlight, shadows, sea, and sand, I knew my loved ones were waiting for me.

COMING SOON

Viaticum

"Paradise has a price."

by

PATRICK MORGAN

Summer 2021

Acknowledgements

First and foremost, I would like to express my sincerest thanks and appreciation to Christopher Bailey and the entire team at Phase Publishing for their continued belief and support in my storytelling. It means the world to have such talented, intelligent, and encouraging advocates in your corner, especially at this early stage of the journey. I am eternally grateful for this opportunity to realize my dream.

I also want to thank Jenny Rudd and Right Word Express for doing such an exceptional job editing this work. On a more personal note, I also wanted to thank Jenny for lending her hospital expertise in helping make that early sequence more realistic as well.

Thank you to my publicist, Kayle Hill, for coming aboard on this project (and hopefully on many future ones). I cannot wait to see what new doors we can open together through our collaboration.

To all of my old teachers, professors, and mentors, from kindergarten all the way through college and beyond, I want to say thank you, thank you, thank you, once again. There is absolutely no way I'd be in this position today without your guidance and encouragement. Also, please don't take it personally that this particular story's protagonist had an "adverse reaction" to school and certain subjects of study (Calculus, European History, Physics, etc.).

From the bottom of my heart, I want to express endless gratitude to all my friends. I hit the cosmic jackpot by meeting each and every one of you. Thank you for enriching the story of my life. A very special thank you as well to all of those friends who read this story (or any of my stories) and gave me honest feedback.

Finally, to all my relatives and family members, thank you for accompanying me on this journey from day one. Grandparents, uncles, aunts, cousins, close and distant relations... Mom, Dad, Megan, Paul... you're all a part of me, and that makes you a part of this story. Whether you're in this realm or the next, know that the love I hold for you defies dimension.

©2020 Patrick Morgan
Photo credit: Robert Atchinson

ABOUT
THE AUTHOR

Patrick Morgan is a novelist, playwright, and poet. His debut novel, *Apparent Horizon*, was released in the fall of 2020 to critical acclaim.

After having spent a long and memorable stint in Los Angeles, Patrick currently resides in Austin with his dog, Cider.

His two great loves are the ocean and the New England Patriots. He's also partial to Nacho Cheese Doritos dipped in cold Tostitos Salsa Con Queso (don't knock it till you've tried it).

You can contact him via his website at:

www.patrickmorganonline.com

CPSIA information can be obtained
at www.ICGtesting.com
Printed in the USA
LVHW020945230221
679712LV00014B/215